Also by Christopher Pike

The Cold One
Sati
The Season of Passage

THE LISTENERS

Christopher Pike

A TOM DOHERTY ASSOCIATES BOOK
NEW YORK

This is a work of fiction. All the characters and events portrayed in this book are fictitious, and any resemblance to real people or events is purely coincidental.

THE LISTENERS

Cover art by Joe DeVito

A Tor Book
Published by Tom Doherty Associates, Inc.
175 Fifth Avenue
New York, N.Y. 10010

Tor® is a registered trademark of Tom Doherty Associates, Inc.

ISBN: 0-812-55039-0

First edition: January 1995

Printed in the United States of America

0 9 8 7 6 5 4 3 2 1

For Teli

The author wishes to thank
Carl Sagan for *The Dragons of Eden*
and Robert K.J. Temple for *The Sirius Mystery*,
which were very helpful in writing this book.

And also Melissa Ann Singer,
who put in long, hard hours editing this story.

CHAPTER 1

avid Conner had shot three people in his life, blown up three, and burned another to death. At the FBI field office in Los Angeles he had been given the nickname "Dirty Dave," and maybe the appellation would have seemed harsh if the seven people hadn't been guilty as sin and deserved to die. Most FBI agents were fans of Clint Eastwood, so the nickname had stuck and was considered a compliment among David's peers. But it wasn't a title David especially appreciated because he had always thought of himself as one of the good guys.

Now he wondered. Now that he was quitting.

David Conner was thirty-nine years old, a fifteen-year veteran of the Federal Bureau of Investigation. His experiences as an agent were varied. He had sent organized crime figures to prison, caught bank robbers, and rescued victims of kidnapping. He was the stuff of legend, as the old cliché went, and because he was handsome with an office located in the same time zone as Hollywood, he was almost a star as well.

Nevertheless, there were two failed cases in his past, one a month old and one seven years gone, that made him feel old. But he blamed the outcome of those cases more on God than on his own incompetence. God must not have been a fan of Dirty Harry's, David thought, or else he would have known that in the end the good guy was always supposed to win. That was one of the reasons David was quitting the FBI—he didn't believe in God anymore, or, for that matter, truth, justice, and the American way. He just wanted out.

The Los Angeles office was one of fifty-six field offices directed by the FBI's ten headquarter divisions. The divisions set policy and became involved in local cases at important junctures. For example, the laboratory division might help a field office by doing an autopsy on a murder victim, while the field office did the actual job of investigating the crime. Each field office was headed by a special agent in charge (SAC). With 570 agents, Los Angeles was the third largest field office in the country after New York City and Washington D.C.

David had spent his first ten years in the FBI in the L.A. office, and his last month there trying to rescue Angela Wilson. He had read in the paper the other day that one of the major Hollywood studios had purchased the rights to the Angela Wilson case. He wondered who would play himself. Clint Eastwood was too old. He had a hard time imagining that Angela's parents, after all they had gone through, had agreed to the project.

Ned Calendar, the L.A. SAC, was also about to retire, but for far different reasons than David's. Ned had been in charge of Los Angeles for the past twenty-two years and was unofficially seventy years old and still on the job. He was a master of organization and inspiration, and his official ID miraculously listed him at a mere sixty-five. Ned still believed in truth, justice, and the American way, but despite that, Ned and David were good friends.

It was Ned who had called David to come down to headquarters with the promise of an important case that only David could handle. David couldn't imagine how important it could be when they were both going to be unemployed in two weeks. Ned's office was on the seventeenth floor, a corner suite that overlooked Westwood Village. Ned's secretary waved David in as he stepped off the elevator. David found Ned at the window staring down at the nearby U.C.L.A. campus.

"I remember when I was in school," Ned said, without turning. "I used to pray for summer vacation. Now I dread retirement. Why is that, David? Retirement is supposed to be like one long vacation."

"It's because you're too old to get laid now," David said.

Ned turned, a slight frown on his face. He was a tall man, gangly, with a cluster of faint liver spots that chased his thinning sandy hair up the northern hemisphere of his skull. He had intense blue eyes that changed shade with the burdens of his position, which, make no mistake, were great. He was fit; he had run 10 Ks until six months ago when he broke a bone in his foot kicking a mob informant who had James Bond fantasies of being a double agent. The injury still caused him to walk with a slight limp. Ned was a pleasant enough gentleman in social situations, but at work he liked to be in complete control—not really a problem since he had, for the last two decades, run the L.A. office with a rare mixture of tyranny and compassion. Many agents, when they first started to work for Ned, made the mistake of thinking him laid-back because of his California tan, his years, his casual dress. But he had been known to transfer agents who screwed up to difficult-to-pronounce places that even the CIA didn't count under their jurisdiction. David had known Ned from the day he walked into the L.A. office. They had solved many tough cases together, working hours that would have killed most men. For those reasons, and a few others, David was the only person in the L.A. office who could speak his mind to Ned and get away with it.

"Am I too old?" Ned asked. "Who told you that?"

"Your wife."

Ned grinned and waved the remark away. "She'd be the last person to know." He nodded to the chair in front of his mahogany desk. Ned's office was relatively austere, especially compared to the days before personal computers. In the good old days he had files stacked everywhere. Now there were only pictures of family on one wall, an abstract painting on another, and a couple of files on his desk. David's own office was equally sparse, with only two pictures: one of Angela Wilson, the other of Sandy Quin, both casualties of FBI involvement. David took the offered chair as Ned sat down across from him.

"You'll have fun," David said. "You can take up fishing."

"I don't like fish."

"You can always throw them back."

"Like the justice system does with all our hard work?"

"I suppose." David put his hands on his head and rubbed his temples. "Why did you want me in so early? You know I don't get up before ten these days."

"Hangover?"

David dropped his hands and shrugged. "My head hurts,

what can I say? Maybe it was the alcohol. Maybe it was the loud music at the club."

"Which club was that?"

"I can't remember."

Ned nodded. "What are you going to do in a couple of weeks when you have no reason to get up?"

"I only drink when it gets dark. I don't have a problem, and even if I did, I don't want to talk about it. Why am I here?"

"I have a case for you."

"I don't want it."

Ned lifted a folder on his desk. "This is an unusual case. It's perfect for you. I think you can complete your investigation and file a report before we walk. I might even help you out with it."

"Is Sanders climbing into your chair already?" Chip Sanders was in line to be L.A.'s next SAC. Headquarters had recently brought him in from New York. A splendid choice, David thought. Sanders took taxis to work because he still hadn't bought a car.

"He sits in my chair after I leave in the evenings," Ned said, opening the file in his hands. "But my secretary likes him. That's all that matters. Besides, I want to do a little more fieldwork before I take up fishing." He paused. "You have to take this case. We're paying your salary for the next two weeks and you're going to earn it. But you'll like it—I guarantee you, no one can get hurt. Are you listening?"

David had returned to massaging his head. He did indeed have a nasty hangover, although, Ned's suspicions aside, he had yet to make drinking a habit. But now it felt as if his blood were being fed through a two-horsepower motor before it was rammed into his swollen brain. He'd chewed four Tylenol dry on the drive in and was wondering if they needed a gulp of whiskey to start working. What club *had* he been at? He vaguely remembered a middle-aged woman with blond hair that curled with the gentle grandeur of straw and lipstick the color of strawberry chewing gum. She'd bought him a couple of drinks and asked, after catching sight of the gun in his coat, if he was an assassin for hire. Sounded like she disliked her husband. He had declined her offer to accompany her back home.

"Yes," David said. "I'm listening. A fish guaranteed you no one would get hurt."

Ned frowned. "One day you're going to have to drop it. It wasn't your fault."

"I never said it was my fault. It was your fault."

"It was nobody's fault. We did everything we could for Angela. It's a hard world. People die. Sometimes they're young and pretty." He paused. "You know, you look like shit."

"Thank you."

Ned shook his head. "What am I going to do with you?"

"Let me go home and go to bed."

"No. You're going to study all day and this evening you're going to take a plane to Boise, Idaho."

David lifted his head from his hands and winced at the sunlight pouring in through the window behind Ned. "Who's in Boise? Don Corleone?"

"Professor Stephen Spear and his channeling group."

"Come again?"

"Do you know what channeling is?" Ned asked.

"Yes. It's a New Age term. Channelers go into trances and a spirit speaks through them. Clearly an activity the Federal Bureau of Investigation should be deeply concerned about."

"Shut up and listen. Professor Spear is a fascinating character, as is his group. For the past two days I've been going over the information we have on them. There's something here besides crystal healing and tarot cards. Spear's group channels an entity called the 'Big Mind.' A number of transcripts from their sessions have been collected into book form and published under the same name. You can't find it at Waldenbooks, but it's available at New Age bookstores, like Hollywood's Boddhi Tree. The majority of information in the book resembles similar New Age texts. There's the usual talk of a new era of peace dawning for mankind, global disasters, reincarnation, higher states of consciousness. But there's also a section where the Big Mind talks about what's going on inside the government. It says that we've already developed the process of cold fusion. That we have supersonic jets capable of attaining shallow earth orbit. That we have the technology to transform waste from nuclear reactors into harmless isotopes."

"So?" David said.

Ned set down his folder and stared at David. "So, my most brilliant field agent, the Big Mind is right. Every time it mentions something specific that we are able to check out, it does check out."

"We already have cold fusion?"

"Yes. Still in the experimental stages, but it has been developed."

David shook his head. "I must read that book. Do we have colonies on the moon, too?"

"Don't be ridiculous."

"*I'm* being ridiculous? Surely you don't want me to fly to Idaho to investigate a channeling group?"

"That's exactly what I want you to do."

David chuckled. "Is this what happens to burnt-out agents before they're put out to pasture?"

"I know it sounds like a waste of time, but that's only because you don't have all the facts. When you do, I think you'll be anxious to meet Professor Spear."

"Is he anxious to meet me?" David asked.

"No. You'll be going in undercover as a magazine reporter."

David laughed. "A newspaper reporter is undercover? Don't these intuitive giants know that *normal* people read magazines?"

"The channeling group is not opposed to outside interest, obviously, or they wouldn't have published a book. But to be approached by a reporter is a lot different from being questioned by a government agent. As usual you'll have to first gain their trust to learn anything of value. That's why I've chosen you, David. You're handsome and, when it suits you, you can be charming. Besides, you could use some fresh air."

"I don't want to go. I can't go."

"Why not?"

"The Big Mind will be able to pierce through my aura and see that I'm a fake."

Ned stood. "On the contrary. The Big Mind has already approved your visit. One of our agents up north stole a video of one of their sessions. I want you to see it. I think you'll find it interesting."

As the two men sat in a dark conference room, waiting for the video to start on the wall monitor, David thought about Ned's referring to his good looks as one of the reasons he was chosen for the job. Since FBI agents had to elicit information from people who didn't want to give it—half of whom were female—the point was valid. However, David believed Ned saw him as a Casanova because most of the agents in the office looked like the lawyers and accountants they had been before joining the Bureau. Certainly David was not being chased by the producers of the Angela Wilson Story.

David stood six foot even. He had been a champion swimmer in college and had come within two-tenths of a second of qualifying for the hundred-meter butterfly for the Olympics. He still had a swimmer's tapered body, but these days got his exercise practicing martial arts. He was fit, quick, strong—he could kill with his hands if he needed to, but he preferred a 10-millimeter semiautomatic pistol for messy work. His father had been Irish, his mother Italian. As a result his cheeks reddened when he drank, and his hands became animated. His hair and eyes were dark. He had inherited his mother's wide, sensual mouth, her olive skin. His stamina occasionally surprised even him. Ned had once invited him to run on the track. Even without regular running workouts, David had worn his boss to the ground over twenty laps.

Yet the same could not be said for the endurance of his liver. Even with Irish whiskey and red wine in his genes, if he spent a night at a bar, he'd wake up beside the toilet. He was not an alcoholic, but knew he would be soon if he didn't get his act together. The trouble was, he had no inspiration to quit. The autopsy had been performed on Sandy Quin, and Angela Wilson would not be going to her prom. Rudy Failla, a close cousin of the mythic Don Corleone, was every bit as dead, a 10-millimeter slug in his burned forehead, buried in a sandy grave outside Las Vegas, where the real losers played the slots. Dirty Dave.

"How did our man manage to steal this tape?" David asked Ned, who sat to his right.

"He picked the lock on Spear's office cabinet. Why?"

"Just wondering. Why doesn't this lock picker pose as the magazine reporter? Why send in an agent from Los Angeles?"

"The Bay Area office is not interested in the case."

"Does that tell us something about the case?"

"Shh. Watch the tape. It's starting now."

A school classroom appeared on the screen, complete with green chalkboard and anatomically incorrect chairs. Five people, three males and two females, sat gathered in a small circle, facing one another, their eyes closed. At the edge of the circle, standing against the wall, hovered a middle-aged man with a bushy gray moustache and a wild Einstein hairdo. He had not shaved that morning; his face was cold, his eyes dark.

"That's Professor Spear," Ned said.

"What's he a professor of?"

"He holds twin doctorates, one in anthropology, the other in psychology. Both were awarded from Stanford."

"What are they doing?" David asked. The point of view of the camera was from the corner of the room, stationary. The image quality was fair to poor. The group appeared to be taking long, slow, deep breaths, nothing else.

"Regressing," Ned said.

"Is that healthy?"

"Watch. Listen."

"So we come to a point of simplicity," one of the men said. He appeared to be from India, in his early thirties. His face was thin and aesthetic, his voice deep and soothing. "We breathe in and we breathe out. We do so with awareness and as a result our awareness comes into the present moment. It is only in the present that we know the past. The past is an illusion, of course, it no longer exists. But if we desire we can step through this illusion and enjoy the sights. We breathe in and we breathe out. We close our eyes and see what is behind us."

"Are they hyperventilating?" David asked.

"No," Ned muttered.

"We close our eyes and see what is," another man said. He was approximately forty-five, big and burly—like a sedentary truck driver. He wore a red and white Pendleton shirt and could have just downed a few beers with Paul Bunyon. His voice was as calm as his partner's. "Between every inhalation and exhalation is a point of simplicity, a moment when creation's pendulum halts. A moment when the fluctuations of the mind cease. We breathe in and we breathe out. We are happy."

"Are they—" David began.

"Don't say it," Ned interrupted.

"We are joy itself," the third man said in a faint Scandinavian accent. He was obviously a body builder, tan and handsome, perhaps a little foolish. The camera focused on him. There had to be a seventh person in the room, David noted. The camera operator. "We breathe in and we breathe out. The inward breath raises us up. The outward breath calms. The present moment is huge. But we choose the illusion. We choose the past."

David shifted in his seat.

"Yes?" Ned said, annoyed.

"Nothing. My ass is going to sleep," David said.

"We choose to go back." One of the two women finally spoke. She was young, perhaps twenty-five, with long, curly red hair, freckles, and the face of a modern angel. David sat up and leaned forward. She held the hand of the woman next to her who must have been her identical twin. The other woman's face quivered as her sister spoke; a tense line appeared horizontally across her forehead. She remained silent as her sister continued, "We move without changing position. We see without vision. There is no personality. There is no emotion. There is no distortion. We breathe in and we breathe out. The ego is tied to the breath. We let the breath go. The process of inhalation and exhalation begins to slow. The breath begins to stop. The ego begins to dissolve. The Big Mind dawns."

The group fell silent, their eyes remaining shut. A minute went by. Professor Spear stirred from his place against the wall. He held a yellow notepad in his right hand and studied it as if to refresh his memory before taking a step toward the group.

"Follow the Nordic chain," he instructed. "What do you see? What do you feel?"

Another silent minute went by.

"The wind," the fellow from India finally said. "The salty air. We are on a boat, on a mission. Our women have been taken, our children killed. We must have revenge. We are strong. We are not afraid. The gods hear our prayers."

"Where do you live?" the professor asked. "What is your destination?"

"We live in our green land," the beautiful twin who spoke replied. "We go to the enemy's land. They steal our women. We will cut their throats and hack off their heads. Our swords are sharp, our hearts hot."

"What kind of swords do you carry?" the professor asked. "Describe them. Are they iron? Are they made of steel? How are they shaped?"

"They are black like iron in the earth," the truck driver said. "They are thick and curved like the crescent moon."

"Describe your vessel," the professor said. "The shape of the sails, their color."

"Our ship is wooden," the Indian fellow said. "It rocks in the cold waves. Our sails are the color of blood. A black hammer on a flag waves atop our mast."

Professor Spear was interested. "What's the name of your main god?"

"Thor," they all said in unison.

The taping abruptly stopped. Ned stood and turned on the lights.

"Is that it?" David asked, disappointed.

"You're not impressed?"

"Well . . ." David said diplomatically. "Are you?"

Ned leaned against the nearby conference table, the folder he took from his office with him. He picked it up and opened it in response to David's question.

"I find the tape interesting," Ned said. "The coherence of the group. That last line, when they spoke the word *Thor* simultaneously, caught me by surprise. It lends credence to one of Professor Spear's central theories."

"Which is?" David asked.

"Before I answer that question let me give you some background on the man." Ned consulted his notes. "Until twelve years ago Professor Stephen Spear was a moderately well-known anthropologist. His primary field of study was the culture of the ancient Australian Aborigines, which until the Europeans arrived hadn't changed much in the last thirty thousand years. The papers he wrote on the subject were well received, and he had even published a small volume on Dreamtime, the Aborigines' mystical tradition. He lived in Australia with his wife for five years. They were childless. After a brief return to the United States, he developed an interest in the Dogon people of Mali in Africa. Have you heard of them?"

"No. Mali? That's between Algeria and the Ivory Coast, right?"

"Correct. Sub-Saharan land—the former French Sudan. The Dogon are an ancient tribe, descended culturally from the Egyptians, that has preserved pre-dynastic Egyptian religious mysteries more accurately than the Egyptians themselves. They go way back, before three thousand two hundred B.C." Ned paused. "I have to tell you what drew Spear's attention to the Dogon. Listen with an open mind."

"Of course," David said.

Ned consulted his file again. "Between the years 1946 and 1950 two French anthropologists, Marcel Griaule and Germaine Dieterlen, managed to gain the trust of two priests, one priestess, and a patriarch of the Dogon people. This was not an easy task because first they had to learn the languages of the Dogon, Sanga and Wazouba. Also, for thousands of years the Dogon have guarded the inner secrets of their religious tradition with great fervor. Even among the tribe, only high initiates were given the type of information Griaule and Dieterlen obtained. The two French anthropologists eventually published the information in a paper entitled 'A Sudanese Sirius System.' I have a translation of this article and want you to study it. Professor Spear read it and it was this article that led him to bring his wife and a number of associates to Mali." Ned paused again. "Are you familiar with the star Sirius?"

David shrugged. "I know it's the brightest star in the sky."

"Then you can understand why it would be of particular importance to an ancient culture. Particularly one as inquisitive as the Egyptians."

"I thought we were talking about the Dogon here?"

"We are talking about what the Dogon know of the ancient Egyptians, facts not found by studying the pyramids. The main deity of the ancient Egyptians was the Goddess Isis, who is usually associated with the star Sirius. I won't go into all the details of how frequently the Egyptians' traditions are linked to the star. Suffice it to say it was important to them, and to the Dogon."

"Just because it was bright?" David asked.

"No. There's much more to it. Let me cut to the chase. The Dogon people believe that their culture, and that of the Egyptians, was formed by a race of heavenly beings that came from the Sirian star system thousands of years ago. Of course, any anthropologist could show you dozens of isolated tribes throughout the world that believe almost the same thing. The difference is that the Dogon people know things about the Sirius star system that modern astronomers are only beginning to discover. The most significant of these facts is that Sirius has a white dwarf for a companion. Do you know what that is?"

"Yes. A star that has collapsed back upon itself. They're usually planet-size, rather than as big as an ordinary star."

"You're right. The white dwarf, Sirius B, was not discovered until the advent of large telescopes. That's because it's extremely faint, only magnitude eight, invisible to the naked eye under the best of circumstances, even if it wasn't completely obliterated by the light from nearby Sirius. It circles Sirius every fifty years. Now you must be thinking, So what?"

"I am," David agreed. "I'm also thinking that I don't believe in little green men."

Ned straightened himself. "The Dogon people have known for thousands of years that Sirius had an invisible companion circling it. They knew its period of rotation around the central sun. They also knew that it was, and I quote, "The smallest and the heaviest of all stars." Wipe that smile off your face, David. They knew about condensed states of matter even before modern physicists dreamed them up."

David kept smiling. "I just can't believe all this is worth a trip to Idaho, or that this discussion is taking place inside an office of the FBI."

"There's more. But before I go on let me impress upon you that the Dogon's knowledge of Sirius is irrefutable according to anthropologists who have studied them. For they also have drawings of exactly how Sirius B orbits Sirius, which is in an ellipse."

"All planets revolve in an elliptical pattern. The earth traces an ellipse around the sun."

"Yes. Kepler explained that over three centuries ago. But the Dogon people had no access to Kepler and his laws of planetary motion. How do you explain that?"

"I don't have to. I'm retiring in two weeks."

"You're playing the smart-ass. I expected that. But I have piqued your interest. I know you, David—you love a mystery. That's another reason I chose you for this case. Let me go on, because the tale leads in an unexpected direction. Professor Spear read these things about the Dogon and quickly decided he had to study them firsthand. As I said he brought his wife and another professor with him to Mali. His sister-in-law went along as well. They stayed six months. From all accounts, they managed to probe even deeper into the Dogon's inner circle than the two French anthropologists had. Spear learned to speak Sanga and Wazouba fluently, no small feat. Then there was a tragedy—Spear's wife died and the sister-in-law went insane. The group returned to the States."

"How did the wife die?" David asked.

"A wild animal killed her."

"What kind of wild animal?"

"I don't know," Ned said. "We're talking about a small group, studying an isolated tribe. The details are sketchy. What information we do have on the death of Mrs. Spear comes from the LAPD, who interviewed the group when they reentered the country."

"Why did the LAPD investigate a death that took place in Africa?"

"Penny was born in Los Angeles. I believe Spear re-entered the U.S. through Los Angeles, without Penny. You can't just lose your wife in a foreign country without somebody asking questions. But it was a cursory investigation. No criminal charges were brought against anyone."

"Has the sister-in-law recovered?"

"No. At present she's in a sanatorium in South Carolina."

"Did the death of her sister bring about the insanity?"

"We don't know, but the two events did coincide. All we know for sure is that Spear was devastated when he returned to America and spent the following year in solitude, before embarking on his current field of interest." Ned paused. "Have you heard of past life regressions?"

"Sure. Another New Age term. Under hypnosis people regress their memories to a time before their births and into the memories of other, previous lives." David added, "I grant the process as much validity as I do the theory of little green men."

Ned nodded. "You might be surprised to hear that Professor Spear doesn't believe in past lives either. The man appears to be an atheist. However, he is investigating a concept that runs parallel to reincarnation. He believes— and I might add that he is not alone in the belief—that each of us carries within us the memories of our ancestors. Embedded in our genes are the pasts of our mothers and fathers, and in turn their mothers and fathers, and so on, back. The videotape you just saw was an example of how his group tries to probe the memories of a particular genetic line. You might have noticed Spear give the instruction, 'Follow the Nordic chain.' "

"When you say others support his theory, do you mean other scientists?"

"A few, not many. But Spear has published his research into genetic memories in a number of prestigious journals. The topic, at least, is being debated in scientific circles."

"But the things his group knows about the government don't seem to be connected to past life regression," David said.

"Yes and no. The group that you saw probing genetic memories also speaks for the Big Mind about current events. Supposedly, what we saw was the Big Mind talking, not individual people."

"I'm confused," David said. "What does Spear's experience with the Dogon have to do with his research into genetic memories? For that matter, what about the aliens?"

"I didn't say anything about aliens."

"Yes, you did. I heard you. I wish I was wearing a wire."

Ned gave an exaggerated sigh. "I simply pointed out that the Dogon people possess extraordinary knowledge of our universe. As for your other question—we're not sure. That's one of the things we want you to find out. Why did Spear shift from anthropology to parapsychological research? We know that Spear uses some type of group hypnosis to bring his five subjects to a deep state, and the Dogon may have taught him the technique."

"Who were in turn taught by the aliens from Sirius?"

Ned shook his head wearily. "That must be it."

"What's the deal with the identical twins?"

"You noticed them?"

"They're hard not to notice."

Ned nodded. "Beautiful women. Their names are Lucy and Vera Temple. Lucy was the one who spoke. She's older by two minutes. They're twenty-eight, graduate students of Professor Spear's, both working on Ph.D.'s."

"What university is he affiliated with?" David asked.

"Stanford."

"What are the girls studying?"

"Psychology. Remember, Spear holds a doctorate in that field as well."

"Does Stanford approve of this research?"

"They're being open about it," Ned said.

"What's he doing up in Idaho?"

"They're on a retreat at some kind of camp for the next few days. He grew up in Idaho and apparently feels the isolation is conducive to his research."

"If he wants isolation, why does he want me there?"

"He wants acceptance as well as isolation. You're a writer. You can make him famous."

David considered it before he burst out laughing. "This is the craziest thing I've ever heard. I keep waiting for the punch line. Tell me the truth, why are you sending me to spy on a group of trance channelers?"

Ned smiled with him. "If the Big Mind knows all it appears to know, maybe it can tell us what next month's lottery numbers are going to be. Seriously, David, have you anything better to do for the next few days? Go up there and see what they're all about. If nothing else, you might hit it off with either Lucy or Vera."

"I have your official permission? Becoming entangled with an informant is grounds for dismissal."

Ned shrugged. "They're hardly informants. Who are they informing on? The Big Mind? Besides, like you said, I don't get laid anymore. You have my permission as long as you tell me all about it. While you're there, I'll pay a visit to Professor Spear's old partner—Professor Buckley. He's in Florida. Supposedly he hasn't spoken to Spear since they were in Mali. They had some kind of falling out."

"You're really going back out in the field? Sanders *must* be driving you nuts."

Ned snorted. "He's biting on my nuts. If the Dogon were cannibals, I'd convince Sanders that Jimmy Hoffa was still alive and underground in Mali and that he personally had to check out the situation."

David chuckled. "What a way for two agents to end their glorious careers. Spying on psychics who worship Thor and Isis. By the way, do you have photographs of everyone in Spear's group?"

"Yes." Ned opened his folder again. "I know you just want Lucy's and Vera's."

"No. Let me see them all." David accepted Ned's stack of four-by-five black and whites. He didn't bother asking where Ned obtained them, nor what the sources for his information on Professor Spear were. There were few activities in the United States that Ned Calendar could not find out about.

David studied the pictures. The young women were every bit as attractive in black and white. Lucy's smile almost burned through the print, David thought. She looked too wholesome to be sailing on a Viking ship seeking vengeance. Vera, on the other hand, appeared as serious as she had on the tape, even with her eyes open. He had trouble telling the two of them apart—they were that identical.

At the bottom of the stack were pictures of two other women who also looked similar to each other.

"Spear's wife and his sister-in-law," Ned said as David separated the pictures out. "Those are copies of their passport photos, before they went to Africa."

A wave of disquiet settled over David. "What were their names?"

"Spear's wife was named Penny. The sister-in-law is called Frances Cumberly. Remember, she's still alive."

"That's no life, being locked in a mental institution." David didn't understand the source of his uneasiness, except that it had hit him the moment he saw the women. Surely, he thought, it couldn't be because of the cruel fates they had each suffered. His career had been an extended exercise in the madness of mankind. He had seen photographs of hundreds of victims over the last fifteen years, many of whom had been ripped and torn by bullets and knives, and even by bare hands. Yet there was something about these two women that felt strange to him—a warning of some kind. Ned noticed his concern.

"What is it?" he asked.

"See if you can visit the sister-in-law while you're checking out Spear's ex-partner," David said softly. "I want to know what drove her mad."

CHAPTER 2

W hy had David become an FBI agent? He thought it would be fun. He believed, when he graduated from the University of Iowa with a degree in chemistry and no desire to go on to medical school—as he had initially planned—that he'd enjoy rescuing kidnapped children and putting serial murderers in prison. He had watched Efrem Zimbalist, Jr. in the reruns of "The FBI." He thought he knew what he was getting into.

He studied the requirements. A candidate had to be-tween the ages of twenty-three and thirty-seven, hold a de-gree from a four-year college, and pass a background check and receive top-secret clearance. There were tests, of course—IQ and moral fiber exams, plus two lengthy in-terviews. The FBI accepted fewer than one out of twenty applicants, but he must have answered the questions well because soon he was off to Quantico, the famed FBI Academy, which was located forty miles south of Washington. The training lasted sixteen intensive weeks.

There was a "town" located in Quantico named Hogan's Alley. It had the highest crime rate in the United States—kidnappings and murders every day. It was where the trainees practiced the skills they learned in the classroom. One day there was a bank robbery, and David and his four partners were to swoop in and save the day. Only this robbery was toward the end of their four-month training and it had a twist. While the five trainees surrounded the bank and shouted for the guy to give himself up, a trash man down the street started his truck and began to drive off. To the surprise of his partners, and to himself, David chased after the truck. That was his first experience with the "gut feeling" that the best law enforcement officers experienced. He just *knew* the garbage truck was the getaway car and arrested the driver over the protestations of his group. It turned out the trash man had a fully automatic Uzi under his front seat. David received a special commendation for quick thinking, yet really he'd acted without thinking. It was a lesson he was to remember—logic could only serve so far.

After graduation he was assigned to the Los Angeles office, with Ned Calendar as his SAC. Besides being the bank robbery capital of the world, Los Angeles had problems that were unique to the city, such as "star harassment" and ferocious gang violence. But bank robberies were the big thing and David was happy to be assigned to a squad specializing in them. The action was fast and there was a lot of it. Compared with working on white-collar or organized crime cases, there was little paperwork. No two days were ever alike. The year he arrived, over two thousands banks were hit in L.A., with the FBI solving more than eighty percent of them, demonstrating that it was the most foolish crime one could commit. The literary quality of many of the holdup notes demonstrated the level of intelligence of the average thief. David collected them on a board beside his desk. *"Give me your money or I will shoot it." "Don't worry I not kill you. I just want kill money." "This is a stickup. Put your hands in the air and keep them there. Put your money in my bag." "Don't be afraid. I have a gun." "Excuse me. This is a hold up. Sorry to wreck your great hair day."*

He loved the funny money as well. To make it easier to catch robbers, bank tellers' drawers had some marked bills that contained dye packs that exploded. Often, the packs exploded while the bad guys were trying to escape. More than a few times David spotted the getaway car by all the red dye pouring out of it. Once a guy robbed a bank and then stopped in a 7-Eleven around the block for a six-pack of beer. David apprehended him in the convenience-store parking lot where he happened to stop for a Coke, after going over the crime scene. The robber, red from head to toe, was calmly sitting in his car getting drunk, twenty thousand in messed-up bills on the seat beside him.

Then there was the big day of life-event number one. It was a Friday afternoon, three years into his stint as an FBI agent. David had the day off and stopped in his own bank to cash a check. He was flirting with the pretty teller when a man in a business suit let out a cry to his right. Sure enough, a guy who looked and smelled as if he had spent the last forty years in a grocery store Dumpster had a gun to the businessman's head. The bank had a bandit barrier installed, bulletproof sheets of Plexiglas to separate the customers from the tellers. Bandit barrier banks were seldom robbed because they were that much harder to crack. When David looked over, he noticed that the teller in front of the gunman had already dropped down behind the counter as she had undoubtedly been instructed to do in the event of a holdup. This had put the robber in a foul mood.

"Give me your goddam money or I waste this fucker!" the guy screamed.

Of course the teller was safe and didn't want to put her head back up, bulletproof sheet of Plexiglas or not. David could understand. He suspected she had already pressed a silent alarm, but he knew this guy was not going to wait around for the SWAT team. There was a wild fury in his eyes, no doubt drug-assisted. Methedrine soaked in Valvoline. PCP spelled backward—something toxic bubbled in the guy's bloodstream. It was one of those few times when David was not carrying a gun. The bank had a security guard, however, and he had one. Unfortunately the gentleman was in his seventies and loved nothing more exciting than playing Clue with his grandchildren. David wasn't even sure the guard's gun would be loaded. The guard knew David was an FBI agent and his eyes immediately went to him for help. David shook his head minutely and wished the teller would stand back up and give the robber what he wanted. He knew a short fuse dipped in gasoline when he saw one.

"Motherfuckers!" the robber yelled. He pulled the trigger. The young businessman in the nice suit suddenly had a red hole in each ear. He went down in a messy puddle. The customers in the bank turned to Jell-O. The gunman grabbed a middle-aged woman. "I'm not waiting!" he shouted.

Everyone else was, including the bank president, cowering behind his desk in the corner. There was terror in the woman's eyes. She struggled feebly with her captor. The robber smacked her hard enough on the back of her head with his gun to let her know he didn't like that but not hard enough to knock her out. David had no choice. He took a step toward the robber, his outstretched arms saying everything was cool.

"I work here, sir," David said in his blue jeans and T-shirt. "I can get you all the money you want. Just relax and give me a minute. No one else has to get hurt."

The robber drilled the muzzle in the woman's ear. He snorted. "You don't work here."

"I sure do," David said. "I'm senior vice-president of this branch. Today's my day off. Just relax and let me get you your money. Would you like large bills or small?"

The guy thought a moment, then yelled, "I want all your bills!"

David nodded. "You'll have them. Did you happen to bring a bag with you?" He could see the guy had not thought of that. Before the guy's frustration could peak again, David hastily added, "It doesn't matter. I can get you a bag. You can have your money and be on your way in one minute." He paused to allow his calming words to sink in. "Would that be all right?"

The guy flashed a wide toothy grin. "No funny shit."

David nodded. "No funny shit." He glanced at the teller he had been flirting with before all the excitement started. At least she had kept her composure and not lowered her head. He said, "Mary, do we have any of those sacks we take our deliveries in?"

"Yes," she said. "In the back."

"Could you please get our guest two of those bags and stuff them full of cash from the teller drawers. Give him everything we have."

Mary quickly fetched the bags, and while everyone stood and stared as the puddle of blood around the dead man spread to the tips of David's shoes, she emptied the front drawers. She was wise enough to work calmly, which helped to relax the robber. When she was done she passed the bags through an electronically controlled door to David, who handed them to the robber, his shoes actually splashing in the dead man's blood. The robber tossed the middle-aged woman aside and leveled his black Colt .38 revolver at David, his expression a mixture of money-bag-high and bad-acid-blues.

"You still don't look like you work in a bank," he said.

"But I do," David said calmly, knowing the guy was half an inch away from putting a round in his belly, where it would hurt worse than almost anything. "I can prove it to you."

"How?"

"I know the combination to the vault in the back."

The guy was interested. "What is it?"

"Left six. Right five. Right five. Left two. Right nine."

The guy grinned. "No shit? I'll remember that. Hey, I'll be back here next year and take your whole fucking stash!"

David chuckled. "Repeat business is the heart of any successful bank." He nodded to the clock. "You'd better get out of here before the cops come."

The guy blinked as if he had just heard the earth was round. "You're right. Thanks." He lowered his weapon. "You have a nice day, you hear."

"You too," David said.

After the guy left, David dashed to the guard. Ed was already pulling out his gun to hand to David. "It's loaded," he said quickly as if reading David's mind.

"Keep everyone here," David barked. "Call for back-up."

Mild-mannered Ed had handed him a .44 Magnum. David was out on the street in a second, scanning for the robber, who despite his dilated chrome pupils, had good leg speed. He was already a hundred yards down the road and starting to climb into the driver's side of a rusty blue Mustang that looked as if it had been parked on Venus for the past year. He glanced back at the bank, as he tossed his loot on the passenger seat, and saw David and the Magnum. He shifted into high gear. David was less than half-way to the car when it lay down twin trails of sizzling rubber. David raised Ed's gun and, taking aim with both hands, fired three rounds at the rear tire on the right. The kick on the gun was like a fastbreak ball tossed by Magic Johnson. David was lucky to land one round in the rubber, but it was enough—a .44 Magnum in a Michelin four-ply. The tire exploded like a Tonya Harding alibi. The front of the car careened into a yellow fire hydrant. Had the scene been on TV, water would have gushed out onto the sidewalk—but it didn't. David sprinted toward the side of the Mustang. Mr. Money Bags slowly climbed out of the car, weapon in hand.

"Halt!" David shouted. "Slowly, drop your gun and put your hands in the air."

Dazed, the guy raised his hands but didn't drop his gun.

"Drop your gun," David repeated firmly.

Blood the color of red Kool-Aid poured from a gash on his forehead. "You said you worked for the bank," he complained.

"I work for the FBI. Drop your weapon this instant or I'll blow your fucking head off."

The guy was annoyed. "You lied to me, motherfucker. That wasn't the combination of the vault."

"I will count to three. If you do not drop your gun by three, your head will explode. It's that simple. One—"

The guy stared at him. "Shit."

"Two."

Since David had lied to the guy about being a bank VP, he could understand why the robber didn't believe him about being an agent. Still, he did have an awfully big gun pointed at the asshole. The guy should have listened.

"Three."

The gunman whipped his arm down and tried to get off a round. His personal poison had to be in the higher-frequency bands; he was fast. But he was also just another low life with the IQ of a lousy blackjack hand. David shot him in the chest. The force of the round sent the guy flying backward, his arms flung out as if he was preparing for crucifixion. Vital organs exploded out the rear of his spine—he landed like something dropped from a skyscraper. David stopped to take a breath. He thought of the young man lying dead on the floor of the bank. Of the two big bags of money sitting on the seat in the Mustang. Of how his right wrist hurt from the recoil of Ed's Magnum. He had just killed someone for the first time, and he should have felt either disgust or elation, some powerful emotion. But all he felt was a great weariness. He heard sirens in the distance. He had walked the mile to the bank. He wondered if a cop would give him a ride home so he could rest.

Later, though, he felt elation when the office heard what he had done. The secretaries looked at him differently. His partners volunteered to buy him lunch. The nickname got started. A .44 Magnum. Just wasted the bastard out in the middle of the street. That's Dirty Dave for you.

Then Ned came to him and asked him to go after kidnappers. The action was a lot slower, he said. The success rate was a lot lower, but the reward could be greater, to return a child to his or her parents. Ned made a persuasive argument. David always liked to try something new. He said OK.

His first case, which he handled with three other agents, concerned a sixteen-year-old boy, Harold Murray, who had apparently been kidnapped while he was alone in his house. His parents had been contacted, and a ransom of one million dollars in cash was the asking price for them to see their son alive again. The family was wealthy. There were no signs of struggle, but by the glasses on the kitchen table, it did look as if Harold had offered one or more people a drink. On top of that, when David questioned the parents, he learned that Harold was home alone rarely. David's brain hummed. The kidnappers not only knew Harold, they knew him well. That probably meant they were young, Harold must be being held in the neighborhood, and the kidnappers could not possibly let him live once they collected their money. David told his partners his deduction but they thought he was moving too fast and with too little information. They believed the voice that had called for the ransom sounded older. David thought that was unimportant. He *knew* he was right. His gut feeling was back.

David instructed the parents to stall for time—to tell the kidnappers it was hard to gather a million overnight—and went to Harold's school to speak to every single teacher. Did they have any troublemakers who had hassled Harold in the past, he asked? Were any of them absent lately or nervous, talking together in corners at lunch? David made up a list of a dozen possible candidates and that same day visited each of their homes. At the third house a long-haired, droopy-eyed boy answered the door. He had a twitch in his left cheek and bloodshot eyes. As soon as David identified himself as an FBI agent, he knew he had hit the jackpot. The kid practically fell over.

"Are you a friend of Harold Murray?" David asked.

The kid held his head so low he might have been trying

to snort coke from the floor. "No. I mean, yeah, I know him. Why?"

"Do you know where he is?"

Shuffling, foot to foot. "No."

"Are you sure?"

"No."

"You're not sure?"

"I don't know where he is, Officer. I swear it."

David smiled. "I'm not a cop. You don't have to call me officer. You can just call me Dirty Dave. What's your name?"

"Ralph."

"Ralph, do you know how I earned my nickname?"

"No."

"I blew away a kidnapper with a .44 Magnum. Blew his balls off. He bled to death in the middle of the street. That's the honest truth. He died screaming." David reached into his coat. "Are you sure you don't know where Harold is?"

The kid jumped back. "I don't know. I heard he was kidnapped."

David took a step into the house. "Are your parents home, Ralph?"

"No." The kid was sweating. "Can you just come in my house like that? Don't you need a warrant?"

"No. Only cops need warrants. I'm an FBI agent, remember? You got any drugs here?"

"No. I swear it."

"You're eyes are red, Ralph. You're lying. You've been smoking, I can tell." David pulled out his gun and pointed it at Ralph. "Tell me where Harold is."

The kid was in tears. "I don't know!"

David leveled the gun at his balls. "One of your partners has already tipped us off. We know you've got Harold. But if you don't want to talk now, that's all right, you'll be talking with a squeaky voice the rest of your life. That is, *if* you don't bleed to death in front of me now."

"You can't shoot me!"

David cocked the hammer. "Why not? I like shooting people. I won't get in trouble. You'll probably be dead and won't be able to identify me."

The boy shook. "Who told you about Harold?"

David chuckled. "Ah. That's a secret. I'm good at keeping secrets. If you tell me where Harold is, I won't tell any of the others you told me. It'll be our secret."

Ralph buried his face in his hands. "I didn't want to do it. They made me do it. They talked me into it."

David put away his gun. He walked over and put a hand on the kid's shoulder. "Ralph," he said, "that's the last thing in the world you want to tell the jury."

Ralph took him around the block to a classmate's house. The parents were home, and the father demanded that David show a warrant. David refused and pushed past him. It was permissible under the law—he had verification that a hostage was being held in the house and that the said hostage was in danger. He found Harold tied up in the guesthouse. The adults didn't know he had been there for the four days he had been missing.

David ended up arresting five youths. He went to their trial, of course, to testify against them. He didn't give Ralph any brownie points for cooperating. Ralph tried to convince the jury that David had almost killed him but David testified that at all times he had treated the boy gently. The jury believed David.

God, if only other cases were so easy, but it wasn't to be. He had far more successes than failures, but each of the latter stayed with him ten times as long. He lost wives and husbands, sons and daughters. But he kept going, he had to keep going. He felt he had a responsibility to society, and knew he was too good to quit.

Then, in the middle of David's ninth year at the Bureau, Ned came to him again with something different. Ned always pushed David to his limits, but this time Ned himself would be overseeing the case, which meant those limits would be blown away like Mr. Two Money Bags's heart. Ned was a workaholic—hundred-hour weeks were standard with him. Ned wanted David with him on an OC case—organized crime. Despite all he had heard about how slow OC work could be, David found himself getting excited as he listened to the facts.

Rudy Failla, the head of the most powerful Mafia family on the West Coast, was the target. Failla's tentacles reached into a dozen Mob-friendly businesses: construction, loan-sharking, drugs, prostitution, topless bars, gambling. It was gambling where Ned planned to strike. While the majority of the public blissfully believed that Las Vegas had been swept clean of the Mob with the construction of family-oriented high-rises on the Strip, the FBI knew better. Failla didn't own any of the major hotels on the Strip but he did control several of the larger downtown casinos, and his influence was felt throughout the city. Because Failla was based in Los Angeles, Ned felt he had the right to kick his ass if he could locate the perfect boot. Ned believed he might have found it.

He had turned one of Failla's men into an informant. The guy was not a low-level wiseguy, but a ruthless lieutenant who regularly traveled with the Don. He had already provided Ned with a list of people Failla had ordered hit. The problem was the lieutenant—Ned called him Gary Garrott, his real name was Gary Guilliani—had never received a direct order to kill from Failla, who had an almost invisible *consigliere* and two underbosses to take care of such details. The other problem Ned told David was that no one had heard from Gary Garrott in a month.

"He's probably dead," David said.

Ned shook his head impatiently. "I did think of that, you know. But I still have the list he gave us. All we have to do is tie Failla to it and we can lock him up."

"Is that all?"

"It's not as bad as it sounds. We have the RICO, electronic surveillance, and any new toys the tech boys can whip up for us. We can bug the roaches in Failla's casinos. Gary Garrott led us to six bodies he personally dumped. We connect Failla to two or three of those and he'll be presumed guilty. Most people on a jury will tell you they loved Brando's Godfather. But Failla's a fat fuck, looks like Marlon Brando before the diet. No jury's going to like him. Place those bugs for me, David. Put one in his lover's snatch."

"Is that within the jurisdiction of the RICO?" David asked, surprised at Ned's crude remarks. He was usually conservative when it came to matters of sex. David could see that going after Failla had affected Ned's psyche. He had a dartboard hung in his office, a map of Las Vegas hotels behind it to catch the bite of his misses. Ned didn't like to miss, David knew. But when he did, the opposition didn't walk away smiling.

The RICO, or the Racketeer-Influenced and Corrupt Organizations Act, was the Bureau's main weapon against organized crime. It had been in existence for over a decade but few in the agency really knew how to use it. The RICO allowed them to build a case against entire families instead of taking out a few soldiers. It was supposed to let them attack the very structure of the La Cosa Nostra. In court, a Mob "family" could be proven to be a criminal organization, rather than a collection of hot-tempered relatives.

Ned answered his question. "It will be after your bug sticks its ear out."

So David moved to Las Vegas. He became Blake Nichols, half owner in a well-established and highly successful pool construction company. The cover was excellent. It gave him a past and money to gamble with. He also got to work on his tan, even though he did most of his real work at night. He began to haunt Failla's casinos, playing blackjack mostly. Because he was using the Bureau's money and was a conscientious employee, he learned to count cards so that he usually left a winner. But he didn't win so much that he drew suspicion, and at Failla's pride and joy, the Silver Shamrock, he always left a few hundred at the tables. It was at the Shamrock, five weeks after moving to Vegas, that he met and fell in love with Sandy Quin, who worked for the casino, for Failla. At first it had seemed a fortunate coincidence, but David should have known how quickly fortune could change to despair in the city of sin.

He was sitting at the counter in the casino coffee shop after playing against a dealer who busted as often as meteors land in the desert, counting his losses and thinking he hadn't even met Failla's lover much less asked her if she had a condom. A slim dark blond with lips the red of Christmas peppermint candy and a smile as sweet as chocolate chased ice cream around a pie plate two seats to his right. Thirtyish, with a tan that said she was local, she wore a smart orange dress and a white ribbon in her hair. Had it been a black ribbon he supposed she would have reminded him of Halloween. Trick or treat. Hello, I love you. Two different ways to say hello late at night. He didn't know which was better, which was worse. But he did believe he loved her the moment he saw her, although he normally didn't indulge in ridiculous sentiments. When had he last let himself care for a woman? In college? For the last nine years his career had been all-consuming. Had Ned asked him right then if he'd use this woman to get Failla, David would have told him he was crazy.

"Hi," he said. "You might want to grab that scoop of ice cream with your hand. It doesn't like your fork."

Blushing, she put down the fork. "I shouldn't be eating this late at night, anyway."

"This is Vegas. It's never late here. There are no clocks."

She smiled and picked up a folder of papers on her right. "It's late for me. I have to have this work on my boss's desk by tomorrow morning at nine."

"What are you working on?"

"An ad for this hotel."

"Are you trying to sell it?"

She chuckled. "I'm afraid I don't own it. I'm just a poor working girl."

David had a sinking feeling, even then. "You work for the Silver Shamrock?"

"Yes. I'd tell you my title if I knew it. Four years ago I started as a secretary but when Mr. Failla—he's my boss—learned I could write, he put me in charge of hotel publicity. Since then I've picked up the jobs of payroll and menu maker and overall errand runner. Occasionally, I still take shorthand and type." She paused, studying him. "What do you do Mr. . . ."

"Nichols. Blake Nichols." The first thing he told her was a lie. It would be the same with the last, when he said everything would be all right. He offered his hand. "Pleased to meet you Ms. . . ."

She took his hand, and although he didn't mean it so, she took the bait.

"Ms. Quin. Sandy Quin," she said.

They started to date. She liked hiking, water-skiing, kite flying, baking, him—most of all him. Why did he use her? Because she was there? His love was as true as hers. It was only a desire for truth that led him to tell her who he really was and what he was doing. At first she didn't believe him—not that he was an FBI agent, but that her wonderful boss was a cold-blooded murderer. David didn't want to tell her the stories of Failla. He didn't want to place the horrific images in her mind, but she made him talk, show her the pictures and secret files. Ned would have nailed David to the Shamrock's craps table if he knew that he told her so much about their case. But David trusted her, with his life, literally.

They covered the dirty details early one morning before the sun came up. "See," he said, "here's what happens when your boss gets angry. The chainsaw that cut up this guy started at the toes, with the guy's legs still kicking. It took forever to get to the head." "The testicles in this guy's mouth belonged to his baby brother."

"This woman used to go out with Mr. Failla." "I recognize her," Sandy cried.

"That's amazing," David said. The woman was missing her eyeballs. "She should never have slept with Failla's poker partner. The partner should never have slept with her." But Sandy didn't want to see that man's body—what was left of it. She ran into the bathroom, locked the door, and threw up. She didn't come out for a long time. But when she did, her clear blue eyes were as colorless as windshields and her voice was filled with resolve.

"I want to help you get him," she said.

He said no, of course, he wouldn't risk anything happening to her for the world, even though her dating an FBI agent put her in peril anyway. What he wanted her to do was quit her job and move to Los Angeles with him. But he couldn't go home yet, not until he got his man.

David never realized how strong Sandy was until too late. Maybe she, too, had watched "The FBI" reruns while growing up. She shocked him when she went over his head and called Ned in L.A., saying she had a plan. Ned listened as she explained she'd tell Failla that they desperately needed to upgrade their phone equipment. Ned's agents could take the place of the phone crew and install all the bugs they wanted in both Failla's offices and private quarters, with her personally supervising their work. No one would question the work order. Sandy had thought the plan up all by herself. Ned was interested, of course he was. He later told David he had visions of Failla behind metal bars while Sandy talked.

David, when he heard about the plan, flipped. Absolutely not, he said, then backed down slightly. That was a mistake, to open the door even a bit. He agreed that Sandy could help them get the bugs in, but then she had to get out. Ned vetoed the idea. He said her sudden departure might alert Failla. With the bugs in place, business had to go on as usual, and that meant Sandy had to stay. Ned also feared that any changes in Sandy's routine might cause Failla to take a closer look at who she was dating.

"The phone company will cooperate a hundred percent," Ned tried to reassure David. "Failla can call them himself and they'll confirm that they had their people out. There's no reason to think he'll look for bugs, and if he does get suspicious, we'll hear about it from his own lips. This is our big break. We can have Failla and his top men in jail by the end of the year. Think about that, David. Think about how much it will mean to have him and his bastards out of society."

He did think about it, and it seemed that the possible

gain outweighed the risks, which appeared reasonably small. Yet his gut said they were making a huge mistake. Ned asked David for his permission because of David's relationship with Sandy. Ned never forced him, and in the end David said OK, we'll use her if she wants to be used. He never forgave himself for that.

Excited, Sandy told David that Failla had only grunted his approval when she asked him about the installation. He trusted her judgment on such matters completely. She was Efrem Zimbalist, Jr.'s girlfriend, playing in the big leagues now. Dancing around her apartment, she playfully mocked David for his lack of daring. But David understood then that Sandy had yet to connect the man she worked for with the photographs David had shown her. She couldn't picture Failla wielding a chain saw himself. David could, and he hardly slept that night.

Failla's private conversations came in loud and clear. Though the mobster was only in Nevada on weekends, preferring his mansion in Malibu to his penthouse on the top floor of the Shamrock, he did most of his business in Vegas.

On the very first weekend they listened, Failla blatantly discussed how he had personally blown off the back of Gary Garrott's skull, and even where he had dumped the body—Lake Mead beside the Hoover Dam. David lost all enthusiasm for tap water after that. With that tape in the can, David wanted to blow the lid on Failla, feeling they had enough to prosecute. But Ned wanted to tear up the whole family, put the underbosses and the consigliere in jail. He was ready to listen for the entire next year if that's what it took.

A month after the bugs were planted, Failla discussed with his consigliere a hit on a local businessman. David listened to the tape several times. He knew the man who was to be killed, James Holt, the largest movie theater owner in Las Vegas. Blake Nichols's company had just put in a pool for Mr. Holt. David had even had lunch with the guy. The tape came to them courtesy of a bug in the painting behind Failla's office desk.

Failla: Holt licks my girls and then spits in my face. I gave him his start. I handed it to him on a silver platter. He thinks he doesn't owe me on his other projects, he's full of shit. Do him this week. Put a rocket in his chest. Make it burn.

Consigliere: Should we give the job to Frankie?

Failla: Fuck. Frankie's too old. He can't even get it up for his hand. Give it to George. He's a fucking lunatic. He'll enjoy torturing the guy.

Consigliere: Do you want it to look like a professional hit?

Failla: No. We don't need the shit. Not after Gary. Holt has to disappear. Put him in a hole somewhere that no one will ever dig up.

It was right then the fates began to conspire to wreck David's life. It was after ten o'clock when he finished listening to the tape and called Ned at home about saving Holt. If he didn't know him personally, Holt would have been just another statistic in Failla's reign of terror. But Holt had spent half their lunch talking to David about how much his three kids were going to enjoy their new pool. David told Ned they had to get Holt, his family, and Sandy out of town. He wanted to obtain arrest warrants with what they had, and take their chances in court. Ned was more daring.

"Let's just put a watch on Holt," Ned said. "Let's be there when they pick him up. Then, after we save the guy, we can put him on the stand. His testimony together with this tape will make it impossible for Failla to walk."

"But we have enough," David argued. "Too many things can go wrong. I know 'George,'—he *is* a fucking lunatic. He gets one whiff of our presence and people will die."

"You can handle him, David. I know you can."

But David was worried about that one line on the tape. *"Not after Gary."*

In his enthusiasm to get Failla, Ned never even mentioned the remark. But to David it spoke volumes. Failla knew Gary Garrott had ratted to the FBI. He had his antenna up. Any minute it might sense the tiny electronic devices around him, and then he would remember Sandy's request for a new phone system.

"If we're doing this, we're getting Sandy out of town—now," David said. "I don't give a damn if it makes waves."

Ned hesitated. "Maybe you should. Get her out now, then. Tonight."

"Thanks," David said.

David wanted to call Sandy right then, but he remembered she had to work late that night, and he definitely did not want to call her at the Shamrock. Failla had spoken of hitting Holt sometime during the week, which David knew could include the present moment. After calling backup and grabbing his gun, David decided to spend the night watching Holt's home. Failla's people were not above dragging someone from his own bed.

Lunatic George was already there when David cruised by. David didn't know the status of Holt's family, but Holt was being dragged down the front steps of his mansion, a gun to his head. It was Friday, close to midnight. David's backup had yet to appear, but he would have bet a stack

of black honeybees that George had people nearby. David
felt he had no choice. If George got Holt in the car, the
man would die. David did what any other agent raised on
TV reruns would have done. He rammed George's car
with his own just as George opened the back door to
throw his victim inside.

The door whacked Holt and sent him flying, probably
unconscious, to the ground. Lunatic George took one look
at David starting to climb out of his car and quickly raised
his gun. David ducked and heard a bullet pierce his windshield and the top half of the front seat. When he looked
up, George was running down the block. David stood up,
his 10-millimeter semiautomatic pistol in hand. He remained rock still, and took aim. Only on TV could people
shoot accurately while running at full speed.

"Stop or I'll shoot!" he shouted, intentionally failing to
identify himself as an FBI agent. He didn't want every
wiseguy on the block to know he was around. George
didn't stop. David shot him in the back. The guy fell like
a raging bull. Farther down the street, perhaps a hundred
yards, headlights went on as a car made a U-turn in the
middle of the street and roared away. David ran to where
George lay. The man was dead. God bless his hairy soul,
David thought. He ran back to Holt. The businessman was
alive but groggy, a nasty bump on his head. David got on
his car phone and called for an ambulance.

Then he thought of Sandy and Failla's quick mind.

He could practically hear the Don shouting at George's
backup.

*How the fuck did anyone know we were going to hit
Holt? There must be a mole here. Or else this hotel is
bugged.*

Failla would pause and check out his office.

It didn't matter what Ned said. Failla would know.

David drove toward the Silver Shamrock at high speed.

He arrived just in time to catch the midnight special into the land of nightmares.

There was a crowd gathered out front beside the silver fountain. Police cruiser lights flashed in dizzying circles. An ambulance stood nearby. David tried to push through the crowd but a teenage boy who looked like Harold Murray the day he was rescued, stopped him with a hand on his arm.

"Man, you don't want to see it," the boy said. "She jumped from the top floor."

David croaked. "Is it a young blond woman?"

"I don't know. Her hair's red now."

"What is she wearing?"

"An orange dress." The pale kid squinted at him. "Did you know her?"

David hung his head. "No. I didn't know her."

Even in that moment, in his black well of despair, the light of revenge shimmered before him like an ancient star guiding him to where the innocent gnawed on the bones of their tormentors. David took a couple of deep breaths, composed himself, and strode into the casino. He was a robot, his program clear. His gun set off an alarm. Security was on him in an instant. No problem. He flashed his badge and said he wanted to speak to Mr. Failla. They said fine, no problem. But they took his gun, something they had no right to do. It was still no problem, not to David. He wouldn't kill Failla now, tonight. He had time, he thought. He would kill him tomorrow.

They led him to Mr. Failla's private office. Failla sat behind a desk as wide as his belly, his stiff hair the color of dirty silver dollars. He was one of those men who had a hippo leg for a throat, fat and wrinkled. He wore an expensive gray suit, though, and his hands were remarkably delicate. He shelled and chewed peanuts as David entered. He snacked while Sandy's blood still lay in a warm pool beneath her head. The rage David experienced right then was beyond emotion. It took him to a place where he believed he was capable of anything. Still, the robot was all he showed. He flashed a grin as he was led forward to meet the great man. Failla's two underbosses stood behind their leader like grotesque stumps grown out of a volcanic hillside, their hands in their fat pockets, fingering guns they wished weren't so much bigger than their dicks.

"Who the fuck are you?" Failla asked.

David's grin widened. "May I sit down?" he asked.

Failla hesitated. Then he snapped a finger. A chair was brought. David sat down and crossed his legs. "So you caught her," he said smoothly. "I knew you would. I knew it was only a matter of time."

Failla's eyes narrowed. "I don't know what you're talking about."

David gestured to the room. "I'm sure you've swept this place clean. We can talk freely. My name's Blake Nichols. I work for the FBI. I've been spying on you for the last two months. I recruited Sandy. She was my stooge." David shrugged. "I let her fall in love with me. She did what I told her."

Failla considered. "You don't sound too shook up by her unfortunate fall."

"What can I say? To me, it's just business. That's why I'm here. I want to do business with you."

Failla was cautious. "What do you have to offer?"

"The details of the FBI's case against you. Also, the name of a highly placed mole in your organization."

"There is no mole in my organization," Failla said flatly.

"What about Gary Guilliani?"

"He's not with us anymore."

"Too bad. You should have talked to him before you laid him off. He could have told you about his partner." David paused. "I have the records. I can prove everything I say."

Failla thought for a full minute. "How strong is the FBI case?"

"A bitch if you don't know what's coming. Bullshit if you've got alibis ready."

"What do you want in return for these records?"

"One million in cash."

Failla snorted. "You have balls asking for that. What if I say you're still working for the FBI? What if I say my boys take you for a ride right now? Dump you where they dumped Gary?"

"You can say what you want. Without my help you'll be in jail in less than six months. And you won't be getting out. By the way, that was pretty sloppy work tonight, dumping the girl beside your own fountain."

David spoke the truth. Failla was shrewd and calculating enough to build and maintain a large empire. But at the same time, he was just another hotheaded thug.

Failla shook his head. "So I have a temper? What can I say? She pissed me off. She seemed like such a nice girl."

"She was a cunt," David said.

Failla slowly smiled. "I'm beginning to like you, Mr. Nichols. But I'm still not convinced that what you've got is worth a million. Tell me the name of the mole now as a sign of good faith and then maybe we can do business."

David stood and removed a card from his back pocket. He threw it on the Don's desk. "I'd like to, but my answer would not be appropriate, given the situation. That's my number. No one in the FBI knows it. Let's meet again tomorrow night, out in the desert somewhere. You pick the location. Leave me a message with directions. I have to go to L.A. now to get everything you need. Don't have me followed; it'll only cause complications for you. Bring unmarked bills, hundreds. By the way, I'll give you most of what I have tomorrow, but not all. Just in case you don't want to pay for my services." David paused. Staring Failla in the eye, he saw a dead man. "I hope we understand each other, Mr. Failla?"

Failla stood and nodded. He offered his hand across the wide desk. "You come alone, unarmed. You understand, Mr. Nichols?"

David smiled and shook his hand. "Yes."

He called Charles Gordon when he got back to his Vegas apartment. Gordon owned a large construction company in Los Angeles. Three years ago his wife had been kidnapped and the FBI had been called in. David had been put in charge of the case. It turned out to be one of the easier kidnappings David had ever worked on, largely because the kidnappers were as shrewd as Harold Murray's. The kidnappers asked that the half million in ransom money be placed in a specific trash can, and when they arrived to pick it up David arrested them. David had Gordon's wife back to him within two days. The man told him if he ever needed a favor, no matter what, to call him. So David called him. Gordon was happy to hear from him, but David didn't waste time on pleasantries.

"Charles," David said. "I need a big favor."

"Anything. What is it?"

"I need two hundred pounds of dynamite, detonators, wiring, and a timer. I need it in the next twelve hours, preferably sooner. Can you get it for me?"

Gordon took a moment. "Can't the Bureau get it for you?"

"This isn't a Bureau job."

"What is it?"

"It's personal."

"Where are you?"

"Las Vegas, but I can leave now to drive to your place."

Gordon paused. "That's not necessary. It sounds like you've got your hands full. Let me bring it to you."

"You can get the two hundred pounds?"

"Yes. But I have to warn you that that many sticks will make one hell of an explosion."

"That's exactly what I want," David said.

David told Gordon where to meet him before hanging up. Gordon's coming to him simplified matters, gave him longer to prepare his own car for the explosives. Before he could set to work, however, Ned called. He had heard about Sandy and wanted David to come home immediately. David had to laugh.

"But you said I couldn't come home until I got my man," David said. He hung up. He didn't blame his boss for what had happened to Sandy. He blamed himself and God. He felt like God as he began carefully to undo the seams of the upholstery in his car. He had the power of life and death in his hands. And he was choosing death. He worked through the night, wanting nothing to appear amiss. He wept only once, when he thought of her. But other than that once he didn't let her name enter his mind. He could grieve later, he decided, if he was still alive. Either way, he didn't care.

Gordon arrived two hours after sunrise and gave him the explosives. David thought of that line from *Apocalypse Now*. "I love the smell of napalm in the morning. . . . Smells like victory." David held the hard red sticks up to his nose before he transferred them into his hacked-up backseat. Gordon watched, worried.

"You must be in deep shit," Gordon said.

"Yeah, I suppose. But now I can blow my way out." David picked up the box of detonators and tossed them in the front seat. "I really appreciate the fireworks, buddy. If anyone ever steals your wife again, just give me a call. I'll find her for you."

Gordon blocked David's way as he tried to leave. "You have to tell me what's happened. If you don't—I can see it—you're going to die."

David stopped. "So I die. So what?"

Gordon shook his head. "You can't say that. You saved my wife's life. You have talents few people possess. You still have other people to save. You have to let me help you."

David didn't know why he listened to him, except that once he had Failla alone, he would need backup transportation if he was going to play Good Godfather/Bad Godfather the way he envisioned. In the end he told Gordon everything that had happened. He kept his voice calm and conversational, which seemed to frighten Gordon more than if he had broken down hysterically. Finally, it was decided that Gordon would follow him far enough into the desert to a point where he could see the explosion. David believed that would leave Gordon at a safe distance.

There were two messages on David's machine when he returned to his apartment. One from Ned—which he fast forwarded through—the other from a Failla wiseguy. Drive here, turn there. Follow the dirt road, then make a left. Look for the squat hill. Come alone. We'll be waiting for you at sunset. David wrote it all down, then tore up the directions. He had an excellent memory. A long memory with a short fuse, as they say.

Gordon watched as David outfitted his car, a black SC400 Lexus with leather interior, for its last day on earth.

David had been driving it for only two years and hated not to collect on his insurance policy. As he worked he quizzed Gordon about the power of the shock wave the bomb would generate, the range of the scrap metal from the blast. Of course, David knew the answers to most of his questions, but the talk helped pass the time and David wasn't in the mood to sleep.

Close to sunset, the two of them drove into the desert in separate cars. David left Gordon at the start of the first dirt road. Gordon had binoculars with him but David didn't think he'd need them. The evening desert air was as dry as salt and as still as David's hands. He had no fear because for the first time in his life he had no expectations for his own well-being. He didn't care if he drew in another breath, or let out the one inside his chest. His idea of what constituted a good time had simplified. He just wanted to torture Failla to death.

They waited for him at the base of a hill that resembled a garbage heap bulldozed over with cat litter. A gorilla with silver-mirrored sunglasses stood outside a black limo as impenetrable as an army tank. David was happy they had brought the armored monstrosity. Otherwise, the gorilla might have signaled him to park at a distance, afraid he might drive by and open fire. But secure inside his plated cocoon, Failla was only too happy to let David park beside him. David had already pressed the button that activated the timer. By his best calculations, he had five minutes before his Japanese-made sports coupe revisited Hiroshima. David grabbed the manila envelope and tiny cassette player and stepped out of the car before the gorilla could reach him. The windows on the limo were pale orange mirrors reflecting the fading sun. The orange reminded David of Sandy but only for a moment. The gorilla had a gun out.

"Put your hands in the air," he barked.

"Fuck you," David said. "I'm unarmed."

Odd, the gorilla didn't trust him. David was thoroughly frisked, and his cassette player and manila envelope examined, before the limo windows rolled down. Failla stuck his fat face out. David noted Failla had company, one of his underbosses and possibly the consigliere. Ned would get his wish after all, David thought. The family would cease to exist.

"Get in," Failla said pleasantly.

"If you wish," David said easily. "But you might prefer to listen to what I've brought alone."

Failla glanced at his partners. The seed David had planted the previous evening had sprouted. *I'd like to, but my answer would not be appropriate, given the situation.* Failla was worried how high up the mole was. The Don nodded to the gorilla. Again, David was frisked, his balls squeezed so hard he had to restrain himself from kneeing the guy in the face. The gorilla moved to the car, searched it quickly, found nothing amiss. He nodded to his boss. Only then did Failla get out of the limo. David noted the bulge under his suit coat.

"Let's go for a walk," Failla said.

"I want my money first," David said.

"You'll get your money," Failla said.

David put a hand on the Don's chest as he stepped by. The gorilla didn't like that, but then again, David didn't like the gorilla. Failla was unperturbed.

"First," David repeated. "Bring it with you. I want to see it."

Failla was amused. He snapped his fingers. A bulky black briefcase was handed out. David hoped they kept the window down to let in a little fresh air, a little Lexus shrapnel. Not that it would matter with his car so close to the tank. Failla held on to the briefcase. He pointed to the curve of the hill.

"Over there," he said.

They walked approximately a hundred and fifty yards away from the others, a reasonably safe distance in David's estimation. Still, they were close enough that Failla should be startled when the timer kissed the big twelve. Clearly, Failla was not afraid to be alone with him now that he knew David was unarmed and had no backup in the neighborhood. Failla trusted in his own weapon, his bulk, his balls. Also, the gorilla still had his gun drawn. David figured Failla's goon squad had earlier searched the area for other FBI agents, hidden weapons. That was the beauty of his plan. His weapon was parked in plain sight. The plan had come to him the instant he learned Sandy was dead. Such was the perverse nature of the creativity of a killer. A pool of blood could serve as a muse. David thought of himself as a killer then. He was no longer concerned about the Constitution, the Bill of Rights, or the RICO. They halted beside a cactus that looked as if its last watering had been at the hands of a Spanish missionary.

"Who's the mole?" Failla asked quickly.

David held up his hand. "I have brought tapes of conversations the FBI has of you and your people. I want you to listen to the first one and the answer will be obvious."

Failla was impatient. "Why don't you just tell me?"

Because there was no highly placed mole, but David couldn't explain that at the moment. He nodded to the tiny cassette player. "Just listen. It's better if you hear the truth for yourself. Then you'll have no doubts."

"But if I was in on the conversation, then I've already heard it."

"You heard the man who betrayed you, Mr. Failla. But

you didn't know who he was or what he was doing. Give me three minutes and you'll understand what I mean." David paused. "But first show me the money."

Failla opened the briefcase. One hundred packs of hundred dollar bills. A hundred bills per pack. They looked crisp and clean—but not to David. He knew how they had been purchased, with blood and pain and death. He picked one out and studied it in the fading light and smiled. To his surprise, it was the genuine article.

He played Failla a tape of one of the first conversations they had bugged. On it Failla made a reference to the execution of Gary "Garrott" Guilliani. Failla listened closely, his impatience fading. He knew such a tape would not sound pretty in court, especially if Gary's body was found. David hardly listened. He counted the seconds, a hundred and eighty of them. He shifted aside, putting Failla between himself and the cars. Once again he thought of the power of the shock wave, what it would feel like if the fat fuck landed on him.

There was an incredible explosion.

The flash of the bomb was brilliant, almost blinding. Even David had underestimated the sheer strength of two hundred pounds of dynamite. He had hoped the bomb would tear the limo in two pieces, turn it over maybe, kill the occupants. But the limo and Lexus detonated as one unit. The black-orange ball of flame momentarily assumed the shape of an atomic blast, a mushroom cloud. The gorilla vanished into flying pieces of dark meat. The cars were no longer cars.

A thick wall of compressed air hit both Failla and David. But David had the almost three hundred pounds of the Don to shield him from the shock wave. Failla fell toward him as if kicked in the lower spine. David caught him as he fell and rammed his right knee up into Failla's face.

Something cracked, something splattered. Failla fell to the ground. Casually David leaned over and removed the gun from Failla's coat. He frisked him quickly then took a step back. Failla groaned, his face covered with blood.

"She was my girl," David said. "You killed her. I'm going to kill you."

Failla opened his eyes, saw he was covered, and sighed. "Shoot then."

David picked up the briefcase. He would keep the money for his troubles. "No. My friend is coming for us in a few minutes. After I drop him in town, you and I are going deep into the desert. My friend smokes and carries a Bic lighter. I'm going to borrow it from him. They don't cost much, you know, maybe fifty cents. But they can be used as instruments of horrible torture." David paused. "I want you to feel a hundred times the pain she felt before you leave this world."

Failla was afraid. "But you're FBI."

David shook his head. "I'm not one of the good guys."

David buried Failla later that night, in a shallow grave. Still using Gordon's car, he drove partway back to Los Angeles and checked into a motel off Interstate 15. He slept twelve hours straight, awakening only once to a nightmare of Failla's screams echoing over an endless black desert. It was a nightmare he was to have often as the years passed.

There was a hearing, of course, after all the shit went down. In real life guns were not fired and bombs did not explode without plenty of second-guessing and paperwork. But from behind the scenes Ned helped and the hearing took on an unreal flavor. It didn't even focus on the deaths of Failla and his men, but on David's relationship with Sandy and the missing money from Failla's casino. Officials were always more interested in illicit sex and missing bucks than whether you got the job done or not. But with Ned's help the board bought the story that Sandy had been his informant, nothing more. How awful David felt to publicly deny any interest in her. And as far as the money was concerned, they couldn't prove anything until it was found or David began to spend it. Even Ned was not sure David had it.

David sort of retired after that. He asked Ned to plant him in a cornfield somewhere. Ned shipped him off to a small town in Iowa, Burkesville, where he was the only FBI agent for fifty miles around. Ned knew what David had done—the whole Los Angeles office did, but nobody said anything directly to him. They were all a little afraid of Dirty Dave after that—and a little proud. But there was no pride in David. There was nothing left for him except time to kill. He never stopped missing Sandy.

Six years in Burkesville were like sixty elsewhere. People moved as slowly as crops grew, and consequently committed few crimes worthy of his attention. His only big case the first year there was when a guy shot his wife for sleeping with his brother—shot her twenty times in her bare ass with a BB gun. It fueled the gossip on the town square for three months. Things picked up a little after that, but not much. David liked that just fine. It was not as if he had to work, not with a million under his bed.

In the end, though, he knew a call would come.

He first heard about the Angela Wilson case, not from Ned, but from the newspapers. Pretty, eighteen-year-old homecoming queen kidnapped out of her own house in the middle of a slumber party with friends. The guy just knocked on the front door and grabbed her, but her friends didn't even get a good look at the jerk. One said he was blond, another bald. The stuff of national tragedy. Angela's

picture was on the cover of *Time*. She was gone, and it
didn't look like she'd be coming back. That was David's
professional assessment. A week had elapsed and the kidnapper had made no ransom demand. All kinds of experts
quoted odds on whether she was dead. A couple of people
in Burkesville asked David what he thought the odds were.
He ignored them. What were the odds that Sandy would
have died so young? Fate spun an odd-shaped roulette
wheel.

Ned did ring David, however, when he got a call from
the kidnapper. It seemed Angela was still alive, but in dangerous company. Ned had come up against the worst slime
the world had to offer, but David believed this was the
first time he had ever heard Ned scared. The kidnapper
had contacted Ned directly.

"You have to hear this guy's voice to believe it," Ned
said. "He sounds like Charles Manson after electroshock.
He said he was tickling Angela the whole time we talked,
and she kept crying. I don't know what he was tickling her
with. He doesn't just want money."

David understood. "He wants to play."

"Yeah. I think with us and Angela both. But he is making monetary demands." Ned paused, his voice rising with
his passion. "I need you, David. I need you to talk to him,
to catch him. We can't let this girl die."

"I'm the last person you should call."

"No. You're the only person I can call. You can save
her, I know you can. Please, David, for her sake."

David had to close his eyes, but the image of Angela's
face remained in his mind—her innocent brown eyes, her
dimples—as did the thought of what her captor probably
did to her after he finished talking to Ned. David knew
that Angela deserved the best, but it was just that David
thought his involvement could seal her fate. He had started

out wanting to save people and had ended up burning off a man's penis in the desert, while the man cried to Mother Mary for him to put a bullet in his brain. He was a monster, there was no doubt about that. But that didn't mean he was the right man to go after another monster.

"What's the guy asking for?" David asked finally.

"A quarter million in cash."

"That isn't much. I have that. I can give it to him."

Ned paused. "The money's not a problem. He is. He calls me instead of the parents. He strings me out, talks about the weather and razor blades in the same breath. Jesus, the President called me last night about Angela."

"Does he want a quarter million, too?"

"David, she'll die. She'll die without you. Can I put it any plainer?"

"What if I come back and she still dies?"

"What kind of question is that? If she dies, then she dies. At least we would have tried. Come back, David. It can help you, you know, to save her."

"Help me what? To forget? That won't happen."

David looked around his office, four bland walls above a bankrupt savings and loan. His eyes came to rest, not on Angela's or Sandy's picture, but on a Bic lighter a cop had left on his desk the past evening. He picked it up, struck the flame, stared at the quivering orange, saw a jack-o'-lantern grin at him from behind it. Trick or treat.

"David."

"All right."

"You'll help us?" Ned asked simply.

"Yes." He let the flame die. "I'll try to help all of us."

The Bureau's code name for the guy who kidnapped Angela was Pokey. When David listened to Ned's conversations with the suspect, he thought it sounded as if Pokey were jabbing Angela with a sharp object. David agreed with Ned's assessment of Pokey's disturbed state. He was definitely not just in it for the money. Curiously, Pokey sounded old as well as unstable. Few kidnappers were more than fifty. Reviewing the tapes, David tried to get a fix on what Pokey really wanted. The talks were so brief it wasn't possible to get a trace on the line.

Pokey: I have the girl. I have the goods. She's being a good girl. You want to hear her? Know that she's alive?

Ned: Sure. Let me talk to her.

Pokey: I didn't say you could talk to her. [Angela cries in the background.] There, that's her, you can ask her mother and father. Shut up, Angie. Now! I read in the paper you want her back.

Ned: We would like it if you could return Angela to us. What can we do to make that happen?

Pokey: I need money.

Ned: No problem. We can get you money. When would you like it?

Pokey: Soon.

Pokey hung up. His next call was the next day.

Pokey: Do you have my money?

Ned: We can get it for you. How much do you want? Where do you want it delivered?

Pokey: A quarter million. Can you get that much?

Ned: No problem. We give you the money and you give us the girl. How about that?

Pokey: I have to give her back? I don't want to. I like her. I think she's beginning to like me.

Ned: We can talk about that. Where do you want us to put the money?

Pokey: In my piggy bank.

Ned: OK. Where is it?

Pokey: [Laughs] In a wet place.

Pokey hung up. But the same time the next day, there was another call.

Pokey: I have chosen a place for you to bring my money. I want her father to bring it. If my instructions are not followed, Angie will cry for a long time. She misbehaved once and I made her cry. She's not quite the girl she used to be, if you know what I mean.

Ned: We want her back unharmed.

Pokey: It's a little late for that. But I can assure you she still works.

Ned: We just want her back. You can have the money. Would you like hundreds? Twenties?

Pokey: Hundreds. I'll call you soon with the details. [Angela cries in the background.] I have to go. My baby needs changing.

Sitting in Ned's office, David listened to the tapes over and over, trying to construct a psychological composite of the enemy.

"I think we should believe him when he says he doesn't want to give her back," David said. "Why didn't you make that a condition of the transfer of the money to him?"

"I mentioned it enough times. But I didn't try to pin him down because of what you just said. He doesn't want to give her back."

David shook his head. "You hope to catch him at the pick up? That's the wrong strategy with this guy."

"Why?" Ned asked.

"We both agree he's old. That means he's waited a long

time to pull off a stunt like this. He laughs, but he also takes what he's done very seriously. He expects you to take him seriously. I think you're missing that. These points seem contradictory but they're not. It's a game to him, and you have to play by his rules. If you make a deal with him and don't keep your end of the bargain, he'll make us pay for it by either hurting or killing Angela."

"You want us to just give him the money and hope he returns her?"

"It might not be a bad idea," David said. "What's a quarter of a million?"

"It's more than the family has, a lot more. We'll be using the Bureau's money on this one. The President said it was OK. Do you think Pokey has a partner?"

"No. *Angie* is his alone. I think that's clear."

"But if he has no partner, and he comes for the money, we'll get him."

"Not necessarily," David said. "You may think you smooth-talked him, Ned, but he controlled the conversations. You can't just go by what he says—he is intelligent, and I suspect he'll force us to deliver the money in an interesting way."

"Do you want to talk to him?" Ned asked.

David was doubtful. "You already have a relationship with him. He specifically called you. I'm a stranger to him."

"But you're quick on your feet. I want you to talk to him. If he objects, I can always pick up." Ned paused. "Why do you think he calls us instead of the family?"

"It's another example of how intelligent he is. He knows we're here. He's saying he's not afraid of us." David shook his head. "I hate cases like this. Already I can tell that he'd sooner kill her than return her."

"Don't tell the parents. I haven't told them about his

not-quite-the-girl-she-used-to-be remark." Ned looked ready to spit. "What do you think he meant by that?"

"Oh, you know. He cut off an ear or something. He personalized her. How are the parents holding up?"

"Good. Both are hopeful," Ned said.

David didn't know if that was such a good thing.

Pokey's fourth call came two days after that, in the early morning hours. David took it; he had been sleeping at the office for lack of a better place. Ned stood close by while David introduced himself.

"I'm special agent David Conner. I've been put in charge of this case. But if you would like to talk to Ned, he's here. It's up to you."

The voice was raspy, pleased. "David Conner? Haven't I heard of you?

"I don't know. Have you?"

"You were in the papers years ago. You rescued people who were kidnapped. You're a hero." Pokey chuckled. "I like that, talking to a hero."

"Good. Let's discuss business." David wanted him to understand he didn't see this as a game. The fact that Pokey was aware of him spoke of his extensive knowledge of the FBI. David had been mentioned in the papers only once, over ten years ago. He tried to avoid publicity. "Where do you want us to bring the money?"

"There's a phone booth in Abolene, Oregon, at the corner of Main and Lincoln. Be there at sunset tomorrow. You and the father. I will call and give more instructions. The money is to be delivered in a waterproof briefcase. If an attempt is made to capture me, Angie will cry again. Understood?"

"Yes. When we deliver the money, you will release Angela. Understood?"

"I didn't say that."

"I did. I mean it. Otherwise, no money. Do we have an agreement?"

Pokey laughed. "We'll see."

He hung up. Again, there had not been enough time to trace the call. Pokey had each of the conversations timed. Ned nodded his approval of the way David handled the call. David was in no mood for praise.

"He didn't agree to bring her," David said.

"You can't force him. Do you know anything about Abolene?"

"It's in northern Oregon, a lumber town, population around five thousand. Lots of trees and rivers in the area." David paused, thinking. "I wonder if the rivers are the reason he wants the money in a waterproof briefcase."

"Really? Throw a briefcase full of money in a river and it would just sink."

"Yes," David said. "But it would be easy to make the case buoyant. He might instruct the father to do so tomorrow afternoon—at the last minute."

"You really think he'll have the father throw the money into a river? That's a great way to lose it."

"I think it is a strong possibility. One thing for sure, he sees the briefcase getting wet. Also, don't forget, the money is secondary to him. His plan sounds clever. The woods are thick in that part of the state. He could wait downstream at any point for the money to come to him. We would be hard-pressed to stake out every river in the area. Not without his knowledge."

Ned was adamant. "But we have to make an attempt to capture him."

David nodded. "I agree. But notice he said I was to accompany the father to the phone booth. In a sense, he's giving me permission to come after him."

"You'll never be able to stake out a river by yourself."

"I realize that. We'll have to outfit both the father and briefcase with a directional beeper. We can follow Pokey that way."

"You'll need backup. You can't do this yourself."

"I want two hundred agents for backup. A SWAT team for that matter, but I don't want them in the immediate vicinity. We mustn't spook the guy. We'll have everybody stationed nearby. You heard Pokey's warning. He meant it, he'll make Angela cry." David made a fist. "But only if he gets back to her."

Ned stared at him. "You can't kill him. You have to bring him in."

"You put me in charge. I'll do whatever is necessary to save her."

The next morning David sat in the front seat of a Jeep Cherokee beside Mr. James Wilson. The man seemed old to have an eighteen-year-old daughter, perhaps sixty, with a full head of silver-brown hair and a beefy body that looked as if it could take a hard punch. Their breath came out in little white clouds. Mr. Wilson was nervous, but he was not afraid, not for himself. A quarter million in real cash sat on David's lap. He patiently explained how the directional beepers worked.

"It's crucial that after you give him the money and he leaves," David said, "you turn off your beeper. The one in the briefcase and the one in your shirt broadcast at a different frequency, but it's not that different. If you don't turn off your beeper, you may confuse us. There's a famous case in FBI annals where a man forgot to do just that and his wife died as a result." David pressed the top of the gentlemen's pocket. The device appeared to be an ordinary pack of cigarettes. "You press the top of the pack and the beeper is activated. Press the bottom and it's turned off. Is that clear?"

"Yes. What if he discovers the beeper in the briefcase?"

"I intend for him to discover it. That's why I have placed a second beeper inside one of the packs of money. It's very small. He'd have to search every pack to find it, and he won't have time, not right away."

Mr. Wilson's lower lip quivered. "Do you think he'll have Angela with him?"

"No. He never said he would bring her. But she won't be far away." David paused. "Is there anything else you want to ask me? Once he calls, neither of us will have much time to talk."

"What will he say?"

"He'll direct us to some place in the area. Listen closely to what he has to say, he may not repeat it. But don't worry. I'll be in the phone booth with you. If you miss something, I'll catch it."

"Why does he want you there?"

"Because he's a fool," David lied. Pokey wanted him around to add spice to the chase. But who would turn out to be the hound? Who the fox? David suspected Pokey had the unexpected up his sleeve.

"Will he try to kill me?" Mr. Wilson asked.

David hesitated. "He might kill you."

Mr. Wilson nodded quickly. "It's all right. I'll do anything for my daughter."

David squeezed his hand. "I'll bring her back to you. I swear it."

They shut themselves in the phone booth a few minutes before sunset. Downtown Abolene was a corner gas station and a coffee shop. The evening light, filtered through the surrounding forest, was a haunting glow of orange and green. Pokey did not keep them waiting long. Mr. Wilson answered on the first ring. David put his ear to the phone.

"Listen," Pokey said. "Strap something to the briefcase to make it buoyant. A couple of boards will do. Take Tattler Road north out of town five miles to Mercury. Make a left. Mercury dead ends in the trees. At the end of the road take the path that leads to the river. Place the suitcase in the water and leave the area immediately. Do this now. I won't wait long."

Pokey hung up. Mr. Wilson stared at him in surprise. David had not told him that this would be the probable scenario. "Where am I going to get a couple of boards?" he asked.

"I have them in the Jeep," David said. "Let's go."

David followed Mr. Wilson toward the drop-off spot in a separate Jeep, but did not turn onto Mercury. His maps showed another road that led to the river, two miles downstream. It was David's hope to come up on Pokey from behind, as the guy snatched the briefcase from the river. David radioed Ned, and once more cautioned his boss and the waiting agents to keep their distance.

The river was called Wild Current. David was unhappy to see it deserved its name. He had hoped for a little creek that wouldn't carry the briefcase far. This river was many feet deep, at least a hundred feet wide, and it flowed as if the Indian monsoon had just passed over. It couldn't be crossed without a raft of some kind. How would Pokey drag the money from the river, David wondered? Perhaps he would have a long net of some kind. Remaining in the shelter of the woods, a gun in one hand and a scanning device for the directional beepers in the other, David hiked upstream. He watched on his scanner as Mr. Wilson reached the river and let go of the briefcase. For a minute the two beepers in the briefcase, and the one in the father's shirt pocket, separated. Then Mr. Wilson's shut off.

"Good," David whispered.

Now the two beepers were moving toward him at breakneck speed, one flashing red on his miniature screen, the other, the tiny one in the money, green, each overlaying the other. The two miles between him and the beepers were quickly cut to one mile, then half a mile. David's heart pounded when, a quarter mile upstream, the beepers stopped.

"I've got him," David whispered, excited.

Not yet. A quarter of a mile upstream the river narrowed in a stony gorge. The walls were sheer granite; David saw no way to hike down to the spot where his scanner said the briefcase must be, where Pokey must be. From behind a tree, David searched the riverbank with a pair of miniature binoculars. The problem was there was no riverbank. Yet the briefcase had come to a rest. Had the flotation boards snagged? Damn, he couldn't even see the briefcase, yet his scanner indicated it was still in the middle of the river, dead center, only two hundred yards from his position. The evening light was failing but still David knew he should be able to see it. He was utterly perplexed.

Then the twin dots, red and green, began to crawl toward the opposite side of the river—and all at once David understood, even with no briefcase in sight. David had tried to anticipate the unexpected but he had been caught up short.

Pokey must have snagged the case from the *floor* of the river. He could have donned scuba gear after calling them and previously prepared the riverbed with strong ropes and cables to cling to. David watched in horror as the twin dots reached the edge of the river and continued *through* the seemingly solid granite wall. Pokey had planned this for a long time, David thought. He understood the second dimension to Pokey's escape route was a cave in the granite wall. At certain times of the year, it was probably visible, but not now. David watched as the blinking dots accelerated away from him. Pokey had reached dry land, removed his fins, dropped his tanks. He was on the other side of an impassable river, on the backside of the granite wall. To put it bluntly—he was getting away, and there was nothing David could do to stop him.

At the moment. The directional beepers had a range of three miles, four if conditions were ideal. David hurried back to his car to call for reinforcements. Carefully, he outlined to Ned what had happened. Ned was still optimistic.

"We can flood that part of the forest with our people," Ned said. "We'll get rafts if we have to. As long as he has the beeper, we can get to him."

"He's smart," David warned. "He'll drop the briefcase soon. He might even find the other beeper and destroy it. We must move fast."

Pokey did move quickly. Fortunately when David ran downstream to his car, a quarter of a mile away, Pokey—on the other side of the river—did the same. Unfortunately, David had to pause to report to Ned and Pokey gained ground on him. Still, David was fast and in excellent shape and, he believed he could catch up to the guy. Especially since, according to his scanner, Pokey was veering back toward the river. The move surprised David until he saw the twin lights stop beside the water. He would have given a lot to have been able to see his adversary right then, but there was a curve in the river that blocked his view. Yet David understood what Pokey was doing because the two colored lights separated and the green dot took off down the river, while the red remained where Pokey had paused.

"A boat," David whispered to himself. "He has a boat." The kidnapper had transferred the money to the boat and left the briefcase lying on the shore. Again, David had no choice. On foot, he couldn't possibly keep up with a boat being swept along by that current. Pokey would be out of range in minutes. David raced back to his car, scanned the map, and felt relief. The river flowed parallel to Tattler Road. At the very least, he should be able to keep Pokey in range for some time, even if he couldn't drive through the trees to the river to intercept him. Momentarily leaving the woods and pulling onto the main road, David radioed Ned and explained the new twist. Ned's optimism remained high.

"As long as the green light blinks," Ned said. "We know where the money is, and we know where Pokey is."

"Yeah," David agreed, feeling far from certain, even as he raced parallel to his adversary with his fellow agents converging on his course. David thought Pokey had considered every angle: the time of day, the amount of light—enough to snag a floating object, but not enough to be spotted underwater—the cave, the bend in the river, the directional beeper in the briefcase. What a brilliant mind. Yet why hadn't Pokey considered the possibility of a second beeper? Clearly, he understood FBI procedures. He had his boat, he was moving fast. But with all that, he was only postponing the inevitable. There were too many agents in the area. The net was tightening. Soon he would be squeezed out.

But David's gut feeling kicked in.

He glanced at his scanner. He had moved out of range of the red light transmitting from the briefcase that Pokey had left beside the river. It was no surprise to David that he was receiving no signal from the red beeper. But if he were to turn around and drive back to the other beeper, he should receive a signal from it then. It had been working when Pokey left it. There was no reason to think it wouldn't be working now. Of course, that would be insane, to turn around. He was closing in on his man. To stop pursuing him, now, after having come so far, would be madness.

Yet the gut feeling would not go away.

The feeling, no, the certainty, that he was being played for the biggest fool of all time.

A hundred agents are after the green beeper. If I turn around, it will make no difference. I don't have to be there to read Pokey his rights. I just have to be there when Angela sees her father again.

David slammed on the brakes and spun the car in the opposite direction. It took him fifteen minutes to reach the point on the road where he should have been a mile from where Pokey had dropped the briefcase.

There was no red light blinking on his scanner.

There was nothing. David called Ned.

"Did you send an agent to fetch the briefcase?" David asked.

"No," Ned said. "Do you think that's necessary?"

"Why don't you. For my peace of mind."

"It's done."

David rang off, consumed with the horrible suspicion that Ned and his men were chasing a decoy. Pokey had not climbed into a boat. He *had* found the second directional beeper. He had sent it downstream while he—what? Where was he now? David felt panic rising. Pokey could be anywhere.

Think man! Think of everything he's shown you.

All right, David told himself. Stay cool. Pokey had

wanted to meet in Oregon. Why? He had probably been
calling from here all along. He had to be familiar with the
area. Indeed, very familiar because he knew about the
cave. He couldn't have just stumbled upon it. He must
have grown up here and been to the river in the middle of
summer, when it was low and part of the cave was visible.
David decided to accept that as fact one. He didn't have
time for doubts. OK, what was fact two? Pokey could
scuba dive. Perhaps he had been taught around here, in a
lake. It might be possible to search through the records of
every dive shop in that part of Oregon to see if anyone remembered instructing— Wait a second! It was simpler
than that! Pokey had been underwater when he grabbed
the briefcase. He must have rented air-filled tanks in the
last few days. Today even, probably locally.

David got on the line to the Portland field office and
asked for a list of the five nearest dive shops. They were
back to him in two minutes. There was only one dive shop
close to Abolene, twenty miles away, in Farside. It was actually a sporting goods store, but they sold and serviced
dive equipment. David called them. This is the FBI. Believe it, buddy. Did you refill a tank for an older guy in the
last two days? You did? This morning? Do you have his
name? Sampson Pincher? Do you have his address? No?
How about his diver's ID? Do you have the number? A
PADI card number 9102027320. Excellent. Thank you for
your time.

David called the Portland office back. Ring PADI and
get the last address of this guy. Quick! They called David
back in ten minutes. Sampson Pincher, it turned out, lived
ten miles outside of Abolene in a remote area away from
the river. David took the address and thanked the Portland
office for their help. He did not bother to contact Ned. If
Angela was in the woods with Sampson, he didn't want a

SWAT team breaking branches at his back while he sneaked up on the house. Just the three of them would be fine, he thought.

David *knew* Sampson was Pokey. What he didn't know was how loyal the guy at the sporting goods store was to his customers. David hadn't thought to order the store clerk not to call Sampson and warn him that the FBI was curious about his air tanks. But it was these little details that made the world such a fucked place to live in.

Parking at a respectable distance from Sampson's, David crept through the woods toward the lone dark log cabin that sat in the middle of the brambly meadow like the witch's house in every fairy tale ever written to give children nightmares. The light in the west was almost gone but there was a moon. David was more than a little startled when a shotgun blast burst from a window and splintered the bark on the tree beside his head. David fell to his belly beside a string of weeds that looked like poison ivy.

"How the fuck did you find me?" a voice called out, Pokey's voice.

"How the fuck did you know I would find you?" David called back. Sampson had obviously been waiting for him, shotgun in hand.

"The sporting goods store called!"

"That was nice of them!"

"What are we going to do now?"

"Let Angela go! Then we can do anything you want!"

"Fuck you!" Sampson fired again. The round tore over David's head, causing him no personal damage but inspiring him to back up another thirty yards deeper into the woods. Sampson probably had no idea he was alone and assumed his cabin was surrounded. David wondered if it might not be a good idea to bring in the SWAT team. But his gut feeling screamed *no*! It didn't matter in the end.

After ten wasted minutes observing the house, David knew he was no longer alone in the woods. Silent as a small army of trolls, agents with high-powered rifles equipped with infrared scopes were spreading out around him in the trees. Ned appeared by his side.

"Where did you come from?" David whispered. "Did the Portland office call you?"

"We had a directional beeper on your Jeep."

"You bugged me? Goddam you, Ned. You don't trust me anymore."

"Quite the opposite. If we screwed up, which we did, I trusted you would be the first to figure it out. I also trusted that you would want to try to save her alone."

"For good reason. This guy will kill her if we piss him off."

Ned was impatient. The last few days had been hard on him. David had to remind himself that the man was seventy years old. "What do you suggest then? That we back off? He has his money. Now he'll kill her."

"He doesn't care about the money. It's a playing piece on his FBI board game. He's upset that we've caught him, but he's happy about it, too. Now he gets to barter with us, face to face. I have to go in alone. I have to talk to him."

"He might kill you before you get to the door," Ned reminded him.

"It wouldn't surprise me one bit."

"How do you know he wants to talk to you?"

"He likes to talk. He couldn't on the phone because he knew we would trace him," David reasoned.

"Why don't we tell him that he's surrounded and that he should surrender?"

"That won't work. Don't even try it. He'll make Angie cry."

Ned considered. "I don't like this. You're taking a big

chance with your own life." He paused. "You haven't become reckless, have you—since Sandy?"

David kept his voice even. "I just want to get the girl back to her family."

"Why don't I go in?"

David chuckled. "He would definitely shoot you before you got to the door."

Ned was insulted. "Well, if you're going in, tell me where you've got Failla's loot stashed. I'm about to retire and could use it. It won't do you any good if you're dead."

"So you did know I had his money?"

"His casino receipts showed he withdrew a million in cash before he went to meet you. Ten thousand hundred-dollar bills." Ned added, "I never showed the people at your hearing those receipts."

"Are you the only one who saw the receipts?"

"Yes."

"Why didn't you turn me in?"

Ned sighed. "You know why."

David understood. He was the son Ned never had. But he was not the good son. He kept breaking things, like Ned's heart.

"It's under the bed in my apartment in Iowa," David said. "I haven't spent a dime of it."

Ned was anxious. "I was only joking. You didn't have to tell me." Ned put his hand on David's shoulder. "Be careful. Your life is as important as Angela's. Don't trade yourself for her."

"I wouldn't think of it," David lied. It was his main option. "Do me one favor, Ned. While I'm in there, keep the boys on the SWAT team back."

"I'll do what I can."

David called out to Sampson, "Let's talk face to face, work out a deal." Sampson was interested if David approached wearing only his shorts. David didn't complain, even though the evening air was brisk. He was happy he had put on underwear that morning. Then he remembered that he hadn't even gone to bed the previous night.

The log cabin was rectangular, plain, a smoking chimney at one end, a propane tank at the other. Shadows clung to the structure like black halos did to TV evangelists. Walking toward it, arms in the air, David wondered what it would feel like to take a round of twelve-gauge shot in the belly. Talk about a gut feeling—that's what had got him into this situation. Yet despite his gruesome thoughts, he found he was not afraid for his own life. There were occasions when suicidal tendencies came in handy. He stopped at the door and knocked. Sampson called for him to enter.

The interior of the cabin was hot. Sampson had a fire going that was large enough to cremate a body. Perhaps, before David showed, that's what he had intended to use it for. Or maybe Sampson had caught a chill during his dive. The crackling orange light flooded the cramped front room. The furniture was old, culled from pieces given away free after an all-day yard sale. Sampson sat on the floor with Angela, near the fire. Sampson had drawn the curtains on the front windows, but the side windows were uncovered. Sampson was probably aware that the FBI had excellent shots.

Sampson looked like a messiah for the homeless. His long white hair fell over his barrel chest like strands of kite string. His face was sun-worn, lined. In the blazing light from the fire, his eyes were twin rubies from a voodoo doctor's private deity. His brown leather coat was scuffed with white worn spots, his blue jeans patched. The shotgun in his hand, however, looked clean enough as he pointed it at David.

"Sit on the floor and keep your hands where I can see them," he said in Pokey's raspy voice.

"All right," David said, going down on his knees, a position from which he could spring up quickly if he had to.

Angela was dressed much like her captor—jeans, a leather coat. The clothes were oversize and probably belonged to Sampson. Her long brown hair was clean, remarkably shiny for a captive's, and there were no marks on her face. A pretty girl with a nice figure, she had a pouty mouth and high, well-defined cheekbones. Yet the innocent brown eyes that had stared out from the cover of *Time* had seen too much in the last few days to ever be innocent again. A bloodstained bandage covered her right hand. David glanced at a glass jar on the mantle above the fireplace. It held a thumb. David was not sickened, but relieved. He had feared worse. Yet he knew there was still time for that. Angela stared at him with a hope so great it was close to despair.

Sampson smiled. He needed dental work. "How did you find me?"

David explained. Sampson listened closely, and nodded with approval as he described his call to the sporting goods store. "Freddy called me after you called him," he explained. "I've bought stuff from him for years."

"I'll have to meet this Freddy," David said.

Sampson chuckled. "Don't be too hard on him. He ran his motorcycle into a tree when he was sixteen, hurt his head. He's pretty stupid." Sampson smoothed his left hand over the twin barrels of his shotgun. Briefly, David wondered if he had reloaded.

"Why didn't you take off when Freddy called?" David asked.

"I was doing just that when you appeared. Hey, I almost got you, didn't I?" Sampson said, changing the subject.

David shrugged. "It looks like you have a second chance."

Sampson was amused. "Where do we go from here?"

"Do you want to surrender?" David asked.

"No. I want you to get us out."

"I can get you out. Not her. She has to stay."

"No way," Sampson said flatly. "I give her up, I'm as good as dead."

"You're wrong. Listen to my proposal. This cabin is surrounded by a SWAT team. That's a fact. You must know that. But if you let her go right now, I can give her instructions to take to my boss to allow you and me to leave here unharmed."

"Your SWAT team will try to take me out before we reach the car," Sampson said. "That's another fact."

"Not if you and I are close together, walking under a blanket. They won't be able to get a clear shot at you, and they won't risk my life to kill you. They'll let us go, and once we're on the road, we can drive all the way to Canada if you want, or Mexico. You can let me go once you're out of the U.S. I'm serious when I say I'm the only one who can get you out of here."

Sampson studied him. "I see that you are." Then he shook his head. "But I don't want to leave Angie. She must come."

David shook his head. "They won't let her come. It doesn't matter what I tell them. They'll open fire, risk killing all three of us, before they let you take her."

Sampson considered. "Getting to the car and on the road will be the most difficult part. Let's compromise. The three of us will leave together, under a blanket, and then once we are out of the woods, I'll release Angie. They can follow us that far to be sure I keep my word."

"But they won't let you put her in the car. They'll shoot you first."

Sampson was getting angry. "As we leave here, you'll explain the situation to them—tell them they have no choice."

David relaxed a bit. Sampson was accepting his basic proposal. "It would be better if you allowed me to explain the situation to them ahead of time."

"No. I don't want you out of my sight."

"Why not?" David asked.

In response Sampson withdrew a hunting knife from his back pocket. The fiery light in his eyes shone with cold malice. "I told you if you tried to capture me what the penalty would be."

Angela trembled, tears running over her cheeks. Her eyes went to the knife, then to David, pleading, imploring. He knew if he failed to save her those eyes would haunt him the rest of his life.

"Please," she whispered to him.

David spoke quickly, firmly. "The time for that nonsense is past. You have been caught. I can help you escape. If you hurt her any more, they will never let you go. Put away your knife."

Sampson grinned, a cold affair. He scratched the blade over the barrel of the shotgun, aggravating their taut nerves. "I have so little of Angie to take with me. Just a finger. I need more to remember her by."

Angela broke down then, sobbing. Like a cornered animal, she made a useless try for the door. It was only then David realized her ankles were bound together. She rolled forward, her face slapping the floor. Sampson reeled her back in by the hair. He pressed his cheek to hers, the knife to her face.

"I think I'll take your nose," he said to her in his hellish voice. "Better to smell you with my dear." He stuck the tip of the blade in her right nostril, which trickled blood from her fall.

"Wait!" David said. "I'm the one who disobeyed you. Why don't you take my nose? It's nicer than hers anyway."

Sampson wasn't interested. "You're a guy," he said.

Angela's terror-stricken eyes would not leave David's. Instinctively, he started to get up, but when Sampson stroked his shotgun, David sat back down. He wouldn't be able to save the girl with his intestines hanging out. At the same time he couldn't sit still and watch as her face was carved up. Desperately he struggled for the perfect thing to say. But what could you offer a madman who wanted a girl's nose?

"Take her other thumb," David blurted out.

Sampson paused, the blade still up Angela's right nostril. "Why the thumb?" he asked conversationally. David replied in the same tone.

"The nose will not come off cleanly. You'll be left with a mess of tissue that won't resemble anything. But if you take the other thumb, you'll have a matching pair. You can put the left one in your jar with the right one."

Sampson raised a bushy eyebrow. "You have a point there." He turned to Angela. "What do you think, my dear?"

Angela shook her head slightly, her gaze straying right back to David. Why was he offering the lunatic parts of her body? Why couldn't he save her? David wished he could explain that the world did not always offer a choice between good and evil. Usually, if you lived long enough, the choices were between bad and worse. Personally, he would rather lose a thumb than a nose. But he didn't know what to tell her, so he spoke to Sampson instead. In doing so, he betrayed the last vestige of hope in her eyes. The fireworks were still minutes off, but it was as if she died as the words came out of his mouth.

"Cut the other thumb off and let's get out of here," David said.

Sampson obliged him. He worked slowly; he had to, so he could keep David covered at the same time. Angela screamed all the while. David stared at the floor and listened to his heartbeat, the wind through the trees, the snapping of branches as the SWAT team shifted uneasily in the woods. With Angela's cries, David knew all possibility of his being allowed to escort Sampson and Angela away from the cabin had vanished. They would try to take Sampson down before he reached the car, blanket or no blanket. Still, David wanted Sampson to bring the blanket. David believed it could come in handy. He changed his plan as he listened to Angela's wailing die to a shocked gulp. He knew he could escort Sampson no farther than the front door. He would rest his chances—and Angela's—on his own trained reflexes rather than a sniper's sweaty trigger finger. And who knew, maybe Angela's thumb could be sewn back on if they got her to a hospital in time.

Time was one reason for his change of plan.

That, and the fact that he wanted to kill Sampson with his bare hands.

Sampson bandaged Angela's gory wound with an oil-stained rag. He stood up cautiously, still crouching, and undid the bonds on Angela's ankles. She was a limp sack of potatoes. Sampson had to pull her to her feet. He gestured to David with the muzzle of his shotgun.

"Grab that blanket," he ordered. "We'll put that over us."

David stood. The blanket was caught under the rocker

of a wooden rocking chair and looked as if a dog had slept on it. David pulled it free and slowly stepped toward Sampson and Angela, two twisted figures in silhouette with the fire at their backs. Sampson was no fool—he continued to keep his head low, his shotgun leveled at Angela's side. Yet David thought Sampson the biggest fool to ever cross his path because he had tortured a young woman right in front of him. Guys like that really pissed him off. David would have liked to have enlightened Sampson about Failla right then. Sampson didn't know he wasn't the only lunatic in the room. David approached to within ten feet, holding the blanket open in front of him.

"Let's do it," Sampson said.

"Let's do it," David repeated. He threw the blanket toward Sampson and took a quick step to the left. Sampson did exactly what David thought he would do, what normal reflexes demanded when an enemy threw up a screen. As the blanket lazily floated toward Sampson, threatening to cover his head, he turned his weapon away from Angela and fired at the blanket. By the time he recovered from the recoil and understood that Special Agent Conner was not standing behind the ripped blanket with a hole in his body, David struck from the right. His left foot lashed out, striking Sampson's hip, sending him crashing into Angela. The two fell to the floor, the shotgun to the side. David went for the weapon first, not Angela. He honestly believed that once he had the shotgun everything would be all right.

It should have been true. Nine times out ten it would have been.

Sandy should have escaped Failla. Ninety-nine times out of a hundred . . .

Sampson scrambled to his feet. Angela got up a bit slower, but had some life left in her. She broke free of Sampson's grip and retreated toward the fire to form the tip of their unstable triangle. By then David had retrieved the shotgun and had it pointed at Sampson's chest. Slowly, deliberately, David cocked the hammer. How tempting it was, the thought of squeezing the trigger.

"Fuck," Sampson said bitterly.

David smiled. "Fuck you."

A bullet whizzed through the uncovered side window. Glass cracked and fell to the floor. Sampson doubled over and dropped to his knees, leaving only Angela and David standing. A member of the SWAT team had finally got Sampson in his sights and rolled the dice. For a moment, it was OK. Sampson was bleeding from the left armpit and although it was clearly not a fatal wound, it was nice to see the guy hurt. Angela was staring at David again. Those imploring eyes and that look—where did it come from? She was saved. She could have her thumb sewn back on and return to being homecoming queen at her high school. Next year she'd go to college. Later, she could marry a doctor and have two beautiful kids, even learn to play the piano. You could play the piano with eight fingers and one thumb, David told himself. Then he noticed the hole in Angela's brown leather jacket, just above her heart. It was such a small hole, it didn't look important. As if in a dream, she slowly raised her right hand and covered the hole. See, now it's gone, David thought.

Wishful thinking.

Blood gushed around her fingers.

Her head fell to the side, her eyes dimmed.

"Oh God," David cried, barely catching her as she fell. "Jesus Christ." He laid her on the floor, one hand behind her head, the other holding the shotgun. He moved his free hand and pressed on her wound, feeling a thick volume of liquid beneath her coat. Her eyes stared up at him, at the ceiling, the sky beyond. "No," David whispered.

She was gone.

Sampson giggled. David glanced over at him.

"I won't even get murder one," Sampson said. "I didn't kill her. I'll be out in five years, eight at the outside." He paused to snort. "Ironic, isn't it?"

David let go of Angela and stood above Sampson. He placed the barrel between the man's eyebrows. "You will not be out in five years. You will not leave this cabin."

Sampson laughed. "What are you going to do, shoot me?"

"Yes," David whispered.

Sampson was afraid, as Failla had been afraid, in the end. Indeed, he said the exact same words. "But you're FBI."

"Yes. But who gives a fuck?"

David shot him. Took off the top of his head. Then he carried Angela out of the cabin, past the SWAT team, to Ned. He asked his boss where Angela's father was. As pale as the moon, Ned told him the man was at the hotel where they had stayed the previous night. David nodded. He carried the girl's body to the Jeep. He laid her in the backseat and drove her to her father. He kept his word to the man. Yeah, he brought him back his dead daughter. His word was as good as gold—fool's gold found on the bottom of cold streams. He had *almost* thrown the sack of ransom money in the fire. But it belonged to the government, not the mob, and he couldn't be bothered stealing it either. All the money in the world couldn't bring either of them back.

There was another hearing. Why did he kill Sampson? Was it necessary? He mumbled his answer, stared at the far wall, the TV cameras. He was a celebrity. They let him go—couldn't reprimand a hero and enjoy the public's support. They recommended counseling, however. Dirty Dave needed a wash. So he went out and bought himself a bottle, and overslept his counseling appointment by two days. No one cared. He was quitting anyway.

David Conner awoke in the middle of his late-night flight to Idaho from a bad dream. Like an old war wound, he knew the nightmare well. Hotel fountains spouting orange blood. A fat man crying in a barren desert. A young girl's eyes piercing through a fiery sky. David signaled for the flight attendant and asked if she could please bring him a drink. He would have preferred a sleeping pill. The alcohol left a bitter taste in his mouth. He was never able to go back to sleep. He just sat and stared out the window at the black night sky.

CHAPTER 3

Lucy and Vera Temple rode their mountain bikes along the last portion of the unpaved path. They had left Camp Paradise twenty minutes earlier, and it had taken them that long to ride through the woods to reach the only road that connected them to civilization. Paradise was located on a mesa-topped mountain at an elevation of four thousand feet. The road was three miles south of the camp. When the group had come to Paradise, three days earlier, they had had the advantage of Dr. Henry's four-wheel-drive truck, the only vehicle besides their bikes that could tackle the rough path between the camp and the road. Since then Dr. Henry hadn't allowed anyone to borrow the truck. Dr. Henry had even taken to sleeping in it. Lucy thought he had a fetish about the stupid truck and that he saw it as the all-powerful male lover he had yet to find. Dr. Henry was unabashedly gay.

"I heard the reporter's supposed to be cute," Lucy said to Vera, who rode a few feet in front of her.

"Who told you that?" Vera asked over her shoulder. "Dr. Henry?"

"Yeah."

"He's never met him. He's never even seen his picture. He just talked to him on the phone."

"Dr. Henry can tell a lot by a guy's voice," Lucy said. "I think he had his EEG wires hooked up to the line. Ran a brain-wave coherence program on the guy. Said the reporter operated from a primal level, on pure sexuality."

Vera shook her head. "All that information on a guy from the ten words he spoke over a static-filled phone line? I swear, sometimes Dr. Henry thinks he knows more than the Big Mind."

"Sometimes Dr. Henry thinks he *is* the Big Mind," Lucy said as she caught up to her sister, bumping up and down as she maneuvered her bike over ruts. The day was bright and warm, the sky the color of the sea as seen from the moon. Summer was not far off, Lucy thought happily. She loved the hot months the way most people loved a long massage, the heat sinking into her bones, the cool sweat on her bare arms. Below them, close to the road, June Lake came into view. Lucy was inspired. "Why don't we go for a swim before the reporter gets here?" she said.

"We didn't bring our suits," Vera said.

"It doesn't matter."

"How do we know the reporter's not here already?"

Lucy nodded to the point where the road met the path, the spot Dr. Henry had told them to meet the man. "I don't see him. Do you? No? Well, that probably means he's not here."

Vera frowned. "But what if he shows up while we're swimming?"

"Then he'll see us naked. He'll get all excited and probably want to have sex. But because we look exactly alike he won't know which one of us to jump. So he'll probably just have to have us both at the same time!"

Vera stared at her, incredulous. "You're sick."

"I'm not. I'm just horny. I haven't had a guy since Neil, and he didn't count."

"What was wrong with Neil? You went with him six months."

Lucy laughed. "I never told you this. He was so afraid of catching HIV or herpes or whatever that he always wore *two* condoms whenever we made love. Do you know how long it takes to put on two condoms? His dick was so insulated I always felt like I had a plastic pear inside me."

"You mean a plastic banana."

"No! A pear! That was the other thing wrong with Neil!"

Vera was disgusted. "You can't seduce the reporter, no matter how handsome he is. Professor Spear brought us here for an important purpose. He paid for this trip out of his own pocket. We have work to do."

"You may have work to do. I'm here to relax."

"We're having a session as soon as we get back," Vera said.

"We are? But we had one this morning."

"Yes, but this morning you kept interrupting the Big Mind to ask what the reporter was like. We didn't do any real work."

They reached the edge of the lake. Lucy set her bike down and undid the buttons on her yellow blouse. She took off the tiny gold crucifix she always wore and put it in the pocket of the blouse. It had been a gift from her mother. She could have worn her white shorts into the water—they were almost as skimpy and tight as a bathing suit—but she loved to swim naked in a cool lake, especially with a cute guy. Not that she was a tramp. She enjoyed infuriating her sister with her loose tongue, but in reality she had only slept with five guys in her life. Not many, she thought, for a twenty-eight-year-old redhead.

"I thought what the Big Mind had to say about him was interesting," Lucy said, finishing with her blouse and kneeling to untie her tennis shoes. "Did you notice it repeated how brave and resourceful the man was? How he'd had a life rich in excitement but also filled with sorrow?"

Vera nodded. "He's probably been all over the world on assignments. But I still wish he wasn't coming this week."

"Why not? The Big Mind said he's important, that he can help us more than we can imagine. It also said we can help him. I'm glad he's coming. I'd like to get some recognition for Spear's work outside of New Age magazines."

"Then we'll never have any peace."

Lucy kicked off her shoes. "Yeah, but we'll have more dates. Just think how many guys will want to go out with modern-day witches." Lucy pulled down her shorts and mooned her sister. "Especially with an ass like this!" She skipped into the water.

"Don't drown!" Vera called.

"You can always save me!" Lucy called back. *Jesus, it's cold.* She ran in quickly and, as soon as it was deep enough, dove underwater. The jolt of the frigid water sent her heart hammering. She screamed as she resurfaced, kicking fiercely. June Lake was a rough circle, perhaps a quarter mile across. It had been her intention to swim across and back, but with her skin already turning blue she wondered if she'd make it. Vera waved and Lucy waved back.

"Ah," Lucy moaned in pleasure a few minutes later as

she moved into a mysteriously warm patch. The water was at least fifteen degrees warmer than in the rest of the lake. Rolling onto her back, she decided to stay in it as long as possible. Relaxing, with only the blue overhead to fill her vision, she felt unconnected to her body. The feeling was not frightening, though. In the presence of the Big Mind, she often felt as if the physical plane was nothing but a drawing sketched on a canvas much larger than the sky. Even though she had objected to Vera about having another session, she did enjoy them. They were no work at all and most often brought deep peace.

Lucy had discovered both her sister's talent and her own while working her way through undergraduate school at Stanford. She had a state license in massage and could charge forty dollars an hour for her services, although from her fellow students she usually accepted half that. Any new therapy caught her attention, so her list of massage techniques was impressive. She knew shiatsu, Swedish, polarity, Raki, and both applied and educational kinesiology. The latter two systems were related in the sense that they both used muscle testing, but were also quite different. Applied kinesiology, or AK, operated under the theory that every organ in the body had a muscle that corresponded to it. For example, the stomach could be tested by holding the arm straight out and turning the palm away from the body. The tester person would then say "resist" and pull down on the arm. If the arm muscle locked, the stomach was probably fine. However, if the muscle failed to lock and the person could not resist then there was either something wrong with the muscle or the stomach. If the stomach was affected, the muscle was always weak, although the reverse was not true. Lucy often used AK at the end of a massage to balance a patient's major muscles and organs. Most people enjoyed the AK more than the massage itself.

Educational kinesiology or EK also used the locking of muscles to learn things, but EK used the body as a kind of living Ouija board. If a question was asked and the arm was tested and the answer was no, the muscle would become weak. If the answer was yes, the muscle would remain strong. That was the theory at least, and Lucy had good success with it. Her accuracy was rather high, yet it wasn't a hundred percent, and that bothered her. Periodically she would test out the EK theory by asking questions she already knew the answers to. For example, "Am I working on a girl?" "Is this person an alien?" Sometimes the person's arm would remain strong when Lucy asked if she or he were a robot. This made no sense to Lucy.

One day a girl told Lucy to ask her body if she was pregnant. Before Lucy could move the arm into position, she knew the answer. It crystallized in her mind, not in the form of words, but as an unmistakable certainty. Yes, the girl was exactly nine weeks pregnant. Lucy blurted the fact out. Her patient was surprised, but not as surprised as Lucy was when the girl returned and informed her that she had been right. She was nine weeks pregnant.

After that Lucy discovered she didn't need muscle testing to get answers. They just popped into her mind. She also noticed that if Vera was in the room, her accuracy was even greater. In fact, if Lucy focused all of her attention on predicting, Vera stopped what she was doing and went dead still. At such times Lucy would feel as if an invisible thread connected them. And an answer would come, a certainty of what was true nevertheless. Lucy was both delighted and slightly frightened. Both women were majoring in psychology and planned to go on to graduate school—neither had a desire to become a professional psychic. But Lucy constantly had new referrals. Soon her "massage" business was booming and she hardly had time to study.

At the end of their senior year at Stanford, Professor Spear gave a talk on his theory of genetic memory. Lucy had heard fascinating things about him and dragged Vera to the lecture. Spear spoke of how he used a technique of mutual hypnosis to take small groups of people to new and previously unobtainable levels of consciousness in which they were able to tap into the racial memories stored in DNA. Lucy found his lecture both enlightening and confusing—confusing because Spear used many New Age phrases and was clearly an atheist. His past lives had nothing to do with reincarnation. Indeed, he angered a few people in the audience when he denounced past life regressions as delusionary and made several pointed remarks about the stupidity of modern religion. Clearly here was a man who didn't care what others thought, yet railed against all forms of human ignorance.

Lucy didn't agree with everything he said but she was anxious to meet this man with the wild gray hair and riveting dark eyes. For someone who believed in nothing spiritual, he gave off an amazing amount of charismatic energy. After the talk Lucy dragged Vera with her to speak with Spear. To her surprise, he gave her a few private minutes to explain her experiences with AK. She even told him how Vera improved her accuracy. Spear was interested. He gave them his home number, asked them to call.

He believed they could be ideal candidates for his practice of mutual hypnosis.

Two years later they were still chasing memories.

Spear had not wanted the reporter to come, but the Big Mind insisted. Spear did not always heed what the group channeled, not when it disagreed with his theories. For the Big Mind said they *were* spirit, souls evolving back toward the divine. Spear didn't buy this. Lucy felt Spear's relationship to the Big Mind was curious—he was a disciple without a master, an astronomer who trusted the stars, but not his own telescope. Spear used the Big Mind but didn't have faith in it. The Big Mind did not seem to mind.

"Lucy!" Vera called.

Lucy rolled over and looked toward shore. She was surprised to see how far out she had drifted in a few minutes. Did the lake have a current? Then again, time often slipped away when she was daydreaming. In sessions with the Big Mind, hours could pass in the flash of an instant. Vera was anxiously pointing to the lakeshore. Lucy saw a man taking pictures of her with a sophisticated camera. Could that be the reporter? The primal sex maniac? Quickly Lucy swam toward shore, hoping he would avert his eyes when she climbed out of the water and give her a chance to get dressed. Vera moved between her and the man.

"I hope he's not a pervert," Vera said.

Lucy had her back to both of them, pulling on her shorts. "Has he put away his camera?"

"Yes. But he's coming this way." Vera paused. "He doesn't look like a reporter."

"What does he look like?"

"Trouble."

Lucy threw on her blouse, the material clinging to her damp skin. Finally, she turned around. The reporter, wearing gray slacks and a long-sleeved white shirt, strode toward them. His gait was smooth, graceful, but Lucy noted that he moved like a man who was used to being in charge. She was perceptive when it came to such matters.

He had an athlete's body. His features were dark, mysterious, but also a little weary. The Big Mind was right, Lucy understood. He had seen a lot in his life, much of it unpleasant. Yet he smiled as he came closer, a black overnight bag in one hand, his camera dangling around his neck.

"Hi," he said. "I'm David Nichols. Are you two the welcoming committee?"

"Yeah," Lucy said. "Where's your car? We didn't see you drive up."

He nodded down the road. "I parked it off the road, under some trees. I was told that I wouldn't be able to drive it to the camp. It's a rental—I don't want anyone to steal it while I'm here."

"That was smart thinking," Lucy said. She stepped forward and offered her hand. "I'm Lucy Temple. This is my sister, Vera. We're Ph.D. students of Professor Spear's."

"Hi," Vera said softly, also offering her hand. "Why were you taking pictures of my sister, Mr. Nichols?"

The question didn't disturb him. "David, please. The lake seemed so inviting with Lucy in it that I wanted to record the scene for posterity. I meant no offense."

Lucy chuckled. "It's no big deal. Just don't let *Time* magazine publish it. OK?"

"Sure." He nodded to their bikes. "Is this how we get to the camp?"

"Yes," Lucy said. "We only have two, but I'll be happy to walk with you—David."

"You can take my bike," Vera said quickly. "I don't want to return to the camp right away anyway."

Lucy was concerned. Vera had been having nightmares since they arrived in Idaho. Lucy slept in the room beside hers and twice she had heard Vera wake up moaning. But Vera had no explanation for the bad dreams and offered no

details of their content. Lucy was puzzled. The camp was
as comfortable as it was beautiful. Indeed, Spear had chosen the spot because of the serenity it offered. The last
couple of days Vera had gone for long walks away from
the camp and seemed unusually preoccupied.

"You were the one who said we have a session scheduled for this afternoon," Lucy said.

Vera crossed her hands over her chest as if she were
cold. "I'll be there. I just want to be alone for a few minutes."

"Keep your bike," David said. "I'd probably run it into
a tree anyway."

Vera studied him. Lucy believed her sister was even
more perceptive than she was about people, except when
it came to men. Vera had not had a boyfriend in ages.

"Are you sure?" Vera asked. "It's a long walk to the
camp. I'm used to it but you might find it strenuous."

"I look forward to the exercise after my plane ride." He
nodded to Vera. "It was nice to meet you. Really, Vera,
you're one of a kind."

Vera smiled at his joke. "We're not so similar as we
look. You'll learn that soon enough, I think."

Lucy set off with their visitor, walking her bike beside
him, despite his protests. "The path only gets worse the
farther you go," she said. "I don't mind walking."

"I'm confused," David said. "This area's beautiful. I'd
think it would be a favorite vacation spot. Why is the
camp so difficult to reach?"

"It's got two strikes against it. It's old and it's small. It
was built before the First World War and can accommo-
date only fifty people. Most groups need more space. As
a result, it hasn't been booked in years and the path hasn't
been kept up. At least that's what Professor Spear says.
Did you know he grew up around here?"

"I'm afraid I know very little about your mentor, Miss Lucy."

She laughed. "You make me sound like the woman in Dracula."

"Funny you should say that. That's exactly what I was thinking. Can you read minds? Are you a good witch or a bad witch?"

"Why," she said, taking the tone of Dorothy in *The Wizard of Oz*, "I'm not a witch at all!" She paused. "I guess we must seem like a bunch of nuts to you."

"I try to have an open mind."

She eyed him. "Except when it comes to stuff like this?"

He shrugged. "Well."

"You just need to be educated. By the time you leave, you'll be a believer."

"Is that what you are, Miss Lucy? A believer?"

"In a manner of speaking, yes. I believe we're all born believers."

"Not me."

"I don't believe you!" she said and laughed. "Isn't there anything that fills you with awe?"

He hesitated. "Beautiful redheads swimming naked in mountain lakes."

Lucy blushed. "I hope you were gentleman enough to avert your eyes as I climbed out of the water."

"Only long enough to fit a more powerful lens in my camera."

"Did you really take a picture of me naked?"

"Of course, I'm a reporter. I need a complete record of what goes on here."

The blood in her cheeks sizzled. She was not the exhibitionist she pretended to be. "Then I can only hope you were able to maintain a steady hand as you shot the picture."

David smiled. "Your sister thinks I'm a pervert."

Lucy shook her head. "It always takes a while for Vera to warm up to people. Also, as far as anything remotely sexual is concerned, she's pretty conservative."

"Hmm. Doesn't seem that she inherited the quality."

Lucy shook her head. "Mr. Nichols, you've known me only ten minutes and already you're embarrassing me."

"I'm deeply sorry, Miss Lucy."

"And stop calling me that!"

David laughed. "Tell me about your group."

"Are you starting work so soon? Are you going to pull out your recorder?"

"I don't need a recorder. I'll remember every word you say."

Lucy glanced over, caught his face in profile. He had a gift for making conversation, and there was nothing fake about him. Yet the things he said seemed remote somehow, not attached to the present situation. Perhaps it was because he had to be detached to be a reporter or because the rest of his life had been so intense or that she was simply boring him. He wasn't boring her, however. Not with that body.

"You know, you don't act like a reporter," she said.

"What do I act like?"

"A spy."

He smiled, obviously enjoying her response. "Maybe I am a spy. Maybe the FBI sent me here to see if your Big Mind knows next week's lottery numbers."

"So you've heard about the Big Mind?"

He nodded. "I've done a little research on you, not much. I have a lot of catching up to do if I'm to write an article on you. Go ahead, tell me about your group."

"Well, first there's Margaret Farrow. She doesn't channel the Big Mind, but she's been with Spear since he started his research into the field. You'll love her. Officially, she's Spear's assistant, but she's more like our mom. She cooks for us and takes care of us when we're sick. Margaret's one of the few people I've ever met who honestly seems to have no ego, but don't get the impression she's dull. She has a mischievous sense of humor. When we first arrived here, she planted a boom box with a tape of exotic African animal sounds in the woods. She set it to go on at three in the morning. Scared the hell out of all of us. Even Spear was up and running around in his underwear."

"She sounds like my kind of person," David remarked.

"She's also crippled, but her handicap doesn't slow her down one bit. She's an inspiration to us all. Wait till you see her in action. Then there's Dr. Henry Deering. We just call him Dr. Henry. He's not a member of the channeling group, either, but he's been studying us for the past year. He's a medical doctor and also has a Ph.D. in neurophysiology—he's an expert on brain waves. He's brought lots of EEG equipment with him. He specializes in how the three levels of the brain interact with each other. He's gay and real out front about it, but not in an obnoxious way. He's the funniest guy you'll ever meet, and like Margaret, he'd do anything for any of us."

David shrugged. "I have friends who are gay. Sometimes I've thought of becoming gay myself."

Lucy paused. "Really?"

"What's the matter? Are you homophobic?"

"No. It's just that—it's just that you don't act gay."

"That's because I'm a spy, Miss Lucy. I have to be careful how I act."

Lucy frowned. "Are you pulling my leg again?"

"What does your intuition tell you?"

"Well, it doesn't seem to be working right now!"

"Yes. I'm teasing you. Tell me more about the others?"

"You are a character. OK, next we have Panda Gopal. He's from India. We call him our sage, although he's not much older than I am. He has an extensive philosophical background. He's quiet, gentle. Unless you're talking about God, he doesn't say much."

"How did *he* meet Professor Spear?" David asked.

"He had a dream about him and searched him out. Next there's Tom Forester, who used to be a long-distance truck driver. You know what it's like driving cross-country with that endless line dividing the road, the whole experience can be hypnotic. Anyway, Tom always wanted to be a country-western singer. He'd sing at the top of his lungs as he barreled down the highway, taping himself as he went along. Well, one time he was playing the tape back and he heard some guy saying all kinds of esoteric stuff. The problem was the guy was talking in his voice! He was the guy! Apparently Tom had spaced out watching that endless line and gone into a trance and channeled a being on the other side."

"On the other side of what?" David asked.

Lucy hesitated. "The other side of death's door."

"So what you're saying is that a ghost spoke through him?"

"It wasn't a ghost, but an angel."

David nodded. "I see."

"Oh brother, I'm doing a terrible job of explaining. Spear's going to chew my ass off. Forget what I just said. Let me finish describing our group. There's Jon Horst, he's from Sweden. He had a show there, where he bent spoons and stuff like that. But Jon's always wanted to be an actor—Arnold Schwarzenegger is his hero—and he came to the States looking for a Hollywood agent. He met Spear instead. I think he hopes to use the exposure from our work as a platform to riches and fame. So he's really excited you're here. He'll probably corner you to show you a few of his psychic abilities."

"Do you think his abilities are genuine?"

Lucy considered. "Off the record?"

"Whatever you say, I will keep in the same safe place as your nude photos."

She giggled. "I think Jon used to possess psychic abilities, but since meeting the Big Mind, those abilities have faded. I don't even know if he can bend spoons anymore."

"Why?"

"The Big Mind thinks it's a waste of time to use one's abilities on sideshow junk."

"What is the Big Mind?" David asked. "Is it a being that you channel?"

"It's not a being per se. It says that it's what we are, our true selves, our higher selves. I know that sounds abstract, and it is, but once you've personally experienced the Big Mind it's hard to doubt its authenticity. But you've raised another point. We don't actually "channel" the Big Mind. By that I mean we don't go into trances, leave our bodies, and become unaware of what we're saying. The Big Mind says that channeling as it's usually practiced destroys mind-body coordination and doesn't develop a person spiritually." Lucy paused. "What I just said is true except for Vera. When the Big Mind comes through, she's gone. She remembers nothing of what is said, and she never speaks for the Big Mind herself."

"Then why is she a member of the group?" David asked.

"Her presence allows us to focus the Big Mind better."

"Forgive me, I think I'm missing an essential point.

How do you contact the Big Mind? What did Professor Spear teach you that allows the group to function as a unit?"

"We call it 'mutual hypnosis' for lack of a better expression. Say for example someone hypnotizes you. He or she has you take a few deep breaths to relax. You imagine yourself sinking down—all the usual things. If the hypnotherapist is experienced, you'll settle into a restful state of consciousness, but that particular state has limits. The therapist is always speaking to you from an awake state, but you're not awake. If I may use an analogy, it's like he's on the surface of the lake, while you're twenty feet under. He can't communicate very clearly with you. Granted, you can hear him clearly, but your minds are not at the same level. Does this make sense?"

"Sort of. Go on."

"Spear taught us a technique whereby we take *one another* deeper. Our individuality ceases to dominate. As I said, we're still there, we're alert, we know what's happening around us, but a larger presence floods our souls and fills the room. It connects us, and at the same time, allows itself to come through. There is group coherence, literally. Dr. Henry has discovered that our separate brains begin to produce the same wave patterns. It's as if the group functions as one big brain, giving rise to a higher state of consciousness. That state is the Big Mind. When it's there, you know things you wouldn't know otherwise. You feel centered, free, as if you're soaring through uncharted realms of existence. Yet, at the same time, it all feels perfectly natural. As the Big Mind says—the experience is nothing more than the experience of our own inner natures."

"But I've heard that Professor Spear, like most scientists, says consciousness is dependent on the human nervous system. When we die, we're dead. That what all this past life regression stuff is doing, at best, is tapping into genetic memories. Otherwise, he says, it's illusionary."

Lucy nodded. "That *is* his opinion and I respect it. Certainly his work with us has shown that most of the past lives we pick up are related to our ancestors."

"Most? Not all?"

"Sometimes we pick up lives and don't know where they came from. Some are so ancient it's impossible to say whether they're related to us or not."

"Who taught Professor Spear this technique you describe?" David asked.

"He learned it in Africa."

"From whom?"

She hesitated. "I don't know. He never talks about who taught him."

"Aren't you curious about the source of the technique you practice? What if it came from a witch doctor of a tribe of cannibals?"

Lucy laughed. "I am curious, but you can't press Spear for information he doesn't want to give. You can't joke with him the way you're joking with me. He won't like it. He dislikes it when the Big Mind jokes with him."

"The Big Mind jokes? I'm gaining more respect for it all the time."

"It's hilarious. It even told us a dirty joke the other day! Of course the joke came out of my mouth, so maybe its source is a little suspect. I'll tell it to you later, when I know you better. I must warn you, Spear didn't want you coming here *now*. If he's less than open, understand why."

"What's so special about now?" David asked.

"We've been running into a wall for the past two years. We regress back along a particular genetic line, and if we're lucky, we end up in the Stone Age, always in Africa. It's a trip being in the minds of those people because they're half human, half ape. Their thought processes are slow. They stare up at the moon at night and wonder why the lit portion keeps changing size. They think there are lots of moons."

"And you're actually in their minds?"

"Yes. It's hard to believe, I know, but you're right there. You feel what they feel. You see what they see. But it's as if from a distance. The peace of the Big Mind smooths out the experience. For example, if someone's about to be killed, you become afraid, but it's the same fear you'd have watching a killing on a movie screen."

"But if someone is killed, then how do you have their memories in your genes? It couldn't have been passed on at that point."

"That's a perceptive question. Actually, we've never experienced the death of an ancestor in our regressions. If you think about it, it adds weight to Spear's perspective. But let me continue explaining about this wall we've hit and why Spear's upset that you're here now. Spear calls it the 'rational thought barrier.' He says that's it's difficult to regress prior to two million years because back then there *was* no humanity. It was the age of the missing link, before men were men and women were eating apples off the wrong trees. At that point in our evolution we weren't capable of storing memories, not in the way we do now. Therefore, there's nothing to remember. Yet, at the same time, he says there is a way to go back before then—way back, sixty million years back in fact. He says he's done it before and plans to show us the technique during this retreat."

"Another technique he learned in Africa?"

"I believe so. He said the one time he did it was with a group in Africa. Why do you keep asking about Africa?"

"Just curious. I'm confused about a couple of things. How can any mind-altering technique, no matter how powerful, allow you to regress to a time when there were no people? Sixty million years ago there were dinosaurs still walking around."

"I don't know," Lucy said.

"Have you asked him?"

"Of course. He says he'll show us. He's not one to boast. If he says he has regressed back that far, then he has."

David scratched his head. "All this takes time to absorb. I'm confused how specifically the Big Mind helps you regress?"

"While the Big Mind is present, our consciousness is more unbounded. We just slide backward. It's easier to do than to explain."

"Essentially you use that state of consciousness as a springboard into the past?"

"A springboard, yes," Lucy said. "That's a good analogy."

"Thank you. I liked yours about women eating apples off the wrong trees. Tell me, what does the Big Mind say about your research into the past?"

"That it's a waste of time," Lucy said.

"Really?"

"Actually, the Big Mind says it's foolish. That we would be better off not doing it."

David halted on the path. "Then why do you do it? If you have such faith in the Big Mind?"

"Spear wants it done. He wants to prove the authenticity of the theory of genetic memory. If we're successful, it will open up a whole new dimension of what we as human beings are. And the research is fascinating. Don't get me wrong, the Big Mind does not oppose him. It opposes nothing. It embraces everything. But it says the past is a lower state of consciousness. The Big Mind is into the present moment. It says, Be in the present moment. Live life now and fully. Drop all regret and anger about the past. Don't be anxious about the future. The past is dead and tomorrow will take care of itself. The Big Mind says this repeatedly."

"Sounds like good advice. Maybe you should listen to it."

Lucy eyed him again. "Is there nothing in your past, Mr. Nichols, that you'd like to keep?"

She must have hit a nerve because he lowered his head. "There are parts I'd like to save. Parts I'd like to forget." He shrugged. "But it happened. It's done."

She reached over and touched his arm. "I'm sorry."

He looked up, smiled quickly. "What are you sorry about, Miss Lucy?"

"For asking such a personal question."

"That's OK," he said smoothly. "You can ask me whatever you want. As long as I can do the same in return."

"Deal," she said. "But I am sorry."

"About what?"

She smiled. She liked him. "That I never met you sooner."

CHAPTER 4

They walked the three miles to Paradise Camp. It wasn't exactly like stepping into a Girl Scout camp. Lucy was right—it was tiny and spread out. In fact, it seemed as if it had been purposely designed so that no visitor would be able to see two buildings at the same time. They passed a small redwood dorm on the right, but it was hidden by the trees before they caught sight of the next building, a stone chapel. David was amused that a place as rustic as this camp would have a church. He said so to his guide.

"Professor Spear says that eighty years ago, in this part of the country, they would put up a church before they built the kitchen," Lucy replied. "That tells you what their priorities were." She nodded toward the chapel. "See the stained-glass windows? It's fortunate this camp has been almost forgotten. Those windows are precious. If vandals knew about them, they'd be smashed or stolen in a week. At certain times of the day colored light floods the interior of the chapel and you feel like you've fallen into a kaleidoscope. We hold our sessions in there. Dr. Henry has all his equipment set up on the altar."

"I smell food but don't see a kitchen," David said.

"It's behind the chapel, down the slope fifty yards. That's where the other dorm is as well. You can stay there, or in the one we just passed, the sorority house."

David stared into her soft green eyes. One of the things about Lucy Temple that he liked already was that she was not self-conscious of her beauty, which was not the same as saying she was unaware of it. She knew how to flirt: bat her long lashes, toss her head of red curls, and giggle. She loved to giggle. Yet her flirting seemed to come naturally. He already found himself forming one opinion of her and then discarding it ten minutes later. She spoke of reliving the lives of cavemen, which made her sound like a New Age flake. Yet in the same breath she could expound on the fine details of computer programs that correlated brain-wave activity. Her world was so different from his own—an academic, spiritual wonderland where the only time someone was tortured was during finals—that his usual standards could not be used to judge her. He liked that about her as well.

Still, he did not believe she had been back in the Stone Age.

"I assume the women are staying at the sorority house?" he asked.

She blushed; she did so often, her many freckles lighting up like fireflies. "Yes. But there's a room available there."

"Then that's where I'll stay."

"Are you sure? For your story, it might be better if you roomed closer to Professor Spear and Dr. Henry."

"I'm sure, Lucy," he said.

She was pleased. "Good," she said.

A tall, burly gentleman in his midforties appeared. David remembered him from the stolen videotape—Tom Forester, long-distance truck driver, channeler of country western angels. He had on khaki shorts, hiking boots, and nothing else. From the film of sweat on his hairy pectorals, it looked as if he had been working, or working out. He was obviously a "good old boy," the kind of teddy bear lonely women loved to meet at bars when they were drunk. His handsome face was lost to too many pizzas and second helpings, but his blue eyes possessed a certain clarity and charm. He strode up to them with such innocent confidence, as if the war on crime had been won and the sun only went down at night so he could sleep.

"Howdy," he said, his fat hand out. "Name's Tom Forester. Are you the famous reporter?"

"I'm David Nichols." He shook his hand. "I don't know how famous I am, but yes, I'm here to write an article about your group."

"For *Time* magazine?" Tom asked.

"That's the plan," David said.

Tom whistled. "Wow, that's big time. Will we be on the cover?"

David smiled. "I can't guarantee that. But I hope it will be a substantial piece."

Tom pointed to the camera around David's neck. "Just so long as I get my picture in the magazine. My momma thinks I'm wasting my time with all this consciousness stuff. She wants me to work on my musical career. Hey, you wouldn't happen to have any double-A batteries on you, David? My CD player died the day we got here."

"Our electricity is from a gasoline generator Spear and Henry brought with us," Lucy explained. "That's another reason you might want to stay at their dorm. It's right next to the power source. Our lights only work half the time."

Tom chuckled. "You don't need lights for everything."

David smiled. "Well said, Tom. I'm sorry I don't have any double-A batteries."

"Gosh darn," Tom said, truly disappointed.

"Tom," Lucy asked, "do we have clean sheets and towels for Mr. Nichols?"

"Am I in charge of housekeeping?" Tom asked.

"You were when we got here," Lucy said.

Tom considered. "We have some but I don't know where. I'll have to look around." He stuck out his hand. "I can take your bag, David, put it in your room for you."

"That's all right, thank you," David said casually. "I've carried it so far I feel like it's an extension of my arm." In reality he didn't want anyone to touch his bag because he was packing a special FBI cellular phone, an ultraportable laptop computer, and his 10-millimeter semiautomatic pistol.

Tom withdrew his arm. "Suit yourself. I'll go try to find some sheets and towels. I warn you, every mattress in the camp is about as firm as my ex's tits. Best you put your mattress on the floor of your room so you don't wake up with an aching back."

Lucy took a step away. "I'll go with you, Tom. I think I saw sheets on a shelf in the kitchen." She patted David on the arm. "Stroll around, try to figure out where everything is while it's bright and sunny. I warn you, at night, without a flashlight, you can't walk ten feet without running into a tree. Everybody knows you're coming, so if you meet anybody, just introduce yourself. Say, 'Hi. I'm the famous reporter!' "

"Watch out for Dr. Henry, though," Tom said seriously. "That guy likes men."

Lucy socked Tom. "Don't listen to him, David. Henry only pinches Tom's butt to get a reaction out of him. Tom's such a redneck. Henry's cool."

"I am not a redneck," Tom said, offended.

"Yeah, you are," Lucy said. "You're neck's getting red right now." Then, to show she was only teasing, she grabbed Tom's arm. "Come, let's not air our dirty laundry in front of our guest. Wander around, David, but don't wander too far. The woods are filled with lions and tigers and bears."

"Oh my," David said softly, watching them leave. He wondered what it would be like to be part of a close-knit academic group that worked on nothing more threatening than past lives. Somehow, he couldn't imagine it for himself. Yet he was sorry to see Lucy leave. He hadn't encountered such a sweet, sexy woman since, well, Sandy. But he didn't want to think about that, not now. He appreciated the Big Mind's advice about dropping the past—he just wished he could follow it.

David heard running water off to his left. A short hike brought him to a stream and a meadow. Beside the water sat Margaret Farrow in her wheelchair. David had imagined her older, but she appeared to be only in her late thirties and, with the exception of her handicap, healthy. She wore her long brown hair in twin pony tails. Her round face was wholesome rather than pretty, a tomboy who should have been playing basketball, not confined to a wheelchair. That was the world for you, David thought. It didn't care who it paralyzed. Margaret wore green slacks and a yellow T-shirt with a picture of a whale on the front. On her lap were a half-completed green and white sweater, a ball of white yarn, and knitting needles. Hearing his footsteps, she stopped working. He expected her to look over, but all she did was stare down at the running water.

"Hi, Margaret," he said when he was about twenty feet away.

She finally looked over, the reflected sunshine glittering on the water behind her, breaking it up like a million shards of glass. "You must be David," she said.

"Yes, David Nichols. I'm the reporter you probably heard about."

"Come closer. Sit on the grass near me. Don't you love the smell of the meadow grasses?"

He approached and knelt down. The spot she had chosen to knit in was idyllic. Along most of the path to the camp, Lucy and he had been in shade. But here the May sun was bright as in the desert. Oh, there was that thought of Las Vegas again. He would have to watch that. The Big Mind might notice.

"Yes," he said. "It's lovely."

Margaret studied him, as he did her. Her face was remarkably smooth and youthful for someone who had suffered the traumas she probably had with her handicap. For some reason, he liked her immediately.

"Have you traveled far today?" she asked in a pleasant voice.

"Yes. I was on a plane part of the night and then had to take a car up from Boise. I've been on the road a few hours."

"You must be exhausted."

"No, surprisingly, I'm not. The air here is invigorating."

"But you must be hungry."

"I'm not sure."

"We'll go back to the camp in a few minutes and I'll fix you some lunch."

"That's not necessary. I can just scrape together something."

"You're a bachelor, I can tell. You're used to taking care of yourself. But I enjoy cooking. I was just thinking about what we should have for dinner tonight. Before you arrived, I decided to ask you, our guest."

"Anything's fine with me. I'm not fussy."

"What is your favorite meal, David?"

He had to chuckle. "You won't be much impressed if you cook regularly. I love roast turkey and mashed potatoes, and gravy and stuffing."

Margaret nodded. "The way your mother used to cook it?"

"Yes." His mother had died while he was in high school. Cancer. "She used to cook it whenever it was a special occasion."

"Today is a special occasion. You're here. And guess what?"

"What?"

"I have a fresh turkey that we picked up three days ago. It needs to be eaten, so you'll have your favorite meal tonight. How does that sound?"

"Really, Margaret, you don't have to trouble yourself. I'll eat whatever everyone else is eating."

Margaret smiled. "Tonight everybody will be eating turkey. It's no trouble at all. I get to eat, too, and I love turkey."

"I would have thought you were all vegetarians," David said.

"Vera is. Panda is, too, but he doesn't count because he's a Hindu. Tom still eats hamburgers. I bought some ground beef as well, to make them for him. Did you meet Tom?"

"Yes. He's a friendly fellow."

"Yes, he is," she said softly.

"Is there something wrong?"

"No. Why do you ask?"

"I don't know," David said. "I was just wondering."

"Do you want to ask me some reporter questions while you've got me alone?"

"Only if you don't mind," David said. "We can always do it later."

"I'm usually so busy cooking and cleaning, there might not be a later. Ask, I don't mind."

"Very well. Who's that sweater for?"

"Lucy. She catches cold easily."

"How did you meet Dr. Spear?"

"I met him at the hospital soon after I awoke from my coma."

"You were in a coma? When?"

"Almost twelve years ago. I was in an accident. The doctors tell me I was probably hit by a car, but I don't know for sure. I have no memory of how I was hurt. I have no memories at all from before I was hurt."

"Are you serious? But what about your family?"

"I don't know if I have any family. I see the surprise in your face, but it's true. Total amnesiacs are rare, but you have the genuine article sitting in front of you. When I came out of the coma, I was paralyzed from the waist down, and a nonentity."

"That must have been terrible."

"Not at all. I didn't have to relearn to speak or eat or any of those things. I remembered what it's like to change the car oil and mop the floor, and even how to work a word processor. But awakening again after being unconscious for two months was like a rebirth for me. I awoke free, content. I feel that way now. There's no reason to pity me, David."

"I don't pity you. I admire you. Do you remember what you looked like?"

"Like I do now." She laughed. "I'm not blind, you know. Why do you ask that question?"

"It just popped out of my mouth. I'm sorry if it offended you."

"No offense taken."

"But what I specifically meant was, do you remember how you used to dress? How you used to wear your hair? How you used to walk?"

She was thoughtful. "No. I don't remember any of those things. Your question *is* interesting. I may look different. Maybe if my husband met me today—if I had one—he wouldn't recognize me."

"When you woke up did you have a wedding ring on?"

"No. But my finger looked as if I had worn one most of my life."

"I'm still amazed that no one searched for you."

"The doctors and the police believe I may have been injured some distance from where I was found, which was in a garbage barrel behind a grocery story in L.A. For all I know I could have lived on the East Coast before I was hit. Professor Spear was in the room across the hall. He had just returned from Africa with a terrible fever. But he padded over to meet the famous patient without a past when he felt better. We got to talking and he told me of his desire to form a special group of sensitive people to peer back into the past. When I was ready to check out, he offered me a job. I had nowhere else to go, so I took it."

"What do you think of the work he's doing?"

Margaret paused. "It's full of possibilities."

"Do you believe his theory is correct? That we carry the memories of our ancestors inside us?"

"I believe we are many wonderful things inside. The past as well as the future."

"Does the Big Mind ever predict the future?"

She smiled, yet there was a hint of sadness in the expression. "I think the Big Mind knows the future."

"But has it ever actually predicted something that did happen?"

"I don't know—maybe a few times."

"Can you remember any specific instances?"

"You're asking me? The woman without memories? You should ask Lucy. By the way, what did you think of her?"

"She seems like a nice young woman."

"I think you two are going to get along great."

"Are you a matchmaker on top of all your other duties?"

"Yes, I love romance."

"Are you married? I mean now?"

"No. Do you want to marry me?"

He chuckled. "Maybe we were married once, in a past life. Maybe our ancestors were married. Sure, I'll marry you—if the turkey tastes as good as you promise."

She nodded. "Then we have a deal. But Lucy will be jealous."

"She hardly knows me."

"She will be. I guarantee it."

"Are you a psychic as well, Margaret?"

"No, I'm just silly. You shouldn't marry me because I think you're going to end up with Lucy. Or maybe Vera. Did you meet her as well?"

"Yes. I don't know if she took to me as well as her sister."

"Oh, that's too bad. Vera's the prettier one."

"But they're identical," David protested.

"Even identical twins can be told apart. I cut their hair. Vera's is longer and softer. Look closely next time and you'll see the difference. Lucy eats too much junk food. I know, I bake her cakes and cookies all the time. Maybe what you need is a hybrid of Lucy and Vera. And that would be me."

David shook his head. "I think I need to discuss this with the Big Mind."

"You'll have a chance this afternoon. Spear plans a session."

"Margaret, can I ask you a couple of questions about Spear?"

"Sure."

"After the two of you left the hospital, did he form a group right away?"

"No. He was too ill and too upset over the death of his wife. It took him time to regain his strength. The same with me. My spine was broken. The bones took a long time to heal. I was not able to get around in a wheelchair for several months." She shrugged. "We took care of each other during that time."

"Was it Spear who gave you the name Margaret?"

"You are perceptive. Yes, of course, I woke with no name, none that I could remember. He just started to call me Margaret as some way to address me. I didn't object. It was better than being 'she' or 'you.' " Margaret paused. "Margaret was his wife's middle name."

"Did he ever talk about how his wife died?" David asked.

"No. Except to say that she passed away in Africa."

"Do you know what he was doing in Africa?"

Margaret paused. "I get the sense that you have studied his background. Do you know what he was doing in Africa?"

David decided to take a chance with Margaret. He trusted her, and in his business he trusted few people. Yet what did he trust her with? To keep his confidence over Spear's? That was asking too much, yet he didn't feel she'd spy on him for anybody, including her mentor. And even if she did, many of the things he knew about Spear could have been discovered by an industrious journalist.

"I know he was studying the Dogon people," he said.

"Do you know what's special about the Dogon people?"

"They were connected with ancient Egyptian culture. And that culture appears to have had contact with alien beings."

Margaret stared at him.

"I read a paper published by two French anthropologists that describes the Dogons' knowledge—and theoretically the ancient Egyptians' knowledge—of the star Sirius and its white dwarf companion. Knowledge that only modern astronomers have been able to prove accurate."

"Do you believe the paper?" Margaret asked.

"I don't believe the anthropologists were lying, but that's not the same as saying I believe aliens from the Sirian star system visited here thousands of years ago. Do you believe the article?"

"I haven't read it," Margaret said.

"Did Spear ever discuss the Dogon with you?"

"A few times. No one in the group knows much about his experiences in Africa."

"Why is that?" David asked.

"They haven't probed into his past as you have."

"But haven't they asked him where he learned his mind-altering techniques?"

"Oh, sure. He replies that he learned them in Africa. He just doesn't go into details."

"Do you know why his sister-in-law went insane in Africa?"

"Where did you find that out? I don't believe that's been published."

"I have my sources. All reporters do. I take it no one here except you knows about the wife and sister-in-law?"

"That's correct," Margaret said. "The sister-in-law might be another question you want to put to him—but not right away. Let him get to know you first."

"Over turkey?"

"Yes. People are more inclined to share secrets while they're stuffing themselves with stuffing."

"Does Spear have secrets? What did he tell you when he discussed the Dogon?"

She regarded him gravely. "That there were never any aliens."

"How did he explain the Dogons' knowledge of the Sirian system?"

"He said it was the past—the ancient past." Margaret looked over his shoulder then. "Let's get back to camp. I have things to do. If you want a sandwich come by the kitchen."

David stood quickly, took hold of her wheelchair, which was manual. It had no battery or motor. "Let me help you," he said. "But I think I'll pass on the food—I'm just not hungry."

"I would have had a devil of a time getting up the hill without help. Thanks." She glanced back at him. Her eyes were unusually kind, but in that moment, it was as if she were blind. Or else she was seeing right through him. He didn't know which image disturbed him more. All he knew was that he felt the same chill he had when he studied the pictures of Spear's wife and his sister-in-law. She added, "Maybe I shouldn't use that word while we're here."

"What word?" he asked.

"Devil."

David smiled. "You surprise me, Margaret. You believe in devils?"

She turned back around. "I would rather believe in aliens."

CHAPTER 5

David met Jon Horst while wheeling Margaret up the slope to the camp. Apparently Jon had come to get her. Once off the incline, Margaret bid David farewell and vigorously pushed her chair over the mat of pine needles in the direction of the kitchen. David knew why Arnold Schwarzenegger was Jon's hero. Although fifteen years younger than the Hollywood star, Jon had a similar build, complexion, and even, to the unsophisticated, accent to his idol. Clearly Jon had worked long hours in the gym to establish the similarities. Yet Jon's face lacked Arnold's power. David would have hated to break it to the guy that he wasn't in Arnold's category. Jon seemed friendly enough, however, as they all did at the camp. David was looking forward to meeting the master asshole himself, Spear, just for variety.

David and Jon shook hands and introduced themselves.

David was distracted, a part of his mind still with Margaret, the odd things she had told him, and the strange matters at which she had hinted. She had cleverly avoided certain points, but he had not been fooled. Spear wasn't chasing aliens, never had been. His fascination with the Dogon and his interest in genetic memory were tied together. David's interest was piqued. He was looking forward to the session with the Big Mind, that is if Spear allowed him to attend.

"Did you know I was the first one Spear chose to make a permanent member of his group?" Jon asked.

"I thought Margaret was."

"Margaret's our cook. She's a wonderful woman but has no special abilities. Do you want to know how Spear found me?"

"Sure," David lied.

"I was working a club in Hollywood called the Magic Parlor, and Spear was in the audience. I was doing tricks with a pack of cards. Picking them out of people's ears, making a queen of hearts change into a jack of spades— the usual things. Then I did a trick no other magician can do because it involves real magic. Spear spotted that. On the far side of the stage, I had a woman draw a card and look at it and then put it back in a pack she held in *her own hand.* Then I told her what card it was, just by reading her mind. I had her do this ten times and guessed the correct card all ten times. What do you think of that?"

"She wasn't working for you?" David asked.

Jon was disappointed in him. "She was picked at random from the audience. But I understand your lack of enthusiasm for what I just told you. If you were a magician you would know that sleight of hand is impossible if the magician doesn't handle the cards. Spear understood that and knew immediately that I had psychic abilities."

"But if you have such abilities," David said. "Why don't you go to Las Vegas and make a fortune?"

"I'm not interested in that," Jon said, indignant.

"But I understand you want to be an actor."

"Who told you that?"

"Lucy."

"She shouldn't have told you that."

"Why? Isn't it true?"

Jon hesitated. "Yes, it's true. I would like to act. I'm not ashamed of it. I'm a very good actor, but I don't see what that has to do with going to Las Vegas."

David put his hand on Jon's shoulder. "Jon, movies are made with money, lots of money. Las Vegas is full of money. Go there and load up on the stuff, then you'll have plenty of Hollywood producers and directors ready to cast you in starring roles."

Jon blinked. "In what film?"

David laughed. "It doesn't matter! You can write the screenplay if you want! They'll let you. They'll let you sleep with your choice of romantic leads as well." David patted Jon's shoulder and took his hand back. "As long as you've got the money."

Jon thought about it a moment then shook his head. "It would be unethical of me to use my God-given abilities in such a manner."

"Then you may as well forget about becoming a Hollywood star."

"Why?" Jon asked.

"Because it just doesn't happen in real life. No one gets discovered anymore. I can't even get discovered."

Jon was interested. "Are you an actor too?"

"I'm always acting."

Dr. Henry Deering came by right then. David was surprised that he had been enlisted to bring the linen for

David's room. Henry offered to escort him to the women's dorm. David accepted, saying a hurried goodbye to Jon. Dr. Henry, as he preferred to be called, was a handsome man who had a bit of a British accent. David remembered from Ned's files that Dr. Henry had had a Rhodes Scholarship to Oxford. So the guy was no dummy. David found him effeminate but charming. He was one of those rare people whose normal expression was a grin. He was short, five-six in shoes, but as fit as David, although he must have been ten years older. He wore a white doctor's coat over a pair of black slacks and a red silk shirt.

"Was Jon hitting on you for space in your article?" Dr. Henry asked.

"I think he was warming up to the topic," David said.

Dr. Henry waved his free hand. "Jon's all right. He's just young, full of dreams. Nothing wrong with that. I have a few dreams myself—I want to be the first gay black man to win a Nobel prize. But I do wish Jon would concentrate more on our research. He's not like the others, who feel they gain substantially from the sessions. Lucy and Vera are both working on doctorates in psychology, so this is class for them—they get credit from Spear. Panda is here because when he sits with the Big Mind he feels he's in the presence of God. And I think Tom stays around because of Margaret's cooking. But Jon has no such focus. I think he's waiting for the group to become famous."

"Is he an integral part of the group?" David asked.

"Oh, yes. Spear wouldn't have him here if he weren't." Dr. Henry nodded to the redwood dorm, so wrapped in branches it looked as if it had been built by a hobbit. They headed up the rickety steps. "They tell me your room is here at the end. I hope Tom didn't scare you away from the men's dorm by telling horror stories about me."

"Well, I think Tom's from the old school."

Dr. Henry laughed. "I only tease him about how cute his ass is because he's so uptight about homosexuals. Otherwise I wouldn't say boo to him." Dr. Henry opened the door to the room. David wondered who was next door. Dr. Henry added, "He does have a cute ass, though."

"So do you," David said.

Dr. Henry glanced back over his shoulder and lit up. "Do you think so?"

"Absolutely. It's just not as cute as Lucy's."

"I heard you took a picture of her while she was skinny-dipping?"

"Several."

Dr. Henry approved. "I'm glad *Time* sent you instead of a stuffed shirt. The Big Mind won't even talk when one of those is around."

They entered the room and David felt as if he were back at two-week, sleep-away camp. There were two sets of bunk beds stuffed into a wooden box too small to swing a bottle of beer in. There was a bathroom, however, and he had it all to himself, rusty sink and all. The slender shower stall looked as if it had been designed to humiliate the chubby kid. David had been fat as a child. Too much turkey stuffing. He only lost weight when his mother died.

"Isn't this cool?" Dr. Henry asked after a moment of silence and broke into a broad grin.

"Way cool," David said, setting his bag down on one of the lower bunks. He decided right then that he'd have to put a couple of mattresses on the floor to get a decent night's sleep, if not all four of them. Actually it didn't matter much one way or the other the way his bad dreams sucked his energy lately. Dr. Henry started to make up one of the bunks with the clean sheets, but David shook his head. "I can get that," he said.

"Just trying to be the proper host," Dr. Henry answered as he glanced at his watch. "We have a session starting in about thirty minutes. You're welcome to sit in on it."

"Would it be possible to meet Professor Spear before then?"

"No. He specifically told me he would talk to you *after* the session. He wants you to get a taste of what we're doing here. He feels it will make you more open to his ideas."

"Are you open to his ideas?" David asked.

"I endorse them a hundred percent. I think Professor Spear will win the Nobel prize before I do, once the scientific community fully understands what he is saying." He added, "I hope your coming here will help to speed up that process."

"But I understand Spear isn't excited about my being here."

"He is and he isn't. He wants publicity, he simply wants it a few months from now when we have completed our research. But the Big Mind said you were to come, so here you are."

"Lucy told me you specialize in how the three levels of the brain interact with one another. What exactly does that mean?"

"How well do you know the workings of the brain?"

David shrugged. "Assume I know nothing."

"To understand the brain and my association with Spear, you have to understand how the human brain evolved. Take a fish. A fish has a spinal cord and a little swelling at the front end of the spinal cord, which is its brain. Its brain weighs no more than a gram or two. Fish are pretty stupid. But even their small brains have the same major divisions as the *core* of our brains. Like us, they have a hindbrain, a midbrain, and a forebrain. Five hundred million years ago there were fish swimming in our primeval oceans with these same basic parts already in place. Three major steps in evolution have occurred since then, and each time a new layer of brain has been added. Yet the old layers have remained, and have to be added to the equation. Do you understand?"

"I'm not sure."

"The principal modern exponent of the view I am discussing is Paul MacLean, who was chief of the laboratory of brain evolution and behavior at the National Institute of Mental Health. He developed an amazing model of brain structure and its evolution that he called the triune brain. I have already mentioned that our core brain is similar to that of a fish's core. It contains the basic machinery for reproduction and self-preservation. Our heartbeat, blood flow, respiration are controlled by the core of our brains. On top of this we have three layers; three different mentalities with which we view the world. When fish moved to land, reptiles evolved what is called the reptilian complex or the R-complex. Reptiles to this day have it, as do all mammals. MacLean was able to show that this reptilian complex plays an important role in aggressive behavior, territoriality, ritual and the establishment of social hierarchies. I see your knowing smile, David. Yes, much of modern society is influenced by this reptilian complex. Have you noticed how often a murderer is described as cold-blooded?"

"Yes," David said.

"Perhaps we react to such people instinctively, knowing that the side of a man that commits murder is dominated by the complex developed by cold-blooded reptiles. Myths are replete with references to reptiles as evil. There were dragons, of course. The knights of the Round Table were always off slaying some fire-breathing serpent. Then there's that most famous reptile of all, the serpent in the Garden of Eden, who offered Eve the knowledge of good and evil. But I have to wonder if the knights of the Round Table, in their search for the Holy Grail, and dragons to slay, weren't really searching the depths of their souls, the depths of their brains. If the myth of Arthur and his men isn't a profound allegory of human evolution. Why were Adam and Eve driven out of the Garden of Eden? Because of a stupid apple? Or was it because they had finally accepted what the master reptile had to offer? That part of themselves that was capable of unspeakable acts."

"Your ideas are interesting," David said honestly.

"They are not my ideas. MacLean developed them. I must give credit where credit is due. The next level of the brain development was the limbic system. It covers the reptilian complex the way the reptilian complex covers the core. The limbic system probably evolved a hundred to two hundred million years ago. This, too, we share with other mammals. It appears to be the seat of most of our emotions. The pituitary or "master gland" is an important part of the limbic system. The pituitary controls the entire endocrine system, and modern scientists have documented how even a slight change in the endocrine system can affect mood. Thus the popularity of drugs like Prozac, which act largely on the limbic system. 'Friendly behavior' started with the development of the limbic system. Mammals and, to a lesser extent, birds, are the only organisms to devote a lot of attention to taking care of their offspring. If you were to ask me, I would say the seat of love in man is in the limbic system."

David smiled. "What about the heart?"

"The heart is a pump. I don't care what the Big Mind says."

"What does the Big Mind say about the human heart?"

"That it's the throne of God," Dr. Henry said.

"I'm confused, Dr. Henry. From several of your earlier comments I thought you respected the Big Mind. Yet you sound so much like a traditional scientist. Where do you stand on this great presence the group says it channels?"

"I am an agnostic as far as both God and the Big Mind are concerned. Many times I've heard the people in the group say things I believe they couldn't possibly know. Unlike Spear, I believe human beings possess nonphysical means of obtaining information."

"Huh?"

"My experience with the group has led me to believe the human brain is sensitive to energies science has yet to acknowledge. For example, for centuries it has been said we have halos surrounding us. Now with the proof from Kirlian photography, it seems that we do. But what energy is this aura or halo composed of? Why does it seem to change with our emotions? Are other people sensitive to that energy? Can they pick it up from a distance of ten feet? From around the world? Does that energy respond to more than emotions? Can that energy transmit specific information over a distance? These are questions I ask myself. Especially when the Big Mind says that there is going to be bloodshed in the Middle East tomorrow and then the next day a madman with an automatic weapon walks into a mosque and blows away dozens of innocent people."

"The Big Mind has made such predictions?" David asked.

"A few, not many. It doesn't often talk about tomorrow."

"Does Spear share your interests in other forms of energy?"

"No. He's only interested in genetic memories. We work in parallel, not in concert. He gives me a group of sensitive individuals who become something greater than the sum of their parts when they sit together with their eyes closed. I give him hard scientific measurements to back up his theories—EEG's that indicate the group is experiencing a state of consciousness that the individual members could not experience. He takes us into the past; whereas I measure where the past is located inside our brains. Yet we've just scratched the surface of all this, in time as well as anatomically. The third layer beyond the core is the neocortex. It is the most recent development, probably appearing tens of millions of years ago, but its development was greatly accelerated when humans came on the scene two million years ago. Most advanced mammals have it. Relatively speaking, a human's is the largest, although an argument can be made that the neocortex of a dolphin is as powerful. But our group has never been able to regress beyond two million years. I don't know where Spear would place our genetic regressions on a model of the brain, but I say we're still stuck in the neocortex."

"What does the neocortex do for us?"

"Many things. It would take me hours to explain everything. Much of our sensory and speech capacity, even the use of our hands, is controlled in the neocortex. But more important, it gives us the ability to experience abstract thought. The neocortex is what makes us human."

"It keeps the wild animal and the evil reptile outside the door?"

"Nicely put, David. You make an excellent student." Dr. Henry glanced at his watch again. "But if you'll excuse your teacher, he has to finish checking his equipment. The session will be in the chapel. Why don't you freshen up and relax for twenty minutes and then come over? Everyone should be there. Have you met everyone yet?"

"No, not Panda."

"He's a wonderful man, but his English is poor. Except when he speaks for the Big Mind. Then, and only then, is his English fluent."

"What does that tell you about *his* brain?" David asked.

"I don't know. I haven't figured it out yet. But if he says very little to you, you'll know why. He's not being rude."

"I won't take offense. Thanks for the lecture—I know the information will come in useful for my article."

Dr. Henry was at the door. "I appreciate your listening. I know once I start talking I'm hard to shut up. See you soon."

"I'll be there."

David closed the door behind Dr. Henry. Sitting on one of the lower bunks beside his black leather overnight bag, he opened it and removed his cellular phone. He checked the time—twelve forty-eight. Ned would be on the flight to Florida. It wasn't necessary to check in, but there were a few minor points he wanted to discuss. He pushed a button that automatically dialed the number. Ned answered immediately.

"Hello?"

"Hello. This is your favorite field reporter calling from the green mountains of Idaho. What is the Big Mind? Why does it want me here? I don't know and I don't care. Lucy Temple is beautiful, she swims naked, and I think she likes me. How are you, Ned?"

"I'm in first class."

"We never fly first class."

"I am treating myself with the Bureau's money. I figure

5555555555555

I deserve it. Do you know how much alcohol you can drink for free in first class if you want?"

"Yes, I do know. I've treated myself with the Bureau's money for years."

Ned sighed. "I hope this call isn't being bugged. It sounds like you're having fun. Have you met Spear yet?"

"I will in a few minutes. I've talked to most of his people. They're a curious group. It's hard to tell the true believers from the damned. They seem to like me well enough."

"I told you that you were perfect for the assignment. I'm scheduled to speak to Professor Buckley this evening at the University of Miami. It should be interesting."

"Ned, Spear has an assistant named Margaret Farrow. She's been with him from the beginning of his research into genetic memories. You didn't have anything in your files on her."

Ned was surprised. "She didn't come up in our research. That's odd."

"Maybe it's not so odd. She only met Spear after emerging from a two-month-long coma, with no memory of her past. Margaret Farrow isn't her real name, but it might be a lead with which to start a file on her. She's a paraplegic, supposedly a great cook, and a hell of a nice woman. See if the boys in the home office can dig up anything on her. I'll find out what hospital she was in during her coma."

"That would help," Ned said. "She sounds like an interesting woman. Did you join Lucy Temple in her nude swim?"

"No. But the day's young and the night is long. Anything is possible. Isn't it great we're quitting? We can break all the rules and it doesn't matter."

"You've always broken the rules, David. Call me tonight, after eleven my time. I might have some information for you."

"Have you made arrangements to see the sister-in-law tomorrow?"

"It's being arranged. Mental hospitals are not easy places to get into."

"Or to get out of," David added.

"Touché. The flight attendant is about to serve dinner. Steak, potatoes, and steamed carrots, cooked to my specifications. Anything else?"

David hesitated. "Ask Professor Buckley what the Dogon people knew about the brain and the evolution of man."

"Why?"

"I'll explain later. But be sure to do it. It could be important."

"Important? Are you becoming a believer, David?"

"No. You forgot, I'm already firmly entrenched in the other group."

They exchanged goodbyes. David put away his phone and used the bathroom. After returning, he checked to make sure his official FBI gun was still in place. In addition to his 10-millimeter semiautomatic pistol he had brought a snub-nosed Colt .22 revolver that fit under his pant leg. He had worn it all day, but took it off now and put it inside the bag. There was nothing dangerous here, he decided.

David heard someone approaching. Standing, he peered out his window and saw Vera. He heard her enter the room two doors down from his. Two minutes later a toilet flushed then Vera reemerged and headed outside in the direction of the chapel. On their walk up the path, Lucy had confided that her sister had been having nightmares since coming to the camp. Twice, Lucy said, Vera had awakened moaning in pain. Lucy had also said that Vera was the most intuitive person in the group.

David wondered what the young woman was dreaming of.

He decided to hang on to his .22, after all. What the hell.

CHAPTER 6

David had been in a church only once in the last two decades. This one was so small it felt like a confessional booth, so instinctively he thought of his many sins. He had been raised Catholic and realized that guilt didn't vanish with the religion habit, it only changed clothing. Counting the spaces on the twin rows of dark wooden pews, David estimated the chapel could hold forty adults. The floor was gray marble tiles, the walls thick slabs of unpolished sandstone. As Lucy had said, the stained-glass windows were magic. In one window Satan tempted Jesus; in the one on the opposite side, Jesus ascended into heaven. David found the stained-glass window behind and above the altar curious. Here Jesus was simply sitting beside a stream by himself, lost in thought. It was nice to see Jesus taking a break. It was through this window that the afternoon sunlight poured, splashing the col-

ors of the tranquil scene across the pews. David wasn't
such a skeptic that he didn't believe places had vibes. He
would have been the first to say the church *felt* peaceful.
Someone had lit a stick of incense. The back doors lay
wide open, and the fresh mountain air brushed his cheek.
All in all it was a lovely place to hold a séance.

The group was gathered at the altar. Professor Spear and
Margaret had yet to appear. Dr. Henry was busy wiring up
Lucy, Vera, Jon, Tom, and Panda to his EEG and EKG ma-
chines. David met Panda briefly. He seemed a nice enough
fellow, although obviously very shy. He was shorter than
the others, with the long black hair and the soulful dark
eyes of so many Indians. His manner was reflective, pious.
By the way the others deferred to him—giving him the nic-
est chair, falling silent when he entered—David recognized
him as the probable leader of the group.

"Do I look like the bride of Frankenstein or what?"
Lucy asked David, referring to the electrodes attached to
her scalp and chest. She sat in the chair closest to the front
pew, where David had chosen to sit after first seeing
where Lucy would be. She still had on her white shorts
from earlier, although she had changed her yellow blouse
for a blue sweatshirt, a tiny gold crucifix around her neck.
The chapel was a bit chilly. Vera sat to Lucy's left, absorbed in a science-fiction novel. She had not lifted her
eyes once since David had entered the chapel.

"Dr. Frankenstein was the man who created the monster," David said. "Not the monster himself. So you could
easily be his wife."

Lucy was surprised. "You mean all these years I've
been calling that monster Frankenstein and I was wrong?"

"Yes," David said.

"What was the monster's name then?" Lucy asked.

"I don't know. I think he was just called the monster.

It's been a long time since I read Mary Shelley's book, but I do recommend it. It's a masterpiece."

Lucy glanced at her sister. "Did you know that?"

"Yes," Vera said, her eyes not leaving her book. "Everybody knows that."

"Oh." Lucy turned back to David. "Margaret was looking for you. She wanted to feed you. Where were you?"

"I just came from my room," David said. "I told her I wasn't hungry."

"That won't stop her from trying. By the way, guess who you're rooming next to?"

"A silly redhead who swims naked in mountain lakes?"

Lucy frowned. "Yes. *Her.* She's rooming next to a pervert with a *powerful* lens."

"Are you implying that my camera is an extension of my penis?" David asked.

"She's a psychologist," Vera muttered, turning a page. "She sees penises everywhere."

"I don't know," Lucy went to answer him. "I haven't—"

"Don't say it," Vera interrupted. "Remember, we're in a church."

Lucy smiled, tossing her head and her many lovely curls the way pretty girls learned when they were young and wanted Daddy to buy them something. She touched David on his knee. "Guess what we're having for dinner tonight?"

"Turkey," David said.

Lucy blinked. "How did you know that? Did you talk to Margaret?"

"It just came to me," David said. "I love turkey."

"I hate it," Vera muttered.

"You must be psychic," Lucy said, eyeing him.

Professor Spear and Margaret Farrow entered the chapel

then. David knew Spear's face, of course, from the video-tape and the photographs in Ned's files, yet he appeared different in person. The wild gray Einstein haircut was still there, as were the bushy moustache and rumpled brown coat he'd worn on the tape. Yet he was taller than David had imagined, thinner. He, in fact, looked as if he had recently checked himself out of a hospital after suffering a high fever. His long fingers were bony, and the skin on his face and hands was the color of old Brie cheese. His demeanor was intense but not arrogant. More than anything he appeared to be preoccupied. He nodded to David as he passed but didn't stop to shake hands. David wasn't insulted. Margaret smiled at him as she wheeled herself toward the altar—that was all the warmth he needed, for the time being. It was nice to be around a group of young women who weren't drinking hard liquor. Since arriving at the camp, he had not missed having a drink. A camcorder rested in Margaret's lap, and David realized she had shot the video he watched at the L.A. office.

With Spear's arrival, preparations for the session hastened. Dr. Henry finished wiring up Panda, and Margaret set her video camera on top of a stand in the corner. The five members of the channeling group—David still thought of it that way despite what Lucy had told him—closed their eyes and began to take long, slow, deep breaths. Margaret peered through her viewfinder, focusing. Dr. Henry bent over a computer terminal beneath a holy picture, and Spear leaned against the chapel's main cross, the nailed and bleeding feet of Jesus Christ pressing into the professor's waist. David sat and watched and tried to feel for the presence of the Big Mind, but felt nothing. The group continued to breathe in and out for several minutes, and David had to stifle a yawn.

Then, just as they had on the videotape, each of them began to speak about the beauty of the breath, coming into the present moment, and the dawning of unbounded awareness. All except Vera, who sat so still her breathing could have ceased. She clutched Lucy's hand, and it was definitely Vera holding on to Lucy and not the reverse. She clung to her twin as if she feared she were about to fall off a cliff.

Then there was a long silence where no one spoke.

"Ah. What is the program?" Panda said finally, his English much improved over twenty minutes ago, his voice clear, resonant. It was as if he spoke in a much larger room. The effect puzzled David.

"We have no program this afternoon," Spear said in a surprisingly gentle voice. "We let you decide."

"Ah," Panda said. Or was it now the Big Mind? David had to assume so. "We have a visitor, do we not? David?"

"Yes," David said, sitting up. "I'm here."

"How are you? How was your trip?"

"It was fine. I'm fine. How are you?"

"Wonderful. What would you like to do this afternoon?"

"Maybe asks some questions. Then regress into the past. See some dinosaurs."

Panda, the Big Mind, chuckled. The faint echoing quality in Panda's voice continued.

"If we see dinosaurs, they might see us. They might be hungry. It might not be a good idea. But ask your questions. I enjoy questions."

"Who am I talking to right now?" David asked.

"No one, everyone. A window into eternity, a blank wall. It is all the same. Words cannot describe me. I can only be described by negation. I am not this, I am not that. It is a paradox. It is confusing. I am the Big Mind. That is as good a name as any. Who are you?"

"David Nichols."

"Is that who you are? Who is David? Is he these clothes you wear? This body? This personality? I don't think so. Those things will fade away in time, but you and I, we're timeless. We have that in common. I think I must be you. Or at least your friend."

"I am curious if you have any individuality?"

"Yes and no. I adopt individuality for the purpose of communication. The same way a wave rises from the ocean to take the surfer to shore. Then, when it has finished its task, the wave dissolves back into the ocean. Do you swim? You're from California, you must be a good swimmer. I see that. You have been treading water a long time. Take the next wave in, David. It's coming soon."

David took a moment to absorb the response. He had almost made the Olympic swim team. Did the Big Mind know that? Or was it just a coincidence? David's curiosity piqued.

"What is your purpose in contacting this group?" David asked.

"I am the group. I am always here. They simply become aware of me when they sit like this."

"But are you here to help them?"

"Yes. I help all living beings. I bring love, peace, expansion. Did you know it is the nature of life to expand?"

"It seems that it is the nature of life to suffer," David said.

The Big Mind chuckled. "Suffering can be expansive. Why should you run toward the sun when you sit in a bright room? Only darkness makes you crave the light. But I understand. What do you want? What do you really want?"

"Proof that you exist. That there is a Big Mind."

"The only proof is in your experience. How do you feel now?"

"Fine. I feel the same as I did when—" David stopped abruptly. He realized he did feel exceptionally fine, the fatigue of his journey had been lifted. He wondered if he was the victim of subtle suggestion but couldn't remember the Big Mind saying anything suggestive. The Big Mind waited.

"Yes?"

"I feel refreshed," David said. "Relaxed."

"Good. I am relaxed as well. Another thing we have in common. See, we must be the same. You want a miracle, I understand. People always do. But miracles sneak up on you when you least expect them, and usually they pass without your knowing. Life is a miracle. I lied to you a moment ago. Every time I speak, I lie a little. I don't mean to, but it happens. Words convey so little. The purpose of life is unknown. It's a mystery, and you know mysteries can be lived, but never explained. Do you understand?"

"I think so. You are talking about a state of life beyond words?"

"Yes. It is like that. The Big Mind is pure silence. Your inner nature is silence. How can you talk about silence? It is not possible. Still, we sit and talk together because it is fun."

"I read a book this group published that contained transcripts from several of your talks. In it you mentioned top-secret projects the government is working on. Cold fusion. Jet planes capable of flying into earth orbit. Technology that can transform nuclear waste into harmless isotopes. You said the government had already developed these things?"

"Yes."

"Is that true?" David asked.

"Yes. You know it is true."

David hesitated and considered the possibility that the Big Mind *could* see through his disguise. Just as quickly he dismissed the idea. He was a master at undercover work. No one knew anything about him unless he wanted them to know.

"What do I know?" David asked, a note of challenge in his voice.

"Many more things than you let on. *You* are mysterious. You play that role. And this, in turn, keeps you at a distance from those around you, those who love you. You believe you must stay distant or your love will injure you as it has injured you in the past. But no love is ever lost. How is it possible? Does death destroy it? There is no death. The form may change but the essence is never lost. Can any wave, no matter how big, leave the ocean depleted? I tell you seriously another wave comes soon—one that can safely take you all the way to the shore. Yet your eyes stay fixed on the horizon. One miracle is not enough for you. You keep waiting for another, and another, the perfect wave to rise out of the sea. But times goes on, the sun nears the horizon. Your life passes. What are you waiting for, David?"

Despite his resolution of a moment ago, David felt strangely moved. The Big Mind spoke in a delightful rhythm that magically disarmed. Yet he had trouble hanging on to what was being said. The comments were like lines drawn on water; they existed for only the moment.

"I don't understand this wave I keep missing. I don't understand this shore I'm supposed to reach." He added, "Could you please explain it?"

"The shore is the shore. It is covered with sand. It is very sandy. That is what you miss most. That is what haunts you. I tell you it is still there. Angels guard the sandy shore. The waves do not wash it away. Yet the angels haunt you as well. Your past is a shark that circles your feet. You worry it will bite, that you will bleed. You think you bleed now. That your blood stains the sand. That is *maya*—an illusion. Drop your guilt. Come into the present moment. It is eternal, as all the angels in heaven and all the particles of sand."

David had to take a moment. Why did it keep bringing up sand? Why angels? Was it talking about Sandy and Angela? That was not possible, he thought. They were dead. They lived only in his memory. He didn't want to drop them. Then he would have nothing. He realized he was trembling and had to will himself to stop. He lowered his head.

"I appreciate your answering my questions," he said. "Thank you."

"Ah. What next?"

Spear straightened himself. "Mr. Nichols. You said you wanted to observe the group regress into the past. We cannot visit the dinosaurs you mentioned but perhaps we can show you another slice of history. What is your preference?"

David looked up and met the professor's eye. "I have always been interested in ancient Egypt," he said. "Predynastic Egyptian culture."

Spear met his stare, his eyes cold, and amused. "Very well." He spoke to the group. "Let us regress. Follow *all* the genetic chains." Spear's gaze returned to David. "I see your surprise, Mr. Nichols. But, yes, everyone sitting here had an ancestor in ancient Egypt. An amazing coincidence, wouldn't you say?"

David shrugged. "It's remarkable." Spear saw that the Big Mind had rattled him, David realized, and wanted to take the opportunity to underline the fact. Of course, with his request, David suspected he could be asking to see Spear's dirty laundry. When David just wanted to know if aliens helped build the pyramids.

What happened next differed from the regression David had witnessed on the videotape. With the exception of Vera, each of them spoke again in turn. They didn't simply slip into a life in ancient Egypt; they jumped around into different bodies. David found the shifts disconcerting. Also disconcerting were the voices of the group. David couldn't understand why even simple-minded Jon sounded as if he were speaking with the voice of Thor, or at the very least the voice of a large and wise man. But when they slipped into a life, they didn't adopt a particular accent or language, which David found a relief. He assumed the Big Mind automatically translated for them.

Jon: "The molecule is an almost endless spiral. We walk the five billion blocks of nucleotides. We carry the code, our way is clear. The human taxon is complex, but it is not the first. The structure is binary. We see yes, we see no. We feel plus, we feel minus."

Lucy: "My lord and master, the king, draws his sword. I am to be knighted. The king thinks I am brave. He is wrong. All I feel is fear of the impending battle. I know I will die."

Tom: "Mutations in the gametes, in the eggs and the sperm cells, are all that matter for the survival of the race. Radioactivity mutates the cells. Cosmic rays alter the building blocks. Sometimes the nucleotides simply fall apart, some destruction must be needed so that the body can evolve. As we walk the spiral, we skip over the damage, over the genes that bring change. Because we choose to go back, not forward. It is our choice. We feel it is right."

Panda: "The water is as blue as my mother's eyes. She

carries a basket of bread to feed the lepers who rot by the shore. My own fingers fall off, yet my mother says I will be well because she loves me. I love her too much not to believe her."

Lucy: "The line of time is not linear."

Tom: "It is not a circle."

Jon: "It is a spiral."

Panda: "It stands before us."

The room fell silent. David stared at the back of Lucy's head; he could not turn away from it. Because even though his eyes told him her red curls had not smoothed out or darkened, that her skin had not changed to black, and her sweatshirt had not been transformed into a long robe, *something* in the room kept trying to tell him things were different. Things that didn't show up on the videotape.

"Isis," Lucy said.

Jesus Christ, David thought, not without a sense of irony. From the point of view of the woman who now sat in front of him Jesus hadn't even been born yet. No matter how hard he tried, he couldn't free himself of the illusion that he was staring at an Egyptian princess. Especially when Lucy turned her head to the side and David saw her ancient profile, carved from the stone wall of a secret pyramid long buried beneath desert sands.

She was very beautiful. This dead person.

"Ast and Asar," Lucy said softly. "Isis and Osiris. It is said Set is the brother of Osiris, but that is a poor metaphor. The night is not related to the day. It is said the black rite is the highest initiation, and that is a danger. Isis is not the bright star in the sky. Isis is the not the statue on the altar. Isis is the star above the head. Isis is the celestial, from where the Goddess pours down the healing white light. The inward breath takes me up to Isis. The outward breath pours her grace down upon me. Between breaths I silently utter her sacred name. She warns me.

" *'Do not take the initiation, child. Do not stare in the mirror. There you will only find the corrupt past—the black one, the old one, the horror of Set.'*

"I listen to the Goddess. I flee the temple without my sister. It is night and I walk alone along the river, but I feel the eyes of the serpents follow me. They think they fool me with their human bodies but their eyes are never the same after the black rite. I have only the light of Isis to protect me. The serpents are many and I am only one. The night grows darker and I feel them close. I begin to run; I am afraid. But I am more afraid to become like them and never see the face of Isis. I hear the hiss of their breath in my ears. They have caught me. Their invisible claws scratch my skin. I am thrown to the ground. Later, I see their faces. They force me to look into their eyes and I am sick on the sand.

"They have brought my sister. She cries for me to help, but I cannot. They hold my face under the river until my chest burns. Then they lift my head up and order me to stare into the mirror. They say they can force me against my will. I pray to Isis for help and she answers. White lights pours down upon my head and Isis speaks to me.

" *'Only human eyes can see Set. If not for my light in this land, the curse would spread like a plague. That is why they need the mirror that reflects no color. Do not look into it. Offer your eyes to me, child, and they cannot use you. Fear not—the eyes with which you will behold me can never be destroyed.'* "

Lucy's head dropped. She finished the tale in a frail whisper. "I shake free of them. I raise my hands and dig my fingers into my eyes. Warm blood soaks my cheeks and my vision fails. There is pain and I hear my sister scream. They take her away and I never see her again. They leave me alone, bleeding by the river, and I never see anything ever again."

The session abruptly ended, without a period of transition. David was confused for a moment until he saw that Vera was responsible for the group breaking out of the trance. Her eyes were open and there were tears on her cheeks. Everyone stared at her, and David would have liked to know exactly what they saw. He no longer saw an ancient priestess, but he had to blink and rub his eyes to convince himself that the tears running down Vera's face were not in fact drops of blood.

CHAPTER 7

Ned Calendar sat in the back row of Anthropology 101 in a large auditorium located on the University of Miami's campus and thought what a lousy teacher Professor Carl Buckley was. Although Ned had missed the first half of the class, he should have had at least some idea of what Buckley was discussing. The title of the course was Ancient Greek Culture, but Buckley seemed to be discussing how to tear down a Parthenon rather than how to build one. Buckley didn't help matters by keeping his eyes glued to his notes so his perfectly round bald head mooned the class. He spoke in a monotone that would have put a hyperactive kid to sleep. Around him, Ned noticed several students dozing. It looked like an old habit with some; they didn't even bother jerking their heads upright once they were down. Despite his rare glances at his students, Buckley must have been aware how little attention he was receiving from the audience. Certainly no one was interrupting to ask questions. At twenty to nine—twenty minutes early—Buckley abruptly closed his notebook and dismissed class.

"I will be in my office till ten if anyone needs help with their paper," he called out as the students—specifically those who had been comatose a minute before—charged for the doors. Two minutes after dismissal, Ned was alone in the classroom with the esteemed professor. True to his habits, Ned had not called to warn the professor he was coming. Ned had a theory about informants: the more nervous they were, the more they said that they later regretted. Of course, he did not classify Buckley as an informant, but had already decided he was not going to say goodbye to the man without getting a better explanation for the death of Penny Spear than the LAPD had received. Ned walked down the steps to counter where Buckley was collecting his papers with the simple-mindedness of a Disney character.

"Professor Carl Buckley," Ned said when he was maybe twenty feet away. "We have to talk."

Buckley finally looked up, startled, a fox caught with a chicken in his jaws. Instinctively, Ned knew that Buckley had secrets to hide, and not the wit to do it. Buckley was a fat man with a body the shape of a stuffed laundry bag. His cheeks and jawline were one smooth slab of twitching flesh. Honestly, Ned could not understand how a man like this had survived sub-Saharan Africa for six months. Maybe the years since then had been hard on him. Buckley eyed him warily.

"Who are you?" he asked.

Ned took out his FBI badge, flashed it so quickly a video camera couldn't have recorded whether it was silver or gold and put it back in his pocket. "Ned Calendar, Special Agent in Charge of the Los Angeles branch of the FBI. I'm here to question you about your activities in Mali, Africa with Professor Stephen Spear, and about the death of his wife, Penny Spear. Would you like to talk here or in your office?"

Buckley drew in a breath and swallowed. He lowered his head and shuffled his papers. "I cannot talk now. I have students waiting for me in my office."

"I doubt that."

Buckley glanced up, fearful. Now that was a new emotion, Ned thought. Fear was not the same as anxiety. Fear often came when there was a victim involved, and a victimizer. Which was Buckley?

"What do you want?" Buckley demanded meekly.

Ned shrugged. "I told you. To talk. Let's go to your office. I think you'll be more comfortable there." He turned toward the door. Buckley hesitated, then began to follow.

"Am I under arrest?" Buckley asked.

"Not yet," Ned said reassuringly.

Ned found the walk across campus refreshing. He enjoyed Florida, the tropical air, the beaches, the flapping white sails on the many boats. Not Miami, though, because of all the crime. He knew it was an odd prejudice for a man who had worked for the FBI in Los Angeles for the last thirty years, but he didn't like crime, period, and occasionally wondered why he had spent his entire life pursuing the destruction of an element he loathed. Yet his career was almost over, as was most of his life. It was too late now to second-guess his choices.

Ned wasn't upset that David was retiring—he wanted David to get away from it all, as desperately as he wanted David to fulfill his destiny. David was one of the few people Ned believed had a destiny. He had only had to work with David a short time to realize that if he pointed him and his energy and intelligence at a problem, it would either be quickly solved or else explode in unforeseen directions. That is what he had loved most about David, that he allowed no major case to sink into a mire of inconclusiveness. He wanted David to retire for his mental health, but he also wanted him to stay on to save that kid or that wife no one else could save. If David had been able to save Angela Wilson, it might have made the incident with Sandy Quin bearable. Maybe not.

Ned had tried to keep his promise to David to hold back the SWAT team. But Angela's screams as her thumb was dissected from her body had strung the men's nerves taut, and Ned couldn't blame the man for taking a shot at Pokey. Ned didn't know if David realized that Clancy had twice tried to commit suicide since the death of Angela. It wasn't exactly the sort of news to cheer David up. Of course, David would probably have smiled and pointed out that no member of a SWAT team should have trouble blowing his own brains out.

And what about Sandy Quin? That had been Ned's call for sure, although David had never blamed him for her murder. Over the years Ned had reviewed what had gone wrong and he supposed he wouldn't stop until the day he died. Yet, logically, he couldn't fault his decision. Had Failla discovered a single bug, he had planned to bring Sandy out of Las Vegas immediately. If only David had not insisted on saving the movie theater owner, Holt, Failla would not have been tipped off. Then, if only David had managed to reach the hotel two minutes earlier, and stopped Failla from pushing Sandy. Ned assumed David knew that Mr. Holt had later been found guilty of murder in the first degree. Sandy's life for that of a con.

What scale of justice must David have struggled to balance to even stay with the Bureau? Ned supposed David had remained because he knew there would be an Angela to save. But now that she was gone, he was going as well. It was sad, Ned thought, but with just a little luck it could have been so incredible. David could have been a legend. Now he was only a phantom hero who failed to rescue the girl. Dirty Dave—Ned hated the nickname.

And he tried not to think about what David had done to Failla. Ned preferred to remember his greatest agent as the son he never had. If he had found Failla's body in the desert, he feared that would have been impossible.

Ned was excited about this case, however. He had been a philosophy major in college and had always been interested in spiritual matters. He was not into traditional religions but he often prayed when he was alone in his office late at night. God was an important part of his life. He was also something of an ancient culture buff, and a lover of astronomy, so the mystery of the Dogon fascinated him. He was happy that David had taken to the enigmatic case surrounding Spear's group. Anything to make the poor guy forget the last month.

Buckley's office was unimpressive, four blank walls and one window that looked out over a huge tree that virtually covered the window with its branches. So this is the expert professor that Spear chose to accompany him to Africa, Ned thought. Teaching general ed classes and stuffed in a closet without a broom. As soon as they were seated, Buckley tried to profess his innocence of any wrongdoing. Ned cut him off with a raised hand.

"You will tell me everything about your trip to Africa. You will start at the beginning, leave nothing out, and continue through to the end. If you don't do this you will annoy me, and when I'm annoyed I cease to be your friendly neighborhood FBI agent."

Buckley stared at him. "What do you do?"

"First, I take out my handcuffs, then I take out my gun." Ned leaned forward and smiled. The gesture on him was not disarming as it was on David. He had grown too old. When he grinned he just came off as unstable. "Would you like to see them now?"

Buckley sat back. "No. I can tell you about the trip. I have nothing to hide."

Ned sat back and relaxed. "We all have something to hide, Professor. By the way, I know about the Dogon people and their special knowledge of the Sirian star system. I have read Griaule and Dieterlen's paper. You don't have to review what they wrote, but I don't want you to skip any points that relate to how the Dogon came by such remarkable knowledge. I do hope I make myself clear."

Buckley looked at him in a new light, and with even more fear. Ned sensed he was rearranging the story he had been about to tell him. "That's very interesting. Few people are aware of that paper." He cleared his throat. "That should have given you a sound understanding of why we wanted to visit the Dogon people. My specialty is ancient Egyptian culture. That's why Spear asked me to accompany him. That, and the fact that we had taught together at Stanford."

"So the two of you go way back?" Ned asked.

"Yes."

"How do the Dogon relate to the ancient Egyptians? Specifically?"

"I can best answer that question by explaining how the Sumerian culture relates to the ancient Egyptians. You may not be familiar with the Sumerians, who gave rise to the Babylonians, in what is commonly called the cradle of civilization, in the Mesopotamian region. But let me start out by saying that phrase is a misnomer. The Sumerians had a highly developed culture of their own. I am speaking of approximately four to five thousand B.C., at which time the Egyptians also had a flourishing culture. That these two cultures were connected by a common origin is, in my mind, beyond dispute. But that is nothing I would utter among my colleagues at this university."

"Why not?" Ned asked.

"Most anthropologists do not feel that the Sumerians and Egyptians had a common origin. But I can support my belief with hard facts. Basic Egyptian astronomy and Sumerian astronomy are identical—twelve months composed of three ten-day weeks each, resulting in thirty-six constellations. That adds up to three hundred and sixty days, and in each culture the five left-over days were considered sacred. In fact, these five days are also important in Mayan astronomy. But I don't want to get into that now or we'll be here all night. Later, of course, the Egyptians adopted a calendar that more specifically related to the sun, but that was not for another two or three thousand years."

"This is all very interesting. But what does it have to do with your expedition?"

"The point is that civilization rose remarkably fast in different parts of the world, but in similar fashions. For hundreds of thousands of years we wandered around, living in caves, and then in the space of a few centuries we had a highly developed understanding of astronomy. Naturally, the French anthropologists' paper describing the Dogon's knowledge of astronomy interested us. I thought to myself that this tribe lives in Mali today, but was it possible that thousands of years ago they had direct contact with the Sumerians and the Egyptians? Spear impressed upon me the Dogon's strong oral tradition. Their spiritual knowledge is passed down from father to son in a very secret and exacting manner. It was my hope to learn more about the connection between the Egyptians and Sumerians through the Dogon."

"What did Spear hope to learn from the expedition?" Ned asked.

"He was more interested in how the Dogon knew that Sirius has a white dwarf companion. I was curious about that as well, but it was not my primary reason for going to Africa."

"After living with them for six months, do you believe that they knew about a star system many light-years from here?"

"Yes," Buckley said. "The evidence is indisputable. They also knew about the four primary moons of Jupiter and the rings around Saturn, objects that can only be seen with a telescope. They have drawings of these planets and stars. I have seen them with my own eyes."

"How do you explain their knowledge?" Ned asked.

"The Egyptians and Sumerians gave it to them. The Dogon are excellent librarians, but I do not believe the knowledge originated with them. However, I should add that it is possible the Dogon could be an actual offshoot of the ancient Egyptians."

"Then let me rephrase my question. How do you explain how the Egyptians and Sumerians obtained this knowledge?"

Buckley hesitated. "I can't."

"You're going to have to do better than that."

Buckley gestured helplessly. "How would you explain it?"

"I don't know. But I didn't spend six months researching the matter. Is it possible that the Dogon were contacted by an alien civilization thousands of years ago?"

Buckley smiled. "I hardly think so."

"Why not?"

"I don't believe in UFOs."

"Yet you're positive that the Dogon's astronomical knowledge is accurate. You and Spear must have a theory, Professor. Tell me what it is."

Buckley lowered his head. "I honestly don't know how they could know such things."

"Why do you avert your eyes when you say you're being honest with me, Professor?"

Buckley's head snapped up, a hint of anger on his face. "Spear knew them much better than I. Why don't you ask him these questions?"

"Perhaps I will. Later. Tell me about Spear. Tell me what it was like to live in Africa with him and the Dogon. Tell me about his wife, Penny, and his sister-in-law, Frances. I am curious about all these people."

"Only three of us—Penny, Spear, and myself—went to Mali at first. Frances came later, at Spear's request. We went at the worst time of year, the beginning of summer. I wanted to go in the fall but Spear was insistent. When he gets something in his head, it's impossible to change his mind. He's stubborn. I didn't like that about him. I don't like several things about him."

"Such as?" Ned asked.

"He's always the boss. He might listen to your opinion, if he's in the mood, but if he didn't like what you said it was as if you had never spoken to him. It just vanished from his mind. My credentials were every bit as good as his. I should have been treated as an equal on the expedition, but I was not." Buckley sighed. "Except by Frances."

"The sister-in-law?"

"Yes. She always treated me with respect. She was also an anthropologist, a specialist in North American Indians."

"Were you romantically involved with her?" Ned asked.

"I liked her. She liked me as well, you know—as a friend."

"Did that upset you? That you were only friends?"

Buckley's pride was evident. "Of course not. We were both professionals."

"I see. When did Spear bring her over?"

"In September. Three months after we got there."

"But why bring her to such a harsh place at such a hot time of year? If the Dogon were not even indirectly related to her field of expertise? Did she want to come?"

"No. She hated it there. We all did, except for Spear. The heat's impossible. Even in the dead of night you feel as if your skin is ready to dry up and flake off. The bugs never leave you alone. I would spray myself from head to toe with repellant and they would still bite me. Frances in particular suffered from the insects. She was there less than a week when she was bitten on the head by a poisonous spider. She almost died. There was no medical doctor in the area, and even the local Dogon medicine man wouldn't help us."

"Why not? Are the Dogon cruel?"

"Not at all. They are exceptionally friendly. They have an age-old tradition of nonviolence and hospitality."

"They why wouldn't they help Frances with her spider bite?"

Buckley hesitated. "Because she was Penny's identical twin."

Ned felt as if the light in the room had dimmed. He thought of the twins Spear had in his channeling group. Still, why had Ned actually felt dizzy after Buckley's remark? Because the last time Spear had been around twins one of them died and the other went insane? Maybe the professor just had a thing about twins, Ned told himself. There were far worse fetishes. Yet he had to wonder what Spear did with them when he had them alone, in the desert, in the mountains.

"What did the Dogon have against twins?" Ned asked.

"They see them as evil. When they're together."

"Did they see Penny as evil as well?"

"Yes. Once Frances arrived, they avoided both sisters. The Dogon have no identical twins in their individual tribes."

"But surely they must. They're human like us. Identical twins must show up every now and then. Wait a second. You're not saying they kill the twins as soon as they're born?"

"No. They have too high a regard for human life to do something that barbaric. But they separate twins at birth. The Dogon are actually made up of three tribes, spread over considerable distances. If identical twins are born, they send one of the twins to another of the tribes. For the rest of their lives, the twins are never allowed to meet. When the Dogon saw Penny and Frances together, they were seeing something unnatural to them."

"But once the twins are separated, the Dogon no longer see the individuals as evil?"

"That is correct," Buckley said.

"Why is that?"

Buckley hesitated, making an effort not to look away, Ned noticed. "I don't know," he said finally.

Ned was impatient. "I don't understand any of this. You and Spear and Penny had been with the Dogon for three months. You must have known this about them. Why did you bring Frances over?"

"Penny and I did not bring Frances over. Spear did. He did so without our permission. God knows how he talked her into coming. And Penny and I did not know about the Dogon's fear of twins."

"But Spear did?" Ned asked.

"Yes. Look, I have to admit something no reputable anthropologist would be proud to admit. When it comes to learning foreign languages, I have difficulties. But Spear is a genius with them. He picked up Sanga quickly, and some Wazouba, which the most remote of the three tribes speaks. Because of that he was on friendlier terms with the Dogon than I was. He often gave their priestesses and priests small gifts. He spent long nights walking and talking with them. They liked him—he had them fooled. He learned many secrets from them. Spear is not generous when it comes to sharing secret knowledge—he doesn't pursue scientific knowledge for the sake of science alone. He is driven by the desire to be the main instrument of truth. His ego knows no bounds."

"OK, he's an asshole. We've established that. Why did he bring Frances to Mali if he knew it would spook the Dogon?"

"I think he brought her there for that very purpose."

"What do you mean?" Ned asked.

"He wanted to scare them. He wanted to show them that he had power. Anthropologists the world over will tell you that what primitive cultures fear, they also respect. Perhaps it's not so strange. We're not so different in the West, if you think about it."

"But why do the Dogon associate identical twins with power?"

Ah, Ned had hit a nerve. Twins and power. Buckley began to perspire.

"I don't know," Buckley said.

"Why did Spear want to scare them? What was he try-ing to scare out of them?"

Buckley considered, his fat neck twitching. "I don't know."

"Professor, if you say that one more time you're going to piss me off. Did Spear speak of his theory of genetic memory while he was in Mali?"

"It was while we were there that he began to formulate it."

"Did he formulate it? Or did the Dogon give it to him?"

"I—I'm not sure. They might have. But Spear took credit for it."

"So he did talk to you about the idea?"

"Yes," he said quietly.

"When? Specifically? When Frances arrived?"

"I believe it was just before she arrived."

"Professor, it seems clear to me that Spear's theory of genetic memory and the existence of identical twins are in-tertwined, at least in Spear's mind. Would you agree?"

"Maybe," Buckley admitted, shifting in his seat, proba-bly wishing it would teleport him far from the merciless FBI agent who drew his salary from the very taxes that came out of the professor's monthly checks.

"Then you should also agree that he brought Frances to Mali to be with Penny because he planned to do *direct* re-search into his theory of genetic memory, which the Do-gon both believed in and feared. Am I correct?"

A bulls-eye. Buckley almost fainted. Panic entered his voice.

"How can I answer these questions? I'm not him. You'll have to ask him."

"Oh, I definitely will ask him. But you can answer these questions as well as he can because you were there and you're an intelligent man and you have a goddam Ph.D.

Now, is there, or is there not, a link between identical twins and the uncovering of genetic memories?"

"I don't know!"

"Dammit, you're lying to me! I warn you, I am not the LAPD. I don't listen to a vague tale about a wild animal killing one woman and driving another insane and then close the case. We're talking about a possible murder here, and you're a suspect until you convince me otherwise. How did Penny die? Why did Frances lose her mind?"

Buckley was having trouble breathing. His fat face had swelled up like a red beet. Ned feared he might have a heart attack on the spot. Maybe he had pushed the guy too hard, he thought, at least for the time being. Interrogation had to be accomplished in waves, hard hits followed by soothing words, or even breaks. Clearly something dreadful had happened in Africa that had scared the hell out of Buckley, yet the professor was trying to hide it. This, despite Ned's opinion that Buckley had not been personally responsible for Penny's death or Frances's breakdown. From the look and sound of him, the worst that Buckley could destroy would be a Big Mac at McDonald's. Buckley bent over as if he might be sick.

"An animal got her," Buckley mumbled into his trembling hands.

"Which one?" Ned asked dryly.

Buckley drew in a shuddering breath. "Penny. She was killed by an animal."

"What was the animal?"

"I don't know."

"What happened to Frances?"

Buckley shook his miserable head. "I don't know."

Ned remembered David's questions. "What did the Dogon know about the human brain?"

"A lot."

"Would you care to elaborate?" Buckley didn't respond. He sat up and blinked as if he were a little boy who had just been told his favorite TV program had been cancelled. Ned added, "What did they know about the evolution of man?"

"A lot."

"They weren't so primitive after all, were they, Professor?"

"No."

Ned stood. "Frances Cumberly is locked in a sanatorium in South Carolina, in a small town called Salutory. She's been there for twelve years, since you left Africa. Did you know that?"

"Yes."

"I'm going to visit her now."

Buckley jerked involuntarily. "Now?"

"Yes. I was going to go tomorrow, but after listening to you, I feel impatient to speak to her." Ned paused. "Do you have a problem with that?"

Buckley paled. "But it's so late. It's dark."

"I'm not afraid of the dark, Professor. Are you?"

Buckley suddenly reached across the desk and grabbed Ned's hand. "Don't go there, please? You don't want to go there. She can't speak. She's too far gone. There's no reason to go there."

Ned noticed how damp the man's grip was. And how Buckley was no longer worried about himself, but about the mean FBI agent who one minute ago wouldn't stop tormenting him. Ned gently unwrapped the man's fat fingers and wiped his own hand on his pants leg.

"I have to go," Ned said. "When I am done speaking to her, I'll return. I know your home address. I don't need a lot of sleep. I may come in the middle of the night. Be there."

Buckley's face crumpled. "If you do see her, for god sakes don't be alone with her. Have someone around, a couple of strong men. And don't look directly in her eyes. Be sure not to do that."

"Why not?"

Buckley trembled. "Because she's so horrible."

CHAPTER 8

·

"At last we meet," David Conner said to Professor Stephen Spear.

They sat in what must have been the camp director's office. Given the dimensions of the retreat center, the room was spacious, with the obligatory moose head on the wall and a half-dozen logs burning in the brick fireplace. The warmth and light of the latter was welcome. Behind Spear, outside the screen-covered window, the evening shadows had lengthened the green arms of the trees into dark outlines of would-be trolls. David had waited the better part of the day for the meeting. After the afternoon session, each of his attempts to talk to Spear had been rebuffed with word that the esteemed professor was resting. David thought Spear looked pretty fried for a man who had napped all day.

The only effort Spear had given to personalize his office

was a two-foot green iguana, which crouched in a straw-littered glass cage off to the left and stared at David as if he, and not the turkey in Margaret's oven, was the feast they were all waiting for that evening. David assumed the lizard was a pet of the professor's since it could not be native to the area. The realization did not make David view the man with more warmth.

"I'm sorry to have kept you waiting," Spear said. Once again David was struck by the gentleness in the man's voice, at odds with his dark eyes, which were as emotionless as a pair of shrunken cue balls. Spear had traded his rumpled brown coat for a neat green sweater, although his gray hair still looked as if he combed it while holding a live wire. Spear added, "It's been a difficult week, coming up here and all."

"That's a pity," David said. "Since I understand one of the reasons you brought your group here was because of the serenity of the location. I was told you grew up around here?"

"Yes, not far from here."

Spear reminded David of Pokey Sampson. Knew the area of his birth well. All the hidden caves and crevices. Probably fantasized about that trick in the river since the time he was a teenager. David brought out his miniature cassette recorder, which all good reporters were supposed to carry. He set it on the desk between them.

"Do you mind if I record this conversation?" he asked.

"That depends."

"On what?" David asked.

"On what you ask me."

"Does it matter what I ask? Your answers are your own." David reached over and put the recorder back in his pocket. "But we can save the official record until later, if it makes you more comfortable."

Spear shrugged. "What brings you to our retreat, Mr. Nichols?"

"Curiosity. I'd like to ask you a few questions."

"I believe it will be more than a few, judging from your questions this afternoon."

"Naturally, before taking on this assignment, I acquainted myself with your past achievements. I know of your interest in the Dogon and their connection to the ancient Egyptians."

"Africa is long ago and far away, Mr. Nichols."

"David, please. I believe your present work is influenced by your experiences in Africa. For example, you went to Mali primarily as an anthropologist. But since you returned you've branched out into what I think we would both agree is parapsychology."

"I had a doctorate in psychology before my degree in anthropology. But let us not quibble. What is your point?"

"Did the Dogon give you the technique of mutual hypnosis?"

"The technique existed in the West before I went to Africa."

"But not as you practice it. I have studied the literature on the subject. Nowhere is there an example of collective group consciousness used to project into the past."

"Do you believe it is only a projection?"

David paused and decided to give an honest appraisal. "I admit I came here ready to dismiss the whole idea. But after this afternoon, I don't know. I was impressed with many of the things the Big Mind said. Also, when Lucy spoke for that Egyptian woman, it was as if—"

"She became the woman," Spear interrupted. "Even her appearance seemed to change. We have all had that experience. I call it genetic transference. Of course, Lucy's appearance had not really changed. If you study Margaret's videotape, you will find no Egyptian woman in it. But during the session, consciousness is fluid. There are fewer boundaries between us. You experienced Lucy as she was experiencing herself."

"And you wouldn't call that a spiritual experience?"

Spear snorted. "That type of interpretation is New Age rubbish. I have fought against it for the past twelve years. People who are desperate to give a spiritual slant to every incident of expanded awareness are sad souls indeed. I use the pun intentionally. In their frantic search for God, they deny the glory of humanity. We are remarkable beings. Contained within our DNA is the secret of how life began on this planet. We can probe that secret using altered states of awareness, which are also, ultimately, a product of that same DNA. What I am trying to do with my work is give a new meaning to human potential, not just redefine it for a modern religion that doesn't even have the decency to call itself a religion."

"I spoke to Dr. Henry today and he explained to me a bit about the evolution of the brain," David said. "He said your probe into genetic memories is related to his probe into the deeper layers of brain functioning."

"That's an oversimplification. It's not as if more ancient memories are stored closer to the core of the brain."

"Yet the core is the oldest, evolutionary wise. Then the three layers that were built up on top of it each correspond to a different leap in evolution. With your genetic regressions, are you trying to tap into these different layers of brain functioning?"

"I believe I have already answered that question."

David smiled. "I'm sorry, I must have missed it. What was your answer?"

"No. We are not trying to regress into the limbic system or the reptilian complex. There is no need to go into the past to find them. Every human who walks this planet is a savage animal and a cold reptile. It is only because we have trained our highly developed neocortexes to suppress these areas of functioning that we have been able to develop a civilized society."

"Then you do believe each level of the brain has specific emotional and psychological characteristics? I know the theory is debated among scientists."

"My answer to your question is yes," Spear said.

"A moment ago you used the word suppress. Do you, Professor, believe we are suppressing a portion of our potential as human beings?"

"We are suppressing the bulk of it. At the beginning of this interview you referred to me as a parapsychologist. That is not a title I willingly adopt, but for the sake of this discussion you can call me that. Because I have seen with my own eyes people bend spoons without touching them, or describe pictures that other people held in their hands two blocks away. I have also seen people remove deep and long-lasting pain just with the touch of their hands. Now, understand me clearly, none of these things are miraculous. None of them mean that there is a beneficent God in heaven watching out for us. They are normal human abilities. Abilities we all should have. They are built into us. That is the goal of my research—to give back to man what he has lost."

"So you believe people had these abilities in the past?" David asked.

"I didn't say that exactly."

"You implied it, Professor. Did we or did we not have these abilities in the past?"

Spear considered. "Perhaps."

"Have you been able to rekindle them with your genetic regressions?"

"I'm not sure I understand your question."

"Have you found a group of people in the past who possessed these abilities? For example, the predynastic Egyptians?"

"There are signs, of course, that they had such abilities. You heard an example of that this afternoon."

"You refer to the young woman who was pursued by bodiless eyes and held down by invisible arms until the evil priests arrived on the scene?" David asked.

"The woman in question saw them as evil. For all we know, she could have been the troublemaker."

"Yet she did not seem interested in having the others' abilities."

"I cannot comment on her personal interests," Spear said.

"I am reminded of a remark Dr. Henry made today. We were talking about the structure of the human brain and he said, 'Yet the old layers have remained. They still have to be taken into account.' I didn't understand what he meant, but I am getting an idea now. Also, a comment you made a moment ago interests me. You said, 'It is only because we have trained our highly developed neocortexes to suppress these areas of functioning that we have been able to develop a civilized society.' I am not misquoting you, am I?"

"No. What's your point?"

"These remarkable abilities we might have possessed in the past—maybe we lost or suppressed them for good reasons. Maybe they had a way of fucking up society, if you will excuse my Egyptian."

Spear frowned. Or perhaps it was closer to a glare. It was hard to tell in the shifting orange light of the crackling logs. The iguana was still staring at David. He had to resist the urge to walk over and open its cage and throw it in the fire. He had never cared for lizards. They reminded him of the desert and Las Vegas. He wondered if there were dinosaur bones buried in the sand surrounding Sin City.

"Your comment reveals the bane of every true scientist the world over," Spear replied in a measured not-so-gentle tone. "That is fear. Space is unknown. The bottom of the ocean is still largely unknown. The future is unknown. The bulk of the past is unknown. What is unknown is feared by most people. But that does not mean it's evil. When we began this discussion, you said you were here because you were curious. You have been here only one day. Aren't you still curious? Wouldn't you like us to go ahead with our work?"

David met his gaze. Spear had a bit of a megalomaniac in him. He liked to stare people down—easy for him with those two black holes in his head. David replied in the same measured, slightly condescending, tone.

"I would urge you to go ahead with your work only after a close examination of your past efforts in the same direction," he said.

Spear was startled. "What do you mean?"

David smiled. He had just been fishing for a reaction and was happy to get one. "We haven't talked about your experiences with the Dogon in Africa. I would like to know if they were aware of the phenomenon of genetic memory?"

Spear found the question insulting. "I did not steal the theory from them—if that's what you're implying. I never said the idea originated with me, but I am the first one to prove it."

"You didn't answer my question, Professor."

"The Dogon have a mystical tradition that does incorporate elements of the theory of genetic memory."

"Do they sit around in groups like you guys do and delve into the past?"

"Not exactly."

"What do they do differently?" David asked.

Spear was still annoyed. "For one thing, they don't have redheads in their groups." He added, "I don't understand the purpose of your question."

"Let's move on. Do you have a special technique for bypassing what you call the rational thought barrier?"

"Who told you about that?"

"Lucy. She said you're planning to have the group regress beyond primitive man during this week-long retreat. Is that correct?"

"Lucy shouldn't be talking about such things. We have never regressed that far before."

"But are you going to try while we're here?" David persisted.

Spear was a long time answering. "That remains to be seen."

"You had a Professor Buckley, your wife, and your sister-in-law with you while you were in Mali. Is that correct?"

Spear's guard went up. He was wondering how this annoying reporter could know so much. "Yes," he said carefully.

"How did your wife die, Professor?"

Spear sucked in a breath which sounded like a hiss. Might have been the iguana. For a moment David had trouble telling the master and the pet apart. Spear shifted in his seat and it sounded as if it was about to crumble beneath him.

"My wife died in an accident," Spear said finally. "I will not discuss it."

"Why did your sister-in-law go insane? Was that an accident?"

Spear stood. He was remarkably tall, looking up at him from a seated position. "Really, these questions are getting too personal and have nothing to do with our present research or your article on our research. I will not answer them. My wife's death is still painful for me. I'm going to eat now. You are welcome to join me if you agree to stop asking abusive questions."

David stood as well. "I apologize if my questions caused you pain; it wasn't my intention. I'm simply doing my job. But I do have one other question, if I may?"

"Yes?"

"Is it your belief that the ancient Egyptians were contacted by an alien race?"

"No." Spear stepped around his desk. "Are you coming with me?"

"Yes." David gestured to the iguana. "What's her name?"

"*His* name. It's Frank. I've had him for twelve years."

"I see," David said.

David did not sit with Spear at dinner, because Spear collected his food and retreated to his office. Probably Frankie had put in an earlier request with his master for a drumstick to chew on. Maybe not. David remembered that reptiles liked to eat living things, when they could.

Well, he ended up asking Margaret to marry him. He had to—the food was that good. Unfortunately for David's stomach, he had second and third helpings and was groaning before dessert, a German chocolate cake topped with vanilla ice cream, appeared. Margaret had accomplished the impossible—mashed potatoes just like his mother's.

David had never met anyone who could do that. Margaret accepted his wedding proposal but wanted a ring to make it official. David then backed off, laughing. He noticed Lucy frowning in the corner.

After dinner the group remained at the dining room table to gossip. David felt at home with them. Indeed, he thought he was going to miss them when he had to say goodbye. To liven things up, he suggested a game of poker but first Jon declined, and the others agreed. But Jon did agree to entertain and bend a few spoons for David.

"You'll bend them right here in front of me?" David asked. "Only using your mind?"

Jon nodded. "Of course."

"You won't touch them?" David asked.

"I will touch them lightly, with my fingertips," Jon said.

"Come on, Jon," David prodded him. "Why do you have to touch them at all if you're going to bend them with the power of your thoughts?"

"I don't like having my spoons ruined," Margaret said, sitting on David's right, Lucy on his left. Jon ignored Margaret and handed David a soup spoon.

"Feel this," Jon said. "It's stainless steel, of high quality and thickness. If I were to hold this lightly between my index finger and thumb, and if it were to melt down before your eyes, would you be impressed?"

David checked out the spoon. "Do it first and then ask me." He gave the spoon back to Jon.

"We should hook the dude up to the EEG," Tom said.

"He'd short it out with that cosmic energy going through him," Dr. Henry said. He reached over and tapped Tom lightly on his arm. "Speaking of which, you had high theta waves inside your head this afternoon. What were you thinking about? Your old rig? A night out with those good old country boys down in Oklahoma?"

Tom quickly withdrew his arm. "I was thinking about the Egyptian priestess, like everybody else. Besides, you shouldn't be discussing my private brain waves at the dinner table. What kind of doctor are you, anyway?"

Dr. Henry grinned. "So, sue me."

"Quiet, everybody," Jon said, closing his eyes and lightly massaging the point on the spoon where the handle joined the bowl. "I have to concentrate."

"I suppose there's a first time for everything," Lucy said, amused by the psychic demonstration. To her left sat Vera, quietly finishing her cake. She hadn't eaten any turkey, only a small amount of potatoes and vegetables. David was happy just to see her because he had been concerned about her after the session, when she left the chapel without speaking to anyone. But she seemed all right now.

"That's one of my favorite spoons," Margaret said.

"We can always bend it back," Lucy said.

"Would everybody please shut up?" Jon asked, his tan forehead wrinkled. He continued to rub the spot on the spoon as if hoping it would climax. Then, much to David's surprise, the spoon magically began to sag. It drooped as if it were roasting in a furnace. Jon opened his eyes and smiled.

"No sweat," he said.

"Let me see that," David said, swiping the spoon from Jon. The spoon was hot. David was dumbfounded. "How did you do it?"

Jon reveled. "I was born gifted."

"So was everyone," Lucy said. She swiped the spoon. "David, did you know that you can do what Jon just did? I can teach you how to do it in a few minutes."

"I don't think so," David said. "I don't have soldering tips for fingers."

"You don't need them," Lucy said. "All you need is to work the spoon as Jon did and have an off focus that it's getting hot."

"What's an off focus?" David asked.

"You focus while you look the other way," Vera muttered.

"You concentrate but you don't strain yourself," Lucy said. "Margaret, give me your spoon."

"No," Margaret said.

"I have a spoon," Panda offered, unsuccessfully searching the area around his plate. Maybe Margaret grabbed it just before he had spoken. Panda hadn't eaten any turkey, of course, but had had plenty of everything else. David wondered where the little guy put it all.

"You can have mine," Dr. Henry said, taking the one beside Tom's plate.

"That's mine," Tom said.

Dr. Henry was sweet. "I was using it before you."

Jon shifted uneasily. "This is not something everybody should attempt. It could be dangerous."

"Bullshit," Lucy said, accepting the spoon from Dr. Henry. Closing her eyes, she began to rock it lightly between her thumb and index finger. "It's getting hot already," she muttered a minute later.

"Hot enough to melt?" David asked. He didn't know the melting point of steel, but figured it must be hotter than two sweaty fingers could produce—by a few hundred, if not few thousand, degrees. Yet, to his astonishment, two minutes later, Lucy's spoon sagged the same as Jon's. She opened her eyes and handed it to David. It was very hot.

"No sweat," she said sarcastically, giving Jon a dirty look.

"I did it in less time than you," Jon said defensively.

"How in Christ's name did either of you do it?" David asked.

"It's done by focusing one of those strange forms of energy inside us that science doesn't yet understand," Dr. Henry explained. "Somehow, by bringing the attention to the fingertips and wishing for heat, the body produces a current that loosens the molecular structure of the steel. Actually, I don't even know if the rubbing motion is necessary for it to work. I think focusing is enough."

"You've seen people do this before?" David asked.

Dr. Henry nodded. "At a party for little kids I handed out a bunch of spoons and asked them to give it a try. Without exception they were able to bend them with the tips of their fingers. As Lucy and Vera explained, the trick is to focus on heat without focusing too hard. Children have a knack for that."

"I never knew you guys could do it," Jon said.

"Ah-ha." Lucy pointed a finger at him. "You didn't know anyone else was *gifted*? What would the Big Mind say about your ego, huh? That it was fully inflatable?"

"I was impressed," David muttered.

Lucy shook her head. "You're a smart guy, David, but you're also too materialistic. There's a whole world going on around you that you've never tried. Grab a spoon. Seriously, give it a try."

Margaret sighed and handed her own spoon to David. "Just promise me you'll try to straighten it out when you're done with it," she said.

David held the spoon warily. He'd have been more comfortable handling a jagged-edged hunting knife— anything that he wasn't required to bend.

"I don't know if I was meant to channel unexplainable energies," he said.

Lucy patted his arm. "Just do it. I promise Satan will not enter your body and possess your soul. I'll stand guard."

What the hell, David thought. He closed his eyes and began lightly to rub the spoon between his thumb and index finger. He thought of heat flowing from his hands into the metal. He thought of the others staring at him with smirks on their faces. After a few minutes the spoon was no hotter. He opened his eyes and set it down.

"Nothing happened," he said.

"Too much heat," Panda said, touching his forehead.

"You were straining," Lucy explained. "You can't *try*. You just have to let it happen."

David felt as if he were back in kindergarten. "How do you try not to try?"

Lucy offered him the spoon. "Do it again. I'll rub the back of your head while you rub the metal. You'll be relaxed and attentive at the same time."

"This is getting kinky," Dr. Henry said. "The whipped cream will come out next."

"I have some," Margaret said.

Once more David closed his eyes and set to work on the spoon. With Lucy's fingers digging into his neck muscles and stroking the back of his skull he did begin to feel kind of hot, but wondered through which part of his body the warmth flowed. A few minutes passed. The session with the Big Mind had given him a boost, but the caressing relaxed him to the point where a fifteen-year backlog of fatigue started to be released. His head fell forward slightly, and he had to catch himself and remember to keep rubbing the spoon. In the middle of all this someone gasped. His eyes popped open. Around the table, except for Jon, they were grinning.

The spoon had melted.

He dropped it on the table. It wasn't that it was hot—the experience was just unnatural.

"Wow," he said.

"Our new high priest," Lucy said, leaning over to give him a congratulatory kiss on the cheek. "O, Master, teach me the ancient secrets. Let thine eternal power enter into my bosom."

Tom nodded to Dr. Henry. "Definitely time for the whipped cream," Tom said.

"I can't believe I did that," David said, enjoying Lucy's closeness. Her hand continued to rest on the back of his head even as she dropped into the chair next to his. He chuckled as he stared into her lovely green eyes, and wondered where he had seen them before. They looked familiar. Must have been a past life. "How do I know it wasn't your touch that didn't make it all possible?"

She flashed a nasty grin. "You might always wonder, David."

The dining hall had a storage room as well as a kitchen. It was in the basement at the end of a steep ten-foot flight of stairs. Together, Tom and David carried Margaret and her wheelchair down into the cool, damp room. She preferred to put away the food herself, she said. While Tom and Dr. Henry cleared the dining area, the rest washed and dried the dishes, David tried to help Margaret. He had known a few handicapped people in his days, but none impressed him as much as Margaret did. It was as if the life she had lost in the lower half of her body had simply shifted to the upper half, and doubled her vitality. She pushed and spun her wheelchair about the cramped storage area as if she were an MTV extra on a skateboard.

"I know I've told you already," David said, "but your

mashed potatoes were the best. I wish I could take you home with me."

"You had your chance," Margaret replied, tossing potatoes into their wooden bin. "You chickened out."

"I saw a dark cloud forming over Lucy's head."

"I told you she'd get jealous. It's just as well. If you ate my cooking all the time, you'd get fat. You want to know the secret to those mashed potatoes you liked so much?"

"Yes," David said. "Please."

"I make them very plain—just a little butter and milk. I knew that about you the moment I saw you—you like your food plain. You'd drive most people who cook crazy."

"Am I that transparent?" David asked, not really worried. Margaret stopped what she was doing to study him.

"No," she admitted. "I agree with the Big Mind. You're a mystery man."

"What makes me so mysterious?"

"If I told you then it wouldn't be mysterious. Did you enjoy the session this afternoon?"

"Very much. Except at the end when Vera got upset. I was worried about her."

"I know you were." Margaret became thoughtful. "I worry about her, too. She's such a beautiful, sensitive girl." Margaret briefly closed her eyes and rubbed her head.

"Is something wrong?" David asked, taking a step closer.

Margaret blinked and shook her head. "No. Everything's fine. Are you going to take the Big Mind's advice?"

"I might if I understood how to translate it into practical terms," David said honestly. He still didn't believe that the intelligence of the universe had spoken to him that afternoon, but he remained deeply affected by the encounter. The Big Mind had touched a sore spot. Yet, ironically, there had been relief in the midst of the pain that he couldn't explain. Sandy and Angela were still dead, and he doubted if he would ever be able to forget how they had died and his role in their deaths. Yet, after the session, it was as if the tragedies—in particular, Angela's—had been pushed farther back into the past. If reincarnation was a reality, he was glad it was arranged so that a person forgot what had happened in a past life. He sure as hell didn't want to remember being an FBI agent, much less be one again.

"Oh, I think the Big Mind gave you very practical advice," Margaret said.

"That I should be happy? What do I do to be happy? It skipped over that small detail."

"It pointed you in a direction. Besides, happiness doesn't come from doing this or that. Or even from thinking happy thoughts. Happiness is what we are, inside."

"Happiness may be what you are, Margaret, but I'm afraid to say you're in the minority. You should multiply."

She smiled. "If there were too many of me, just think how congested the malls would be at Christmas with all the wheelchairs." She threw a carrot at him. He caught it easily. "Go see Lucy. She's waiting for you. I can manage down here. Tom and Dr. Henry can carry me back up when I'm through."

"Isn't Lucy still doing dishes?" David asked.

"Lucy never does dishes. She's too lazy."

David headed for the steep stairs. A thought made him stop. "Margaret?"

"Yes?"

He glanced over his shoulder. "Do you have any idea at

all who you were before your coma? Any image—even a faint one—from your past life?"

She looked at him a long time before answering. "When I awoke, I remembered the sun and the moon and the stars. Mostly the stars."

"Is that all?"

"Yes," she said softly. "That's all."

CHAPTER 9

Ned Calendar chartered a private plane to Salutory, South Carolina. The night was clear, the visibility excellent. The pilot chatted nonstop beside him about how his wife was cheating on him with a guy who designed clothes store mannequins. But he couldn't leave the fucking bitch because of the kids. The pilot sounded as if he enjoyed his kids about as much as he liked finding his wife's lover's used condoms under the bed. Ned advised him to talk to an attorney and not an FBI agent.

Salutory had its own airport, one of those narrow country affairs where the runway was mowed rather than paved. Ned could have had a local agent waiting to take him to the hospital, but he took a cab instead. As he climbed out of the plane, he told the pilot not to go far.

The sanatorium looked like a prison that had been dropped from a great height. The building was a squat rectangle with welded bars on the windows. There was no landscaping except for a few scraggly bushes that would have been better off with a nice layer of asphalt above their roots. It was a cheery place. He told the cab driver to wait as well.

The physician in charge of the night shift was expecting him. Ned had pulled strings to get in to see Frances Cumberly at such a late hour. That was another good thing about retiring—he could call in all his markers as if there were no tomorrow. The way Buckley had gripped his hand before he left, maybe there wouldn't be. Not that Ned was afraid of an insane woman who had been locked up for twelve years.

Dr. Simon Goldberg was younger than Ned expected. He was the nerdy first-year medical student who never washed his hands after gross anatomy. The lenses on his glasses more rightly belonged on the old and out of focus Hubble telescope. He even had a few zits left over from college all-nighters fueled by chocolate bars and girlie-magazine posters. Simon acted happy to meet a genuine FBI agent, especially at one in the morning.

"Did she kill somebody?" he asked when Ned explained that he was there to see Frances Cumberly.

"Not that I know of." Ned paused. "Has she killed somebody while she's been in here?"

"She might if she had the chance. We have her on heavy doses of Thorazine, wrapped in a straitjacket in secured isolation. The whole nine yards." Dr. Goldberg flipped open the folder in his hands. "Would you like me to review her medical records with you?"

"Yes. Please."

"Frances Cumberly. Forty-four years of age. Primary diagnosis: acute schizophrenia. She believes she is the direct descendant of an ancient godlike race. Has delusions of supernatural powers—telekinesis and mental telepathy—but has never demonstrated any paranormal abilities, although she is extraordinarily strong. Perception of reality is intermittent. Spends the majority of her time wrapped in hallucinations. Has failed to respond to traditional psychotherapy or even repeated shock therapy. Prone to exceptionally dangerous outbursts of violence." Dr. Goldberg closed his folder and looked at Ned as if he should be impressed that his hospital had such an interesting patient. "Are you sure you want to interview her?"

"Yes. Have you awakened her?" Ned asked.

"We didn't have to. She doesn't sleep much. I have taken the liberty of having three orderlies secure her for your visit. While you're here, I am responsible for your safety." He added, "I must also be present during the questioning. Hospital rules."

"Why is it a hospital rule?" Ned asked.

"It's for your protection as well as hers."

"But if she's in a straitjacket and secured, I should be safe. And I doubt my questions can harm her more than twelve years of Thorazine, not to mention all the voltage you've run through her brain." Ned paused. "I'll speak to her alone."

Dr. Goldberg did not insist. If anything, he looked relieved. "Very well. Let me show you to her room."

"Just a moment. You mentioned she has a *primary* diagnosis of acute schizophrenia. Does she suffer from anything else?"

"Yes. She has severe psoriasis. It has failed to respond to treatment. For hygienic reasons, we keep her completely shaved."

"When did this start?" Ned asked.

"She's had it since her initial breakdown, twelve years ago."

"I see," Ned said.

Dr. Goldberg led him to Frances's room, a padded cell. The room's only illumination was from a dull red emergency light on the ceiling, encased in shatterproof plastic. Ned requested more light before he entered the cell but was told it wasn't possible. Frances, it seemed, straitjacket and all, had managed to break every light that had been installed in her room. She didn't mind the red night light, however. Ned felt as if he were being shut in a volcanic cave as Dr. Goldberg wished him happy hunting and closed the door. Dr. Goldberg insisted the door be closed. As one last tiny bit of medical history, the good doctor added that Frances had once escaped from her cell and gouged out and eaten both eyes of a severely retarded twelve-year-old boy. Took three strong men to get her back in her room. Wonderful, Ned thought.

Besides being dark and claustrophobic, the cell was permeated by a peculiar odor. To Ned it was like a tropical rain forest after a fire. The odor was specific to the room—the rest of the hospital smelled simply stuffy. Ned wondered at the source of it.

There were no chairs available, so Ned sat on the floor across from the bed bolted into the wall, a toilet and sink to his right. Frances leaned upright against the far wall as if she were fixed in place by a spear. In combination with the sober red light, her straitjacket and bald head made her appear mummy-like, dug from a tomb. Her expression was grotesque. Had the electroshock destroyed the nerves in her face and left them permanently expressing pain? Her mouth was twisted into a voracious maw, her nostrils stood up like dripping snouts. Her eyes, as Buckley had forecast, were the stuff of nightmares. A speck of gold swam in the center of each. Her long pointed tongue raked the air in search of invisible flies. The hiss of her breath was the death rattle of cobras in a pit.

"Frances," he began, "my name is Ned Calendar. I'm an FBI agent in charge of finding out what happened to you and your sister in Africa. I'm here to ask you a few questions." He paused. "Do you understand me?"

The central gold dots in her eyes swelled. Her head bobbed from side to side but it steadied when she gazed in his direction. "I understand," she said in a hiss.

Ned swallowed. Jesus. She needed a fucking exorcist, not Thorazine. That was the trouble with psychiatrists today, he thought. They weren't trained in the dark arts. He felt for his gun under his coat and was happy she was chained down.

"Do you remember what happened in Africa?" he asked.

"No Africa. One land." Her head jutted forward. "Come closer."

"I'm comfortable where I am. Do you remember your sister?"

"Yes. The mirror. We came out of the mirror." She hissed. "Hungry."

"You and your sister came out of the mirror?"

"No. Want to bite you."

Ned felt inspired. "Who is *we*?"

"We are your master. Made you. Came before you. We can do anything."

Ned took the wedding ring off his finger and held it out. "Do you know what this is?"

"Yes."

"This is a ring. If you can do anything, please make it disappear."

"No. The mirror cracked. No power."

"What is the mirror? Was it in Africa?"

"No Africa. One world. Sister cracked. No power."

"Your sister was related to the mirror?"

"Yes. Cracked."

"When it cracked you lost your power?"

"Yes."

"When she died?"

"Yes."

"Did you lose your mind when she died?"

Her neck stretched toward him, impossibly long. It was as if she were an ostrich. "No. Hungry. Feed me. Give me arm."

"I would like to keep my arm, thank you. How did she die? Did you kill her?"

"No."

"Who did kill her?"

"Don't know. Dead. Power dead."

"Frances, do you remember your name?"

"Yes. Zenath. Master of Frances. We made you."

"Zenath exists in the past inside Frances?"

"Zenath now and past. Zenath hungry. Water. Thirsty."

Ned went to get up. "You want a glass of water?"

"Yes." The maw twisted into the facsimile of a grin. "Then meat. Blood."

Ned sat back down. "I'll get your water later. Let me understand you. Zenath existed in the past. Is she an ancestor of Frances?"

"Yes. Ancient. One land. We were the masters."

"Were you the Dogon?"

"No."

"The ancient Egyptians?"

"No. Before the warm ones came. We were there."

"Are you saying there existed a race of people before the Egyptians?"

"No people. Only masters. People are food. Come closer."

Ned felt a cold wave rise from below, from a place where things were best left buried. He couldn't believe the thing sitting in front of him had once been a friend of Professor Buckley's, or anyone else's for that matter. He couldn't quit staring at her. She had some kind of hold on him.

A race more ancient than mankind dreamed?

I am talking to a schizophrenic. I must not forget that.

Yet everything she said, no matter how absurd, rang true. Why?

"I don't want you to eat me, Zenath," he said, "so I won't come any closer."

"Oh."

"What kind of race are you from, Zenath?"

She must have bitten herself. Blood trickled out of her mouth and onto her straitjacket. The gold in her eyes liquified. "Beautiful. Powerful. Intelligent. We are your masters. We come for you."

"You come for us? Out of the past?"

"Yes."

He discovered he was trembling. He couldn't make himself stop.

"How do you come? Through the mirror?"

"Yes. Hungry. The past burns."

"Why does past burn?"

"We burned it. Everything black. Cold. No food."

"Did your race destroy itself?"

"Yes."

"How?"

"Hunger. Power. Hate."

"Did you hate each other?"

"Yes."

"Why?"

"No why. Nature. Power. Hunger."

"Do you hate people?"

"Yes."

"How long ago did your race live?"

"Ancient."

"Did you have an advanced civilization?"

"Yes."

"More advanced than humanity's?"

"Yes. More power."

"Was your race able to travel to the stars?"

"Yes."

"Did you ever go to Sirius?"

"Blue white star. Bright. Yes. Three stars there."

"Not two?"

"Three."

"You come from the past into the present through the mirror?"

"Yes."

"Is the mirror constructed of identical human twins?"

"Yes. Perfect."

His heart pounded. That was the key, he thought—before recalling his vow not to be influenced by her insanity. But who was the patient here? He thought he'd go nuts just looking into her eyes. He wished he could stop himself.

"Like Frances and her sister?" he asked softly.

"Yes. Came through that mirror." A satisfied hiss. "Swallowed Frances."

"Was Penny swallowed?"

"She died. Mirror cracked."

"Do you come into the present through the process of genetic regression?"

"Yes."

"Did Professor Spear guide his wife and sister-in-law through this process?"

"No. Zenath did."

"Did Spear help?"

"Spear is food. Ned is food. Come closer."

"I will come no closer. What's so special about identical twins that you can manifest in our time through them?"

"Perfect reflections. Mirror faces mirror. No holes. No cracks."

So that was it. Logical. Genetically identical twins could not be told apart. The coherence between them during mutual hypnosis would be flawless. How did this thing—he had ceased to think of it as human—know that?

"Genetic regression only works perfectly when identical twins are used?" he asked.

"Yes."

"Did the Dogon know this?"

"Yes."

"Did the ancient Egyptians?"

"Yes."

"Did you manifest in the time of the ancient Egyptians?"

"Yes. Powerful. Spread from mirrors. Ruled people. Ruled land."

"If you were so powerful, how did you lose your power?"

"Don't know."

"Do you mean you spread out from the mirror? Can people other than identical twins manifest your race in our time?"

"Yes. Need mirror. Only short time. Control brain. Heat core."

"You can alter people's brain and they become like you?"

"Yes."

"But you lost your power when Frances's sister died?"

"Yes."

"Did you alter anyone before you died?"

"No answer."

"You don't know?"

"I know. No answer you."

"Why not?"

The thing giggled. "You are food!"

Ned fought to get a grip on himself. It was tied up. He had the gun. He was safe.

"I may be food but you're locked up in a mental hospital. Do you know that?"

"Yes."

"Can you break out of here?"

"No."

"Zenath is trapped? You don't sound so powerful."

"Another mirror. Another Zenath."

He spoke with a conviction he didn't feel. "I don't think so. Only the Dogon and Spear know how to manifest you. The Dogon know you're dangerous and keep twins separated. And I will stop Spear. The knowledge will be lost. Zenath will be forgotten."

It continued to giggle. "I will touch you."

Ned put his gun away and stood. "No, you won't. Even if everything you say is true, which I doubt, you'll never get close to me."

"Oh."

Ned headed for the door. "Zenath, before I leave, describe to me what your race looked like?"

In response the thing suddenly sucked in a deep, hissing breath. Ned heard a ripping sound, but it took him a second to understand what was happening. By the time he did, it was too late. The monster had torn a large hole in its straitjacket and lurched forward. Ned tried to back away, but a crushing grip closed around his right wrist. He momentarily lost his footing as the cackling beast yanked on him. It raised his right hand to its teeth, its long tongue darting out in anticipation. Ned thought of the retarded boy and his eyes as he groped for his gun with his left hand. The stench from the thing's mouth made his head spin. It smelled like a corpse in a cesspool in deep Amazon land. Ned's terror was a black wave crashing from the nightmares of human infancy. It washed away all reason. This thing was hungry and he didn't want to be its food. He tried to shout for help but nothing came out of his mouth.

Jesus help me!

The thing licked the back of his hand with a tongue made of burrs and slowly looked him over. Ned thought that something deep in its brain ignited in that moment, burning through its optic nerves, bringing a hot sheen to the coldness of its dragonlike eyes.

"I look like this," it said.

Ned got his gun out. He pressed the barrel to the thing's temple. "Let me go," he croaked. "I'll blow out the core of your fucking brain, you goddamn witch."

The thing was pleased. Slowly, delicately, it licked his hand again. Ned didn't know why he didn't pull the trigger. He knew it could take off his fingers in one bite. Perhaps it had him hypnotized and his will belonged to another. Yet it didn't put his flesh in its mouth, and in a strange sense this disturbed him more than if it had bitten him, especially after all its talk of hunger. He realized then that its craving was not physical.

It wanted something else from him.

It moved his hand to the top of its bald head and stroked his finger over the sandpaper-rough skin. Psoriasis, my ass, Ned thought.

The thing had scales.

"I feel like this," it said.

"Oh, God," Ned whispered.

It was a reptile.

The thing grinned. "No God." It shoved him back. Ned almost fell as he smashed into the opposite wall. Fortunately it was padded, or he would have been knocked out. Then the devil only knew what would have become of him. He had dropped his gun but quickly scampered to pick it up. That is how he felt; like a beast raised for food groveling at the feet of its master. Even as he leveled the pistol at the thing, it was still in control. "I will touch you again," it said.

Ned found his voice and yelled to be let out. He was halfway down the long sanatorium hallway before Dr. Simon Goldberg caught up to him. He wanted to know how his interview had gone, but Ned was in too much of a hurry to tell him. He ran to the cab, and once inside it demanded that the driver take him to the airfield as quickly as possible. Ned rolled down the window, wanting to vomit. He felt as if he had absorbed a large portion of Frances Cumberly's psychosis during his brief time inside the sanatorium. He wondered how Dr. Goldberg maintained his cool so well, but perhaps he'd never had his prize patient put on such a special performance. Or perhaps the good doctor knew which patients were best left alone. No wonder the man had acted relieved not to have to accompany him into that cell.

At the airport Ned ordered the pilot to spare no fuel getting him back to Miami. He had to confront Buckley immediately with what he had seen. What was left of Frances had exploded his belief system. He had to ask the learned professor if it was not all some bad dream. Or if humanity was, in fact, cursed.

CHAPTER 10

Lucy Temple and David Conner drifted on a starry lake. Lucy rowed gently, lest the ripples ruin the reflection of the black dome from above. They sat facing each other in the boat, but the darkness was so thick her date could have been a shadow. She liked to think of him that way—as a blind date, an enigmatic stranger who just happened to show up at her door, as David had done only thirty minutes earlier. They hadn't hiked to the lake where they met, but to a pond behind the camp. Here the water was warmer—she hoped they could swim. In her bag she had brought two towels as well as a high-powered flashlight. No bathing suit, though. Now all she had to do was get his clothes off.

"Did you know this boat would be here?" David asked, leaning back, relaxed, his outstretched legs near hers.

"Yes. Dr. Henry and I found this spot yesterday." She added, "The water is clean here."

He yawned, stretched his arms up and tilted his head back. "I don't know if I've ever seen so many stars in the sky at once. Are there more in Idaho than the rest of the country, do you think?"

"We're a long way from a major city, where even a smattering of light can ruin the night sky view. Guess how many stars you can see in the sky with the naked eye? I'm not talking about the fuzzy light of the Milky Way."

"I'd guess *billions* and *billions*," David said, imitating Carl Sagan.

"A little over two thousand," Lucy said.

"No way. I see more stars than that."

"You just think you do. Two thousand is a lot of stars. There are only two thousand stars of a magnitude six and less. The smaller the number, the brighter. The human eye can't distinguish anything fainter than magnitude six. Trust me, I grew up playing with telescopes. I wanted to be an astronomer when I was young."

"And now you're old, Lucy."

She smiled. "Do you think of me as a little girl?"

He continued to stare at the sky. "No. I think you're an alien. Strange words come out of your mouth at odd times. Where's Sirius? Is it up now?"

"No. It's a winter star. But that blue star you see directly overhead is important. It's named Vega and it's twenty-six light-years from Earth. I read an article once that said it might pose the limit of a man's universe. If the speed of light is the maximum we can hope to achieve, then a man could conceivably travel to Vega and back in fifty-two years. But he would use up the majority of his adult life on the journey."

"Don't you believe in the possibility of warp drive?" David asked.

"I'm a born believer. I don't rule it out."

David pointed east, just above the trees. "What's that star there? It's bright."

"That's Jupiter. And that's Mars over there. It's not nearly as bright but it has that wicked red color. I used to dream about traveling to Mars when I was young. I wanted to be an astronaut as well." She paused. "You know, I'm always telling you about myself but you never say anything about your past. Why is that?"

"I told you, I'm afraid you're an alien. I don't know what you'll do with the information." He gestured to the sky as a whole. "How did the ancients see so many constellations and gods and goddesses up there? I don't see any. What do you think they were smoking?"

Lucy laughed softly. "Many of them stared at the sky every night. It was a major part of their lives, as it should be. We forget how small the earth is in the greater scheme of things. The ancients let their imaginations flow, so the stars spoke to them."

"You believe they channeled the myths?" David asked.

"I don't know, maybe," Lucy said. "The word *channeling* can be applied to so many different states of mind. All I know is I loved those myths as a child. But many of the stories we classify as Greek mythology actually came from the Egyptians. Professor Spear explained several examples to me: Jason and the Argonauts, the Golden Fleece, the great god Hermes—all those legends came from the Egyptians."

"What about Zeus? Was he really Egyptian?"

"The Egyptians worshiped a queen before a king."

"Isis?" David asked.

"Yes. She was *the* Goddess."

David sat up, making the small boat rock. Lucy stopped paddling—she had been going in circles anyway. When he touched her bare leg, she liked the feel of his fingers. It had been too long since a real man had touched her. Yet it wasn't as though she just wanted to be seduced. She had only known him twelve hours but already felt as if he were a large part of her life. Of course, anybody else would say she was just riding high in the infatuation phase. He couldn't be that important to her life because she knew so little about him. Yet, deep inside, she felt she knew David Nichols.

Lucy had joked earlier with her sister about her last boyfriend, Neil Hardell, but her remarks had just been a smokescreen. The truth was much darker. Unknown to Vera, Lucy's six-month relationship with Neil had been highly damaging to her psyche and her body.

And he had seemed like such a nice guy.

She had met Neil at a health food store near the Stanford campus, which should have been a safer place to meet a guy than a bar in downtown Oakland. She had gone there for her glass of fresh carrot and celery juice, a daily ritual. Waiting for her vegetables to finish pulverizing, she noticed the long-haired, blond guy who looked as if he had just climbed off a surfboard. He was scrutinizing the vitamins. He didn't appear as if he could tell a B-complex from a herbal laxative. Since the only help in the store was making her drink, she asked him what he was looking for. He was kind of cute, a little sloppy maybe. He smiled when he saw her. Great mouth, lots of white teeth.

"I'm looking for something to straighten out my glands," he said.

"What's wrong with your glands?" she asked. He looked as healthy as a porpoise.

He leaned closer, very close. Maybe he liked redheads, she didn't know.

"They never go to sleep," he confided in her.

She didn't have sex with him on their first date, but they made love most of the second. Never had she felt the way she did in Neil's arms, so much like an animal that for a time she saw the big three—sex, food, and sleep—as the be-all and end-all of human experience. When they were together even the simplest acts of getting undressed or eating a candy bar were coated with a silver lining. They spent most of the time in his bedroom, music blaring and clock ticking loudly in one corner. They ordered out for pizza and when he ate it off her belly she came before he could burp. It was the kind of love affair she had always dreamed of—sort of.

It was a dream. What she didn't know at the time was that from the start Neil had been feeding her X&L, candy flips, a combination of LSD and ecstasy that produced a long-lasting psychedelic trip with soft, loving edges. A million years later she asked herself how she couldn't have known she was drugged. She regularly drank her vegetable juice and did her deep breathing. She was a natural kind of girl, so she thought she was tripping on a natural high. Love and sex with a tan California hunk. It was way cool. She saw Neil every night. How was she to know he was a drug addict? He never smoked anything, much less drank. How was she to know *she* was ingesting illicit chemicals? Maybe she should have known by the depression that flattened her whenever she was away from Neil too long? She passed that off to her messed up cycle— which had never been messed up before—and true love. She was such a fool.

He told her the truth in his own subtle way when after a month of dating he outright offered her a pill instead of grinding it up and mixing it in with her Perrier water. She flipped, screamed at him for two hours straight. How dare he fuck with her body and mind? What a scum bag. Piss off, buddy, no way I'm going to keep seeing you. I would just as soon call the police and have you arrested. Yet, her words aside, she did take the pill and spent the night with him. Just this one last time, she swore to herself. One last good fuck for the road. But the road Neil Hardell had put her on was a weary spiral. There was every bit as much uphill as downhill. She was an addict for his body as much as his pharmacy. Well, at least he didn't charge her for the stuff.

Of course, that financial arrangement didn't last.

Things probably would never have gone so far as they did if she had been having regular sessions with the Big Mind during that time. Unfortunately, Spear was traveling in Europe and they had curtailed their meetings for several months. When he returned and the group contacted the Big Mind, it immediately launched into a stern lecture about her behavior. Yet it respected her privacy. Even when it was done speaking and she was left sobbing, no one knew what her problem was. Vera, of course, knew something was wrong. She had known for a while, she said. They were too close to hide things from each other. Yet, even if Vera knew there was a problem, she didn't know how serious and what the specifics were. She could not even imagine them really. The hardest thing Vera ever took was a Tylenol.

Somehow, Lucy brushed off all their questions. It's nothing; it's personal; it's over. Vera was not so easily put off, so Lucy made up a convincing story, which Vera bought, sort of. Lucy did confide in Spear, however. She trusted him to understand what she was going through and not judge her. And he was wonderful about the whole thing, but firm. Quit being a baby. Stop seeing the asshole and stop taking the pills. You'll be your old self in a month.

Easier said than done. The truth was she didn't want to stop sliding and grinding to sensual heaven every night, plus when she halted the drug for even two days she got terrible headaches and felt suicidal. She made discrete inquiries about what was happening to her. Psychotherapists she knew personally swore LSD and ecstasy were not addictive. They were nuts! By its own nature every chemically induced high had to be classified as addictive if the person in question wanted to keep getting back to the high. She could have written a dissertation on the subject. She didn't listen to the Big Mind or to Spear.

She traveled the usual route of all respectable addicts, but perhaps in a shorter time. She lost weight, skipped classes, blew all her spending money, looked like shit, and fought with her pusher and her boyfriend, who—lucky for her, since it saved her driving—were the same person. Despair was her new identical twin. Something a little harder from Neil's personal medicine cabinet began to look attractive. On top of everything else, the Big Mind was not talking to her anymore, although it did continue to allow her to sit in on the sessions. Remarkably, except for Spear, no one knew she was a wreck. But with each passing week she sensed the presence of the Big Mind less and less. She felt as if she were losing her soul as well as frying her nervous system. But maybe the despair it brought was a friend in disguise. Certainly the Big Mind allowed it to build to the breaking point without intervening.

During one session, when they were sitting silently and breathing, she prayed to the Big Mind to give her the strength to get away from Neil and quit the drugs. Nothing sensational happened. The hand of God did not zap her with golden light. Yet from that moment on she felt a quiet certainty that everything would be all right. After that session, she marched over to Neil's apartment and told him that she wouldn't be needing his stupid pills or his stiff dick anymore. He took it all right. She suspected he had another girl in the back room when she gave notice.

She was fine in less than a month. From then on her faith in the Big Mind was unshakable. Literally, she believed it had saved her life.

Now David Nichols sat before her in the dark—in her boat. She wanted to kiss him. Hadn't kissed anybody since Neil. She had a feeling, with David, that she wouldn't need drugs to swoon. God, she thought, he was handsome, even though she could barely see him.

"What did you say?" she asked.

"I didn't say anything," he said. "Are you hearing voices again?"

"I don't hear voices. What were you going to ask?"

"About Isis. I love the sound of that word. It's followed me throughout the day."

"Isis is one of the words in the mantra the woman in ancient Egypt meditated on. When I was in her mind, I understood the technique she used. It was very powerful. It brought the flood of white light from the *chakara*—the center—above the head."

"Is there really such a thing?" David asked.

"Yes. It is subtle but real. I experienced it today."

David shook his head. "You scare me sometimes, you know that? I don't know how many of you there are in there."

She smiled uncertainly. She didn't want to scare him away but she also wanted him to understand who she was—no pretenses. Neil had never been interested in her work, just her body, her money, and her hands to rub his bony back. What a sick relationship they'd had, she thought sadly. She wanted so much more.

"There's just me in here," she said softly.

His fingers played with the skin on her knee. "At the moment, Lucy. But in the session this afternoon, were you really in that woman's mind?"

"Yes. I experienced what she did. But, like I told you earlier, it was from a distance. I didn't suffer as she suffered."

"But Vera did."

"Perhaps. Vera is Vera. She's very sensitive."

"That's the second time I've heard that about her tonight."

Lucy paused. "I know this will sound silly, but when I was with that woman I felt as if I were with my sister."

"You mean you think it was Vera in a past life?"

She pursed her lips. "I had a powerful feeling that I knew and loved that woman. Even when the session was finished, I couldn't free myself from the conviction of kinship."

"What was the black rite?" David asked.

"I don't know. Something awful that permanently altered a person."

"Do you think it was real?"

Lucy shuddered then at the horror of the woman's thoughts when she had contemplated the secret initiation. Yet there had been awe inside her when her meditation on Isis's name helped her to prevent the black rite from being spread over the land. Lucy wondered briefly if she could practice the technique the woman had used, if it would work in modern times. Even the memory of the white light was wonderful.

"Yes," she replied. "I think the black rite was completely genuine."

"Hmm." David was thoughtful. She put her hand on his. "Now you tell me a few things about how you feel."

"About what?" he asked.

"About what's happening right now."

He was amused. "Nothing's happening. It's very peaceful."

"Are you teasing me?"

"I wouldn't think of it, Cleopatra."

"Yeah, right, I believe you. Have you any family, David?"

"My father's still alive. He has Alzheimer's. He doesn't recognize me."

"I'm sorry."

He withdrew his arm and shrugged. "It happens. He's been that way a long time."

She missed David's hand. "Do you have any brothers or sisters?"

"No. No ex-wives or kids either. Just me."

"That must get lonely. I don't know what I'd do without Vera. Both our parents are dead. They were killed when we were seniors in high school."

"Was it difficult growing up with an identical twin sister?"

"Everybody asks me that. Really, it was the most wonderful thing in the world. Even though we're quite different personality-wise, Vera understands me like no one else." She paused. "I should say, she understands most things about me."

"But not your dark side?"

She laughed softly. "You are perceptive, Mr. Nichols. You should have been a psychologist. Yes, I do have a dark side. And I must warn you, it comes out most forcibly in the dark."

He sounded interested. "How does it do that?"

She took his hands and raised them to her lips and lightly kissed his knuckles, the tiny crucifix hanging from her neck brushed against his fingers. "There," she said quietly. "I've made the first move. Now you can do what you want and will still be considered a gentleman."

He scooted closer and reached out to touch the side of her face. He stared at her for an eternity, but what he saw of her in the dark was a mystery. His hand was warm.

"You're very dear," he said finally.

She smiled nervously. "Is that a no?"

"You don't know me."

"You don't know me."

He brushed her hair back. "I'm not what I appear."

She grabbed his hand, kissed it again. She was dying for him to kiss her. "I know, you're a spy. Your real name's James Bond."

"Close." He brushed her hair aside again. "Close," he repeated.

Because of the sadness in his voice, she froze. "*Are* you a spy?"

The question floated in the air between them. The gods debated it and tossed it back to earth. David's whole body seemed to sigh, although he still didn't speak. She reached over and caressed his face.

"I don't care," she whispered. "It's you I care about."

He shook his head. "It isn't that simple, Lucy."

"Why not? I'm a simple girl. You don't have to tell anything you don't want to."

He drew in a breath. "I must be insane talking about this."

"The stars can do that to you late at night. Make you silly." She waited. "David?"

He struggled with himself. "It must be because I'm quitting."

"Quitting what?" Lucy asked.

"My name's not David Nichols. It's David Conner."

"That isn't such a big deal."

"I'm not a reporter."

That did startle her. "What are you? A cop?"

He slid back, away from her. The boat rocked. The reflected stars on the lake surface shifted. He spoke to the water, to the sky, at the same time. "I'm an FBI agent. I was sent here to see how your group knows so much about what's happening inside our government. Several of the Big Mind's comments were too insightful for the powers that be."

Lucy tried to absorb this. She had never met a spy before. No matter, she told herself, he was trying to be honest with her, but she was confused.

"Are we going to be arrested?" she asked.

He chuckled dryly. "No. Government agencies are not as evil as they're portrayed in movies. We're just a group of men and women trying to do our jobs. We mean you and your friends no harm."

"But why didn't you just tell us what you wanted at the start? We have nothing to hide."

David hesitated. "*You* may not. I'm not so sure about Spear."

"What do you mean? Has he broken the law?"

"Not that I know of, but let's just say he has a complex past. Look, I shouldn't be telling you these things. But I trust you, Lucy."

"I don't know what to say. Are you on duty now? Is that why you can't kiss me?"

"That's not the reason. I want to kiss you—just because I'm an FBI agent doesn't make me inhuman." He lowered his head and added, "I hope it doesn't."

"Then why don't you kiss me?"

He was taken back. "You still want to? After knowing I've lied to you?"

She didn't have to consider long. "Yes. I understand your position."

"Really?"

"Well, maybe not. But as long as you're not here to hurt us, I don't mind. David, please." She slid off her seat and came to rest on her knees between his legs. His nose was two inches away. She rested her hands on his strong shoulders. She wondered if he could fight like the heroes in the spy movies. The thought was sort of stimulating in a non–New Age fashion. She added, "Tell me what's really bothering you."

He frowned. "Haven't I said enough?"

She ran a hand through his hair. She wanted him so bad! Could they do it in the boat? Would it sink? Would she care? "No. You're afraid to get close to people. The Big Mind said as much this afternoon. What happened? Did the bad guy get away?"

The moment the question was past her lips she regretted it. He stiffened.

"Twice," he whispered.

"Jesus, I'm sorry. I'm an ass. What happened? I mean, you don't have to tell me. Was it terrible?"

He looked weary then, an outline of a story best left untold. The stars seemed to weigh down on him. He took a long time to reply. "Did you hear about the Angela Wilson kidnapping?"

"Sure. Who didn't? It was in the papers and on TV every day. Did you work on that case?"

His voice was strained. "I was in charge of the case. I dealt with the kidnapper directly." He coughed. "That night, I was the one who went in the cabin with her."

She took her hand back and put it in her mouth. She had

read what had happened, the whole country had. "Oh, God. You were *him*? But what happened wasn't your fault. Someone fired a rifle when he wasn't supposed to. You tried your best to save her."

He buried his face in his hands. "You don't understand. I was responsible for her safety. I had her life in my hands. Everything was under control, then I let it slip away. Her father was waiting for her back at the hotel, and I let her die."

"That's ridiculous! You can't blame yourself. You did what you could. You risked your life for her. No one could ask more."

"It doesn't matter how hard I tried, Lucy. I learned that a long time ago. All that matters is that people who were alive are now dead."

Carefully. "People?"

He slowly sat up. "There was another person I allowed to . . ." He stopped himself, shaking his head. "It doesn't matter. It was long ago, and Angela should have graduated from high school this month. Anyway, you're right. It happened. It's done. I'm not God, and I can't control fate." He paused. "Still, I should have been able to control myself."

"What do you mean?"

He took a painful breath. "I mean, my dear Miss Lucy, that the newspapers seldom get the whole story. Angela was dead and the kidnapper was injured. The SWAT team had stopped firing. Still, Special Agent David Conner was upset. He didn't like the way things had gone, not at all. He wanted a little payback, for himself as well as for Angela and her family. While the kidnapper lay helpless on the floor, he took a shotgun and put the barrel to the motherfucker's forehead and blew his brains through the hard wood floor and into the dirt beneath the cabin." He chuckled bitterly. "He didn't even read the guy his rights." David tossed something in the water, a small stick perhaps, and watched as it sank. He glanced over at her. "Do you still want to kiss me?"

Lucy wept. "You have been so hurt. Do you even want my love?"

He stared at her a moment, then up at the sky, then back at her. "Yes."

Lucy hugged him. "Then, yes, David, I want you."

CHAPTER 11

When Professor Carl Buckley answered his apartment door, he didn't appear as if he'd just jumped out of bed. He had changed into large red sweat pants and a bulky white sweater that made him look like a department store Santa who had received an electric shaver for Christmas. Even in the eighty degree night air, the guy was dressed for the next Ice Age. Behind him Ned could hear the TV on loud—sounded like a Shirley Temple movie. *Grandfather! Grandfather! I just remembered that you abused me when I was in the womb.* Buckley looked psychologically abused. The dark bags under his puffy eyes drooped like misplaced silicon implants.

"You saw her?" he mumbled.

Ned nodded. "I saw her. May I come in?"

Buckley stood back and let the door drift open. There

was alcohol on his breath. "Please do. Don't mind the mess. It's the way I feel."

A minute later they were seated in Buckley's small but smartly furnished living room. The place was not that messy, except for a few books and magazines lying about. But perhaps the professor had been referring to the half-empty bottle of Seagram's 7 sitting on the coffee table when he had made an excuse for the place. He offered Ned a drink, which was the best offer Ned had had all night. They drank to each other's health. How different this meeting from the earlier one—the time for pretense was over, and they both knew it.

"Did you know," Buckley began without prodding, staring at the residue of whiskey left in his glass, "that human beings are born with three instinctive fears. They are afraid of the dark, of falling, and of reptiles. After seeing Frances, don't you find that interesting?"

"Yes," Ned said grimly. "She scared me."

Buckley was drunk but not close to falling down. The liquor seemed to broaden the range of his personality. He was more sure of himself, and his face had stopped twitching.

"I knew she would," he said.

Ned sighed. "Can you just tell me if it's real?"

Buckley reached for the bottle again. "Yes. It's more real than either of us wants to believe."

"Do you know that Spear has a channeling group with twins in it?"

Buckley swallowed directly from the bottle. "Yes. Since Africa, I have followed his career. I have written him letters warning him, but he ignores me. I know it's only a matter of time before he tries another experiment."

Ned shook his head. "I'm not ready to talk this way. I

still can't believe that an ancient super-race of reptiles once ruled the earth."

Buckley looked at him with something akin to pity. "Then why are you here?"

"I told you. Because she scared me. She wasn't like a normal crazy person. She wasn't a person at all. Do you know she almost bit my hand off?"

"Ouch."

"Is that all you have to say?"

Buckley spread his hands. "Do you want me to talk about Africa? About lizard monsters? The combination of the two?"

"Explain to me how such an advanced civilization could have existed in the past, and that we know nothing about it. I just don't buy it."

"Yes, you do. You bought the whole farm when you went up to Salutory. You see, I've been to the sanatorium. I know what you saw. You just want me to give you reason to believe Frances is just another mental case rotting away. She's not. She's not even a *she*." Buckley burped. "She's an *it*."

"But there would be ruins of their ancient cities," Ned protested. "Some sign that they had been here."

"Not necessarily. You're not an anthropologist. I am. In daily life you're used to thinking in years, at most decades. Until I met the Dogon, I was accustomed to thinking in terms of thousands of years. That's a long time. The average person cannot really imagine a thousand years, never mind eight thousand years, the length of human history. They think they can, but they can't. You have to mold your point of view over a lifetime to develop that kind of perspective. Yet eight thousand years is nothing compared to sixty million years ago. It's a drop in the bucket. The world has changed a lot since the great reptiles were here. Continents have come and gone. Mountain ranges have risen and fallen. Oceans have filled and dried up. Why do you think the remains of a civilization would be lying around for us to pick up? We'd be lucky to find anything. Besides, they burned it all down when they destroyed themselves. If we went searching for a clue to their existence, it would be a search for ash. That's all that's left."

"How do you know that for sure?" Ned asked.

"Didn't Frances mention their Armageddon?"

"She did say that they had destroyed themselves."

"They destroyed themselves and practically everything else on earth. You must have heard the old question. What happened to the dinosaurs? Why did they suddenly vanish after millions of years of life? There are lots of theories to explain their extinction. The most popular is that an asteroid or comet hit the earth and stirred up so much dust the sun was blacked out for several years and all the vegetation died. I believed that theory myself until my stay in Mali."

"You don't believe this race had a war that blocked out the sun for years," Ned said.

"Perhaps not. But I think they had a war that liberated as much energy as a collision with an asteroid. I'm sure they scorched the world in their fury—this race that went to the stars. In our time we can hardly get to the moon. They controlled physical energies that we can't even conceive of. They had *mental* powers we have never dreamed of."

"How do you know that?" Ned asked.

"I saw a demonstration of them in Africa. That may be another answer to your question about their cities. Because they were so highly developed mentally, I don't know if they required extensive cities. For all I know they teleported themselves to neighboring stars without the use of spaceships. Of course, now I'm just speculating."

"You speak of how developed their minds were. But it's my understanding that reptiles are stupid. Their brains are small compared to the rest of their bodies. Dinosaurs in particular were supposed to be simple."

"I'm not saying this super-race was made up of gigantic dinosaurs. On the contrary, I believe they were approximately our size. There are various evolutionary reasons why our size is conducive to intelligence. We are large enough to have developed brains, but not so large that we couldn't acquire hands to manipulate our environment. The use of our hands stimulated the growth of our brains. We didn't get smart until we stood up. Still, you make a good point. The reptilian complex is only one layer above the core brain. Humans have the limbic system and the neocortex in addition to what reptiles have. Our brains are much more evolved, much more complex. How could they be so smart? I pondered that question myself after returning from Africa. I did research into the field. Spear has a respected neurophysiologist—Dr. Henry Deering— working with him now. I read his papers and talked to other experts in the field of the evolution of intelligence. Then it occurred to me that I was looking at the situation backward."

"What do you mean?" Ned asked.

"I was trying to understand how they could have been as smart as we are. A more realistic approach would have been to try to understand how we could be as smart as they were. But the more accurate approach would be to accept that their intelligence wasn't the same as ours. What I mean by that is that we judge intelligence largely by the ability to solve logical problems, retain information, and see the relationships among various situations. But since they had only one layer of the brain above the core to work with, I reasoned that their intelligence was basically *instinctual.* They didn't sit and discuss things as we do—they acted, but not randomly, as animals and other reptiles do. Their instinctual capacity was so great that they invariably moved forward—perhaps even unconsciously—developing a more and more advanced understanding of the universe and themselves. I know that sounds paradoxical but that is only because we examine them as human beings must—from a human point of view. We cannot see them as they saw themselves. I believe they lacked our consciousness of self, but were far more perceptive."

"They couldn't have been that perceptive if they wiped themselves out."

Buckley chuckled. "That's a weak rationalization when you consider how close we've come to wiping ourselves out. Anyway, you forget a fundamental point—for all their power, they were still reptiles, and reptiles are cold-blooded. They're aggressive, dominating, but unemotional."

"Aggression is not an emotion?"

"Our society labels it as one, but emotion is a product of a level of brain functioning reptiles do not possess."

Ned drummed his knee with his fingers. "I still can't believe this. Everything I've read on prehistoric creatures states that their brain size was simply too small to support intelligence."

"You didn't read enough. Scientists have discovered the fossils of a man-size dinosaur that resembles an ostrich. It had a large brain, relatively speaking. It was not as large as ours, and I'm not saying it is the remains of one of our superbeings, but this creature could have been related to them. It's very possible in fact. Few people know that birds are the descendants of dinosaurs. Ostriches have hands, warm-blooded with four fingers on each. As I've already stated, hands are crucial to the development of intelligence. You must drop the concept that we *have* to be the first intelligent race on this planet. The idea is egotistical. The earth has been around for four billion years. Human beings have only been here two or three million years, which is nothing. Plenty happened before we got here. God only knows how long *they* were in charge. God only knows how long we will be."

"Do you believe in God?" Ned asked.

Buckley took a sip from his bottle. "No."

"But after Africa you believe in the devil?"

"I don't know what I believe in." Buckley's expression was ironic. "High-powered weapons, maybe. If they can stop those things."

"I don't understand that remark. Maybe I will after you explain what happened in Africa. But before we move on, I have to point out that Frances displayed emotion. She giggled several times while I was there and seemed to take pleasure in my discomfort."

"It was a cold pleasure, I'm sure. Besides, she still has a human body. She may be a hybrid of what they were and what Frances was. Or else . . ." Buckley trailed off.

"What is it?" Ned asked.

"It's possible that only a portion of the reptilian intelligence in her genetic past was able to come through. Or perhaps, I should say, only a portion was able to remain in our time."

"Is that another insight from Africa?" Ned asked.

Buckley gave him a dark look. "You think I'm a fat fool. When you came to my class eight hours ago, you had me shaking in my boots. I was scared, but not for the reasons you thought. The FBI can't do shit to me after what I've been through. I just wanted to tell you that up front."

"You're drunk," Ned said.

Buckley laughed proudly. "You'll get drunk with me when I'm done. Then you'll fly to Washington, D.C., and try to talk Congress into exterminating the world's population of identical twins. They won't listen to you, though. From experience I can tell you that ahead of time. From now on, whenever you see twins together, you'll think of death. You'll never be the same after you hear what I have to say."

Ned crossed his legs. "I'm here to listen, Professor."

Ned's using Buckley's title seemed to cheer Buckley somewhat. He set his bottle down and began where he left off.

"As I said, before Spear brought Frances to Mali he began to talk about the idea of genetic regression. He was spending time with a Dogon priestess. Her name was Kalu and she was wonderful to look at. Thirty years old, tall as I am, with black hair that fell to her knees. She wore it in braids and often painted her face with red and black pigments. Kalu was a wild woman, high up in the tribe, but not entirely trusted. Penny didn't like her because she could see that her husband had more than a scholarly interest in her. Spear was wooing Kalu for secret knowledge, giving her small gifts and coins, when he wasn't fucking her brains out. Kalu told him things she wasn't supposed to tell any outsider. Spear confided in me when it suited him, which was not often. One night, after Frances had recovered from her spider bite, Spear and I got drunk and he told me more than he intended. That was the first time I heard about the Listeners."

"Who are they? The reptilian race?"

"No. The Dogon called that race the Setians. The word comes from the name Set. Set was an Egyptian god and the brother of Osiris, and the supposed brother-in-law of the

Goddess Isis, the highest of all Egyptian deities. The Dogon word for the Listeners was *Hotri*, which means 'to listen' in Sanga. Spear called them the Listeners because he thought in English. And to the Dogon that's what they were, a group of initiates who were able—through a technique we would describe in the West as mutual hypnosis—to listen to the inner voices of their distant past. They had to listen closely to regress through their genetic codes back to the lives of their ancestors. Spear confided that he had seen them in action and that the knowledge they accessed about ancient cultures was genuine. Even though he was drunk, Spear spoke with authority. I was intrigued because I knew Spear could tell real information from garbage. If he believed these Listeners were seeing back in time, I couldn't dismiss the idea."

"Did he invite you to observe them regress?" Ned asked.

"No. He said they wouldn't let me be there. They trusted only him. But he was right when he pointed out that my observing the initiates wouldn't do any good because I wouldn't be able to understand what was being said. Let me go on. The reason he was courting Kalu so fervently was to obtain the details of an even deeper secret. She had already told him about the super-race of reptiles and the reason the Dogon were so fearful of identical twins together. Spear told me about the Setians that long drunken night, too, but I didn't give any credence to the idea. Who would? And Spear himself laughed as he said it. I had no idea he was already convinced of the validity of everything Kalu said."

"Why would a highly educated man like Spear be so quickly influenced?"

"You jumped aboard pretty quickly after you visited Frances," Buckley observed.

"You're enjoying the fact that she scared me. I think you wouldn't have minded seeing me lose a few fingers as well."

"I tried to warn you."

"That you did," Ned agreed. "Please continue."

"To answer your question, I don't know. It could have been a combination of factors. When you're living in that part of the world, so isolated from civilization as you know it, you're much more likely to believe things you'd never consider in America. The deserts of Mali have a hypnotic quality, and sometimes at night when I stared up at the stars through the swarms of insects I wondered what the hell had gone on in Africa before man arrived. As Spear began to talk openly about the Setians with me, I listened. He was an anthropologist and could question the Dogon's information, see if it matched our knowledge of the ancient Egyptians. He was able to validate what they said. That's important to remember."

"So the Dogon *are* descended from the ancient Egyptians?" Ned asked.

"Probably. We were never able to establish it as a fact, but they definitely were connected. The Dogon initiates were able to regress to the days when the earliest pyramids were being constructed. When they need to know anything, they search for the answers in the past. According to the Dogon, there are many huge structures still buried under the desert sands. To find them would be a major archaeological discovery, yet in Spear's mind, it paled in comparison to what he was digging out of Kalu. Before Frances arrived, Kalu had already told him that the way the larger pyramids were built was by the use of mental powers reawakened from the ancient past. She said if a human was transformed into a Setian, he or she could do anything."

"Do you believe that?" Ned asked.

"Hold that question till I'm through. All I'll say now is that it would solve the central mystery of the pyramids. I'm sure when you were going through grade school you were given texts that showed colored drawings of how the Egyptians built the pyramids. Rolling the large stone slabs on tree trunks—two dozen smiling slaves pushing from behind. The idea is patently ridiculous. Today, even with our most sophisticated heavy equipment, we could not build the pyramids. We simply could not lift a rock slab the size of a small house and fit it into a space cut to a centimeter of accuracy. There is not a crane on earth that can do that. That's a fact. So how did those rocks get up there? Kalu said when you became a Setian, you could just float them into the sky as if they were kites."

"Kalu knew about the pyramids?"

"Yes. And she had never been to Egypt. Nor had she ever spoken to a white man before Spear. Like other Listeners, she knew of them from the past."

"Earlier this evening you mentioned that our civilization sprung up all of a sudden. Now I assume it's your belief that it was handed to us by the partial reemergence of the super-race from the past?"

"Correct. The ancient Egyptians' knowledge of astronomy was staggering. The Mayans, also, were very sophisticated. The average person has no idea how much these people knew."

"Do you believe that the Mayans also stumbled upon the doorway to the past?"

"The question is intriguing. But I wonder if it happens simply by chance. Maybe there is something deep in our genetic code that comes out only when identical twins are together. That pushes them, so to speak, to experiment." He paused. "I wonder if the Setians cursed us somehow."

I will touch you again.

Ned shivered. "Cursed us and said that they would one day return?"

"Yes. It's not an idea I like to contemplate in the dark."

"I understand. Did Kalu warn Spear about the dangers of trying to reawaken the Setians?"

"I believe so, but he promised her so many things that she kept telling him more secrets. He was going to take her out of Africa. He was going to buy her a house by the ocean. She would wear beautiful clothes and have sparkling jewelry. He filled her head with so much nonsense that she forget her sacred vows. Finally, maybe two months after Frances arrived in Mali, Kalu told Spear the big secret. How identical twins could punch through the memory of the dawn of mankind and reach all the way back to the time of the Setians."

"There is a specific technique?" Ned asked.

"Yes. Like most profound secrets, it's very simple once you know it. The twins have to sit close together facing each other—their knees touching, their hands clasped—and stare into each others' eyes. They must synchronize their breath so that one inhales while the other exhales. Then they must lead each other back in time."

"How do they do that?" Ned asked.

"Through suggestion. But the process is much more profound than ordinary hypnosis, or even, for that matter, mutual hypnosis. Suggestion plays only a small part in it. Once the process starts, it continues by itself. The understanding of the breath is crucial. The Dogon do not see the breath as something that travels in and out of our lungs. They believe that there is an energy associated with it. When we exhale, the energy goes out from our bodies. When we inhale, it comes back in, revitalized by the elements in the air. The energy goes out farther when we breathe hard. That's the reason, they say, we get tired when we exercise. When twins sit together and breathe in this manner, they function like a single organism, as one nervous system, one big mind."

"The being Spear's group now channels is called the Big Mind," Ned said.

"I know. I read the book the group has published. The coincidence is disturbing. Let me continue. That the twins stare into each other's eyes is also critical. Usually, Spear told me, the Dogon initiates keep their eyes closed while regressing into the past. But with identical twins, their focusing on each other increases the power of their mental coherence manyfold. Spear likened it to two mirrors set in front of each other. The reflections go back and forth, down an infinite tunnel. Think about it—sixty million years back in time. That's as good as infinity to the human mind, don't you agree?"

"Frances mentioned a mirror to me several times," Ned said.

"I'm not surprised. She's the only being alive on this planet that I know of that has looked into it." Buckley's head hung heavy. "And look what it did to her."

"I'm sorry. As we analyze this, I forget you were close to her."

Buckley coughed, deep in his lungs. "I wanted to be a lot closer. You were right when you implied I hoped for a romantic relationship with her. I was a lot thinner when I was in Africa. I had a great tan. But she wasn't interested, and I understood. Still, she never ceased to be a close friend until the night Spear opened the black door. Frances and I would often swim together in a lake in the hills far from the main tribe. Afterward we would lie naked on the stones and talk about being back home. I felt close to her then. It was almost as if we had a satisfying physical relationship without making love."

"What about Penny? What was she like?"

"Very quiet, reserved. I think Spear had worn down her natural personality over the years. Penny did not have Frances's sense of humor and seldom started a conversation. She was a good person, though. She never gossiped, never had an unkind word to say about anyone, except Kalu. Spear didn't even try to hide his affair with the priestess. Even the Dogon—liberal by nature—had to wonder at him. They feared Penny and Frances but they meant them no harm. Secretly, I think, they worried that Kalu was sharing secrets with Spear. The knowledge of the Setians was their deepest taboo, as well as their greatest insight. They understand the workings of the breath and the genes and the evolution of the brain like no one in the civilized world. And this same civilized world sees them as savages." Buckley paused. "How did you know to ask me about the brain and its evolution?"

Ned was not worried that Buckley was going to warn Spear. "I have a partner with Spear and his group now. He's undercover—they think he's a reporter. He told me to ask you those questions."

"What prompted him?"

"I don't know."

"Hmm. I would advise him to grab one of the twins and get the hell out of there."

"I've decided the same thing myself. I'll call him after we finish. Please continue."

Buckley reached over and touched Ned's knee. He spoke seriously, as he had when he warned him to stay away from Frances. "Are you sure you want me to? It's gets ugly from here on. You might not want these things put in your brain. Once there, they're hard to forget."

"If what you say so far is true, then they're already in my brain. Just buried."

Buckley sat back. "Very well, don't say you weren't warned." He drew in a shuddering breath. "Frances and Penny heard from Spear about the Setians and how identical twins could regress into the past. The women had wondered why the Dogon were so frightened of them. But Spear gave them his version of the Dogon's fears, passing them off as childish. It was a challenge for him, I'm sure, because he had to give the idea of regression enough weight that the women were curious, but not provide so much detail that they were concerned for their own safety. Now you must be wondering what kind of monster would risk his wife and sister-in-law for the sake of a scientific experiment. In defense of Spear, I think he honestly believed the Dogon were exaggerating the dangers. Remember, he had observed many genetic regressions with his own eyes, and the initiates always came out of their trances smiling. So what if the women went back farther in time, he said to me. It was all in the mind. Nothing could physically harm them. They'd be fine, he assured me, and it would be exciting if it worked. He had us all excited at the prospect. Also, he promised Penny and Frances if the experiment was successful they could leave Africa the following week. That was incentive enough. Believe me, you cannot imagine how nice it is to have a bathroom and a kitchen when you've done without them for as long as we had."

"Was Kalu present when you did the experiment?" Ned asked.

"Yes. Penny didn't want her there, but Spear insisted. Kalu was stoned that night. She was addicted to a leaf that grew in the vicinity called *posos*. The Dogon, as a general rule, were opposed to their people taking psychoactive substances, but Kalu never followed the rules. She was a liberated woman. Posos was usually smoked. It worked something like mescaline, from what Spear said. I think he, too, was high a lot of the time he was off with Kalu. But he was clearheaded the night we hiked up toward Lucian Point. *Lucian* is Sanga for demon, and the hill was called that because it had once been an active volcano. The smell of sulfur was still strong in the area. Lucian isn't much of a peak—it rises at most two thousand feet above the desert plain—but its tip is black with tar and smells awful. It can appear intimidating when viewed from a distance. I had been to it once before with Frances to swim in the heated sulfur baths, but since it was so hot in Mali all the time, we had no incentive to return. The place gave me a headache, but Kalu said it was a powerful spot to perform a Setian regression.

"Frances and I trailed the others as we climbed the rocks. The moon was out, three-quarters full, and there was plenty of light to see by. I remember Frances talking excitedly about where we could eat when we got back to the States. I know that it must sound odd that before an important experiment we were talking about food, but none of us saw the experiment as a life-changing event.

"Finally we arrived at the sacred spot, a flat stone ledge that overlooked the sulfur pools I mentioned. A cave led away from the ledge, deep into the hill. I shone my flashlight into it but didn't explore farther. A lion in that area would have been rare, but Spear and I each carried a high-powered rifle, just in case. Kalu was laughing and flirting with Spear, annoying Penny. The sisters were both panting from the long walk. I have to admit I needed to sit down and rest myself. Only Spear was clearheaded and bursting with enthusiasm. He had almost unlimited energy. It was one of the qualities that made him such a good anthropologist, and at the same time an egomaniac. He wanted to get started right away.

"The women sat cross legged on the rocky ledge, facing each other, their knees touching, their hands clasped. Earlier Spear had gone over the secret instructions with us. I remember how the moon shone straight overhead. It illuminated the entire plain with silver light, and it was easy to imagine we were back in time sixty million years. I half expected to see a dinosaur raise its curious head from around the wall of the cliff that shot up another three hundred feet above the ledge. Once again, I emphasize how powerfully hypnotic parts of Mali can be at night. And we were at a spot where, according to Kalu, the Dogon themselves had long ago awakened the beast inside. I noticed, as the women sat and began to breathe in rhythm together, that Kalu fell strangely silent. She fingered an amulet the Dogon occasionally wore around their necks to ward off evil, a gold-colored string necklace with a single snake tooth. The Dogon do not ordinarily believe it takes evil to combat evil, but I guess when it came to the Setians they made an exception.

"Kalu fidgeted nervously as the women began to whisper to each other about going back in time, back through the Middle Ages, the Roman Empire, the Grecian civilization, the ancient Egyptians. The sound of their voices changed as the process proceeded. They spoke more softly, yet their words echoed into the night. I had the impression they spoke to each other from a great distance, even though they had unconsciously leaned toward each other until their noses almost touched. I sat to one side, near the cave entrance, Kalu close on my right. Spear knelt on the ledge beside the women. He couldn't take his eyes off them. Nor could any of us. Their forms seemed to shimmer beneath the moon. I had trouble focusing on them and had to rub my eyes to convince myself I wasn't hallucinating. For brief moments I imagined I could see through them. It was as if they had fallen into another reality. I remember having the thought that maybe history didn't exist in the past, but in another dimension beside us, just out of earshot, just beyond the horizon, laughing at us, knowing that it could catch up to us when it suited its needs.

"After perhaps thirty minutes the women fell silent, and nothing seemed to happen for a while. They didn't blink, they hardly appeared to breathe. Yet if nothing was happening outwardly, plenty was changing on the level of their consciousness. As an FBI agent, you must have had the experience of arriving at the scene of a crime not long after someone's been violently killed. Unfortunately, I've had a similar experience. I once visited a 7-Eleven late at night just after it been held up. The owner of the store had been killed, and although the police and paramedics were present, the body was still lying on the floor in a pool of blood. The atmosphere in the store was devastating, and it lingered for months. I never went back to the place.

"That night, on that rocky ledge, as the sisters sat facing each other, the atmosphere was similar. It was as if a silent swarm of insects had come between us and the moon. The light dimmed. The sulfur fumes may have worsened because suddenly I was having trouble breathing. The tension was unbearable. I thought if I tried to stand I would fall over. Yet physically there was nothing present. To a remote TV camera, nothing would have appeared to have changed. It was all on an intuitive feeling level. The vibrations were like spiders' webs. All we could do was wait for the monster to arrive and slowly devour us. Kalu began to sob quietly, then steadily louder. I wanted to cry myself but didn't want to draw the attention of the women in my direction. There was no question in mind that whatever had come to us, had come especially for them. It was as if a huge, black, fathomless pupil had formed between their rock-still forms.

"Maybe Spear was immune to the bad vibes, I don't know. Kalu's sobbing annoyed him. I think he was afraid it would disturb the women. He motioned for me to take Kalu away, and I was desperate for an excuse to leave. I wanted to get out of that place more than anything I had ever wanted in my life. It was hard to move, though. It was as if my body had gained an extra two thousand pounds. Somehow I managed to get to my feet. Stepping past the opening of the cave, I pulled Kalu up as well. She clung to me like a terrified child. Her posos high was gone. Patting her on the back, I tried to comfort her, but she wouldn't be comforted. I knew I had to get her away from the women. Carefully, leading her as if she were blind, I began to retrace our steps down the side of the cliff.

"We had gone maybe a hundred yards when Kalu suddenly broke free of me and looked back up at the stone ledge. One of the sisters had turned and was staring down at us. To this day I don't know which one she was. I know that must sound odd but they were dressed identically—khaki shorts and T-shirts. It didn't really matter who it was. In my opinion, it was already too late for both of them.

"Then the madness began. I could feel the gaze of the woman as if she were projecting a green laser light from a black crystal buried deep in her cranium. It brushed past me and settled on Kalu, the high priestess who had sold her secrets for the lies of a power-drunk American. Kalu's sobs ceased and her shoulders slumped forward as if the carcass of a large animal had been thrown over her back. Yet she continued to look up, her head pulled slightly forward as if she were a puppet dangling at the end of string.

Her body jerked spasmodically. Spear was on his feet now, trying to get a better view of what was happening. I was about to hike back up and demand that he stop the experiment when Kalu took three long strides and dove head-first off the side of the cliff. She didn't scream as she fell, and that made the fact of her suicide that much more shocking. She was just gone. I heard her body strike the rocks below with a moist crushing sound. Then there was nothing, and I knew she was dead. I knew that Kalu loved life dearly—this had been no suicide. The sister above had made her do it. Slowly, she turned her head in my direction. I had seen enough and didn't give her a chance to get a fix on me. Turning, I fled down the side of the cliff. Christ, I never ran so fast in my life."

Buckley paused to wipe the sweat off his brow. "I suppose you think of me as a coward. I left my partner alone with two dangerous females. I had left the women. I hadn't even made an attempt to snap them out of their trance. But you have seen Frances with your own eyes. You must have an inkling of what she and her sister were like that night. Maybe you can understand why I kept going. No matter how bad Frances seemed to you at the sanatorium, that night the two of them were a thousand times worse. The mirror was not cracked. It blazed with cold fire. They had incredible power, and I didn't think anything could stop them. I assumed Spear was a goner.

"I neared the Dogon camp close to dawn. With the coming light, I was suddenly plagued by doubts. What if Kalu had survived the fall? What if she could have survived with some first aid? I questioned what I had witnessed. So much of the experience was purely subjective. Penny and Frances were my friends. They couldn't have changed into creatures from a super-race of extinct reptiles. Such things didn't happen in the real world, I told myself. My steps faltered. I was exhausted, but knew I wouldn't be able to rest at the camp without knowing what had transpired on that rocky ledge. After a brief period of internal debate, I turned and headed back toward Lucian Point. The sun was rising as I closed on the tar-scarred slope. It shimmered in the orange morning light like a volcano on the verge of erupting.

"Between the hill and the camp was a pool. It lay a quarter mile to my left, to the west, in a cluster of large granite boulders. Even over that distance, I heard human cries—like those of frightened children. My heart pounded in my chest. I was afraid, but people were in pain, I told myself. I had already fled once that night. I could not run away a second time. I changed direction and ran toward the pool."

Buckley sighed and shook his head. "I shouldn't have bothered. What I saw next is difficult to repeat, even after all these years. I found a mother and her two children at the edge of the pool, their bare feet in the water. The mother held a spear in her hand, pointed at one of the women. I think it was Frances. I'm pretty sure it was, because her hair was a little longer than Penny's. But I couldn't swear to it. It doesn't matter, really. I peered at the four of them from behind a boulder. The mother was trying to defend her children from the woman. They were all clearly terrified of her. I don't know what Frances did before I arrived to invoke the fear. Maybe nothing. Just the sight of her, with the black aura that radiated from her, was horrible. She stood shaking like a being possessed with demons. Her eyes were as empty as a snake's. She hissed as she stalked the mother and her children. But she wasn't afraid. It was if she were playing with her prey before the kill.

"Finally the mother could take no more. She flung the

spear at Frances. Here was the first clear demonstration of Frances's mental powers. The spear splintered in midair. It exploded as if detonated from the inside. The debris didn't even touch Frances. At that the mother charged her. What a brave woman she was. Frances struck her on the side of the head and I heard bones break. The mother collapsed in a battered heap in the shallow water.

"Frances turned her attention to the children, two young girls approximately six and eight years of age. They knew their mother was dead, and clearly wanted to flee. But the older girl couldn't move. It was as if her feet were glued to the bedrock. I know you must be thinking that she was too terrified to move, but that wasn't the case. As Frances came closer and the littler girl drew back, the older one tried to free her feet. But they were stuck—the monster was holding them in place with only the power of its mind. The little girl backed in my direction, unwilling to leave her sister but not willing to attack the beast. Here was my chance to redeem myself, I thought. Frances was not looking in my direction. I jumped out from behind the boulder and grabbed the little girl. She started to scream but I smothered the sound by putting my hand over her mouth. Quickly I ducked back down and held the girl's head so she couldn't watch. But I felt compelled to see for myself what my dear friend had become. What Spear had changed her into with his mad thirst for secret knowledge.

"Frances stood beside the older girl. The poor thing was so terrified she couldn't even scream. She trembled as Frances stroked her long dark hair. The Dogon women have the most beautiful hair in the world. There are so many wonderful things about them. I wish we had been able to honor their knowledge and not steal it. I wish we had been able to bring them something other than pain and death. I wish I had never stayed to watch what Frances did to that little girl. But I did stay, and what I saw I will never forget. I wake up every night thinking about it."

Buckley began to cry. Ned didn't know what to say. He didn't know what to believe, except that the professor was making up none of his story. No human being was that powerful a liar. Buckley reached over and poured himself a drink. Not all the whiskey made it in the glass. He stared down at the floor as if the poor Dogon girl lay buried beneath his carpet.

"Frances killed the girl?" Ned asked delicately.

"Yes," Buckley whispered. "She ate her. She ate her alive."

Ned felt sick to his stomach. "Oh God."

"She started with the girl's right shoulder and kept feeding. There was so much blood. The entire pool turned dark. The girl died slowly, still standing up, her feet fastened down in the red water."

"But you saved her sister?" Ned said after a moment's silence.

"Yes. She was a beautiful little girl."

"You did the best you could." Ned remembered he had said the same words to David.

Buckley sadly shook his head. "We were anthropologists. Other people could think the Dogon were savages, but we knew better. We lived with them for half a year. We knew they were one of the greatest people to walk the earth. Yet we ignored their warnings about the danger of awakening the Setians. We passed the warnings off as those of superstitious fools. We behaved like the ignorant white men we were. We murdered that mother and that child as surely as if we had butchered them with our own knives." Buckley looked at him. "You can see why I've become the way I am—a fat and frightened caricature of the man I was in Africa. I wasn't always this way, though. I want you to know that. I was a great scientist once."

"Don't be so hard on yourself. You did more than most men would have done under similar circumstances." Ned added carefully, "What became of Spear and Penny?"

Buckley nodded, getting a grip on himself. "I carried the little girl back to the path that stretched from Lucian Point to the Dogon camp. There I set her down and told her to run to get help. I couldn't take her with me. She was scared but she listened. She set off at full speed. Then I turned back toward the cliff. I had little hope of finding Spear alive or Penny unchanged, but now I was determined. These monsters could not be allowed to invade the Dogon village. I started toward the peak. I prayed that Frances's hunger was satisfied for the time being and that she wouldn't come after me.

"My strength began to fail. I had been up all night with nothing to eat or drink. My vision swam as I started up the path that led to the sulfur baths and the cursed ledge. Several times I was forced to stop and rest. Everywhere I looked I saw blood. I reached the spot where Kalu had fallen and saw that she was beyond my help. At least it had been quick for her, I thought.

"Near the top I found Spear lying unconscious on his back at the edge of the ledge. His breathing was erratic and he burned with fever. I had a hard time awakening him. But once he was up he seemed alert enough. His eyes were strange, though. The whites had turned yellow and his pupils were completely dilated. Yet there wasn't a mark on him. He gripped my arm, and despite his fever, his hands were cold. It might have been from lying so long on the hard stone.

" 'What's happened?' he demanded.

" 'Frances is on the loose. She struck down one woman

and ate a small child.' I wept. 'What's happened to Penny and Frances? What are we going to do?'

"Spear was grim. 'We know what's happened,' he said. 'We were warned. Was she headed in the direction of the Dogon camp?'

" 'Yes,' I said. 'I don't know what can possibly stop her. She can move things with her mind, make them explode.'

"Spear stood and grabbed me by the shoulders. His eyes were freaky but they were clear. His thoughts were way ahead of mine. He was a brilliant man. I hate to acknowledge that after all the pain he caused, but it's true. While I was falling apart in my boots, he was making plans. He said, 'I know how to stop them. But we must act quickly. First there is hunger, but then the need to reproduce will dominate. We can't let it go to that step. We'll all die.'

"The way he said the word *all*, I knew he meant the entire human race would perish. Kalu must have explained to him how the Setians reproduced. Spear clearly stated that twins were no longer necessary from that point on. Any human could carry the Setian consciousness. He handed me my rifle, which I had left on the ledge, and urged me to hurry back to the camp to try to slow her down. Spear had a rifle as well. I asked him what he was going to do but he wouldn't answer me.

" 'Never mind,' he said. 'Just try to stop her from killing anyone else.'

" 'But will a gun stop her?' I begged.

"He shook his head. 'No.' He hugged me then, something he had never done before. 'Go, my friend. Go with luck. Wish me the same.'

"What could I do? I wished him luck. I didn't know what he was doing, where he was going. But as I scampered back down the hill, I thought I saw him enter the cave. Maybe Penny was in the cave. I was never to know for sure.

"On the long road back to the Dogon camp, I came across a group of tribesmen, who carried spears and bows and arrows. They were gathered around Frances. Her clothes were torn, soaked with blood. She groveled on the ground as three strong men pinned her down with their spears. To my immense surprise they had gotten the better of her. I knew then that she was not the beast I had watched eat the child at the pond."

"So it was Penny you saw the first time?" Ned asked, confused.

"I believed then and know now I saw Frances in both cases. What I'm saying is something different. The woman the Dogon were pinning down didn't have the power she had at the pond. She had lost it."

"How?" Ned asked.

"I don't know. Spear said he knew how to stop it. Apparently he had. But he never explained to me what he did. Later, I was able to establish for a fact that it was Frances the Dogon had captured."

"But what about Penny? How did she die?"

"I don't know. Spear only told me that he killed her. Since he had his rifle with him, I assume that he shot her."

"But he told you bullets wouldn't stop them," Ned said.

"I know. Yet he did stop them. I never saw Penny's body. He buried it somewhere up on Lucian Point. I only have his word that he killed her. He was as anxious as I was to stop them from hurting anybody else. I accompanied Frances back to the States on a separate flight. A French physician traveled with us. She was tied down and heavily sedated, unconscious actually. It was the only way to transport her. I was there when she was checked into

Salutory. Since then, I have been up to see her twice. I don't know why I go. Frances is gone forever."

"But Frances still possesses supernormal powers. With my own eyes I saw her rip through a straitjacket. Her doctor said it took three strong men to hold her down when she escaped from her room."

Buckley shook his head. "Neither of these is a demonstration of supernatural power. It is not abnormal for an acute schizophrenic to demonstrate tremendous strength. Note also that when you were with her she broke the straitjacket, but not the chains that held her to the wall. Believe me, before Spear did whatever he did, a hundred men could not have stopped her. She is still horrible, true, but only a shadow of what she was immediately after the transformation."

"I'm frustrated with this account," Ned said. "There's too many loose ends. You must have spoken to Spear after all these events?"

"Only briefly, when he returned from Lucian Point. He told me that Penny was dead, and to tell the authorities it was a wild animal that caused all the problems. Then he collapsed with a high fever, a hundred and ten. It should have killed him. The Dogon medicine men treated him with special herbs. They helped transport him to the Ivory Coast. After all the heartache we had caused them, they still wanted to help. From there Spear flew to a clinic in Spain, and eventually to a hospital in California. I tried to visit him during his convalescence but he refused to see me. I have since written him a dozen times but he never writes back."

"Didn't the police question you concerning Penny's death?" Ned asked.

"You know they did. You wonder why I agreed with

Spear's lie? At the time I felt I had to. I didn't want to go to jail. What purpose would that serve? I didn't want to plant suspicion in the authorities' minds. I went along with Spear's account, just as I went along with him when he talked us into going up to Lucian Point."

"I understand," Ned said, and he did. He probably would have done the same.

Buckley grimaced. "What was I to do after such a nightmare? I couldn't tell anyone about it. They'd never believe me. I did my research, trying to come to terms with the nature of the Setians. But it was purely intellectual research. I don't think my theories would help anyone nowadays, certainly not the victims of our experiment. Maybe they can help you—that is my hope. My mental state was fragile for a long time after Africa. I couldn't sleep unless I had a light on. I had no money, and couldn't teach. Eventually, however, my strength returned. I landed the job at the university. I know my students find me a bore, but it pays the bills." Buckley shook his head. "If only they knew what Professor 'Buckass' had gone through. Maybe they wouldn't use my class periods to nap."

Ned took a minute to absorb it. "Now what?" he asked finally.

Buckley nodded. "That's the important question, isn't it? I guess you know why I decided to tell you what really happened."

"You want me to stop Spear? You want the Dogon's knowledge to die with you two?"

"To die with us three."

"I don't know," Ned said.

Buckley leaned forward. "You said it yourself, he's got another pair of twins."

"I can't arrest him based on what you've told me tonight. You know it would never hold up in court."

Buckley stared at him with something that might have been hope if it hadn't had such a disturbing edge. "I'm not asking you to arrest him," he said seriously.

Ned shook his head firmly. "We don't do things like that."

Buckley accepted his reply without surprise. Still, he wanted something more than words from the big-shot FBI agent. Perhaps it was the chance to sleep one whole night without waking up screaming in a cold sweat.

"But you do believe me, don't you?" Buckley asked. "What I've told you?"

Ned shrugged. "It's hard to believe."

"Do you?" he persisted.

Ned thought of Frances's eyes, the gold in the center of her pupils liquefying and then igniting. The stench of the ancient forest. Her last words to him.

I will touch you again.

"I believe the inexplicable happened to you and your friends in Mali," Ned replied.

Buckley's grin was bitter. "What if the inexplicable happens to your friend while he's with Spear and his new pair of twins? What if *he* gets a high fever, and is never the same afterward?"

Yes. Need mirror. Short time. Control brain. Heat core.

Ned shivered. "Do you think one of the women altered Spear?"

Buckley sighed. "I don't know. After their hunger to feed had been satisfied, perhaps their hunger to reproduce was also met. Who knows what Spear *really* did in that cave with his wife? Who knows what she did to him?

Spear stood face to face with the horror of the Setians, but he hasn't given up on trying to bring them back. You think about that when you tell me you can't stop him because the facts won't hold up in court. Because what comes next won't be easy to stop." Buckley nodded gravely. "If he awakens them again, and they do have a chance to multiply, then they might just wipe out the entire human race."

CHAPTER 12

D avid Conner dreamed of the past and the future. He was scuba diving in the deep end of the Silver Shamrock swimming pool in Las Vegas. He sat on the bottom and watched as the bubbles from his regulator rose and tickled the bellies of the brown bodies of the people swimming above him. He felt good being under water, except for two minor concerns—his air was going to run out eventually, and it was going to be dark soon. He was more worried about the dark than the air in his tank, however, and for that reason he didn't want to return to the surface. He believed when night came, it would get too cold.

After some time a pretty woman in a one-piece orange bathing suit swam down to see him. She looked like Sandy but he knew Sandy was dead. He was happy to see her anyway. He reached out and she clasped his hand and they smiled at each other under the water. Her blond hair floated above her head like sunlight blowing in a turquoise wind. She was so close, and he wanted to kiss her, but he had the stupid regulator in his mouth and was afraid to take it out.

Sandy blew kisses in his direction, bubbles that raced to the surface faster than he could follow. He knew she had to return to the surface soon to breathe, but he was worried about the approaching cold. He wanted to protect her from it and keep her close. That was the only reason he continued to hold on to her hand, even when she stopped blowing bubbles and began to struggle. He didn't want to hurt her. He loved her, for Christ's sake. But he held onto her because it seemed the lesser of two evils. Even when her eyes pleaded with him and she began to thrash and her face turned blue, he continued to hold onto her. Then her expression went blank. Her eyes dimmed; the lights went off, and no one was at home. It was weird, it was tragic, and it made no sense at all, but it was only then that he could finally let go of her. Sandy's body floated to the surface and drifted lazily above his head. Everyone else in the pool got out, and he felt bad, real bad.

Later another girl dove down to see him. She had long brown hair and wore blue jeans and a brown leather coat. He thought it was pretty weird that she didn't have on a bathing suit, but he was happy to see her, at least at first. It was lonely sitting on the floor of the pool with Sandy's body floating overhead. It took him a moment to realize the new girl was Angela. He knew she was dead as well and for that reason he didn't offer her his hand. Yet she took it, anyway, and hung on to it tightly. He didn't want that. He knew what had happened the last time. But for the life of him, he couldn't shake free of her. Not until her eyes clouded over as Sandy's had and she ceased clinging to him. Like Sandy, Angela's body floated to the surface, where he had to look at it all the time.

He felt miserable. His air gauge was sinking toward zero. He knew if he stayed where he was, he would drown. Still, he was afraid to brave the surface, especially with the two bodies floating there. It almost seemed as if death were the preferable option. It was a dilemma of the worst kind, and he couldn't see a way out.

It was then a third woman dove down to see him. He recognized her immediately—Vera. She was naked. Her red hair floated above her head like the flames of a dragon; her green eyes sparkled like emeralds. He knew it was her and not her sister because he had made love to Lucy once long ago and Lucy had a scar on her right hip that Vera didn't have. There wasn't a mark on Vera; she was perfect. After swimming straight to him, she pulled out his regulator and began to kiss him, hard. For a moment he forgot everything except how nice it was to have her mouth on his. He forgot even his need to breathe. But then her tongue slid into his mouth and he shook in horror. It was forked; she had the tongue of a snake. It slid around the inside of his mouth like a tapeworm crawling through the intestines of a corpse.

He felt nauseous and tried to draw back, but Vera gripped his head with both hands and she was very strong, much stronger than he was. He didn't know how to get free. He only knew that he had to get her tongue out of his mouth. Closing his eyes, he bit down as hard as he could. Cold acid burned the inside of his mouth and he gagged. He opened his eyes and saw Vera floating before him with red blood dripping from her open mouth. He assumed she would be furious with him but she wasn't. Her arm was outstretched and a crooked finger with a long, sharp nail pointed at him. Her mouth was twisted in a grotesque smirk. You're mine, she seemed to say. You stayed under too long.

Then the light started to fail.

David whipped his head upward. Far beyond the surface and the dead bodies, somewhere out in deep space, he could see a huge, taloned hand move over the face of the sun, devouring it as if it were just another solar system on the way to the center of the Milky Way, swallowing humanity's only source of light and life. It happened so fast; he had no chance to react. The sunlight failed; the pool turned dark and cold. The floating corpses froze in place. A crack formed on the surface and ran down to the floor of the pool like a crack in a pane of thick glass. Vera froze before his eyes, her floating blood now a permanent stain for the darkness to peer through, a stained-glass window hung before a devil's tabernacle. He reached for the regulator, but was too late. His arm was frozen in place, his eyeballs. He could not turn his gaze away from Vera, and he knew, as the world turned black and cold as an asteroid tumbling aimlessly through space, that she would always be before him, for all of eternity. The curse was old, the pain raw. He was an Egyptian mummy stored in a pyramid raised on the spilled blood of tortured slaves. No goddess waited to take him to the safety of the other side. His soul was entombed with a monster.

David awoke to silent darkness. He heard his heart beating, that's all, the endless rhythm of circulating blood, a red drum set beside a narrow stream in a forgotten forest. For a moment he imagined his mother was near. Yet the external silence did not last. The night thawed; he became aware of the falling rain, and remembered the clouds that had swept in as Lucy and he hiked back to the camp from the lake, eager to make love. Along with the rain he heard the gentle rise and fall of Lucy's breathing as she lay naked beside him on the mattresses piled on the floor of his room. She had stolen his blankets; his legs were cold. But then he remembered his nightmare, and everything became cold. His dream was like no other. So real, a memory rising from a strand of DNA. He didn't want to know what his ancestors had suffered. He didn't want to meet what his children would see. The pain of his own life was all he could bear.

I won't have children. I'll never have a wife. Who would take me?

Yet Lucy said she loved him. What could that mean? He had known her for only a few hours. Was it possible to love someone that quickly? He hadn't told her that he loved her but he felt something for her that he thought had died forever when he saw Sandy's body splattered on the front steps of the Silver Shamrock. It was a wonderful feeling. Why couldn't he let it be? The wave had arrived. The sandy shore waited. Angels stood guard. It was safe to love her, the Big Mind had promised him.

David rolled over and peered at Lucy's face in the dark. Even in shadow, it was all innocence. She had a glow, a warmth—it was as if her flesh healed him where it touched him. There was passion, too. Even now he felt the moist warmth radiate out from between her legs. Never had he made love to a woman for so long, with such abandon. What had Vera thought, two doors down? Vera, whom Lucy had said slept lightly. Yet her sister's proximity had not prevented her from moaning in pleasure. Lucy's affection for him possessed her to the core. She let it go; that was her special ability, to give herself over completely. She let go and trusted that everything would be all right. That was what he loved most about her and what worried him as well—that she was trusting in him to make everything perfect, as had Sandy and Angela.

Loved most about her.

He had not said it aloud, he reminded himself. Only thought it, so it didn't count.

His cellular phone beeped softly. Lucy stirred, sighed, and rolled over. David sat up and picked it up quickly. Lightning flashed in the distance as he pushed the Talk button. He counted to himself but the thunder never came.

"Hello?"

"David, I need to talk to you," Ned said.

"I'm not alone." He paused. Lucy's breathing was deep, regular. "It doesn't matter, she's asleep."

"You're not going to believe what I have to say."

"Bad news?" David asked. He glanced at his watch. Five-fifteen in the morning.

"It's not just bad. It's a nightmare."

David thought of his own nightmare. "I might believe more than you think. Talk."

"You know the story of the serpent in the Garden of Eden?"

"Yes."

Ned sounded scared. "I think that story had a lot of truth in it."

David listened to his boss for well over an hour: the meeting with Buckley, the visit with Frances, the talk with Buckley. Ned often quoted Buckley and Frances word for word and David remembered the phrases well. Both men had excellent memories, particularly when it came to bad news. Oddly enough, nothing Ned told him surprised David. He recalled his own dread when he had first seen Frances and Penny's photographs. In the pictures they looked only somewhat alike, but subconsciously he must have realized they were identical twins, and connected their fate to that of Lucy and Vera. With Spear and Dr. Henry and the Big Mind, he had been chipping away at the same mystery Ned had pursued. Good old Frank the iguana—Spear was a lizard lover from a long time ago. Yet when his boss finished, David was left with the big question. Did he believe any of it? A long silence settled between them.

"Are you still there?" Ned asked finally.

"Yes."

"What do you think?"

"Her eyes were that weird?"

"God doesn't make them like that. They looked like something dug out of a robot's head."

"Maybe they are from the future. Maybe these people aren't regressing at all, but moving forward. Maybe the Flintstones were more prophetic than we realized."

"David, I'm serious. You've got to get out of there. Get your girlfriend out as well. Which one are you with?"

"I don't know. It's hard to tell them apart."

"David!"

"I'm with Lucy. I don't know what I can tell her. She has a lot invested in Spear and she just met me. To tell her to throw it all away on the ravings of a broken-down professor on the other side of the country is asking a lot."

"David, remember how you begged me to get Sandy out of town and I wouldn't listen to you? Well, you were right and she died. I fucked up. Now I'm begging you to get out, and take the girl. Buckley wasn't raving. He had seen people eaten alive and he was scared."

David glanced down at Lucy. He couldn't imagine her or Vera harming anyone. Still, Ned didn't panic easily and the way he sounded, it could have been he who'd been in Africa instead of Buckley. Besides, Spear gave

David the creeps anyway. The guy looked like someone who'd had the core of his brain cooked by laser eyes. David would just as soon get Lucy away from him—if she'd go. Big if, and then what? Was he going to ask her to move in with him? He would have to start picking up after himself, couldn't leave his pizza boxes lying on the floor for a week at a time. He might have to stop drinking, not that he enjoyed it anyway. Life could get complicated. But he supposed he could worry about those things later.

"I'll leave here today with Lucy," he said. "You have my word. But I'll have to tell her some of what you told me to get her to leave."

Ned hesitated. "Does she know you're FBI?"

"Yes."

Ned sighed. "Be careful what you say to her."

"I understand. You sound like you're on a plane. Going somewhere?"

"Denver."

"Why Denver?"

"It's on the way to Idaho. It's the only flight I could get so early in the morning. I want to make sure you get the girls out of here. I might even arrest Spear—I'm thinking about it."

"Why don't we just kill him? Save the taxpayers the money."

"You joke, but after what I've seen and heard, I've thought about it. Buckley asked me to waste him, and I agree that Spear's a menace to humanity."

David chuckled softly. "This doesn't sound like the boss I said goodbye to in Los Angeles. When do you arrive in Denver?"

"In two hours."

"Call me from there if you wish, but I'll be out of here by noon. Honestly, Ned, you don't need to come up. It's not an easy trip. The camp's in the middle of nowhere."

"If you and the girl leave the camp immediately, I won't bother with the flight. Don't wait until noon."

"As soon as Lucy wakes up, I'll have her pack. By the way, did you find out anything about Margaret?"

"I haven't checked with the office lately. It's still too early. I'll call them as soon as I get to Denver. What's your interest in her?"

"There's something about her that fascinates me. I can't explain it."

"She's not another Frances, is she?" Ned asked.

"No. She's very kind." David paused. Lucy stirred again. "I have to go. Happy flying."

"Next time we talk I want you to be on the road to Boise," Ned said.

They exchanged goodbyes. David stared down at Lucy, the curl of her red hair over her pale ears, the way she pursed her lips like those of a young child. The intensity of his feelings for her shocked him. If there was even a remote chance she could be harmed using Spear's mental techniques, he wanted her as far from the guy as possible. He wasn't about to lose another woman to bad timing. Sliding back onto the floor beside her, he heard the floor creak beneath the mattresses. She turned in his direction. What a wonderful thing her warm skin was. Maybe there was a God, after all. Her sleepy green eyes blinked in the poor light, although it was not nearly so dark as when Ned first called. It would be a gray and wet morning.

"Were you gone?" she whispered.

"Secret agent business. I had to use the bathroom."

She smiled. "You're cute. I was dreaming about you."

"Was it a nice dream?"

She frowned. "I'm not sure. I don't remember it that well. There was some kind of eclipse, and it was dark and cold."

David stiffened, but pulled her close. "Go back to sleep, Lucy. We can talk about it when the sun's up."

CHAPTER 13

Ned Calendar picked up a phone in the Denver airport. After dialing his home office, he talked to a new receptionist and ended up with Special Agent Carol McCormick. Carol was a tough-assed agent from Harlem. He used her with L.A.'s east side gangs, mainly to keep an eye on where they were getting their drugs. Not one of them dreamed she was FBI. She had a black belt in karate, could drink a bottle of tequila standing up, and still blow the bottle out of the air with one shot if it was thrown high enough. David liked Carol, too. Once, practicing karate together, she broke three of his ribs. Ned had put her in charge of investigating Margaret Farrow's past history.

"That woman's got no past," Carol said. "For all we can tell, she crawled out of the ground a year ago. It's spooky. I spoke to her doctors and the police, who said they had plastered her face across the country. Not a soul called to claim her."

"Did you run her fingerprints through the computer?" Ned asked. He assumed the police had got them; it would have been standard procedure with an unidentified comatose patient.

"Yeah, that's the other weird thing about her. No prints."

"The police didn't take a set?"

"Oh, they took them all right. She just has no prints."

"What? Her palms are featureless?"

"That's it, boss. I spoke to the doctor who printed her."

"There must be some mistake. It's medically impossible not to have fingerprints."

"I know. The doctor said he never saw anything like it. He wondered if she broke her back falling out of a UFO."

"But you get fingerprints in the womb," Ned protested.

"Maybe this chick wasn't ever in anyone's womb."

"Carol."

"Well, boss, she doesn't have a past. They dug her out of a garbage bin. God knows where she came from. And right away she hooked up with that weird professor. They're a pair, I tell you. If David's with them, you tell him to watch his back. They might put a spell on him."

"Do you have the numbers of the doctors who treated Spear and Farrow?"

"The same doctor took care of them both, except for Farrow's back surgery. That was done by an orthopedic surgeon. I haven't been able to locate him. I'll give you the doc's info. You call and talk to him yourself. He'll have a thing or two to tell you."

Ned took down the information and rang off. He checked his watch—eight thirty-nine. It would be an hour earlier in Los Angeles, but doctors often worked that early.

Ned rang Cedars Sinai and asked for the internist, Dr. Ralph Barnes, saying it was an emergency. The receptionist left the line to have him paged. Ned was on hold ten minutes before the man came to the phone. Ned introduced himself, told him why he was calling. The doctor sounded suitably impressed. He didn't ask for his credentials. Instead, Dr. Barnes asked the question everyone asked first.

"Have the professor and Margaret done anything wrong?"

"That has yet to be established," Ned said. "We're doing background checks at present. I would appreciate it if you kept this conversation confidential."

"No problem. How can I help you?"

"I understand you treated both the professor and Margaret. Is that correct?"

"Not precisely. I was in charge of Professor Spear's care, but was only a consultant for Margaret. She had a serious spinal injury. While she was in her coma she developed pneumonia, and I was called in to treat it. She was under the care of Dr. Ruth Thompson, who no longer works here. I could find her number if you want."

"It's not necessary. My associate, Agent McCormick, has already told me about Margaret's lack of fingerprints. I want to know if you've ever seen such a thing before?"

"Personally, no. It confounded many of us here at the hospital. But I have read about such cases. They're very rare, but I can safely say Margaret is not alone with her smooth hands."

"What creates the condition?" Ned asked.

"Medical science doesn't know, but it would appear to be an inherited condition."

"Did Margaret have any other conditions that medical science cannot explain?"

"No. But complete amnesia about one's past while maintaining day-to-day clarity is rare. When a person suffers loss of memory because of an injury to the central nervous system, she usually forgets how to read and how to make coffee or even dress. Margaret had a serious concussion as well as a broken back, but she was exceptionally clearheaded after she awakened. Her IQ was in the genius range. Yet she hadn't a single memory from her past life."

"How do you explain that?" Ned asked.

"I can't. I'm not a psychiatrist. But in talking to psychiatrists here, they say it's possible her injuries were inflicted by someone close. That the trauma of the incident caused her to selectively block out her memory."

"Did Margaret act psychologically traumatized?"

"No. Once she awakened from her coma, except for her loss of memory, she was one of the most rational people I ever met. Because of the severity of her injuries, she was here a couple of months and was well liked by staff and other patients. I got to know her quite well."

"I was just going to ask you that. I'm surprised you remember the details of her case so well. You must see many patients each year."

"Margaret was very special. I must tell you another unusual incident related to her. When she was first brought in, she was placed in a trauma wing for spinal injuries, along with perhaps two dozen other patients. None of the others were unconscious like Margaret, but the severity of their injuries was such that none was expected to walk again. Yet all of them did."

Ned had to take a moment. "What are you implying, doctor?"

"I'm implying nothing. I'm simply stating a fact. All the spinal injury patients who were roomed with Margaret made full recoveries. It's unprecedented in medical history."

"But what could Margaret possibly have to do with their recoveries?"

"She couldn't have had anything to do with them. Yet she was viewed by the nursing staff and doctors as a lucky charm."

"It sounds like you should have kept her as a patient," Ned muttered.

"I had the same thought myself."

"But she never regained the use of her own legs? I understand she's still paralyzed from the waist down?"

"That's my understanding as well. We would expect her to remain a paraplegic. Her spine was severed at T6—the sixth thoracic vertebra."

"Did any of the patients roomed with her have severed spines?"

"I think a number of them did. But they didn't when they walked out. Don't ask me how."

"I am asking you how, Dr. Barnes. This woman had no fingerprints, no past, and she heals others like a modern Jesus. I'm surprised you didn't keep closer track of her after she left the hospital."

The good doctor sounded offended. "Margaret Farrow is a private citizen like the rest of us. We're not the FBI. We don't keep track of people. Besides, no one is stating categorically that she had anything to do with the other patients' recoveries. Other factors could have been involved."

"Such as?" Ned persisted.

Dr. Barnes considered. "I don't know."

"Tell me about Professor Spear. I heard he came to you with a high fever after being in Africa. What was his diagnosis and treatment?"

"I was his personal physician, but I was never able to make a positive diagnosis. Initially we treated him for meningitis because he showed a definite swelling of the brain, which we attributed to infection. Yet he had no other signs of a bacteria or virus in his system, and we later decided he was suffering from an injury to the soft tissue of the brain stem. His brain wave activity was extremely erratic."

"By erratic what do you mean?" Ned asked.

"His EEG showed hyperactivity, even in sleep. It was as if his brain operated in high gear. He was literally burning up. The bulk of his treatment consisted in keeping him cool and giving him heavy antiinflammatories. The man should have died. He had a fever above a hundred and seven degrees for over a month."

"Did he have an injury to the brain stem?"

"To be frank, I don't think so. We were just shooting in the dark with him. But I was glad to see him recover. I understand he and Margaret work together now?"

"Yes. While Spear was in the hospital, did he ever demonstrate supernormal abilities?"

"Pardon me?"

"Did he ever move things with his mind? Or show signs of unusual strength?"

"No. Not that I ever saw. May I ask why you ask that question?"

"It's too long a story. Was there anything about Spear you found distasteful?"

"I'm afraid I don't understand your question. He wasn't the most personable man, if that's what you mean."

"Did he ever scare you?"

"Scare me? Why would I be scared of a patient, Mr. Calendar?"

"I know one in South Carolina that would scare the shit

out of you, but that's another story. Doctor, I want to thank you for your time. I know you must be a busy man. If there's anything else unusual that you can remember about Margaret or Professor Spear, please call the Los Angeles office of the FBI. We're in the phone book. Ask for me or Carol McCormick." Ned paused. "Do you have anything else to tell me?"

Dr. Barnes hesitated. "Just that when Professor Spear was delirious, he often spoke in a foreign language."

"He knows many languages. He had just come from Africa, where he spoke Sanga and Wazouba. That must be it."

Dr. Barnes was uncomfortable. "I don't think so."

"What do you mean? Did you recognize the language?"

"No, and that's my point. It didn't sound like a human language."

"Did it sound like an *animal* language?"

"Sort of. I know this sounds silly."

Ned was afraid to ask. "Did it sound like a language that a race of reptiles might have? Assuming, hypothetically, that there existed reptiles intelligent enough to develop a language."

Dr. Barnes swallowed heavily. "Yes. He used to hiss a lot." He added, "Come to think of it, it did kind of scare me every now and then."

"I understand," Ned said.

Ned said goodbye to the doctor. The conversation had not reassured him. He made a vow that he would neutralize Spear, one way or the other. If he didn't he would never be able to enjoy his retirement. If David got Lucy and Vera clear of the professor's influence, however, he would have time to mount a legal case against the man. Perhaps he could get Spear for the murder of his wife. It would be preferable to just blowing him away. Ned had killed two men in his life—one a mob assassin, the other a kidnapper—and had not enjoyed the feeling. A long hot shower didn't wash it away, nor did time. David understood that.

Close to three hours had elapsed since Ned had last spoken to David. He tried David's number, let it ring for a while but got no answer. No reason to panic, Ned told himself as he set down his phone. David could have left the phone in his room while making preparations to leave. It was still early in the day. At the camp David probably didn't carry the phone with him at all times. Still, Ned would have felt better hearing from him. He had a bad feeling about the situation, lizard monsters notwithstanding. Spear had sought publicity for years for his theories, and yet he had resisted a visit from a supposedly important reporter. He had also gone to extremes to isolate his group. David had not been exaggerating when he said Camp Paradise was in the middle of nowhere. Ned remembered the map of Idaho. The place was about as far from civilization as a person could get and still be in the continental United States.

Why did Spear need isolation?

Why had he hiked up to Lucian Point in the middle of a dark Mali night?

Ned checked the airline schedules. A Delta flight for Los Angeles left in forty minutes. Northwest had a flight to Boise that departed in twenty minutes. The flight to Boise was ninety-seven minutes long. If he reached David on the phone while he was in the air, it wouldn't be a major problem—he could always spend the day with him in Boise and decide there what to do about Spear. It might even be better than trying to rendezvous in Los Angeles. But if he got on the flight to Los Angeles, and didn't reach

David for the rest of the day, then he'd go out of his mind with worry.

Ned hurried to the Northwest counter and bought a ticket to Boise.

First class. Because he wanted the free booze. Needed it.

I will touch you again.

What was the story with this Margaret woman? Who the hell was she?

She's not a she. She's an it.

CHAPTER 14

David Conner sat eating breakfast with Margaret Farrow. Or rather he ate and she served him. Between courses she knitted the green and white sweater she had been working on when he first met her in the meadow. She had made pancakes that tasted exactly like his mother's. The coffee, too, was much to his liking, although he couldn't say the same for the weather. David did not know if Idaho often got rainstorms like this one, but if it did then it should have had a Great Lake of its own. The sky was not filled with gray clouds but black nozzles. He should have brought scuba equipment rather than his waterproof Patagonia coat, which had not kept him from getting wet on his walk from the dorm to the dining area. Yet the thought of scuba diving was not pleasant this morning. The gloom of his nightmare continued to linger. He could not dispel the image of his hand freezing in place before his numb eyes or the scaled hand reaching out to smother the sun. Camp Paradise was no longer a happy place to be. Yesterday he'd only been concerned about government leaks, but now he had to worry about super-reptiles. The Vera in his dream had had a tongue like a snake, and that had been before Ned's call. He may not have believed what Buckley had to say, but he couldn't disbelieve it either.

"Can I get you more butter?" Margaret asked.

"You have done too much for me already. Sit and relax. I mean—I didn't mean that. I'm sorry."

Margaret smiled, a ball of white yarn on her lap, her knitting needles in hand. "I know I'm crippled. I'm not ashamed of the fact. It's the body God wanted me to have. He must have His reasons."

"But it didn't start out that way. Could God's reasons have changed?"

Margaret stared at him for a moment. "You know what you are, David?"

"What?"

"A deeply spiritual man whose head has chosen to be an atheist and whose heart still yearns for the divine."

"I thought I only yearned for a good turkey dinner." He shrugged and added, "There's nothing spiritual about me."

"I disagree. You care deeply about other people. You never think about yourself. You never make room for your own happiness. That can be a redeeming quality as well as a failing, but I prefer to look at your positive side. You are the perfect servant. The Big Mind said it is only a servant who can become a master."

David chuckled uneasily. "You read too much into what the Big Mind said yesterday to me. I didn't even recognize the man it was talking about."

Margaret went on knitting. "I did. Did you see Lucy last night?"

"Yes."

"Good."

"Do you really think so?" He realized he wanted her approval.

"Yes."

David didn't want to leave without saying good-bye to Margaret. That was the main reason he had come to the dining hall. He'd already explained to Lucy that they had to get out of the camp. As he expected, she had demanded an explanation and he was forced to recount some of what Buckley had told Ned. Lucy had listened carefully and badgered him for details as to exactly what the women had done in Africa that allowed them to punch through the rational-thought barrier. But he held back on specifics, afraid curiosity might get the better of her and she might experiment with her sister. He had *not* told her about the super-reptilian race that supposedly ruled the planet sixty million years ago, but had simply said Spear's wife and twin sister had gone insane and harmed a lot of people after fooling with mutual hypnosis. He figured that would be hard enough to swallow, but his choice seemed to be effective. When he was finished, she agreed to go. Yet she had asked for a couple of hours to get ready.

"I'm glad you approve," he said to Margaret. "And I hope you won't hate me too much for leaving with her this afternoon."

She didn't act surprised, and he had thought the remark would floor her. Or rather, he thought it *should* floor her. He was beginning to see that Margaret had a strong inner core, and not much threw her. She continued to knit.

"You're going to have trouble getting out of here with the path flooded," she said.

"You're not upset that I'm ruining Spear's experiment?"

"It's his experiment. It's not mine."

"But you must support it. You've been with him for so long."

Margaret paused, thoughtful, her head lowered. "I support the Big Mind. I *listen* to it. The Big Mind is never worried, but Spear is racked with concerns." She shook her head. "He and I see things a lot more differently than you'd think."

"Can you continue your sessions with Lucy gone?" David asked.

"No."

David felt bad. "I have my reasons for leaving with her. I would like to explain them to you, but I can't. Too many issues are involved."

"That's all right."

David stood. "Margaret, it's hard to say goodbye to you. Why is that?"

She beamed up at him, her dimples showing. "Because I'm so cute." She held up the almost finished sweater in front of her face. "What do you think? Will Vera like it?"

"I thought you said it was for Lucy?"

Margaret slowly lowered the sweater, her smile fading. "It's for one of them," she said softly. "I'm not sure which."

David hugged her in farewell. He washed his dishes in the back and left the dining hall. Margaret had told him that Dr. Henry had left at the crack of dawn in the four-wheel-drive truck to pick up supplies in Augustine, fifty miles away. He had set out before the heaviest rain started, but she believed he was going to be forced to return. Apparently, ten miles past the point where the path to the camp met the road, the road frequently washed out. At least that's what Spear said, and he knew the area well.

David hoped to use the truck to get back to his own rental car. But if worse came to worst, he'd carry Lucy's stuff to his car, or he might even be able to hike down and bring the car partway up the path. He could wait only so long for Dr. Henry. It was like a full eclipse morning; the sky was as dark as an evening on the moon. He had a bad feeling about the day and just wanted to be gone.

David went looking for Lucy. He wondered what she was doing.

But he didn't find her.

CHAPTER 15

What David Conner did not know, when he spoke to Lucy Temple about the danger of her attempting a private regression with her sister, was that they had done it already. After they met Professor Spear and learned his technique of mutual hypnosis, it was one of the first things they tried. It worked well, in fact, better than the sessions with the others. But they had not continued to experiment with it because Vera always got a headache when it was just the two of them. Lucy remembered—especially after talking to David—how Spear's jaw had dropped when they told him they had regressed alone together. He had quizzed them about their experiences, and when they were through he had suggested they confine their experiments to the group. Yet he had not forbidden them to try again. The prospect did not terrify him the way it did David. Lucy had to laugh at David's concern. No doubt he was an incredible spy, but when it came to research into the field of consciousness he didn't know tarot cards from a Ouija board. She had done hundreds of sessions and never been harmed. She believed David simply disliked Spear and wanted her to run away with him.

Not that running away with him was an unpleasant prospect. She hadn't lied to David when she agreed to leave with him in two hours. The last night in his arms had opened a doorway inside her, and through it she saw a large part of her life that wasn't being lived. She saw a great man who deserved true love. David was like no one she had ever met. A gentle soul with the heart of a lion, but a sad man who had lost more than he realized. She wanted to spend time with him, give him back what the rest of the world had wrestled from him—faith in God and in love. She honestly believed she could love him for the rest of her life.

Lucy had no intention of permanently abandoning Professor Spear. But she no longer wanted him to dominate her life in so many ways. He had become a surrogate father for her and that was not healthy, not at her age. She still planned to get her Ph.D. and help validate his theories, but she was no longer going to jump every time he said jump. Leaving abruptly like this, she felt, would serve notice that she was her own person. He would be angry but the anger could serve to reinforce the personal step she was taking. Naturally, she planned to tell him her reasons for departing before simply vanishing. She couldn't be rude.

What about the things Spear had done in Africa with his wife and sister-in-law? Murdered her, David's boss had said. Sounded like a plot straight out of an unfilmed episode of "The FBI." The idea amused Lucy as much as David's anxiety about the danger that lay beyond the rational-thought barrier. She had heard enough about

Buckley from Spear to know that he was nothing but a jealous academician. Even now he was trying to tarnish Spear's reputation. Spear couldn't or wouldn't hurt a fly—she had known him too long to believe otherwise. Yet she believed Buckley had mixed some truth in with his lies. Most accomplished liars did, and many of David's remarks had sounded authentic. Buckley had spent a long time with the Dogon, and David had told her far more about the unique method of Dogon regression than he realized.

Lucy was much more experienced in these matters than David knew.

First, David had said that the twin sisters had flipped out when they stared into each other's eyes. That must be a salient point. Vera and she had never attempted to regress with their eyes open. Logically, it would seem to keep their attention focused outward, when they were trying to focus inside. Perhaps the Dogon had unusual insights into identical twins. Certainly, if one-tenth of what Buckley had said was true, then they had taught both him and Spear a great deal about the mind. It bothered her that Spear never acknowledged the debt he owed to the Dogon. She knew he had spent a long time there, but she hardly remembered his talking about them.

Second, David had accidentally revealed to her that breathing was crucial to the unique style of regression. When contacting the Big Mind, it was important that they all took long, slow, deep breaths together. It was difficult to reach a deep state otherwise. When Lucy had pressed David about the specifics, he had thrown up his hands and said, "I don't know! They did everything backward. It was dangerous, that's all that matters." To Lucy that meant the women had breathed in rapid rhythm, or opposite each other. One inhaled while the other exhaled. It would not take much experimentation to figure out which was the case.

And Lucy planned to do just that before leaving Camp Paradise.

She was not worried that she or Vera would go insane.

They could always stop if they felt uncomfortable with the technique.

They could just close their eyes and the Big Mind would come to their rescue.

Lucy found Vera in her bedroom, reading. Vera read two or three novels a week. Her special love was science fiction, but fantasy was a close second. Lucy, on the other hand, preferred movies to books. She was visual and liked action. Vera had always been contemplative by nature, even when it came to romance. But her knight in shining armor never materialized. And she was such a pretty girl, Lucy thought. As pretty as me! Vera had dated too many students who had to stretch their student loans just to spring for popcorn. Lucy decided Vera had to be with a strong man or nobody at all. Her thoughtful silences would swallow a lesser soul. As Lucy knocked and walked in, Vera set aside her book and appraised her sister as if from an amused height.

"Don't say it," Lucy said.

Vera raised an eyebrow. "What was I going to say? Did you practice safe sex? Was he as good as *you* sounded? Are you getting married? Are you sore?"

Lucy closed the door and sat on the bunk opposite Vera's. Her sister had the heater way up. Vera was sensitive to cold. Lucy unbuttoned her coat.

"All of the above," Lucy said. Then she giggled. "Yes, yes, yes, yes."

Vera sat up. "You're not getting married. You just met him."

Lucy shook her head. "Well, maybe not yes to that question. But he's adorable, really. I can't tell you how great he is."

"I think you told the whole camp how great he was last night."

"Was I that loud?"

"It's a quiet forest, Lucy. But don't worry, I don't think any of the men heard you."

"But you think Margaret did?"

"Yes. Margaret hears everything."

Lucy waved her hand. "But Margaret doesn't judge. What are you reading? *The Tao of Sex?*"

Vera showed her the cover. "*Frankenstein*. Your boyfriend's favorite. I just happened to have it in my suitcase. But he's right—it is a masterpiece. I haven't read it since I was a child."

"When I was a little girl I read Nancy Drew and you read *Frankenstein* and *Dracula*. I don't know, maybe we're not sisters. Have you ever thought of that?"

Vera picked her book back up. "I think it's true how some people say sex destroys brain cells. You are living proof."

"If they have to die, there are worse ways to kill them. Vera, put the book down. I have something important to tell you. David knows a great deal about Spear's past. He's researched him thoroughly. This morning he told me some of the stuff Spear picked up while he was with the Dogon people in Africa. Remember them? Spear mentioned them a couple of times but never went into detail."

Vera frowned. "I remember that when he spoke about them he was always uneasy. What happened while he was with them?"

Lucy hesitated. She didn't usually lie to her sister, but she didn't want to frighten her either. Then Vera would

never be able to focus for a regression. For that reason
Lucy had decided to wait until after the regression to tell
Vera she was leaving with David. Vera would be upset.
Her sister's loyalty to Spear knew no bounds.

"Nothing in particular," Lucy said. "But Spear picked
up a few tricks from them that he hasn't taught us yet. David just told me one. It involves the regression of identical
twins, but with a new twist."

Vera shook her head. "I don't want to try that again. It
always gave me such a pressure headache."

"This will be different. We keep our eyes open the
whole time and stare at each other. Also, we breathe differently. Let's give it a try. It's supposed to be how the
Dogon penetrated the rational-thought barrier."

"If Spear knows it, why don't we wait until he shows us
how to do it properly?"

"That's my point. We've been with him all this time and
he hasn't shown us. I wonder if he ever will. Come on,
what can it hurt? Think how exciting it will be to go back
before cavemen were even walking around."

Vera considered. "If we go back that far, into the minds
of beasts, we'll lose our focus. We'll just dull out and forget what we're doing."

"That won't be so awful. At least we'd have tried. And
who knows, maybe we'll see something we never expected. It's possible. The Big Mind says anything is possible."

Vera thought for a moment, then chuckled. "All right.
But if we run into Fred and Barney, I'm going to scream.
Do you want to do it in my room or yours?"

"Neither. We might be interrupted. Let's go into the
closed dorm down by the meadow."

Vera seemed doubtful. "We'll be soaked by the time we
get there, and it'll take a while for the heaters to warm that

place up. I don't even know if the heaters work there. Do you have a key?"

"I have an umbrella. You can use it. I have a raincoat as well. The heaters work as efficiently there as they do here. After all, that dorm is hooked up to the generator. It takes ten minutes to warm up one of these rooms. Also, I have a key. Tom gave it to me when I got here. He was afraid he'd lose it. Come on, let's go now, while David's at breakfast."

Vera got up slowly. "Why are you so worried about David?"

Lucy smiled. "How can I fly into the past when I'm moaning in the present?"

Minutes later they were headed for the unused dorm. Lucy found the short hike difficult, as did Vera from the number of her complaints. There were minor streams everywhere. Their feet were cold and wet as soon as they left, even with waterproof boots. Lucy hated to think what the deluge was doing to the path that led to the road. It was just a dirt trail, and would be a ravine by tomorrow if the downpour kept up.

Along the soggy road through the trees, Lucy thought of the night her parents died. Vera and she had been eighteen, one month shy of graduating from high school. They were both in bed, asleep, when the knock came at the door. The pounding was loud—it sounded like thunder to half-conscious minds. Vera was slow to get up. She always took her time getting out of bed in the morning, even when it was a bright, sunny morning. That night she clung to her blankets as if they were another body, while Lucy hurried to see who it was. Just the sight of the highway patrolman was enough for Lucy to know her Mom and Dad were gone. The cop didn't have to say a word, but he did anyway—a few choice phrases. A drunk driver had crossed the center line, hit them head on. They had died instantly, *painlessly*. That word was to echo in Lucy's head for the next few days. Could any change as radical as death be painless? Could any afterlife deserve the name of heaven when the new residents must know how the ones they had left behind suffered? Lucy had been close to both her parents, and knew her mother especially would grieve over her daughters' grief. At least she and Vera had had each other to comfort.

Lucy had once asked the Big Mind about death.

It had just laughed. No such thing, child.

Thunder boomed nearby as they settled inside one of the dorm rooms, their boots beside the door. The heater creaked loudly as the electricity poured through its wires. The place was dusty but dry, and was surprisingly free of the mildew that affected several of the rooms in the other dorms. Vera had brought a candle with her. She lit it and welded it to the top of a table with a bubble of hot wax. The orange flame stood tall, like the sail of a ship caught by the rising sun. Yet it smoked as well. Lucy had never seen so much black soot pour off a single white drugstore candle. She mentioned the fact to Lucy as they both sat on one of the bunks. Vera stared at the candle as if it were a crystal ball.

"A candle is supposed to purify the atmosphere of negativity," she said finally. "Maybe there's lots of bad vibes in here that need burning up."

"Maybe it's a cheap candle." Lucy gestured for Vera to sit facing her. They fiddled around for a moment, trying to get comfortable on the exhausted springs and paper-thin mattress, and ended up reclining on their knees. The little girl posture was easy for both of them; they were blessed with limber joints.

"What do we do now?" Vera asked.

Lucy reviewed the point about focusing on each other's eyes and admitted her uncertainty about how they were to breathe. She half-expected Vera to complain again that they should wait for Spear to show them what the Dogon did, but apparently her sister was committed. Lucy repeated the two options—rapid breathing or alternate inhalation and exhalation. Vera feared hyperventilating. They decided to experiment with the alternate method first. The mattress sloped down slightly between them. They clasped each other's hands because they always held onto each other during a session. It made them feel closer.

Lucy slowly exhaled. Vera slowly inhaled. Lucy smiled and blinked. Vera did likewise. It was not so bad, Lucy thought, staring at the person she cared most about in the whole world. She wasn't embarrassed, any more than she would have been embarrassed kneeling before a mirror. That's how she felt—as if she were opening herself to herself. They kept few secrets from each other, and it seemed a minor lapse that Lucy had failed to tell Vera that what they were doing might be dangerous.

Lucy slowly inhaled. Vera slowly exhaled. Lucy felt a shift in the room with the exchange of the first breaths, as if the walls had closed slightly, and a damp wave had arisen from beneath the floor. Lucy shivered and wondered if the heaters were failing, even though she could hear them clearly as they protested the expansive quality of the energy pouring through them. Lucy felt no expansion herself, on the level of consciousness, as she almost invariably did the moment they attempted to contact the Big Mind. She wondered if the Big Mind was observing their experiment, but then chided herself for the naïveté of the question. The Big Mind was omnipresent. Surely it was watching.

Lucy exhaled. Vera inhaled. Lucy became centered on

the sheer blackness of her sister's pupils. Of course all pupils were dark on all people, but Lucy had never considered how the world of color was perceived through a tiny colorless circle. It was one of those paradoxes of nature that human genes seemed so fond of organizing. She noticed that Vera had not blinked in a couple of minutes and wondered if the same was true of her. She wanted to ask her if that was the case but found she couldn't speak.

Lucy inhaled. Vera exhaled. Lucy felt a definite pull inward. But it was not a gentle, expansive feeling as in a normal session. Rather, it was as if the very energy that gave life to her body was focusing in her head. But not between her eyebrows, as was symbolically depicted on yogis as a third eye on their foreheads. This energy—it was actually more of a sensation of power—moved over her face from sense to sense. It was in her eyes, then her mouth. It crawled up her nostrils, where it burned slightly, like a parasitic firefly. Her ears tingled; she heard an unpleasant ringing that only ceased when another wave of thunder shook the room. Each sense, as it was touched by the power, grew in intensity, particularly her vision. She saw deeper into Vera's pupils, and they could have been bottomless.

And she knew her sister was experiencing exactly the same thing she was.

Lucy exhaled. Vera inhaled. Their breath was one rhythm, a single pulsing, although pulling in opposite directions. There was no conflict. The heart had to squeeze the blood out before it could draw more in. Lucy felt as if she were drawing from Vera's life, and Vera in turn were drawing from hers. Deep in her sister's eyes, in a place her genetic chain had never revealed before, she saw the Egyptian priestess whose mind she had entered the previous day. Only now she saw her from a different angle:

what *would have* been the woman's fate had she failed to gouge out her eyes. In other words, she saw an alternative path for the woman if she hadn't listened to the Goddess Isis. A path where divine vision had never intervened.

Lucy inhaled. Vera exhaled. The priestess was forced to sit upright and stare into her twin sister's eyes. Cold blades were held at their throats. If they blinked, if they lost the rhythm of the breath, lost their focus, they would be cut, not enough to kill them but enough to make them feel their own mortality. The blood was a reminder not to veer from the black rite. That was what it was all about. An occult path that led off the normal course of human evolution. Yet it was not a short cut into a realm of light and love, where mankind joined the angels on the joyful journey to God, but a detour that forced one back into a blasphemous history where the light of the Goddess Isis never shone. Only a mirror could turn away all light. Only a mirror could show what had always been present from the start, deep in the brain, waiting to crawl out and begin nibbling on the warm flesh of mammals. Truly it was a wicked secret that only the conscious fusion of identical bodies and minds could open this portal to hell.

Lucy exhaled. Vera inhaled. Lucy did not want to see the end result but felt compelled to watch. Forced to do another's *bidding*. That was the most frightening realization of all. As they came so close together, closer than two human beings had a right to, *something* came between them. Something came *out* of them, and its will was greater than the sum of theirs combined. They had to watch—ignorance was not an option. Too late, Lucy realized she had made a serious mistake by not listening to David.

She found she could not stop the process.

Lucy inhaled. Vera exhaled. The Egyptian priestess

stared deep into her sister's eyes. She breathed as her sister breathed. She moaned as she moaned. The "I" of the priestess began to dissolve, but it was not the extinguishing of small ego in exchange for spiritual realization. A great ego flooded the hearts of both women. A single entity that required—at least for a short period—two nervous systems to support it. The influx of reptilian consciousness made the blood heat, the brain burn, especially at the core, where forgotten powers had lain dormant for millions of years, waiting for the day to awaken.

Lucy choked. Vera choked. Lucy felt her own temperature soar as the priestess began to shake violently. The evil ones withdrew their knives. Fear was no longer necessary when mastery was all but achieved. The priestess's body convulsed as if caught in the throes of a viper's deadly venom. Then it went so still it could have been dead, if it weren't for the agony that burned behind its eyes. Lucy felt that agony as well because she *was* the priestess, the foolish human who had not listened to the goddess, the damned soul who had exchanged mortal eyes for a vision of the beast.

Lucy did not breathe. Vera could not. They stared at each other through pupils that had swollen to the size of black holes and saw the priestess and her sister begin to change. Yet ultimately only one body was required to carry the will of each member of the super-race—the masters as they called themselves—who scorned their warm-blooded hosts as being simply fresh and bloody meat. Only one nervous system in each set of identical twins had encoded in its genes the information that triggered the metamorphoses that supported full possession. Yet such a wild genetic scheme was not nature's doing. It had been deliberately placed in the DNA by the race of reptiles when they saw their own impending doom. They had only their instinctual feelings of importance and could not accept death. They hated the thought of the missed opportunities to feed, to conquer, almost as much as they hated one another. Their hatred reached as high as the stars. And it was possible that somewhere far off in the shimmering mist of the Milky Way, the Old Ones still lived. Still watched the cradle of their civilization and wondered when it would spawn a new generation capable of doing battle with them.

Lucy went numb. Vera froze. Only one permanent host was required, although two nervous systems were needed to support the transition. To support the time between feeding and reproduction. The mirror required its own reflection to see past all limitations. The priestess watched as her sister shed her flesh and grew scales, lost fingers and sprouted talons. Was the change physical? Or was it all just in the mind? And did it really matter anyway? The barren desert sprouted a tropical forest thick enough to bury an unborn civilization—ancient Egypt, lost to the spread of the black rite. Simultaneously, the dorm in modern Idaho changed to a warm pool of large lizards. Lucy felt slime seep over her legs and into her crotch. With her eyes she watched as Vera's face became that of the priestess's sister. Vera's lips split open and pulled back over a mouth that elongated into a hungry maw.

The priestess screamed. Lucy screamed.

No one heard her, though. There was no one to save her but herself.

The trial of the priestess was only an illusion. She had faced her fear and chosen the path of the righteous. What was left of Lucy's mind knew it had a similar choice. She could reach up now and rip her eyes from their sockets and break the spell. The transformation would be halted. Yet she was afraid. No white light poured down to comfort her. The goddess became remote, distant. Tentatively, Lucy released her grip on her sister and raised her hands to touch her eyes. They hurt as she pressed down on them. They pleaded with her not to wound them. The cold gaze of the intelligence that filled the room penetrated the flesh of her fingers and mocked her attempt to stop it. It knew she was a coward, not strong enough to thwart the will of one such as it. It knew it had only to push a little harder from inside her brain and the hands with which she sought to hold it down would fall. And with that fall, despair would swallow her as surely as the desert sand had buried the greatest of all pyramids. She would plunge back in time to where thought became irrational and the whole world burned.

Warm tears burst from Lucy's eyes as she pressed down. A star twinkled in the black sky that had roped the earth for ten years after the final battle. The star was white and shone with the grace of Isis.

"Vera," Lucy managed to whisper.

Her sister smiled with human lips. But the hands that reached out to touch Lucy's were claws. They tore into Lucy's flesh and casually ripped the skin off them as if peeling the indigestible skin off vegetables. Blood dripped from Lucy's hands and she moaned because she knew she didn't have the will to tear her eyes out. The thing inside Vera made a cruel hissing sound.

"Do it," it taunted. "Or don't it. We always give humans a choice."

Lucy's tears were cold. She would never be able to do it if she were given a thousand years. And that was nothing to these monsters. Their reach stretched over the millennia, as well as the light-years. She was doomed.

It lightly scraped Lucy's lower lip with a sharp nail.

"Nothing will stop us this time," it said.

Lucy shook her head. "Vera."

The thing shook its head, as if it were only a reflection. "It's too late."

There was a flash of silent lightning. It hit with the power of the stormy sky's wrath, and was as cold as an ice age. Lucy's human eyes failed her. In quick succession she felt the ancient Egyptian priestess sitting blind and alone beside the Nile; a leper crawling alone on a crab-covered beach; a wild woman running naked from a large tiger. Next she entered a series of disjointed bodies where it was difficult to comprehend what was being done to her, except that most of it was painful. She was a hairy woman, being raped by a powerful man. She was a young boy, drowning in a pit of quicksand. Then, finally, she lived in a cave, and had two children. When it was cold, they huddled close to the fire. They were always hungry. When the moon rose at night she stared at it and tried to remember something she knew that she had long ago forgotten. Something that had to do with white light that shone from above.

That was her last rational thought.

Images poured in. A cauldron of biological soup. There was birth and death, heat and cold. Most of all there was feeding and famine. Never any peace, never any understanding of why things happened the way they did. Of course there was no why. The return road was not natural. And eventually, thankfully, there were no more questions. Her mind became as dull as an animal's. Yet she could still see and feel. She fell through an unsanctioned path of terrestrial evolution toward a bright light like the afterglow of the Big Bang. Yet this explosion had sent a shock wave that had wiped out an entire race. Entering into it, she felt the agony of a million flames lick her from all sides. The reptilian race had not died easily. They would not be re-born without sacrifice.

Understanding returned. Of an altered nature.

A primeval world spread out around her. All was still, for the moment.

She opened her eyes.

A hideous creature of extraordinary cunning *stood* be-fore her.

Vera, she thought. It was not a name to her, simply a sound that she clung to without reason. The creature drew back its arm. *Lucy and Vera.*

A powerful blow struck the side of Lucy's head. Then everything went black.

CHAPTER 16

Ned Calendar sat beside a crazy pilot as he flew from Boise, Idaho, toward the small town of Augustine, which was located in the northeast portion of the state approximately fifty miles west of Camp Paradise, and sixty miles south of the Canadian border. Ned considered the pilot insane because he had agreed to fly him to Augustine in the first place, when the sky was ready to split open and return Noah and his ark to earth. Plus the guy—his name was Gabe Steel, and it suited him—had worse marital problems than the pilot Ned had had in Florida. After twenty years of marriage, Gabe had recently learned his wife was not only having an affair with the local high school football coach, but was also on intimate terms with a number of the team's linesmen. It seemed Mrs. Steel taught sex education at school, as well as American literature. But Ned was having trouble sympathizing with Gabe's problems because it was taking everything he could muster not to throw up. They were not flying through a thunderstorm; they were trying to paddle through an electrical tidal wave. A bolt of lightning had already caused Gabe's instruments to fail for five minutes. Ned had forgotten how much he had agreed to pay the man to take him to Augustine, but whatever it was, it wasn't enough. The plane took a scary fall as Gabe gestured excitedly and described how one of the guys on the team had had the nerve to leave his football helmet in Gabe's closet.

"I mean, I can understand that she's an attractive gal," Gabe said, a wad of tobacco in his mouth. "I can see those young fellas wanting to bone her. But they should clean up afterward. I wouldn't do that to a guy if I was screwing his wife."

Ned felt as if he was missing something. "Would you screw another guy's wife?"

"Sure. I've done it lots of times. I make sure they're clean, though. I'm no fool."

"But you are upset that your wife is having multiple affairs?"

"That's what I'm telling you. I come home and she doesn't even try to hide it anymore. She's lost all respect for me. I don't think the marriage is going to work out."

Ned had to wonder if commuter pilots suffered from special problems. "Would you prefer she hid it from you?" he asked.

Gabe shrugged. "What you don't know can't hurt you. That's what I always say. How's your stomach feeling? Ready to hurl? Keep that bag handy. I don't want to have to clean up your mess. Last guy who threw up in my plane ended up having a heart attack as well. He was dead before we got back to the airfield."

The plane dipped sharply. Ned felt a wave of nausea. "I'll try to keep that in mind," he promised. His cellular phone rested on his lap. He tried David again, without any luck. Why wasn't his partner answering? "How long to Augustine?" he asked.

"Twenty minutes, if we don't crash."

"Is it possible their runway will be flooded?"

"Let's just say right now I wish this plane didn't have fixed landing wheels. I don't think they're going to help us much. We'll do a flyby, have a look down. We can always detour to Fallston. That's only thirty miles west. A regular crew services that field."

"We won't detour unless we absolutely have to."

"Better safe than sorry."

"Better early than late. I have a car waiting for me in Augustine." Ned paused. "And I believe I have an old friend who needs my help."

CHAPTER 17

An hour had elapsed and Dr. Henry still hadn't returned from his trip for supplies. David Conner couldn't find Lucy or her sister. Worried, David had barged in on Professor Spear, who was reading and smoking a pipe in his make-shift office. The man seemed genuinely confused as to where the women could be. David decided it wasn't the time to confront Spear about his thorny past. He just wanted Lucy and a clear road back to civilization. Next, he went to Tom for help. The ex–truck driver suggested they check the dorm beside the meadow. All the rooms were locked up tight, and Tom said he was the only one with a key to the place.

"They must have gone for a hike," Tom suggested.

"In this weather?" David asked, wiping the rain from his brow. The storm continued unabated, but strangely, the temperature had risen dramatically in the last hour, as much as fifteen degrees. The water on his face now felt as if it had fallen from the sky over Hawaii. Tom noticed the shift as well.

"The cold has passed," he said. "And Lucy loves the rain. At Stanford, she's always out in it. I wouldn't be surprised if she talked Vera into taking a hike up to the caves."

"Where are they?" David asked.

"Two miles north of here. I can show you if you're seriously worried about them."

David considered. Lucy might have confided to her sister many of the things he had said about Spear. Vera could have taken the information hard. Spear was, after all, their personal mentor. For all David knew, Lucy had told Vera he was an FBI agent, although he had asked her to keep that detail private. It was possible Lucy had suggested a walk to calm Vera down. Or else Vera had brought up the hike as an excuse to talk her sister out of leaving the camp. He wasn't worried that they had gone off to practice Dogon rites. Lucy had not struck him as that implusive, and in either case he hadn't completely explained how the regression was accomplished. Actually, he was most worried about how they were going to get out of the camp that day. He felt pressured to check on his car, see if what was left of the path would allow him to move it closer to the dorms. He dreaded the thought of carrying what sounded like five heavy suitcases all the way to the road.

"Tom," David asked, "I know this is asking a lot, but I'd like it if you could check to see if they've gone to the caves. I'm worried about them, but I need to check on my car."

Tom was surprised. "You're not leaving today, are you?"

"Yes. Something's come up. I have to go."

"Do you have enough information for your article?"

David patted him on the shoulder. "I have enough for many articles. Just find the women, Tom."

David was a mile down the path when he remembered that he hadn't checked in again with Ned. He wondered if the lapse was entirely accidental, if he wasn't avoiding his boss with the secret hope Ned would freak out and fly up for him. David wasn't to the point where he felt he needed reinforcements, but he was disturbed. There was the women's disappearance, of course, but more than that, he felt, well, watched. Like many experienced agents, he had a sixth sense when it came to being stalked. He felt eyes on his back, and this particular set were not following him kindly. He had his snub-nose .22 revolver with him but not his 10-millimeter semiautomatic pistol. That was back in the room with his cellular phone. The .22 wouldn't stop a grizzly, but neither would the 10-millimeter, for that matter. Anyway, there weren't supposed to be grizzlies in Idaho. What the fuck was out there and observing him? He stopped and scanned the woods, his vision impaired by the merciless patter of rock-sized drops.

There was nothing.

Portions of the trail turned out to be nothing more than an overflowing gully. The more he saw, the less hope he had of bringing his car closer to the camp. Yet he remained determined to leave. His sense of being followed stayed with him almost the whole way to the road, only leaving when the lake where he had first met Lucy and Vera came into view. The disappearance of his stalker disturbed him almost more than its shadowing him. At least when it was on his back, he knew it wasn't up to mischief elsewhere. He tried to convince himself Ned's stories had gotten to him, that there was no one there. But his gut feeling was back, and Rolaids weren't going to make it go away. Maybe that's how the Big Mind communicated with him. So he didn't have higher intuition. God spoke to him the same way a hamburger did.

But God did not reply to his cry when he reached his black Infiniti rental.

The hood had been ripped open. The distributor cap and carburetor were in ruins. The windshield was shattered; a gaping hole allowed the rain to pour through to the dashboard. The steering wheel had been torn out and lay on the ground beside a nearby tree stump. David studied the damage, saw no signs that a crowbar or sledge hammer or any other man-made tool had been used to destroy the car. He was perplexed until he remembered a line Ned had used to describe Frances's strength.

She tore through her straitjacket like it was made of newspaper.

The accumulation of water in the front seat was not that great, not considering how hard it was raining. Whoever had done this had been only ten minutes in front of him. Someone didn't want him to leave.

"They couldn't have tried it," he whispered to himself. "It couldn't be true."

He hadn't *really* believed Buckley's tale.

He had thought Ned was exaggerating his concerns.

Not now though. David spun and raced back to the path, two hundred yards down the road. To his horror and frustration, he saw that Dr. Henry had returned while he had been preoccupied with his car. A fresh set of tire tracks left deep ruts in the mud, replacing the earlier ones that had been all but washed away by the rain. David figured the rain had drowned out the sound of the truck engine. Again, he thought miserably, it was all a question of timing, bad timing. He had missed Dr. Henry by minutes. Now he'd have to hike the entire three miles up to the camp. And what would he find when he got there?

Then she ate the little girl. Ate her alive.

CHAPTER 18

Jon Horst worried about his not having a green card as much as he worried about his image. Only because Professor Spear used his influence to get him an extended student visa had he been allowed to stay in the United States, even though technically he wasn't enrolled at Stanford. Jon was concerned that if Spear's theories gained notoriety as a result of David Nichols's article, many people would volunteer as research subjects and the professor would no longer need him. Then he would go back to Sweden where he'd be forced to give up his dream of being a famous actor and return to work as a lounge magician. Jon hated magic tricks. When you knew the secret of most of them, they seemed stupid. Besides, his skills were rusty and outside of Las Vegas and a few other vacation spots, there was no money in it. Jon had a longing for the security he believed money could bestow. He had grown up dirt poor on a dairy farm outside of Stockholm, where the cows stared at him as if he were a sex offender. He hated the smell of their udders; when he milked them, he felt like an overgrown nurse in a pediatrics ward tending to infants who resented female breasts. To this day, he couldn't stand the taste of milk.

When Lucy had embarrassed him at the dinner table the previous night, he had been devastated and retreated to his room to figure out a comeback strategy. It was important that David Nichols not treat him as a fool in his article. Jon still had high hopes of using the reporter's influence to jump-start his acting career. What none of them understood was that his gifts were genuine. When he was young, he had routinely bent spoons and forks *without* touching them. But the ability had atrophied with use. The more often he did it, the less it worked. In the early days of his magic show, he had only resorted to the backup method of rubbing the metal between his index finger and thumb when his magic fingers took a leave of absence. As the years passed, however, massaging the spoons and forks became the norm.

At present he sat alone in his room, with a half-dozen forks and knives spread out on the table before him. He had specifically asked Margaret for spoons but she felt too many had been ruined the night before. He could understand. What he was trying to do was get one of the utensils to bend, not even all the way. If one would just curl up at the edges without his touching it he'd be happy. But these were American knives and forks, he thought. They didn't like foreigners without green cards. He had been at the task an hour and so far all he had to show for his troubles was a headache. He was thinking of returning to the dining hall and asking Margaret for an aspirin when there was a knock at his door. Lucy poked her head inside before he could answer. She stared at him strangely.

"Hello," she said. "May I come in?"

"Yes," he said, not rising from his seat. He assumed it was Lucy because she had on the tiny gold crucifix she often wore. Even after knowing the sisters for two years, he still had trouble telling them apart. But he preferred Vera to Lucy, definitely. The other night was a perfect example of why. Lucy was always kidding him, pushing his buttons. Vera was much more respectful. She knew Jon was destined for great things. Lucy sat across from him and stared at his knives and forks.

"What are you doing?" she asked.

He shrugged. "Practicing an old magic trick for fun. Nothing special."

"Are you trying to bend the knives and forks with your mind?"

He flushed. "No. I'm trying to eat an invisible meal with my nose."

She ignored his sarcasm. Leaning close to the utensils, she peered at them as if she were seeing forks and knives for the first time. "Bend them for me. I'll help you."

He snorted. "I don't need your help, thank you."

She sat up and smiled mechanically. "You look healthy, Jon Horst. That is good."

"Huh?"

She reached across the table and took his right hand. Her skin was wet, cold. The texture of her fingers, of her palm, were odd—they felt *slick*. Her eyes focused on his.

"Bend the fork on the end," she said. "I want to see."

Jon was annoyed. "Well, I can't very well do it while you are holding on to me." He tried to shake her off, and to his surprise, failed to do so. He hadn't known she was so strong. "Let go of my hand."

"Bend the fork," she repeated.

"Lucy?"

"Do it," she hissed.

Something in her voice startled him, even scared him a bit. If truth be known, lots of things frightened him. He had yet to get a driver's license for fear he would get in an accident. And his health was a constant concern, particularly the threat of skin cancer. A cousin had recently developed melanoma and died three months after being diagnosed. The sun was dangerous, the roads killing fields. He resettled himself in his chair.

"Very well," he said. "I can try. You want me to bend the fork?"

"Yes."

"You understand it's thicker than an ordinary spoon. I might not be able to do it."

"Begin."

"OK." Jon closed his eyes. "Give me a moment to prepare myself mentally."

"Open your eyes. Look at me. Bend it."

Jon opened his eyes. Lucy had leaned in closer. She continued to stare at him and he wished she'd stop. Her sense of humor usually irritated him, but he would have welcomed it now. There was something wrong with her eyes. The pupils were dilated—they looked as if they had been left overnight in the freezer.

"What's bothering you, Lucy?" he asked.

She smiled again. "I am hungry."

"Why don't you get some breakfast? I'm sure Margaret will fix you something. We don't have a session scheduled until this afternoon."

Her smiled remained fixed, stuck. "I will eat. Bend the fork."

Jon drew in a breath. He tried to focus on the fork but

found his gaze drawn back to her eyes. They were much greener than he remembered, and brighter. There were also flecks of gold near the centers, gold that swam around the black pupils like expensive fillings cracked loose and spat into the watery vortex of an emptying sink. The drain beneath them seemed so very deep.

"Jon Horst," she whispered intently.

A surge of energy soared up his spine; it rose like a magnetic column set vibrating by invisible copper wires buried in his sacrum. His back straightened with a jerk and he heard several vertebrae pop. A wave of blood rushed into his brain. He felt momentarily dizzy and his vision blurred.

Yet the peculiar sensations passed as quickly as they came. Lucy withdrew her hard stare and grinned easily. Jon let go of a held breath and relaxed. What was that? He had no idea. But when he glanced down a beatific smile broke out on his face.

He had bent the fork!

"I did it!" he cried. "Look, Lucy, I did it!"

"Yes." She stood and went to the door and locked it.

He laughed. "What are you doing?" He couldn't get over how quickly his power had returned. Now, if only he could do it in front of David Nichols. He would be on the cover of *Time* for sure, maybe even in *People* magazine. All his relatives back home read *People*. Lucy returned and stood by her chair. She unzipped her coat.

"I do not want anyone to disturb us," she said.

He blinked. "What are you talking about?"

She tossed her coat aside and then reached down and in one fluid motion pulled her gray sweatshirt up and over her head. She wore nothing underneath. He had never realized her breasts were so nicely shaped. Her erect nipples made his smile grow larger. He sure had impressed her!

"We have to be alone," she said.

He bobbed on the back legs of his chair. "Are we going to make love?"

She unbuttoned her pants. "I don't want to stain these clothes."

He nodded quickly. "I understand. We won't even wrinkle them. You can set them on that chair there. This is good, this is great." He shook in wonder. "Lucy, I didn't think you found me attractive."

She pulled down her pants, underwear and all. Jon felt another wave of dizziness, this one pleasant. Her body was flawless. She kicked her pants and panties into a pile in the corner. Naked, except for the tiny gold crucifix around her neck, she sat in the chair opposite him. Her eyes narrowed on his face.

"I am Vera," she said.

He had to laugh. "Really? Wow. This is turning out to be one incredible day. I always knew you liked me, Vera. Why did you pretend to be Lucy?"

"Confusion is our way. Cunning is our nature."

"Oh. Some women are like that. Should I get undressed?"

"No. Put both your hands right side up on the table beside the knives."

He gave her an exaggerated leer. "You really need another demonstration? Shouldn't I save my energy for better things?"

Her eyes went hard again. "Put your hands on the table now."

He hastily obeyed. He had never realized Vera was so moody. Well, that could be a good thing, in small doses. He had found unstable women to be the most uninhibited in bed. God knows Stanford was full of them. He tried to joke with her.

"It's going to be hard to concentrate with you not wearing anything."

"Look at me," she said.

The gold flecks around her pupils drew his attention immediately, and it was odd because he did not like staring at them. They appeared so unnatural, metal implants from a race of computerized wizards that used body parts to make fireworks. Yet they were preferable to her hollow pupils. He still couldn't understand why they were so dilated, and why when he looked into them he felt as if he were falling through uncharted space. He'd had a fear of heights since his father threw him in the air on his third birthday and accidentally dropped him. He wished to God she would at least blink or something.

"The knives bend," she said.

He stammered. "You want me to try to bend them now?"

Her dark tongue moistened her lower lip. "Jon Horst," she whispered exactly as she had the first time the energy had raced up his spine and he had performed his minor miracle. Only this time he felt the air sucked out of him. It was as if a living vacuum had reached across the table and attached itself to his heart and lungs. His shoulders slumped forward, his head—he could hardly keep his eyes focused on her. He did notice her mouth, though—she was smiling again. He wondered if he had somehow done it again, moved the unmovable. His eyes flickered downward.

The knives were bending!

Even as he watched, the blades magically turned upward and around toward his open palms. He watched with the awe of a three-year-old child who had discovered that the new bump on his head allowed him to make all his wishes come true. This was unprecedented! Uri Geller had never bent two knives at once, and certainly not American brands.

"Do you see this?" he asked, excited.

"Yes. Your hands will not move."

He hesitated. "What?"

"Your hands will not move."

Now that she mentioned it, he couldn't move his hands. He tried and it was as if they were glued to the tabletop with the kind of glue that could lift up cars without breaking. That wouldn't have been such a bad thing in and of itself, but the tips of the knives were steadily moving closer to his palms. And he realized that he didn't know how to stop them any more than he knew why a young woman who had only treated him with reserved affection for the past two years should be sitting naked across from him on a rainy morning in the mountains of northern Idaho. No, Jon Horst definitely did not understand why this woman should be staring at him with eyes that would have been more attractive covered with rolls of masking tape, or better yet, gouged out and buried under six feet of mud. Jon began to perspire heavily.

"Stop them," he whispered.

Vera got out of her chair and went around to stand beside him. She was so close—her pubic hair touched his right bicep. He had to twist his head to look up at her. She stroked his hair.

"No," she said.

He couldn't move his hands! The knives were coming! "Please!" he cried.

She put her hand over his mouth, a hand that felt like a mermaid's paw.

"I am hungry," she said.

Oh, God, he thought. He tried to scream but her slimy hand muffled the sound. Straining to stand, he found his ass was mysteriously fixed to the chair. The tips of the knives touched his moist palms. This could not be happening! He had done nothing wrong! He had not tried to remain in the country illegally! The blades dug into his flesh. Blood spilt out over the tabletop. Burning pain throbbed up in his arms and into his brain. His blood puddled and dripped on the floor. He heard his bones cracking. The knives dug through his hands and into the tabletop. Vera, her hand still over his mouth, leaned down and licked his right earlobe.

"I need you to remain still," she said.

Jon felt a rough tug on his ear. Ignoring her instructions, fighting against the force of her grip with a terror that momentarily transcended even the power to bend spoons and forks and knives from a distance, he managed to twist his head to the right side. Her mouth was closed; she chewed something and he couldn't see what it was. But he knew the blood that dripped out the sides of her mouth belonged to him. After taking a moment to work her teeth, she swallowed.

"You do not listen," she said. "But I understand."

He understood as well. She had bit off his ear.

Her free hand caressed the top of his head once more.

She closed her eyes, whispered in the stump she had left behind.

"You are healthy, Jon Horst."

She licked him again. Opened her mouth wide.

"That is good."

CHAPTER 19

The landing at Augustine proved uneventful. The asphalt field had a slight slant so no major puddles had accumulated. Gabe Steel put down his plane as easily as if it were a calm, sunny day. Ned Calendar wished him luck with his wife and the football team and ran to the four-wheel-drive truck he had arranged to be waiting for him. The car rental man provided him with a detailed map of the area, penciling in the most direct route to Camp Paradise. But the man was worried about two sections of the road.

"I used to go up to that camp when I was a kid," he said. "I know the road. It floods on days like this. I don't think you're even going to make it to the path. For sure you won't be able to get the truck all the way up the path. It narrows the farther up you drive, and with weather like this it might vanish altogether."

Ned looked out at the dark sky. "Do you often get rain like this in May?"

The guy shook his head. "I've lived here all my life and never seen a storm this bad—any time of the year." He brushed the back of his arm across his face. "But at least it's warm rain. Feels like it blew in from the tropics."

"Yeah, it does," Ned said, thoughtful.

Ned left the airport at high speed. The truck was a brand-new Toyota, with only three hundred miles on it. He hoped it was watersealed the way many modern vehicles were. If he came to a washed-out section, he was going to drive through it. He'd drown before he turned back. The only reasons David wouldn't have called to check in were if he was physically unable to call or if he wanted to scare Ned into coming. Either way Ned didn't expect a Boy Scout welcome when he arrived at Camp Paradise.

The first spot the man had marked Danger was nothing, but when Ned reached the second spot, he reconsidered his vow to drown. He was an hour from Augustine, well into the mountains and woods, on a broken-down one-lane road that dipped down for fifty yards between two tree-clad hills. The half-a-football-field distance was definitely the low point of the forest, if not the entire state of Idaho. As a result it looked mighty deep. But exactly how deep Ned couldn't tell. The way the muddy water churned as it made its merry way toward the plains, he wasn't about to wade in and use his body as a measuring stick. Going around it, off the road and into the trees, was out of the question. Ned dialed David again, got no answer. He climbed out of his truck and stood looking down at the swimming pool.

"Shit," he swore, getting back into the truck. He would just have to see how efficient the Japanese were at making submarines. He backed up several yards and then plowed forward, holding his breath.

He was slowed to a crawl almost immediately. Water offered a lot more resistance than air. He reasoned that the water could reach halfway up the sides of the engine before he was screwed, but maybe he was being optimistic. The sealing on the doors was sound but it wasn't up to the task he was demanding. He was a quarter way into the pool when he sprang his first leak. The next ones came hard and fast. Soon he had to splash down to find his accelerator and brake. His tires vanished; he had to apply heavy thrust just to keep moving. The engine roared; it choked. The carburetor coughed: mix air with fuel, not water with gasoline, you stupid man!

Ned passed his optimistic limit and then some. The muddy wash swam over his hood, ruining the wax job. Water gurgled at the bottom of his window. For two eternal seconds the current lifted him up and tilted the truck at an awkward angle and he was sure he was going to die. But the kick in the ass might just have saved his life. Close to the side of the road, his wheels momentarily caught on solid earth. He floored the accelerator. The four wheels dug in and he jumped forward through a series of spastic leaps. In a few seconds, he was free of the pool and feeling grateful.

"Goddam!" he exclaimed, pounding on the steering wheel. That had been close.

He reached the path twenty minutes later. Ned knew David had planned to park his car at the foot of the path and have the people at the camp pick him up. Ned didn't see David's car right away, and though he understood David might have stashed it nearby in the trees, he didn't bother searching for it. All that mattered was that he got to the camp as soon as possible. He turned and started up the path; it was like trying to drive up a polluted creek. Even with his four fat wheels and extra gears, he slipped repeatedly. He was on a carnival roller coaster, and all the operators were smoking dope. He knew it was only a matter of time before he was forced to abandon the truck.

That happened approximately a mile and a half up the path, at what should have been the halfway point to the camp. Another four-wheel-drive truck blocked the path. It had been abandoned, and Ned had only to look beyond it to understand why. A large tree had fallen across the path. He'd have to walk from here on in. Fortunately he was in excellent shape. He wished he were wearing waterproof hiking boots, but his Nike walking shoes were sturdier than what he usually wore to the office. He reached in his bag for his 10-millimeter semiautomatic pistol, checked to make sure it was loaded and stuffed it in his coat. He hadn't shot anybody in a long time.

He was climbing out of the truck when he saw the woman standing a hundred feet farther up the path. The dark green hood of her coat covered most of her face, still, he caught a glimpse of red hair. Lucy or Vera Temple, he thought. Walking slowly toward him, she kept her head down as if deep in thought. It was odd how he had not seen her coming earlier, and wondered if she had just stepped out of the woods and onto the path. He patted his weapon in his coat pocket but didn't take it out. Ten feet from him, with his heart pounding in his mouth, she finally looked up. Her green eyes startled him; they were so bright, so beautiful. No way she was like Frances, he told himself, relaxing. Not with that face of an angel. She smiled faintly but didn't speak.

"Hello," he said. "My name's Ned Calendar. I'm a friend of David's. Are you Lucy or Vera?"

She hesitated, glanced past him, then stared directly into his eyes. "Lucy."

"Where's David? Is he at the camp?"

"Yes." She gestured over her shoulder. "That way."

"What are you doing out here alone? Are you looking for somebody?"

"Yes." She stepped closer, throwing back her hood. Even with the dark sky, her wet hair shone like fire. "I am looking for my sister."

"For Vera?"

"Yes."

"You don't know where she is?"

"No."

"How long has she been missing?"

"An hour."

"Do you want me to help you look for her?"

In response Lucy glanced up and down the path, then stared at the two trucks as if they figured heavily in her answer. Then, to his surprise, she reached out and took his left hand. He had just climbed out from the truck's heated cabin; his fingers were warm, but hers were as cold as wet stones. Her gesture was somewhat bold, yet she hung her head shyly.

"I feel I know you," she said.

He smiled. "Did David tell you about me? I warn you, all of it's true."

"Yes." Releasing his hand, she nodded up the path. "Go see him. I will be there shortly."

"Are you sure you don't want me to accompany you? Hiking in a storm like this can be dangerous."

She patted him on the shoulder. "Do not worry. Tell David, I am coming."

"All right," he agreed reluctantly. "Don't be long."

She nodded and carefully replaced her hood, using both hands. Ned started up the path. After about two hundred yards, he paused and glanced over his shoulder. He was surprised to find her still standing by the trucks, watching him. He waved, and she waved back. Outside of her great beauty, he wasn't sure if she was David's type. She seemed kind of quiet.

I feel I know you.

An odd remark, to be sure. He was sure he had never met her before.

Ned quickened his pace.

CHAPTER 20

David Conner was dirty and exhausted when he finally reached the camp. He had been relieved to find Dr. Henry's truck, although blocked by a tree, undamaged. With its four-wheel drive, it was their best way out of the camp. Yet David had to ask himself if escape was now the priority. He needed to have a hard look at who he led to safety. Given that his rental car had been attacked by someone stronger than a normal human being, he had to face the fact that the situation might already be severely fucked. He found Dr. Henry, Tom Forester, and Panda Gopal in the chapel. He didn't waste time on pleasantries.

"Did you find the women?" he blurted out.

Tom jumped up. "No. They weren't at the caves. We've just been discussing where they might be."

"Where is Spear?" David asked.

"He's in his office reading," Dr. Henry said. "I saw him a minute ago."

"Does he know Lucy and Vera are missing?" David asked.

"I told him we didn't know where they were," Dr. Henry said.

"What did he say?" David demanded.

Dr. Henry shrugged. "Nothing."

David looked around. "Where's Jon?"

"I haven't seen him today," Tom said. "Have any of you?"

No one had. David turned toward the church entrance. "Show me his room."

Jon Horst's door was locked. They called but there was no answer. David had had enough of the bullshit. The others jumped as he kicked in the door.

The room was empty. A small wooden table sat in the center between the bunk beds. Bent knives and forks littered the top. David picked one of them up, noticing that the tabletop was badly scraped. There was an unpleasant odor in the air.

"Did Jon bend all these?" Tom asked, gesturing to the ruined utensils.

"Not with his mind," Dr. Henry said. "Not with his IQ."

David sniffed the air, fingered the bent knife. "There is something wrong here."

"Blood," Panda said softly.

"Huh?" Tom said.

"He's right!" David exclaimed. He dropped to his knees beside the table, felt the wooden floor carefully with his fingertips, and put his nose to it. His nails picked up faint red scrapes. His nostrils detected death. He looked up at the others. "Someone wiped up a puddle of blood here."

Dr. Henry crouched down beside him. "Are you sure? I don't see it. I don't smell it."

David showed him his nails. "It was here, but was carefully removed."

Tom paled. "What do you think happened? Is Jon all right?"

David stood. "I don't know, Tom. It doesn't look good. I just came from the road. My car's been sabotaged."

"What are you talking about?" Dr. Henry asked.

David found it hard to concentrate. Images of Buckley's story kept bursting in his mind, over images of Lucy in his arms last night. He had to fight to remain calm, to take long deep breaths. Already the others were looking to him for direction.

"Somebody does not want us to leave here," David said calmly. "We must speak to Spear, but first I need to check my room. I want you all to come with me. From now on, it's crucial we remain together at all times."

No one asked why. The trace of blood was self-explanatory. As a group, they hurried to the other dorm. David's door was unlocked, when he clearly remembered having locked it. Upon closer inspection, he saw that the lock was in fact broken. Snapped by sheer force. Knowing that it was a waste of time, he searched his bag. He ended up throwing it against the far wall.

"Shit!" he swore.

"What's wrong?" Dr. Henry asked.

"My cellular phone and my 10-millimeter semiautomatic pistol are missing."

Their eyes swelled. "What the fuck are you doing with a piece, man?" Dr. Henry asked, not sounding like a Rhodes scholar. David whipped out his badge.

"I'm an FBI agent. I was sent here to check out your boss." David bent over and pulled his .22 from under his pant leg. They instinctively backed off. "Trust me, he's got a rotten past. Come on, I want to talk to him."

David burst in on Spear without knocking. Indeed, David was so tired of playing Mr. Nice Guy that he grabbed Spear by the collar and thrust him up against the wall and buried the tip of his small revolver in the professor's throat. Spear's pipe fell from his hand and lay smoking on the floor. Frank the iguana looked over, but didn't say anything. David breathed fire on the professor's clammy skin.

"I know everything that happened in Africa," he said in a deadly voice. "Buckley spoke to my partner. I know about the Setians, the secret of the black rite, the little girl your sister-in-law ate. I know why Lucy and Vera turn you on. But there's blood in Jon's room and I don't know where the women are. I'm worried about Jon. I'm worried about Lucy and Vera. But I'm not worried about you. If you should die from a bullet wound in the next two minutes, I won't shed a tear. Do you understand me, professor?"

Spear regarded him with his dark, emotionless eyes. "You don't know half of what happened in Africa, Mr. Nichols," he said. "Or are you going by another name now?"

David leaned closer, if that was possible. "Where are they?"

"I don't know."

David throttled him. "What have you done with them?"

Spear choked. "I never told them about the black rite," he said quickly.

David released him. "Dammit! I told Lucy about it! But I didn't tell her how to do it! You're the expert on these fucking techniques. Could she have done it with Vera without knowing all the details?"

Spear thought a moment. "Jon's missing? There's blood?"

"Yes! Yes! Could they have done it?"

"Did you say anything to Lucy about their staring into each other's eyes? About the breath?"

David put his hand to his head. Could he have been the cause of it all? As he had been the cause of Sandy's and Angela's deaths? "I talked about those things. I tried to be vague."

Spear was grim. "Even a blunt key can open Pandora's box, once you know where to insert it. Yes, they could have done it. Who saw them last?"

None of the others had seen the women all day. "I was with Lucy this morning," David admitted. "It must have been three hours ago."

Spear picked up his pipe and regarded it gravely. "We have to find her before she makes another."

David had been ready to blow the man's brains out a moment ago. Now he looked to him for reassurance. "But they could be all right. It doesn't have to be like Africa all over again, does it?"

Spear nodded. "It's possible Jon simply cut himself. The girls could be hiking. Lucy is addicted to the rain. She could have dragged Vera off."

"I told him that," Tom said anxiously, sounding like he wanted everyone to chill out and stop talking about black rites. Panda stood thoughtfully, as if listening to strange sounds in the distance. Dr. Henry was shaking his head.

"I don't understand," he said. "Are we afraid someone murdered the women? Or are we afraid they've murdered someone?"

David and Spear exchanged glances. "Both," Spear replied.

David jammed his gun in his belt. "I want to return to

the unused dorm I was shown earlier. Let's go now. No, wait. Let's get Margaret. Then we'll go."

"It will be difficult to wheel her through the mud and rain," Dr. Henry said.

"We can carry her," David snapped. "I told you, we all stay together. I want no one out of my sight."

"I haven't been able to find the key," Tom said, embarrassed. "I think I might have given it to Lucy to hold."

David nodded. "More the reason we should go there, then."

Margaret was in the kitchen, peeling potatoes. She came with them without question. Didn't even ask about the gun in David's belt. David helped wheel her through what was turning into a swamp. The rain had faltered; the damp was so warm it had begun to mist. The haze clung to the low bushes like a cloak. How had the vegetation changed, he wondered, in the last sixty million years? How would it change in the next six years? He didn't trust this storm, it didn't feel natural.

David kicked in each door. Behind number four he found a burning candle and a fallen beauty. She lay stretched on her back on the bed across from the orange flame. He leapt to her side. Her breathing was ragged. Blood leaked out of her right ear. Her skin was the temperature of the room. Her right temple was swollen and turning purple. But which Temple was it? Lucy or Vera? David turned to the others for confirmation even as Dr. Henry attempted to gauge the severity of the wound. Tom was the only one to speak.

"It must be Vera," he said. "She doesn't have on the gold crucifix. Lucy always wears her cross." Tom pointed to the ceiling, the wood tiles missing above the bed. "It looks like Vera was trying to fix the ceiling and she fell. Or else she was trying to hide something up there."

David looked up. "Maybe," he said. He clasped the woman's hand. He had to tell himself it was Vera, the twin he had not made love to, particularly when Dr. Henry's expression changed from cool professionalism to silent gloom. Yet David hated himself for wishing for one sister's well-being over the other's, as much as he hated her failure to respond when Dr. Henry pinched her Achilles tendon. Dr. Henry shook his head, and David thought the gesture should be outlawed among physicians for all time.

"She's got a bad concussion," Dr. Henry said.

"How bad is bad?" David asked. The question summed up his life, and God always gave him a hard answer. Dr. Henry carefully probed the bone around the main swelling. The bump was as large as a flattened orange.

"Her skull's cracked," Dr. Henry said. "We have to get her to the chapel. An EEG will tell me what we're looking at."

"But should we move her?" David asked. "It might cause her more harm."

"We can't do anything for her here," Dr. Henry said. "I have a med kit, various drugs. If I can figure out the extent of her injury, I might be able to give her something. We can lift the mattress as a whole, two of us on each side. David—is that your real name?"

He stared at her face. She looked so much like Lucy. "Yes," he whispered.

"David, if there is pressure on the brain due to swelling," Dr. Henry said, "I can slow it down with steroids. But I can't risk giving her a massive dose without a few tests. And we can't move the equipment in here. It would take hours, and it wouldn't fit anyway. We must move her and we must move her now."

"Do any of you have a cellular phone?" David asked.

"No," Spear said.

David nodded and tucked her hand back by her side. He stood. "We'll move her. But let's cover her with a blanket first. I don't want rain to fall on her face."

Or tears to fall from her eyes, he thought. He was ready to cry himself. But he knew he mustn't do that. He might be responsible for what had happened, maybe even more than Professor Spear. He had to remain strong to make it right. Yet his guilt would not leave him free to act. When he stared at her, he saw Sandy and Angela. When he brushed Spear's side, he felt Failla and Pokey near. Why, he could even hear Ned yelling to him. Telling him that the case was important, that no one could possibly get hurt.

"David!"

"Wait a second," he muttered. "That is Ned." He looked at the others "My boss's here. He'll have a phone. We can call for help." He stepped toward the door. "I'll be back in a second."

Tom grabbed his arm. He was scared. "You said we have to stay together."

David paused. Then he leaned his head out the door and cupped his mouth with his hands. "Ned! We're here! Ned!"

Ned Calendar came stomping into view a minute later, looking soaked and tired. David was so happy to see his boss, he embraced him on the dorm porch. Ned seemed glad to see him as well, going by the number of times he slapped him on the back. But the moment they let go of each other, Ned's anxiety became apparent.

"Is this clan of the cave lizards or what?" he asked.

David shook his head. "I don't know yet. Weird things are happening. Just inside this door one of the women is lying seriously injured. We don't know if it was accidental or if she was purposely knocked down. Christ, we don't even know if it's Lucy or Vera."

"Lucy's fine," Ned said. "I passed her on the path about a mile and a half back. She's looking for her sister."

David almost exploded. "You saw her? She's all right?"

Ned smiled nervously. "Why, yes, she seemed fine."

David paused. "Are you sure she was *normal*? We have bloodstains in another room, and the occupant missing."

Ned hesitated. "Well, she was worried about her sister. I don't know if she could be feeling normal. She seemed a little stiff. Is Lucy normally that way?"

David frowned. "No. But these are unusual circumstances. Listen, do you have your phone with you? Mine is gone."

"What happened to it?"

"Somebody stole it. They stole my gun as well."

Ned snorted. "That doesn't sound good. Yeah, I have a phone. It's back at my truck."

"Why the fuck did you leave it at the truck?"

"Because the only one I wanted to call in this fucking state was you, and I was walking up the path to see you in person. Don't worry, I'll go get it. We can call for an ambulance helicopter. Not that I'm sure one will come out in this weather." He turned. "I'll be back soon."

David stopped him. "No. I don't want us to scatter while there are still so many unknowns. I'll go for the phone after we move Vera into the church and Dr. Henry performs an EEG on her. I want to search for Lucy as well." He pulled out his .22. "Do you have your pistol?"

"Yes. Of course."

"Let's trade guns."

"Why?"

"I'm a better shot than you. I deserve the firepower. Give me your gun."

Ned handed over the 10-millimeter reluctantly. "She has amazing green eyes." He paused. "Doesn't she?"

David sighed. "They amazed me."

They moved Vera to the church without mishap and rested her on the altar. Dr. Henry wired her quickly, monitoring her heartbeat as well as her brain activity. Bumpy green lines traced across dark screens, falling stars on a rough road to extinction. The *beep* of her fluttering heart sounded like a broken answering machine. *I'm not at home at present. Please leave a message and if I don't die I'll call you back.* David fretted about the delay, but didn't want to leave until he knew if there was hope for Vera or not. Bent over his instruments, Dr. Henry didn't look encouraged.

"Will she live?" David asked finally. It was the only question that mattered.

Dr. Henry showed pain. "I don't think so. Her EEG is virtually flat. The brain damage must be extensive."

David had to take a breath. "There must be something we can do for her."

A tear ran down Dr. Henry's cheek. "She's not going to wake up."

David felt great pressure on his chest. He looked at Spear. "Have you ever seen anything like this before?" he asked.

Spear was a carving on a mummy's coffin. "Yes."

David nodded. "In Africa."

Spear stared at Vera, lying like a sacrifice on the altar of a God who had forgotten His creation the day after He took off to rest. The professor looked sort of dead right then, but which memory killed him most he didn't say. He only nodded. Yes, in Africa. It all began in Africa.

David was bitter. "Well, that's just fucking great. What

does your experience do for Vera now? What does it do for Lucy?"

Professor Spear wasn't given an opportunity to respond. The doors at the rear of the church swung open, with fanfare, as if the arrival of the royal virgin bride had just been announced. Nature was impressed. Lightning flashed at her back; thunder sounded as she stepped forward. Her hair shone like an angry volcano, her eyes burned like treasure. Her hood was thrown back, her arms swung loose at her sides. Yet it seemed, as she moved, that her feet never left the floor. They slithered over the stone slabs, newborn limbs rediscovering their way. Her feet were bare, her stance arrogant; nothing in the church could threaten her, and she knew it. Her face was the worst nightmare of all, so beautiful, so inhuman. She reached the altar. Taking her time, she scanned each of them. Her gaze came to rest on David, and he understood what it felt like to be stabbed in the heart, although no blade had ever broken his flesh. She wore the gold crucifix.

She smiled. "Who wants to be first?"

CHAPTER 21

David Conner took out his pistol and pointed it at her. "If you try to harm any of us," he said. "I will kill you."

No one moved, except their visitor. Its head rocked slightly from side to side in a gesture no human in a rational state of mind ever made. There was blankness as well as strength in its eyes. It was cunning; it knew how to manipulate them, that was obvious. But did it understand them? Perhaps it felt understanding was not necessary, not with its psychic powers. The field of energy radiating around it was as palpable as the buzz of a high-tension wire on a foggy night, an invisible cyclone of astral pollution. They stared at it as if they weren't seeing a human being. Their combined fear was so tangible the creature seemed to draw strength from it. The fact that it wasn't pretending to be Lucy any longer led David to believe it could not be stopped by physical means. Still, he clung to his pistol, putting pressure on the trigger as it slowly moved in his direction. The smile remained fixed on its face, a line scraped in blood-stained plaster.

"Will you kill me?" it asked. "We sit below the human mind. We have only to glance upward and your thoughts are visible." It shook its head. "You will not kill me."

"For the love of God, shoot, David," Ned pleaded. He, too, had his gun out and pointed at the creature. Yet he hadn't fired, either. "It's not Lucy. It's one of them."

The thing ignored Ned. It continued to stare at David, and he in turn stared at it. He did not have to look deep into its eyes, however, to know the danger of probing its black soul through such uncensored windows. But already it had him under a spell. He wanted to shoot and could not. He was unable to add the two extra pounds of pressure to the trigger necessary to send the bullet hurtling into its heart. There was no threat if he disobeyed, he simply lacked the will to carry on with the act. The core of his brain was keeping him from firing as much as the monster's psychic force field, which was a truly scary thought.

It moved closer to his side and rose up on its toes until he felt its breath on his cheek, cold as a fossil beneath arctic snow. It was older than that, though, more ancient than the last hundred ice ages combined. It stared at him with eyes that had seen a million species rise and perish. He wondered if its mind was always there, inside them, within all its thorny descendants, witnessing their trials, mocking their dreams, knowing that one day it would reawaken and wipe out all humankind as easily as it had wiped out its own race. The thing seemed pleased at his unspoken insight.

"We are you," it hissed softly. "You simply buried us.

You forgot us. You lost all power." It leaned forward and kissed his cheek. "Who am I, David?"

He drew back in revulsion. His vision blurred with tears. "You are not Lucy," he cried. God, it was so horrible! Its smile widened.

"I am not Lucy," it agreed. "But you will join with the body of her sister. The fire of her brain will burn yours. You will remember what you lost." It turned and gestured to the rest of the group. "You will all burn. Or else you will serve as food." It paused and touched its stomach. "Jon Horst."

David struggled to move—it was hard enough to breathe, to think. It said it was not Lucy. Assuming it had no need to lie, that meant it was Lucy who lay nearby dying, her brain hemorrhaging. A silent cry wailed deep inside him, raising up the wave of darkness he knew only too well. He struggled to hold it at bay, knowing he could not give in to despair. Why hadn't it simply killed Lucy? It must have known they would find her.

"Why must you awaken?" he asked. "You have powers we lack, but you have no wisdom, no compassion. You destroyed yourselves the last time. You will only destroy yourselves again, and take us with you."

Its eyes returned to David's face. It seemed to reflect on his words. "Your young awake when they are hungry. It is the same with us."

"But it's humanity's time," he said. "Your time has passed."

"Our destiny has arrived." It raised its hand when he started to speak again. "We do not talk. We do not discuss. We do what we do." It surveyed them. "Who will be first?"

Big surprise: there were no volunteers. David wondered if he met it alone, head-on, if he could fight it the most effectively. A foolish thought, he knew, but required of a supposedly brave man. Knowing he was throwing his body in front of a speeding train to stop it, he spoke again.

"I will go first."

The monster was amused, cruel. "You will be last. You will hear each of the others scream. And you will pray for their screams *not* to stop. Because each time they do, another portion of your precious humanity dies. I know your mind, your deepest fears. You will pray for help, David Conner, to a God you know is not there. And He will not listen."

"It doesn't matter what I believe," he said, sick of its arrogance. "The only thing that matters is what is. You were beaten before. You will be beaten again."

It reached out and took the gun from his hand. "Not by you," it said. Then it turned abruptly, as if feeling a disturbance at its back, and moved toward Spear. He did not fidget at its approach, but rather, focused on it intently, his dark eyes narrowing. Yet his mental efforts did not slow it down. In a mocking gesture, it tapped the top of his head with the butt of the pistol. "You will not stop us again, either. You earned the honor. You will be first."

With that remark Spear's face changed. For a moment he could have been the one possessed by an intelligent reptile born of a super-race. Cold rage flared from his mouth and nostrils. He raised his arms and shoved it hard in the chest, and to everyone's immense surprise it toppled backward. Yet he did not press his advantage. Instead, he turned toward Lucy. Poor Lucy, who lay flat on her back on the altar, oblivious to the fading twilight of the human race. Spear leapt in her direction.

He did not make it to her. The creature recovered with blinding speed. In a move too swift for the human eye to completely follow, it lashed out and struck Spear on the side of the neck. He didn't simply crumble, but went flying across the floor, his head smacking the cold gray marble tiles with a series of sickening thumps. In a crumpled ball, he rolled to a halt close to David's feet. David felt his paralysis momentarily lift. He knelt by the professor, cradling the man's head in his lap. Blood poured from the wound at Spear's temple, and from the tilt of his neck it looked as if several cervical vertebrae had been crushed. Spear was not going to make it and the man knew it. He spoke with great weariness and painful regret.

"I wasn't going to do it," he whispered. "Believe me, I had decided not to do it."

David nodded and leaned close. "I believe you, professor. But how do we stop it? How did you stop it before?"

"You see," Spear said, blood leaking out his mouth. "My wife was fine."

"What do you mean?"

"Penny was fine," he gasped.

Those were his last words. Spear's eyes lost their focus. They rolled up into their sockets and the whites stared at David as if challenging him to guess what the dead man had been about to say. David became aware of the redhead with the bad attitude standing above him. For some reason, he didn't feel like raising his head.

"Ned Calendar will be the first, instead," it said. "I promised to touch him again."

CHAPTER 22

They heard Ned begin to scream even though they were locked in the storage room under the dining hall. It had put them there: Margaret, Panda, Tom, Dr. Henry, David, and even poor Lucy. It had smiled when David lifted his love into his arms, when the creature demanded they leave the chapel. It hadn't tried to stop him. "I know you will take good care of her, David Conner," it said. Not that there was anything he could do for her.

David knelt, cradling Lucy in his arms. Tom had angrily punched out the tiny windows near the ceiling of the storage area. It was through these openings that they heard Ned's cries, and David wished Tom had not bothered inviting the sound in. A kitten could have crawled through the shattered windows, nothing else. Also, unfortunately, the storage room door would not respond to a stiff kick, especially with the heavy metal bar in place. Breaking out was not the key to their salvation, anyway. They would have needed a cloaking device to shield their minds as well as their bodies from the creature. Bummer, David thought, and soon there would be half a dozen of them for the world to contend with. How had the Egyptians stopped them? The white light of Isis? Somehow, David couldn't see her materializing in the next few minutes.

But he had been wrong before.

I promised to touch him again.

The remark was interesting. It carried profound philosophical implications. Was the creature that possessed Frances the same one inside Vera? Or were they simply related? Go back that far in time and probably every human on the planet had embedded deep in their genes some of every Setian that ever lived. Clearly, Frances had allowed Ned to escape, knowing that it would catch up to him again, and do worse things than just bite off his hand. Probably no individual Setians were returning to the modern world, just a collective reptilian spirit. Certainly, though, once they had taken over enough human bodies, and staked out fresh personalities, they would start fighting again. The thing that was inside Vera didn't act like a team player.

David couldn't forget the look on Ned's face when they had said goodbye. Two weeks more and his boss would have been retired. But he had wanted to get into the field one last time, have a final taste of action. Good God, David grimaced, it sounded like the thing was skinning Ned alive! How could a grown man scream like that and not die in the next breath? David clenched his eyes shut as he stroked Lucy's back. She was getting cold and he didn't want that to happen. Corpses got cold.

Ned had looked to Margaret, not to David, when they

were being led away. "Can you do anything?" he asked her. She shook her head.

Why had Ned turned to Margaret?

David opened his eyes and looked over at the crippled woman. She was knitting her sweater. The balls of yarn and her needles had been tucked in the rear bag of her wheelchair when they had gone for her in the kitchen.

"Isn't it a little late for that?" he asked dryly.

She looked up and snapped a piece of yarn. "No."

David sighed and hung his head. "Fuck."

Dr. Henry knelt nearby. "We have to talk. We have to figure out where it's vulnerable."

"It isn't vulnerable!" Tom cried, pacing restlessly. "That's the problem! It can do anything! We're all going to die!"

"Shut up and sit down," Dr. Henry said.

"We're going to die screaming like him!" Tom moaned.

"It isn't killing him," David said quietly, squeezing Lucy tighter. He had already given the others a condensed version of what had happened in Africa. They had not enjoyed the story. "It's changing him, making another like itself."

"How does it do that?" Dr. Henry asked.

David snorted. "You're the expert on the brain, you tell me. But I think it stimulates the reptilian complex layer somehow, perhaps by the power of its attention. Spear had a violent fever when he returned from Africa, after combatting it the last time. I think it tried to change him, but was interrupted for some reason."

"Is that how Spear was able to resist it briefly?" Dr. Henry asked. "He had a trace of its power?"

David nodded. "It's possible. You guys knew him better than I did, but he always struck me as someone who'd had a part of his brain burned out. Anyway, he wasn't able to resist it long."

"But Spear did confront it and stop it in the past?" Dr. Henry asked.

"Yes," David said.

"But how did he stop it?" Dr. Henry insisted.

"I don't know. I tried to ask him, but all he had time to say was, 'My wife was fine. Penny was fine.' " David was thoughtful. "His wife had not changed."

Ned let out a particularly frightening wail that echoed through the trees like that of a wounded animal. The rain had settled down to a warm soft patter. David wished the creature would just hurry up and get it over with. But he wouldn't pray to God to help. The creature had him pegged. He didn't believe there was anyone above or below to listen to his or anyone's prayers. Two feet away, sweat glistened on Dr. Henry's forehead, but the scholar was not ready to quit yet.

"What do you mean, the wife had not changed?" Dr. Henry asked. "I thought that they regressed together? I thought that's what allowed this thing from the past to awaken? Identical twins working together."

"They were—like this," Panda said, sitting in the corner. He nodded and clasped his hands together. Then he yanked them apart. "Then—like that. Weak."

David studied the quiet Indian man. "What are you saying?"

Panda didn't have enough English, not without the Big Mind to help him. He had to gesture with his hands. He held them out, then firmly pressed them together. "Right holds left," he said.

David gasped in understanding. "They need each other! They needed each other to bring the thing into this time, and in the same way, it needs them to *exist* in this time. At least until it can make another. That's it."

Panda nodded.

"I'm not going next," Tom said. "I don't want to go next."

"What do you mean, to *exist* in this time?" Dr. Henry asked. "It's already in our time. I want to know how to get it back to where it belongs."

David shook his head. "No. You misunderstand what it is. It's not just a being from the past. It's a part of what we are today. It said so itself. We cannot send it back. We can only hope to bury it again in our time."

"Splendid!" Dr. Henry said impatiently. "I can live with that. How the fuck do we do it?"

David began to answer but a lump in his throat stopped him. He paused to stroke Lucy's red hair. It was so beautiful, maybe not quite so long and fine as Vera's, but close. He was careful not to touch her head wound. He didn't want to hurt her. Yeah, he had heard that one before, and that was the cosmic joke, wasn't it? The Big Mind had set it all up; it knew the punch line. It had said as much in the session. Another wave on the horizon, David. You see it coming, you had better move fast. He had wanted to save Sandy and Angela from death, but he hadn't, and now Lucy was dying in his arms. Now he had only a few minutes to be with her. Now it seemed he couldn't even have those. *Now*, David, the present moment is the place to be. He didn't buy that. The wave was cresting. Ned's screams were starting to subside.

He understood how Spear had stopped it the last time.

He understood a lot of things.

David turned to Margaret. Another piece of yarn snapped in her hands.

"Who are you?" he asked.

She set the sweater aside. "Margaret is as good a name as any."

I don't even know who I am. I am the Big Mind. That is as good a name as any. Who are you?

Ned had turned to Margaret for help because he knew something about her that no one else did. A crippled woman with no past, David thought. But Ned must have found something in her past that made him believe she could stop a seemingly omnipotent monster. Who was Margaret anyway? Why had she suddenly entered Spear's life after he returned from Africa? Who had sent her? How could she know how to cook just like his mother? Why did everyone love her so much? They were all scared. Why wasn't she?

I support the Big Mind. I listen to it. The Big Mind is never worried.

The Dogon had called their high initiates the Listeners.

"Who are you?" he repeated.

"Let's have a session with the Big Mind!" Tom suddenly cried. "It will help us! It will tell us what to do!"

David let go of Lucy's hand and raised his arm. "Relax, Tom, we don't need a session. We have the Big Mind here. We've always had it here. The same way we've always had the creature with us." He paused. "Isn't that true, Margaret?"

"What are you talking about?" Dr. Henry demanded.

"Shh," David said. "Let her answer. You will answer me, won't you, Margaret? You answered all my questions yesterday afternoon, in the session."

She stared at him, her face as kind as always. "It's up to you. It's always been that way and always will be. You have free will. You can choose."

"What are the choices?" David asked.

"To go forward. Or to go back. Spear always wanted

the past. He thought real power resided there. He didn't believe in the future, in the spirit of man. What do you believe in, David?"

"Is that what the Big Mind is?" he asked. "The future?"

Margaret shrugged.

"No, answer me," David insisted angrily. "It looks like we have the devil in the past, and humanity's in the middle. Are you an angel? Is that what we're to become?"

"I'm not understanding this," Dr. Henry said.

"I just don't want to get eaten," Tom said, holding his belly, no doubt thinking about Jon Horst. Margaret again reached for her yarn and knitting needles. The yarn snapped again in her hands.

"I understand the symbolism," David said. "You can stop doing that."

Margaret stopped and waited.

"What is she doing?" Dr. Henry exploded. "How do we stop it?"

"It's very simple," David said. "The creature was able to enter our time through a unique portal in consciousness, constructed of the fusion of two identical beings. It's only that fusion that sustains it in our time, at least until it can make another of its kind. While the twins are linked, the portal remains open. But break that link, snap it the way Margaret keeps snapping her green and white yarns, and the portal closes. Spear must have understood that." David paused. "I know what happened to his wife in Africa."

"What?" Dr. Henry demanded.

"Spear said she was fine. She hadn't been changed, like Frances. Spear must have gotten away from Frances, and then later returned for his wife. But maybe Frances zapped him a little before he escaped, I don't know. She could have been adjusting to the transformation, and wasn't at full power yet. Anyway, when Spear returned, he probably carried Penny into the cave. Buckley saw Spear go in there. Perhaps Frances had knocked Penny out as Vera knocked Lucy out. We know for a fact that it was not Frances who killed Penny. No, that wouldn't do. Frances *needed* Penny, and Vera did not kill Lucy because Vera *needs* Lucy. That's why it smiled when it said, 'I know you will take good care of her.' It wants Lucy here with us. It wants us to keep her alive until we're all changed. Then it won't matter. By that time the portal will be wide open. Then Lucy can die." David paused. "But Penny died in Africa too early. Penny was specifically killed in order to stop it."

"Who killed her?" Dr. Henry asked.

"Spear." David chuckled. "I thought he was just an asshole, but you have to hand it to him, he made the ultimate sacrifice. He killed his own wife and there was nothing wrong with her. Just to make right what he had done wrong."

"How do you know this for sure?" Dr. Henry asked.

David was grim. "Because ten minutes ago Spear went for Lucy, not the monster. He knew where the weak link was. Am I right about this, Margaret?"

"Yes. You have insight."

David gave a fey laugh. "Oh, we all have insight. Panda has insight. Even Tom has insight. He doesn't want to get eaten. None of us wants to get eaten or go through the black rite. Ned has the most insight, but right now I bet he just wishes he could stop screaming. I have to make a decision soon. I have to decide to set everything right." David's voice cracked. "Is it true? Do I have to kill her?"

Margaret looked at him. "You know what's true. You don't need to ask me."

"Dammit!" David cried, and Lucy shook in his arms.

"That's not good enough! You have to tell me why she has to die!"

"You have just explained why," Margaret said calmly.

"No! You have to tell me why *you* let it happen this way! Why the Big Mind has such a fucked sense of humor? Why God plays with our heads like we're fucking pawns in a fucking game? I tell you I'm sick and tired of having the people I love die on me! I'm not going to kill her!"

"That's your choice," Margaret said.

"You gave us no choice! You didn't even warn us!"

"But you were warned. All of you were."

Actually, the Big Mind says it's foolish. That we would be better off not doing it.

"But you were right there—*you knew*—and you just let us walk into this trap!"

"I watch. I witness. It was your choice. It still is."

"Shit! That's no answer!" David screamed. "I have gone through shit my entire life! I deserve an answer!"

Margaret sighed. "David." She picked up the sweater and smoothed it over her lap. "I think it would look nice on either of them. The green brings out the green in their eyes, don't you think?"

David's fury, his pain, knew no bounds. "You are a cold bitch."

Margaret did not look up from her handiwork. "Children don't often say that to their mothers. But I suppose they sometimes think it."

David felt a hand on his arm, looked over. Dr. Henry had tears on his face.

"If killing Lucy will stop it," Dr. Henry said gently. "Then maybe you'd better do it now. She's going to die anyway. Her EEG's flat. She's hemorrhaging in the neocortex." He patted his arm. "She won't last the day, David."

David was having trouble breathing. "Oh, I'm sure it's just her neocortex that it injured. The creature wouldn't have hurt the deeper layers of her brain. It needs those to keep working until it's through. It needs—I need—" He couldn't finish. Sobs racked his body and again Lucy shook in his arms. He ran his fingers through her hair but it only made his agony worse. How could he kill her when he wanted to kiss her and have her eyes open and her mouth smile up at him. She could tell him that she had just been having a nightmare, but now it was over and everything was wonderful because he was beside her. His hand fell limply to his side. "I can't do it," he moaned. "Will somebody please do it for me?"

No one moved, and he understood their refusal to help. He was the FBI agent, the stuff of legends. He had killed before and could kill again. He leaned over and kissed Lucy on the forehead. He could feel their eyes on him. Just this one last female victim and they and the rest of humanity would be eternally grateful. He slipped his hands around her neck, feeling the base of her skull with the tips of his strong fingers. He had kissed her neck last night, many times. She had liked it. Now just this one last caress, he thought, and his career would finally be over. He could retire; he could even follow her and Sandy and Angela to the grave. But where was her tiny gold crucifix? They said Lucy always wore it. He wished he could find it now, press it to her lips. He leaned over and kissed her again, on the lips this time.

"Jesus," he whispered, getting a grip on her frail bones.

Then he heard a sound, they all heard it. Not Ned screaming, but heavy footsteps approaching rapidly, pounding across the dining room floor above their heads.

Of course, it could read their minds. It must have taken a peek at his in the middle of its brain surgery and saw he was no wimp when it came to killing girlfriends. The human almost caught by surprise. But now it was moving fast. Above them, at the top of the stairs, the creature attacked the door. It just exploded open, as if touched by dynamite, showering splinters down the stairs over all of them. David glanced up the stairs, saw the mass of red hair, felt the rake of poisonous green eyes. But he knew better than to look into those eyes.

David yanked Lucy's skull back as hard as he could.

Every bone in her neck popped. So loud. It must have hurt.

Lucy went still. Just settled back in his arms and stopped breathing.

The creature stumbled down the stairs. It carried David's gun in its left hand.

David quickly set Lucy aside and stood to greet it. The creature moved like a drunk. It brought up the weapon, took aim, lost its grip, and fired into the floor. Its head wobbled backward as if its own spinal cord had been snapped. It managed a surprised grin.

"You are like us," it said.

Then it collapsed. David caught it as it fell. The pistol bounced on the floor. A cold shudder went through its entire body. Its eyes opened briefly. No, it was Vera who stared up at him, her expression one of relief and puzzlement.

"David," she whispered. "I was having the worst nightmare."

Then her eyes closed and she died. Yes, like her sister, she just stopped breathing. Why? Frances had not died. But maybe there was no why, no nothing. Her body sagged toward the floor, and it was there David let her go.

He glanced over at Margaret, who had worked too hard on her green and white sweater to have no one to give it to. No one with green eyes, that is. David wanted to take the gun and shoot her in the head. He went so far as to pick up the pistol and point it in her direction. But you couldn't shoot the Goddess, that wouldn't be cool. It was much better to gouge out your own eyes than to do something foolish like that. He threw the gun against the far wall and fell to his knees beside Vera. Burying his face in his hands, his tears ran through his fingers as the blood must have run through the fingers of the Egyptian priestess, who so trusted in Isis that she offered her own mortal eyes in exchange for freedom from the black rite and a promise of divine vision. But all he wanted was to know why he was crying again.

A warm hand touched his arm.

"David?"

He opened his eyes. Margaret had wheeled herself over to him. "Yes?" he said.

"When you came here, I asked you what you wanted for dinner, more than anything else in the whole word. You said turkey and mashed potatoes and I gave you that. Remember?"

"Yes."

"David, David." Brushing his hair from his eyes, she smiled at him with such love that he honestly felt his mother had returned to comfort him. "Now, tell me, what do you want more than anything else in the whole world?"

His throat was choked; he could hardly speak. "Huh?"

"What do you want?"

His lips trembled. "Lucy."

Margaret nodded. "All right."

"What?"

Margaret smiled again. She called for Tom to lift her

out of her chair and set her on the floor beside Vera. Tom was happy to oblige, now that the screaming had stopped. He helped Margaret sit upright while she put one hand on Vera's head and the other over her heart. Closing her eyes, Margaret inhaled a breath it seemed she never released. A moment of silence went by, or perhaps it was longer than that, years, centuries, sixty millennia, or even as long as the eternity that exists between each and every moment, and between each and every breath. David watched, fascinated, although he didn't know what he was seeing.

The purpose of life is unknown. It's a mystery, and you know mysteries can be lived, but never explained. Do you understand?

He would never understand. Why Vera began to breathe, to stir. Why Margaret opened her eyes, and smiled at him one last time, and told him not to worry, that Ned would be OK as well. Why she then went up the stairs in Tom's arms without saying goodbye, and was never heard from again. David could not see the white light of Isis, which might have given him understanding. Probably no ordinary mortal ever would be able to see it. But Lucy had spoken highly of its power.

Vera opened her eyes and looked over at him.

"David," she whispered.

He took her hand and kissed it. "Vera."

She frowned at him. Silly boy. "No. It's me. It's Lucy."

It took David several seconds to realize that she was not kidding.

EPILOGUE

A cruise up the Nile was for romantic fools, the man thought as he stepped outside and away from the bar to plop down on one of the many benches that ringed the large ship. He was not drunk but needed to clear his head, and had decided the desert night air would be best for that. The trip was no honeymoon for him. He was alone, escaping from business as well as personal pressures at home in England. They were three days out of Aswan, and would see the pyramids soon. Maybe he had drunk a little too much. The stars seemed to pulse above the barren landscape, as close as his outstretched fingers. He had never seen so many in his life.

A couple stood nearby, leaning against the railing, looking at the stars, the desert. The woman's hair was a wonderful red, the man's face strong and grave. By the way they stood, their hands clasped, their bodies never far apart, the man from England could tell they were much in love, and the sight of such a couple brought unexpected gladness to his cynical heart. The woman pointed to a bright blue star.

"There's Sirius," she said. Slowly lowering her arm, she pointed to the embankment, two hundred yards away. "And that's where they caught the priestess."

"You're sure that's the spot?"

"Yes. I still see the—red stains."

The man shook his head in wonder. "So long ago."

The woman leaned over and kissed his cheek. "It won't be so long for us."

The man put his hand on her belly, above the sweater tied around her waist. "What will we name her?"

"Her?"

He nodded. "We both know it. What do you want to call her? After your sister?"

"Would that be all right with you?"

"Yes, of course. I love the name."

The woman laughed softly. "I love you." But she grew serious as her eyes returned to the embankment, and to the bright star. "Let's call her Isis. My sister and the priestess—they both loved that name. And maybe it will bring her good luck."

Turn the page
for an exciting glimpse
of Christopher Pike's
newest novel,

The Cold One

Available in hardcover
from Tor Books
January 1995

PROLOGUE I

There are logical reasons. There are strange coincidences. When the power failed at Kabriel Clinic in southeast Iowa during a thunderstorm, and the backup generators also failed, Penny Hampton didn't know if God was playing a joke on her or if she was simply unlucky. Not until later did she think of a third possible reason. When the crazy man with the knife came to visit.

But that was not until much later.

Penny was a thirty-year-old physical therapist with great hands. Kabriel Clinic was an intensive care facility with forty beds. Penny had worked part time at Kabriel for two years with mixed feelings. The money was OK, she received ten bucks for each patient she stretched and massaged. Since she could do three an hour, she was happy with the thirty bucks. Also, the brain-dead patients never complained. But Penny was outgoing by nature and liked to babble as she worked, and it was no fun talking to people who never answered, except to drool now and then. Even the regular nursing staff at Kabriel spoke only in whispers, as if they were caretakers of a graveyard. And in one sense Kabriel was like one huge tomb—None of the patients who checked in ever checked out. In fact, every one of them had been checked in by someone else. Sometimes Penny liked to imagine that late at night, when no one was watching, the comatose patients rose from their beds, donned Halloween masks, and did a long, slow dance to the rhythm of the wind blowing outside.

Yeah, Penny liked the money but the place had her spooked.

And nothing bothered her as much as Patient 111. First, the woman didn't have a name tag above her bed as the others did. She was just 111—if she had been 666 Penny wouldn't even have touched her. Penny supposed she could have had one of the nurses check the files for her name, but she had never felt the inclination strongly enough. Also, 111 was old and emaciated; a mummy with a dreary green hospital gown for bandages. There was so little flesh left on her that when Penny stretched her limbs, she feared one of them would break like a stick in her hands. It would just snap off with a dry brittle sound, and Penny would be left holding it and thinking, Oh shit. She wasn't sure how long 111 had been at the clinic. When she'd asked the head nurse, Sylvia Thompson, Sylvia had only told her that 111 had been there when she arrived at Kabriel eighteen years earlier. A long time to have a plastic tube rammed up your nose. Penny just wished someone would pull the plug on the woman. Every time she worked on 111 she thought about it.

Then the big thunderstorm came late in the evening on

the last day of April and nature itself pulled out the plugs. It was one of those storms people love to see roll in when there's nothing else to talk about. Clouds huge and black as evil mountains, lightning flashes bright as phaser fire. The rain came down as if it hadn't seen the ads for water-saver nozzles. Penny had a bitch of time getting to the job. Then, after she had dried off sufficiently and rolled up her sleeves to work, Sylvia handed her a list of six patients to treat, and it included the infamous 111. Penny started to protest but thought better of it. She needed the job and the money. She didn't know anyone who wasn't hurting. Except maybe 111. She decided to do her first and get her out of the way.

The physical therapy treatment for a comatose patient was fairly routine. The primary goal was to stretch the major tendons and ligaments, which had a tendency to shorten during unending convalescence. Actually, in Penny's humble opinion, if any of the patients at Kabriel Clinic were to awaken miraculously, most of them would wish they hadn't bothered. Few would ever be able to walk or dress themselves, and certainly 111 wouldn't have been able to get out of bed, even with a full-fledged brain transplant. Penny conscientiously stretched and massaged her patients, but she could have been working on Barbies and Kens for all the good she thought she was doing humanity.

She always started with the legs, but one end was as good as another. Working on 111's lower extremities, Penny tried not to glance at the old woman's face. Her legs were bad enough, knobby clubs with gray bristles. Penny quickly rubbed the bony sticks up and down to get the circulation going, then began to work the Achilles tendons. Few people realized the strength of that particular tendon and how much force it took to rupture it. But

Penny barely leaned on 111's toes to lengthen the tendons, worried that if the damn things did snap, the woman would suddenly sit up and vomit a bellyful of blood in her face. She feared that there was something very unsavory in the old woman, just waiting to wake up and make a mess of things.

Yet there was no logical reason for her fear.

Not one Penny could pinpoint, anyway.

She finished with the legs and moved to the arms, abdomen, and chest. To stretch a patient's spine, Penny would sit the person up and bend her forward as if she were a doll reaching for her toes. The move caused her to get a good whiff of whomever she was working on. 111 always smelled like spoiled milk, and that night was no exception. There was no explaining it because the woman never got milk through the nasogastric tubes that fed her miserable body. The smell reminded Penny of that of infants; in 111's case, infants who had been left alone in their cribs for weeks.

Penny completed her therapy by manipulating the woman's neck. Turning 111's head from side to side was like twisting the radiator fan on a rusty Mustang. Penny's worst concern about working 111's neck was that one day she would be rotating the woman's head, slowly loosening the long tendons that ran into the skull from the shoulders, and suddenly be seized by an uncontrollable desire to break the woman's fucking neck. Just rip off her scrawny head, drop it to the floor, and kick it under the bed as if it were a punctured football. It was a thought she didn't share with anyone.

Yet, for all that, Penny believed that 111 had once been a beautiful woman. She could tell by her delicate bone structure, which was, in fact, all that was left on display, the bones, capped by a tangle of fine white hair that could have been stolen from a retired scarecrow. Penny didn't know the woman's eyes, their color, their size. They remained closed, and for that Penny was grateful. Never, never would she have reached over and raised the lids to peer under them. Not for ten dollars a treatment, anyway.

Penny was just finishing 111's neck when the lights went out.

"Shit," she whispered, and immediately let go of 111.

Kabriel Clinic was divided into four wings. Penny and 111 were in the south wing, which had ten beds—one long line of mechanical respirators and computerized EEG and EKG monitors. When the lights failed, Penny was alone in the wing with 111 and three other patients. Although fully half the patients at Kabriel could not breathe on their own, that night by chance 111 was the only patient in the south wing who had a plastic tube rammed up her nose. The steady hiss of the mechanical respirators was an unpleasant sound Penny associated with working at the clinic. But when that hiss shut off with the lights, she knew panic. Particularly as time went by and the backup generator didn't kick in, as it should have according to state regulations, and the nurses began to shout anxiously to one another in the halls. Penny couldn't hear every word that was being said, but the meaning was clear.

They, the staff nurses, and she, the part-time help, had to start breathing for the patients on mechanical respirators or many of the well-preserved vegetables were—in five minutes or less—going to turn into applesauce. For an instant Penny thought, That wouldn't be so bad.

She thought it for maybe one whole minute.

Finally, though, she realized exactly what she was being called to do. It was her worst nightmare. She was supposed to take a deep breath, lean over, and press her lips to the *thing* while exhaling slowly. The woman was only a thing as far as Penny was concerned, and Penny was not really heartless. From her perspective 111 was brain dead, and that meant she had no mind. Finished, end of discussion, no moral issue at stake. Why should she mess her lipstick and risk catching a disease to preserve a foul-breathed mannequin? No, she thought, she wasn't going to do it. She didn't want to do it. She had to go out with her boyfriend later that night, and if he smelled 111 on her he wouldn't hold her hand for a month, much less sleep with her that night. Bill was kind of a wuss when it came to cleanliness.

Yet all of Penny's thoughts were just thoughts. As she lowered her hand and felt under her trembling fingers 111's dry flesh and wavering pulse, she realized with a force stronger than simple reason that she could be directly responsible for a death. That she was, in a sense, ready to commit murder.

"Oh, shit," Penny whispered.

Penny was trained in CPR. Every health professional in the state of Iowa had taken the class. The skill was simple, not something even someone as anxious as Penny was could forget. Yet it was a long way from remembering the basics of CPR to being an expert at it. The last person Penny had done CPR on had been George, in her initial class, and George had been the dummy.

Penny, however, did have one advantage with 111 that she didn't have with George. 111's heart was still beating, she assumed. All she had to do was respirate 111 until the power came back on. There was no need for rib-crushing maneuvers to massage her heart. Penny had broken George, trying to keep his plastic heart massaged.

Now that she was decided, Penny moved quickly. Leaning over, she opened the woman's mouth to check for obstructions. Finding none, she tilted the woman's head

back, reached up with her right hand, and pinched 111's
nose closed. In the dark Penny couldn't be sure if 111's
lips were coated with gross substances, but she had to assume they were. With the back of her left forearm she
wiped them off. Then, finally, taking a deep breath, she
pressed her lips to 111's. The kiss of life for the brain-dead
woman. She didn't taste like spoiled milk—more like a
Kirby vacuum cleaner. Penny didn't so much exhale into
the old woman's lungs as she felt the breath being sucked
out of her own lungs. Penny filled 111's lungs once and
then sat back up.

"Wow." She panted.

She took another deep breath and returned to her task.
Once again she felt as if 111 pulled the air out of her lungs
rather than placidly accepting it like the living corpse she
was. Penny's fear of the woman returned. As the seconds
turned to minutes in the dark clinic, she felt a strange weariness overcome her, as if 111 took not only her breath but
something more subtle. Something inside her breath that
reminded Penny of the soul she didn't believe anyone possessed. Yet she believed in 111's possession, in the something evil inside the woman. Penny struggled to keep 111
alive even as she prayed for her to die.

Then the power returned, and with it the lights, the hiss
of the respirator, reality.

Penny literally jumped back from 111. She spit out the
taste in her mouth. The act should have shamed her, but it
didn't. Once more the plastic tube started to fill 111's
lungs. But the old woman still had Penny's last breath inside her. A last mouthful of life to exhale. As Penny's
breath came out, 111's head rolled to the side and her eyes
popped open to stare directly at Penny. They were blue,
dark as the ocean during an eclipse, but to Penny they

seemed black as a Halloween sky after all the children had gone home to bed.

A word flew out of the woman's mouth as she exhaled. One clear word followed by a second distorted sound. Perhaps a whispered sigh of pain. A sound of grief certainly.

"Child," the woman had said. Followed by the other sound, the word Penny preferred to believe, for a long time afterward, she hadn't heard.

The word that made her swear never to work on 111 again.

PROLOGUE II

The Voice had stopped.

The Cold One sat at the edge of the warm sea and watched as the bloated sun settled through a wide band of red clouds that resembled a fresh festering scar. The air was hot and dry, the rough sand beneath Its body moist. Yet for the first time in Its life the Cold One was not particularly aware of Its surroundings. The Voice had stopped, the words that made up Its worldly stream of being. Now there was nothing left of the Cold One except what It was. Yet that was the enigma, even to Itself. Still, it didn't bother the Cold One. Nothing ever had, and It doubted anything ever would.

Yet in the silent void there was cognition. It came in an instant, though it had probably always been there—Its purpose. The Cold One slowly stood. A crab crawled over Its bare foot, the right one. The Cold One stared down at the small creature, perhaps curious as to what it would do, perhaps not. The crab rose on its posterior legs and leaned toward the big toe with its claws. The Cold One felt a pinch, Its body did. Blood appeared on the toe. A wave came and the foam washed away the crab. The toe continued to bleed, a bit. The Cold One turned and walked toward the old road a mile inland. The sun beat down but the Cold One did not perspire.

It was far south. Here the roads were poorly tended, and travelers few. The Cold One had to stand by the side of the road a long time before a car appeared on the horizon. The Cold One had originally come in a car of Its own, but someone had stolen the vehicle while It sat on the shore of the sea. It had come to the sea, in this particular spot, because that was what the Voice had done. The Cold One had not felt commanded by the Voice—because It felt nothing—but had merely followed the Voice because that is what It had always done. But now that the Voice had stopped, the Cold One reasoned, It would follow the Voice no more.

The approaching car was expensive, sporty, the type middle-age men bought to feel younger. The Cold One registered the fact without judgment. It saw that the man behind the wheel was approximately forty-five, chubby, tan, with a wide mustache that made his mouth appear fat. His shirt was open in a sloppy way and the hair on his chest was much whiter than the growth over his lip. He was coming from the south, heading north—the direction It wished to go. The Cold One noted all this from a distance of half a mile. Since birth Its sense had been more acute than a human's.

The Cold One stuck out Its thumb to hitch a ride. Half a minute later the car came to a halt beside It. The car was a red convertible, coated gray with dust from the dry road.

The driver perspired heavily, but smiled as he placed his arm on the top of the driver's door and checked It out. The Cold One smiled in return.

"You're a long way from nowhere," the man said.

"Yes," the Cold One answered. "I went for a stroll down to the water and some bastard stole my car while I was gone."

The man shook his head. "That's a bitch, but to be expected in these parts I can give you a ride. Hop in."

The Cold One considered. The man had a reliable car that would probably take It as far north as It wished to go. But this man was no ordinary tourist. The Cold One smelled cocaine on his nose, his breath, a stash of it in his trunk. It was obvious the man intended to take the drug across the border and into California, which could cause problems for the Cold One if the man was apprehended. On the other hand, the Cold One thought, It could kill the man, bury his body and his drugs in the weeds, and take the car for Itself. It was very easy for the Cold One to kill. It was much stronger than humans, and It didn't mind killing, although It got no pleasure from the act either. The Cold One was not even sure what pleasure was.

"What's your final destination?" the Cold One asked.

"Los Angeles. Where are you heading?"

"Malibu."

"Do you want to alert the authorities here that your car's been stolen?"

The Cold One shrugged. "The authorities might have been the ones who stole it."

The man reached for a cigarette. "Ain't that the truth. Well, it's up to you. If you want a ride, I'll give you one. You'd be a fool to wait here for your car to reappear magically."

The Cold One considered further. It had another alternative. It could *change* the man. This act, this change—It had never done it to anyone before. But now that the Voice had stopped, it was time. The Cold One knew this fact without logic or reason or thought. The idea was just there like the crab on Its toe. The man would be Its first. It smiled again.

"That would be great," the Cold One said. It walked around to the other side of the car and climbed in. The man put the engine in gear. They rolled north, toward the States, driving with the roof down. The sun drifted closer to the horizon but the air continued to bake. The man smoked his cigarette and wiped the sweat off his fat mustache and glanced over at the Cold One.

"I'm burning up," the man said. "I wish the AC on this damn thing worked." He paused to study It closer. "How do you stay so cool?"

The Cold One leaned back and closed Its eyes. "It's the way I am."